Acclaim for *New Yo...*
JANE...
and her first Ca...
A Wicked Gentleman

"Intriguing and satisfying. . . . The captivating romance is buttressed by rich characters and an intense kidnapping subplot, making this a fine beginning for Feather's new series."

—*Publishers Weekly*

"Consummate storyteller Feather entices with a mystery tinged with humor that will enchant readers who desire a sprightly story filled with marvelous characters—and just enough suspense to keep the midnight oil burning."

—*Romantic Times*

More praise for Jane Feather's extraordinary novels

"An accomplished storyteller . . . rare and wonderful."
—*Los Angeles Daily News*

"[A] boundary-pushing page-turner . . . rich with details that put 'historical' back into historical romance, this tale seethes with breathtaking tension."

—*Publishers Weekly* (starred review)

"Delightful . . . fascinating and entertaining characters."
—*Booklist*

"A devour-it-like-chocolate page-turner that takes the reader through the vivid landscapes of the time."
—*BookPage*

Also by Jane Feather

JANE FEATHER

TO WED A WICKED PRINCE

POCKET STAR BOOKS

New York   London   Toronto   Sydney

Pocket Star Books
A Division of Simon & Schuster, Inc.
1230 Avenue of the Americas
New York, NY 10020

This book is a work of fiction. Names, characters, places and incidents are products of the author's imagination or are used fictitiously. Any resemblance to actual events or locales or persons, living or dead, is entirely coincidental.

First Pocket Star Books paperback edition April 2008

POCKET STAR BOOKS and colophon are registered trademarks of Simon & Schuster, Inc.

For information regarding special discounts for bulk purchases, please contact Simon & Schuster Special Sales at 1-800-456-6798 or business@simonandschuster.com.

Cover design by Lisa Litwack; illustration by Aleta Rafton

Manufactured in the United States of America

10 9 8 7 6 5 4 3 2 1

ISBN-13: 978-1-4165-2552-3
ISBN-10:   1-4165-2552-1

To Wed a
WICKED
Prince

Prologue

CORNWALL, AUGUST 1771

THE CRASH OF THE SURF on the rocks far below was the only sound in the chamber in the stone house on the cliff top. The room's occupants were each absorbed in their own silent reflection. The woman in the bed was gazing down into the face of the sleeping babe in her arms. The man stood by the open latticed window, looking out into the summer night.

A knock at the door disturbed the quiet. The man turned and looked at the woman, who gave an almost imperceptible nod. He called softly, "Enter."

The door opened to admit a man dressed in the green uniform of a major in the elite Preobrazhensky regiment of the czarina of Russia's palace guard. "Forgive me, Prince, but it is past time for the rendezvous." The words were courteous, the tone almost conversational, but no one was under the illusion that this was anything other than a final demand.

"I'll be down in five minutes," the prince said, and

waved a hand in dismissal. The major left, closing the door softly in his wake.

The woman in the bed looked up to meet her companion's steady gaze. Tears glittered in her eyes, accentuating their blue brilliance, but her voice was firm. "Go, then," she said quietly. "Take him now."

"If there was another way . . ." The words trailed off as he shook his head helplessly. "You could still come with me, Sophia. We could be married . . ."

She shook her head in response. "You know that's not possible, Alexis. The empress would never forgive you. Your career would be in ruins, your family's honor destroyed." A smile softened her set expression for a fleeting instant. "You forget, my love, how well I know you. I know you could not live forever in exile, it would break you."

"With you I could," he said simply.

She tried to smile again, but it was effortful and did nothing to hide the pain and grief in her eyes, or lessen the deep purple shadows beneath them. "The empress will embrace your son, where she would not embrace either your wife or your mistress." She looked down at the child again. "Catherine does not hold illegitimacy against children, she takes the greatest care of her own, does she not?"

"True enough," Alexis agreed somberly. "Her son is brought up at court, given every advantage. Catherine has a certain fondness for children."

"And she will be fond of your child, because he is *your* child," she said. She touched the baby's cheek with a lingering fingertip, tracing the soft curve of his jaw. Her voice was thick with unshed tears as she said, "Alexis, this little one must have a future. The best possible future. If he stayed with me, the stigma of illegitimacy would deny him that future. He would grow up in obscurity, with an outcast mother."

She looked up at him and met his gaze this time with an almost ferocious stare. "I have nothing to give him. You have a noble name, a position of power in your society. You can give him education, opportunities, everything that I can't."

"I would go into exile with you, Sophia," he repeated. "Together, we could make a life."

She shook her head and a hint of iron entered her voice. "You would condemn our child to a life in the frozen wastes of Siberia at Catherine's whim. You know she would never forgive you . . . or me. And our child would suffer."

She shook her head again, more vigorously than ever. "I cannot give our son the opportunities you can give him. And I will not sacrifice you and him for an ephemeral ideal of romantic happiness."

A smile touched his mouth. "Ah, Sophia, you are a woman made of steel. Catherine would appreciate that in you."

"I doubt that," Sophia stated with a touch of derision. "She would see me as a rival for her bed, no more, no less. And while you might with tact and skill avoid being her bedfellow again, she would banish you rather than see you in the arms of another woman. You know how jealous she is of her erstwhile lovers. They must still dance attendance on her, even if she doesn't want them in her bed any longer."

Alexis inclined his head in acknowledgment of this truth. They had been over and over it for so many months now and they both knew there was no escape from the inevitable. "Well, then . . ." He took a step towards the bed.

Sophia lifted the child and kissed his brow, then closed her eyes on her tears as she held him out. "Take him and go. *Quickly.*"

He hesitated. "My love . . ."

"For God's sake, Alexis, have pity. *Go.*" There was no concealing the agony in her voice.

He took the child from her, cradling him close, as he bent and kissed Sophia's lips. They were cold and unresponsive, so unlike the warm, deeply passionate woman he loved that he felt his own tears prick behind his eyes. But to linger now would merely prolong the pain. He turned on his heel and left, closing the door behind him.

She lay listening to the sound of his steps receding on the stairs. And when she could no longer hear him, then and only then did she allow the tears to flow, as she cursed the woman in her grand palace in St. Petersburg whose thoughtless power had destroyed all possibility of happiness for a woman of whose identity she was probably unaware, and whose existence she considered merely a nuisance, as irritating as a mosquito and as easily dealt with.

Chapter One

LIVIA LACEY TAPPED HER CLOSED fan into the palm of her hand, trying to conceal her impatience as the orchestra struck up the beginning strains of the cotillion that as always made her toes twitch. Her dance card was full, but her designated partner for this dance was conspicuous by his absence, and the music was going to waste.

She was vaguely aware of the interested glances from a group of elderly chaperones gathered in a circle at the far side of the ballroom and she knew she was the subject of their chatter. They must have heard the story of her indecorous jaunt to the masked route at Vauxhall the other evening. Ordinarily she was the soul of discretion, obeying the constraints of this etiquette-ridden society, but just once in a while the urge to throw off the traces took her by storm. An excursion to Vauxhall in the company of a group of young bloods, dressed as one of them, had seemed irresistible at the time, but the thrill had palled soon enough and she was left with the irksome consequences.

Of course, if Aurelia had been in Cavendish Square instead of visiting Nell and Harry in Scotland, Livia reflected in hindsight, she would never have indulged such a ridiculous scheme for an instant. But loneliness and boredom had overcome her customary common sense. However, she told herself firmly, it would be a nine-day wonder. The gossips would soon find something else to amuse them, and she would conduct herself with impeccable correctness from now on.

She looked across the ballroom where couples were forming for the elaborate dance. If Bellingham didn't claim her soon, the sets would all be formed and there'd be no place for them. And the cotillion was her favorite dance.

"Lady Livia, you're not dancing. May I present Prince Prokov as a partner."

Livia turned her head and looked in surprise at her hostess, the duchess of Clarington, who now stood beside her with a slender, fair-haired gentleman.

The gentleman bowed. "Would you do me the honor, Lady Livia." He extended his hand. He had a slight accent that she found attractive and as exotic as the massive ruby carbuncle in his signet ring. A gentleman of means, it would seem, and there was something about the lean physicality of his frame that promised a competent dance partner.

Livia consigned Bellingham to the devil. He was a

dreary partner at best, always watching his steps and expatiating on the origins and social significance of the dance. He would never have been her preferred choice for the cotillion, but unfortunately he'd been the first to mark her card, so short of refusing to dance altogether, she'd had no option but to resign herself to half an hour in his somewhat tedious company. However, if he couldn't do her the courtesy of presenting himself for the dance in a timely fashion, then he had only himself to blame if she accepted another offer.

She smiled and took the proffered hand as she rose to her feet. "I'd be delighted, sir."

His fingers closed over hers as he led her to the floor and she was aware of a certain frisson in a warm, dry clasp that felt strangely authoritative. He guided her to her place in the set and bowed with a little flourish that made her smile. She responded with the requisite curtsy as the dance began.

He was a very good dancer. As good as herself, she reflected without false modesty. She knew herself to be graceful and light on her feet and her present partner certainly matched her in the complex steps of the set piece. Conversation was not the point of this particular dance, and he seemed content to exchange complicit smiles as they came together and parted according to the stately rituals of the dance. When it was over, they exchanged salutations once more and he offered his arm to lead her off the floor.

"I enjoyed that, thank you," she said as he led her

towards a window embrasure where the light summer curtains were drawn back to let a cool breath of air into the overheated ballroom. "You're a good dancer, Prince . . . Prokov, is that right?"

"Absolutely correct, Lady Livia," he returned with another little bow. "Alexander Prokov, at your service." He held the curtains aside so she could step onto the narrow railed balcony that looked down over the rear garden of the mansion. "May I procure you a glass of lemonade . . . or champagne, perhaps?"

"Champagne, I think," Livia said definitely. There was a tingle in the air, rather like champagne bubbles, she caught herself thinking, and instantly castigated herself for such a romantic fancy. It must have something to do with the huge harvest moon hanging over the garden.

"Yes, it's an evening for champagne," he agreed with a solemnity belied by the gleam in his eyes, which were an astonishingly deep blue. "Wait here."

Livia watched him move through the crowded ballroom; a hand on a shoulder here, a soft word there, and the crowd parted like the Red Sea for Moses. Where on earth had he sprung from, this Prince Prokov? London had been bare of company all summer and only now, towards the middle of September, were people beginning to trickle back, so perhaps it wasn't surprising she hadn't met him before.

She watched his return, two glasses in hand, the same deft progress through the throng, and then he was beside her, handing her a glass.

"A toast," he said, raising his glass. "To new friends."

Livia touched his glass with her own and drank the toast, eyebrows raised a trifle at such an unambiguous statement. "So, we're to be friends, are we?" she said, her tone a little dry.

He looked at her, his eyes narrowed. "Is there a reason why we shouldn't be? I see none."

Livia shrugged and delivered what she hoped was enough of a snub to puncture a confidence that now struck her as arrogant. "I don't choose my friends lightly, sir. I like to take my time before making up my mind about something so important." She regarded him through slightly narrowed eyes and he returned the look with a quizzical air that discomposed her somewhat. Her snub appeared not to have hit its mark.

After a minute she turned away from him to look back into the ballroom. "I don't understand what could have happened to Lord Bellingham. He was supposed to partner me in the cotillion."

"Ah, Bellingham, so that was his name," her companion murmured, nodding his head thoughtfully. "I'm afraid I didn't know it when we met a little while ago."

Livia spun around in surprise. "You met him . . . where?"

"Oh, forgive me. I should have mentioned it earlier. I'm afraid Lord Bellingham met with a little accident, which prevented him from claiming your hand in the dance," he returned.

Livia stared at him. "A little accident?"

"Yes, he . . . uh . . . he fell into the fountain," the prince informed her with a sorrowful shake of his head. "Most unfortunate." He gestured towards the spouting water in the middle of the garden below.

Livia began to feel as if her hold on reality was slipping. She was convinced the man was laughing, although his expression remained grave, but he could do nothing to hide the deep-seated gleam of amusement in his eyes. "I think you had better explain," she said, trying to inject a little frigidity into her voice but aware that she was failing miserably. The image of the stout and pompous Bellingham falling into the fountain was too absurd.

The prince waved one hand in an all-encompassing gesture. "There's nothing really to explain, ma'am. The unfortunate gentleman just happened to topple into the basin." He shook his head. "Most unfortunate for him. I daresay he's had to return home for dry clothes and was thus unable to keep his appointment with you."

Livia looked at him in startled and dawning comprehension. "Uh . . . you wouldn't perhaps have had anything to do with this accident, Prince?"

"Oh, very little," he assured her, taking a sip from his glass.

Livia's voice trembled with laughter as she said, "Exactly *how* little would that be?"

He shrugged. "Just a touch to the shoulder, a mere brush, I assure you. Unfortunately it appeared to be sufficient to throw the gentleman off balance. I've noticed that some people are less well balanced than others. Perhaps you've noticed the same thing?" He raised an arched eyebrow as he looked at her over the lip of his glass.

"Just why would you push Lord Bellingham into the fountain, Prince Prokov?" Livia demanded, trying to control her mirth. It would be too unkind to laugh at the unfortunate Bellingham, a man for whom dignity was more important than anything.

"Well, he was in my way," her companion explained, as if it were the most natural and logical way of removing obstacles in his path. "And the fountain was there, and he was standing beside it . . . indeed, I believe he had one foot on the rim of the basin. It seemed an obvious thing to do."

"How could he possibly have been in your way if he was standing by the fountain? It's a good five feet from the path," Livia demanded, feeling once again the reins of reality slipping from her grasp. It was the most ludicrous conversation.

"Ah, no, you misunderstand. He wasn't in my way to anywhere, he was in the way of my desire to dance with you. I requested most politely that he yield his place on your card but he saw fit to give me a lecture on the dire impropriety of altering the order of the dance. He had rather a lot to say on the subject, and most of it struck me as somewhat irrelevant . . . I have never cared to be lectured." He smiled benignly as if all must now be explained to her satisfaction.

"You wanted to dance with me?" Livia was incredulous. It was flattering, or would be if the compliment weren't coming from someone who had clearly lost his mind.

"Yes," he said. "I have been watching you all evening, and I wished for an introduction."

"And you couldn't simply have asked our hostess for one? You had to push someone into a fountain instead?"

"Well, it seemed to kill two birds with one stone," he said, sounding apologetic. "I wanted an introduction, but I also wished to dance with you, and it seemed the only way to do that would be to remove one of your prospective partners. And since I particularly enjoy the cotillion, that seemed the obvious choice. Besides," he added, "I didn't consider this Bellingham to be much of a dancer when I saw him in the country dances. You were much better off with me. And he was most inconveniently intransigent about a perfectly civil request, you understand."

Livia didn't know whether to give way to the gales of hilarity threatening to overcome her, or deliver an icy snub for his impossible arrogance and stalk off. The problem was that he spoke only the truth. And while she knew she should feel sorry for Lord Bellingham, she'd often enough been tempted to douse his pomposity herself with a jug of very cold water.

She laughed, and he stood leaning against the railing, watching her and smiling until she had herself in hand again. He took her fan from her slack grasp and flipped it open, fanning her until the flush on her cheeks had faded somewhat and she'd dabbed at her eyes with a flimsy lace handkerchief.

"Oh, dear," she said. "That's so unkind of me to laugh . . . poor Bellingham." She shook her head as if to dispel the last threads of amusement and looked at him. "I have to tell you, Prince Prokov, that that's a very un-English way of handling an inconvenience."

"But of course I'm not English," he pointed out, giving her back her fan. "The Slav temperament tends to the impulsive. We choose the quickest and most efficacious solution to our . . . our inconveniences."

She looked at him more closely now, noticing the high, broad cheekbones, the long, thin nose, the finely drawn mouth, and the luxuriant head of wheat-colored hair brushed back from a broad, intelligent forehead. It was a refined face dominated by those amazing blue eyes.

And there was that slight, attractive accent. Slav? Strangely, she'd always thought of dark complexions and black hair in such a context. But there were exceptions and she made a guess. "Are you Russian . . . or perhaps Polish?"

"Mostly Russian," he told her. He took her glass and set it on the balcony rail. "Shall we dance again?"

"I'm afraid I can't," Livia said, glancing at her dance card, suspended from her wrist on a silken ribbon. "Unless you think you could arrange for the next six gentlemen on my card to have a contretemps with the fountain."

"Whom should it be next?" he asked promptly, and she went into another peal of laughter. But she turned from him and resolutely went back into the ballroom, where her next partner was looking rather disconsolately around the floor.

Alexander Prokov remained on the balcony gazing down into the garden, a fairy-tale garden on such a beautiful late summer evening, lit by pitch torches and myriad little lamps suspended from the trees. He had no interest in dancing with anyone else tonight.

∞

Livia found it difficult to pay attention to her partner and was glad that her feet at least performed the steps without too much mental guidance.

"So, I was thinking that Gretna Green would be best . . . we could elope the day after tomorrow. How would that be, Livia?"

Her gaze focused abruptly and she blinked at her partner, Lord David Foster. "What, David? Sorry, I didn't quite catch that."

"Gretna Green," he said gravely. "I was suggesting we elope the day after tomorrow and drive straight to Gretna Green."

She stared at him. *What?*

"You haven't listened to a word I've said for the last twenty minutes, Liv," he declared. "I'm beginning to feel like a wooden doll with moveable feet."

"Oh, David, I'm sorry." She was instantly remorseful.

"I admit it, I was miles away. But I'm listening now. Do you really want to go to Gretna Green? This is all very sudden . . . but I've always wanted to elope, climb down from my chamber on a rope made out of sheets. And you could wait in an unmarked carriage in the alley . . ."

"Enough," he said, laughing with her. "Not that I wouldn't marry you in a heartbeat if you'd have me."

"That's very gallant of you, David, but you couldn't possibly afford to marry me. I don't have nearly enough of a fortune," she said with blithe candor.

"Alas, I fear you're right," he said, sighing. "I shall just have to live with a yearning heart."

Livia kept her mind on her partners for the remainder of the evening, but she was also looking around for the mysterious Russian. He appeared to have vanished as discreetly as he'd appeared, and as the orchestra finished the last dance, she excused herself from her partner and went in search of her hostess, ostensibly to make her farewells.

The duchess was holding court at the head of the sweeping staircase, greeting her guests as they prepared to descend to the hall below, where maids scurried to retrieve evening cloaks and footmen stood in the doorway, calling out the names of departing guests to coachmen and grooms waiting for their own summons in the carriages lining the street.

At last Livia was close enough to the duchess to offer her own thanks and farewell. "I did enjoy dancing with Prince Prokov," she said, shaking her grace's silk-mittened hand. "Is he new to town? I don't recall meeting him before."

"Oh, yes, quite an asset I think he'll be," the duchess trilled. "One grows so tired of the same faces every season. And such a distinguished addition to our little circle. Of course, Russian princes are ten a penny," she added in a stage whisper, "but nevertheless there's a certain cachet in the title, don't you agree, my dear?"

"Oh, yes, I'm sure," Livia murmured. "I look forward to meeting him again. Thank you, Duchess, for a delightful party." She moved away, yielding her place, and turned to descend the stairs. A hand came under her elbow and a voice murmured, "Ten a penny, are we? I'm crushed."

She glanced up at the prince, who had somehow materialized on the staircase and was now escorting her steadily downwards. "Not my words," she said.

"Ah, but you agreed with them," he chided. "I heard you."

"I was merely being polite," she returned smartly. "And if you will eavesdrop, you can only blame yourself if you hear things you don't like."

"True enough," he agreed, sounding cheerful about it. "I wish to escort you home. You don't have a chaperone here, I trust?"

"Someone else to be disposed of in the fountain?" she queried. "As it happens, my chaperone tonight was purely nominal, and Lady Harley has already returned home with her daughters. My carriage is waiting for me and I have no need of an escort, thank you."

"Oh, I disagree," he stated, turning to beckon a waiting maid. "Lady Livia Lacey's cloak."

The girl curtsied and hurried off to the cloakroom to retrieve the garment. The prince walked to the door and instructed the footman, "Lady Livia Lacey's coach."

The footman bellowed to a linkboy on the street at the bottom of the steps. "Lady Livia Lacey's coach." The boy, with his torch held aloft, went off at a run, calling out the name as he ran along the line of carriages.

A huge round berlin separated itself from the line and progressed in stately fashion to the front door of the Clarington mansion. The groom jumped down to let down the footstep and open the door.

"My carriage," Livia said, accepting her cloak from the maid with a smile and a discreetly palmed coin. "Thank you for the dance, Prince Prokov."

"That's your carriage?" For once he sounded startled. "What an astonishing equipage."

"We call it the teacup," she informed him, gathering up the folds of her cloak and ball gown and moving down the shallow flight of steps to the pavement.

"Oh, yes, that's exactly what it is," he agreed with huge amusement. "Allow me, ma'am." He was by her side, taking her elbow to ease her upwards into the carriage before she could muster any objections. And then he had climbed in beside her, pulling the door firmly behind him. He sank down on the faded crimson squabs and looked around the interior with an air of fascination. "When did these go out of fashion? It must have been at least twenty years ago."

"At least," Livia said, deciding that objecting to his presence was going to be futile at best and undignified at worst. Besides, she wasn't certain she did object to it. "It belonged to a distant relative of mine. I think she insisted on a degree of state when she went out and about."

He looked at her closely, his eyes suddenly a bright glow in the dim interior. "Did she? How interesting."

"Why should you find that interesting, Prince? I'm sure she was a woman of her time. She died at the end of last year," she added.

"Ah, I'm sorry to hear it," he murmured.

"I never knew her," Livia said. "As I said, she was a distant relative . . . I'm not even sure how we were connected, but we shared a surname and for some reason that was important to her, so she made me her heir." Even as she gave this explanation, Livia wondered why she was being so expansive; it was none of this gentleman's business. Yet somehow he seemed to provoke confidences.

"So, tell me about yourself, Lady Livia."

"There's nothing to tell," Livia said shortly, deciding that there'd been enough confidences for one evening. "But you could tell me why a Russian prince is in London at a time like this. Don't you expect to find yourself looked upon with suspicion? Russians are hardly persona grata since your czar signed a treaty with Napoleon."

"Oh, politics, politics," he said, waving a hand in dismissal. "Dreary stuff. I want nothing to do with it. Besides, I am only half Russian."

"Oh? And what's the other half?"

"Why, English, of course," he declared in a tone of such delightfully smug satisfaction that Livia couldn't help another chuckle. The man made her laugh too much and too often.

"I would never have guessed," she said. "Apart from your fluency in English, of course."

"Oh, we Russians are fluent in many languages except our own," he said airily. "Russian is spoken only by the peasants."

Livia was about to question this when the carriage came to a halt and the groom opened the door. "Thank you, Jemmy," she said, accepting the lad's hand to assist her down to the pavement.

"Well, Prince Prokov, here is where we part company. Thank you again for the dance, although I by no means condone your methods of achieving it." She gave him her hand with what she hoped was a purely friendly, if firmly dismissive, smile.

He raised her hand to his lips, however, turning it over to press an unambiguous kiss into her palm. "You will permit me to call upon you, my lady." It was a statement rather than a request.

Livia could see no reason to object to the declaration except that she preferred to feel that her wishes were in some way to be taken into account in such matters. She contented herself with a vague smile, another murmured good night, and turned from him to hurry up the steps to her own house. Tonight of all nights it would have been nice if Morecombe, the ancient butler, had been on the watch for her return. Of course, as she'd expected, she had to bang the knocker three times before she heard the shuffle of his carpet slippers across the parquet within, and the slow, painful drawing back of the bolt, before the door opened a crack and the old retainer peered suspiciously around.

"Oh, 'tis you," he declared, as if it could have been anyone else.

"Yes, Morecombe, it's me," Livia said impatiently. "Open the door, for heaven's sake."

"Oh, patience, patience," he muttered, opening the door wider. "Come you in, 'tis time respectable folk were in their beds."

Livia whisked herself inside and resisted the urge to look back to see if the Russian prince had been watching this little sideshow from the pavement.

❧

Alexander waited until the door had closed and then he stepped back into the street to look up at the house. It was a handsome building, in keeping with its fellows around the gracious London square. There were signs that work had been done on the brickwork and the window frames, and the railings were black-leaded, the door knocker glowing copper, the steps white-honed. Its caretakers were clearly fulfilling their responsibilities, he thought.

He sauntered away, smiling slightly at the memory of the evening. His informant had been quite correct about Livia Lacey. She would do. In fact she would do very well indeed. And unless he was wildly off the mark, that irreverent bubble of laughter that she had such difficulty suppressing promised an amusing and somewhat unconventional collaboration.

He paused on the corner of Cavendish Square, debating his destination. Home, or one of his clubs? He found himself disinclined for further social chitchat and had little interest in cards tonight, so he turned his steps towards his lodgings on Bruton Street.

He had a commodious and comfortable suite of rooms attended by his manservant, and a bootboy. An excellent cook reigned in the small kitchen. An all-male household suited the prince's temperament. His father had preferred it and the young Alexander, once he'd outgrown the wet nurse, had been surrounded exclusively by male minders and tutors, until the Empress Catherine had taken him under her wing as an older companion for her grandson. But even then, in the royal schoolrooms, women had been few and far between, and the boys had grown up under the watchful eyes of the military tutors and senior diplomats chosen by the empress, in order to give her heir an education suited to a boy destined for an imperial throne. Once his unsatisfactory father had been disposed of, of course.

How successful an education that had been was a question Prince Prokov often asked himself these days when he contemplated the actions and decisions of his friend and emperor, Alexander I.

The prince let himself into his lodgings and grimaced at the sound of voices coming from the small drawing room to the right of the hall. His man appeared as soundlessly as always from his own quarters.

"Visitors, sir," he said, bowing. "Duke Nicolai Sperskov, Count Constantine Fedorovsky, and one other. They said they wished to await your return." He moved to take his master's evening cloak, cane, and gloves.

Alex nodded briefly. "What are they drinking?"

"Vodka, Prince."

"Then bring me cognac as well." Alex opened the door to the drawing room.

"Ah, Alex, I trust you don't object to our waiting for you." A plump, pink-cheeked gentleman turned from the fireplace, vodka glass in hand. He waved the glass appreciatively. "Excellent vodka, I congratulate you. Did you bring it with you from St. Petersburg?"

"A dozen or so bottles, Nicolai," Alexander said easily, using French, the first language for all of them. "You're welcome to one."

The duke twirled a magnificent moustache, black as coal, and beamed. "Generous as always, my friend."

Alex smiled and extended a hand in greeting to Constantine Fedorovsky. "Constantine . . . I didn't know you were in England . . . and . . ." He turned with a faint questioning smile to his other visitor.

"Ah, allow me to present Paul Tatarinov, Alex," Constantine Fedorovsky said. "We arrived from the court two days ago."

"You are most welcome, monsieur," Alex said courteously. "Ah, thank you, Boris." He acknowledged the soundless arrival of his manservant, carrying a decanter and goblets. "Set it down there." He gestured to a console table. The man did so and bowed himself softly from the room.

"I find I prefer cognac these days," Alex said, filling a goblet. "May I tempt anyone else?"

"No, no, thank you . . . vodka's the stuff," Constantine said appreciatively, raising his glass to examine the clear liquid in the lamplight. "Smooth as silk, this one, Nicolai's quite right."

"You shall have a bottle," Alexander said, seating himself comfortably in an armchair beside the fire. He crossed his legs and sipped cognac, regarding his visitors with an air of polite attention.

"Ah, you wonder why we're here, I daresay," the duke said with a tug at his moustache.

"It's always a pleasure to see my friends," Alex demurred with a twitch of his eyebrows that spoke volumes.

Tatarinov frowned and went quickly to the door. He opened it sharply and stood peering into the dimly lit foyer. After a minute he closed it and turned back to the room. His eyes darted to the heavy velvet curtains drawn tight at the windows, and he strode across, opening them a few inches to gaze into the darkness of the street beyond.

"Tatarinov is a cautious man," Duke Nicolai murmured.

"Wisely so, I'm sure," Alex returned, regarding his visitor through slightly narrowed eyes. "You suspect eavesdroppers, Tatarinov?"

"Always . . . one can never be too careful," the other man said. "Ever since the czar established that damnable Committee for General Security, their secret police are everywhere." He stood in front of the fire, his legs braced as if on the deck of a moving ship, and glowered into his vodka.

"Well, if you've satisfied yourself on that score, perhaps we could come to the point," Alex prompted, taking another sip of cognac.

"Tatarinov brings some disturbing news from court," the duke said. "It seems that the emperor has heard some whispers about our little enterprise."

Alex's relaxed posture didn't change but his eyes sharpened. "Does he have names?"

Tatarinov shook his head. "Not as far as I know, he's become aware simply that there are some around him who are . . . dissatisfied, shall we say . . . with his imperial performance on the world's stage."

"Which is only the truth," Constantine stated. "While the emperor preens and postures on the banks of the river Niemen, making much of his treaty with Bonaparte, Bonaparte laughs behind his hand. He will use

Russia and drop her the minute he's wrung her dry, and the czar can't or *won't* see it. As far as he's concerned the Treaty of Tilsit made Napoleon his bosom friend, and unassailable ally."

His voice rose with his frustration as he paced the small room. "He won't even listen to his mother on this. The Dowager Empress makes no secret of what she thinks of this rapprochement with Bonaparte."

"It's true. Normally Alexander listens to her, but not on this subject." Nicolai shook his head dolefully. "If he can't be persuaded, he must be removed . . . one way or another."

"Gently, gently, my friend," Alex admonished. "Some things are best left understood but unsaid."

"Quite right," Tatarinov agreed. Constantine grunted and refilled his glass, draining it in one swallow.

"You're the one man he will never suspect, Alex," Nicolai said. "You grew up with him, you shared a schoolroom, you're his most trusted confidant." He looked closely at Alex from beneath thick gray brows. "It can't be easy for you to contemplate such an act of betrayal."

A tense silence fell over the room until Alex said quietly, "I don't see it as betrayal. That's an ugly word and we are talking here of saving our country, even if it must be at the expense of one man."

"The czar's an arrogant fool," Constantine stated. "Too much of his father in him and not enough of his grandmother, the Empress Catherine. If you ask me, I'd say we need to get rid of the czar, his wife, and his mother . . . give the throne to the czar's sister, Grand Duchess Catherine, she's the only one of them with the old woman's brains and spirit."

Alex said nothing as the debate went on around him. He was thinking of the czar's childhood, of the way he had been protected, cosseted, encouraged to consider himself almost a god, as near to perfection and infallibility as any human could be. His mistakes had never been acknowledged, his wishes always took precedence. What chance had a grown man to achieve wisdom in such circumstances? It had long struck him as strange that the czar's grandmother, the great Empress Catherine, a woman of surpassing wisdom, intellect, and education, who corresponded freely with the greatest minds in the civilized world, should have so bungled the molding of her heir.

"You're very quiet, Alex."

Nicolai's question brought Alex out of his reverie. "I beg your pardon, I was thinking."

"Useful thoughts, I trust," Tatarinov said somewhat sourly.

"Maybe, maybe not." Alex regarded this newcomer to the London émigré scene with interest. It was a world that attracted all sorts, fools and wise men, rich or poor, but they were all aristocrats who either were compelled or chose to leave Mother Russia. Tatarinov was of a different kind—he was a rough diamond lacking the polish of the usual émigré—the kind of men like those in this room, who loved their country and their country's honor above all else. What motivated a man like Tatarinov? He would bear watching.

"I was thinking it would be helpful to discover exactly what the czar knows . . . or suspects," Alex said.

"You have his ear. Can you find out?" Constantine asked.

Alex nodded. "I was intending to write to him in the next day or two anyway. I'll bring up the subject and see what it leads to." He stifled a yawn.

"Ah, we're keeping you up," Nicolai said, getting to his feet. "Forgive us."

"Not at all," Alex denied, but he rose to his feet with his visitors. Indeed, he wasn't in the least fatigued by anything except present company. He had several hours' work ahead of him and was anxious to get started.

He saw his visitors out and returned to the drawing room, where Boris was clearing away glasses. "Make up the fire, Boris, and leave the cognac decanter," Alex instructed as he went to the secretaire. "Then you may lock up and go to bed."

"As you wish, Prince Prokov."

Alex drew a sheaf of paper towards him and picked up his quill. He sharpened the nib, frowning in thought. His visitors were not aware that he was in London at the emperor's bidding, about to become Russia's unofficial eyes and ears in London. The czar was going to recall his ambassador in the next few weeks and once diplomatic relations with England were officially broken, he would need someone placed to keep him informed of the English political and diplomatic schemes and opinions. Alex, playing for society's benefit the part of a carefree aristocratic émigré, uninterested in politics, intent only on the pursuit of idle pleasure in the glittering ballrooms and salons of London's society, was perfectly positioned as that informant. He had just a few weeks in which to get thoroughly established in the right circles.

But he had another string to his bow. An entrée to the secret association of Russian revolutionaries based in London. Information he gleaned from them would also be of vital interest and importance to the czar.

Alex began to write.

Chapter Two

◈

"AUNT LIV . . . AUNT LIV . . . WAKE up, we're back."

The excited tones of a small child brought Livia struggling blearily from the depths of a dreamless sleep. Little fingers were tapping her cheek urgently.

"Franny, darling, don't disturb Aunt Liv," the calm voice of Aurelia Farnham admonished. "Liv, I am sorry, I didn't realize she'd come in to you."

Livia opened her eyes and smiled. She hitched herself onto an elbow, brushing her dark hair away from her face. "Ellie, you're back," she said with delight. "Franny, love, I'm awake now, there's no need to keep tickling my face. Come up on the bed." She patted the coverlet in invitation.

"We had such a long journey, Aunt Liv, miles an' miles all the way from Scotland to Grandpapa's house, an' Susannah was sick all over Linton an' Stevie," the little girl prattled as she clambered onto the bed.

"I'm glad I wasn't in the coach," Livia said, with a grin

at Aurelia. "Although, if my father hadn't needed me the other week, I would have liked to have visited Nell and Harry in Scotland. Where are they now? Still in Ringwood, or did they come back to London with you?"

"No, they're still in Hampshire, at Dagenham Manor. Harry has Markby twisted around his little finger . . . it's a miracle. You wouldn't believe it."

"No, I wouldn't," Livia agreed, pulling herself up against the pillows. The earl of Markby, the father of Nell's first husband, who had died in the war, was a formidable gentleman. "So he's come round to Nell's marriage, then?"

"Seemingly," Aurelia said. She went to open the door at a discreet knock. "Ah, tea, thank you, Hester." She held the door for a young maidservant struggling under the weight of a laden tray.

Hester set it down on the dresser and bobbed a curtsy. "Will I pour, ma'am?"

"No, I'll do it," Aurelia said, picking up the silver teapot. "Could you ask Daisy to come and collect Franny for her breakfast."

"Yes, ma'am."

"Thank you, Hester," Livia said in smiling dismissal. The girl bobbed another curtsy and hurried away.

"Don't want breakfast," Franny declared, pouting. "I want to stay here with you."

"You were famished ten minutes ago," her mother said, pouring tea into two delicate Sèvres cups. "And you don't want to upset Miss Ada or Miss Mavis by not eating the breakfast they will have made for you. You know how they always put honey on your porridge."

Franny looked doubtful but went off without too much protest when her nursemaid appeared a couple of minutes later.

"I adore that child, but she does exhaust me," Aurelia said, closing the door on their departure. "She chatters ten times more than Stevie and Susannah put together." She smiled ruefully at the contrast between their friend Nell's children and her own chatterbox of a daughter. She came over to perch companionably on the bed with her teacup. "So, what have you been up to?"

"Nothing particularly remarkable," Livia said, dipping a macaroon into her tea. "I did have a rather unusual encounter last night . . . but first, tell me how Nell and Harry and the children are. I haven't heard from Nell since they left Scotland to come home. I want to hear all about how Harry charmed the earl. I would have thought Markby would have had an apoplexy about the elopement."

"He probably did when he first heard of it," Aurelia said. "But he had to accept the fait accompli in the end."

Aurelia and her sister-in-law, Cornelia Dagenham, had both been widowed at the Battle of Trafalgar, and Cornelia's father-in-law, the earl of Markby, had been the chief trustee for their children's inheritances. When Cornelia had fallen in love with Harry, Viscount Bonham, and eloped with him six months ago, everyone had expected the earl to unleash his wrath on all and sundry.

"But he didn't have to accept it graciously," Livia pointed out, leaning sideways to set down her teacup.

"True enough, but there's something about Harry . . . more tea?"

"Yes, please. I know what you mean, he's some kind of an invincible force," Livia said with a chuckle. "Nell couldn't resist him after all, and she tried hard enough."

"She did," her friend agreed with a responding chuckle as she handed her a refilled cup. "But she's so happy now, Liv." She sighed a little. "I envy her. It's wrong of me to envy her happiness, but I can't help it."

"It's not wrong of you," Livia said swiftly, reaching out a hand to her friend. "And there'll be a Harry out there for you too, Ellie. I'm sure of it." Her fingers squeezed Aurelia's tightly.

Aurelia shrugged and smiled. "Maybe so," she said. "But now I want to hear about this peculiar encounter you had last night."

"A Russian prince, would you believe," Livia said, settling back against the pillows, her gray eyes gleaming with fun.

"A handsome Russian prince?" Aurelia inquired, the amusement in her own eyes now banishing her moment of gloom.

"Very," Livia said. "And something of an invincible force himself. He pushed Bellingham into a fountain." She watched Aurelia dissolve into laughter and within seconds joined her at the renewed image of the stuffy Lord Bellingham immersed in Clarington's fountain.

"Tell all," Aurelia demanded, and Livia obliged.

"Most intriguing," Aurelia said when her friend had finished the recital. "I can't wait to meet him. It sounds as if he intends to come calling."

"That was certainly the impression he gave me," Livia agreed, pushing aside the bedclothes and swinging her legs to the floor. "But I'm engaged to ride in the park with Lilly Devries this morning, so if he does come he'll be disappointed." She went to the armoire and flung it wide. "Will you ride with us, Ellie?"

"No, I don't think so," Aurelia said, going to the door. "Not this morning. I'm somewhat fatigued after the journey. We left Basingstoke at six this morning, and Franny was up at five."

"In that case, you may get the opportunity to meet the Russian prince if you decide you're not too fatigued to receive callers in my stead," Livia said with a chuckle as she reached into the armoire for a riding habit.

"Maybe," Aurelia responded. "I'll see you downstairs for breakfast."

"I'll be down right away," Livia promised, shaking out the folds of the dark green habit. "If you see Hester, ask her to come up. This skirt needs pressing."

"I'll tell her." Aurelia left the bedchamber.

Livia spread the habit out on the bed, then wrapped herself in a taffeta dressing gown that had seen better days. She was brushing her thick black curly hair when Hester reappeared, a pair of Lakeland terriers prancing at her heels. The dogs rushed at Livia, yapping in excited greeting, dancing on their back legs as if she'd been absent for a year.

"Lady Farnham said you wanted me, ma'am," Hester said over the noise of the dogs.

"Yes, Hester. Could you press my riding habit, please . . . Quiet now, dogs. I'm pleased to see you too." Livia set down her hairbrush and bent to greet the terriers, who were trying to climb onto her lap. "I'm going down for breakfast now. If you could bring up hot water in about half an hour I'd be grateful."

"Yes'm." Hester gathered up the habit and hurried away. Livia followed her, the dogs at her heels.

Aurelia was reading the *Morning Gazette* in the cozy parlor that Livia and her friends had made their own private apartment when they'd first arrived at the house on Cavendish Square. The house bore little resemblance now to the cold, drafty, neglected mansion that they'd first inhabited early that year.

"Your prince is mentioned here in the court circular," she pointed out, looking up from the paper as Livia and the dogs entered. "He was presented to Prinny at one of the queen's drawing room receptions two days ago. See . . ." She held out the paper and nibbled a piece of toast.

Livia sat down and perused the item. "He didn't say how long he'd been in London," she observed, reaching for the coffeepot. "But from this it seems that he's been here only a week or two. I suppose that would explain why I'd never come across him before."

"Prince Prokov," Aurelia mused, taking another piece of toast from the rack. "Do you think he's an émigré or just a foreign visitor?"

Livia shrugged. "He didn't say. But he did say that politics were dreary stuff and he wanted nothing to do with them. I think he's just here to play."

"A dilettante, then," Aurelia observed with a raised eyebrow. "Are you inclined to play with him, Liv?"

Livia, to her annoyance, felt her cheeks warm. "It depends on the game," she responded with a lighthearted shrug.

Aurelia nodded, her brown eyes shrewdly assessing her friend across the table. "It might be diverting," she commented casually, and returned her attention to her breakfast.

❧

It was a beautiful morning for a ride, Livia reflected as she left the house, drawing on her gloves as she stood on the top step. Her heart sank a little when she saw the horse awaiting her in the street. The livery stable had sent her the piebald gelding again. He was a dull, plodding ride at the best of times and, even with the utmost modesty, Livia knew she was a better than good horsewoman and the mount didn't do her justice. But she couldn't afford to keep her own horse in London, so beggars couldn't be choosers, she told herself resolutely as she descended the steps.

The livery stable had sent an elderly groom with the

horse and he gave her a leg up into the saddle. "Where to, ma'am?"

"Hyde Park . . . the Stanhope Gate," Livia said, settling into the saddle, feeling the gelding's broad back shift beneath her.

The groom mounted his own cob and whistled through his teeth. Immediately both horses started forward. Livia guided her stolid mount through the thronged streets. Not even the rowdy chaos of Piccadilly disturbed the animal's placidity. Ideal for a nervous rider, she reflected, but dull as ditch water for one who liked a mount with some spirit.

She couldn't help the stab of envy when she saw Lilly Devries waiting with her groom just inside the entrance to Hyde Park. Lilly's mount was a lively gray mare with fine lines and a dainty high-stepping movement. But then, Lilly's husband possessed a considerable fortune.

"Good morning, Livia. Isn't it a delicious day?" Lilly bubbled with customary enthusiasm as her friend joined her. "How was the Clarington ball last night? I was sick at not being able to go, but Hector insisted we dine with his parents . . . such a bore, I can't tell you." She turned her horse onto the tan, the broad band of sandy soil running alongside the paved coach path around the park. Her horse pranced delicately along beside the broad-backed piebald gelding.

Livia chatted idly about the ball, surprised that for some reason she avoided all mention of the Russian. Lilly would have been all ears, as always fascinated by any tidbit of gossip. There was no reason Livia shouldn't mention her encounter with Prince Prokov, although she wouldn't tell anyone except Ellie and Nell about Bellingham's involuntary swim in the fountain, and yet she found herself reluctant to say anything about it.

"Oh, look, there's Colonel Melton," Lilly said suddenly, breaking into Livia's desultory account. "In the party coming towards us."

Livia looked up. A party of three horsemen trotted down the tan towards them, two of them in the scarlet coats of dragoons, the other in civilian riding dress. Prince Prokov was the other. A little prickle of excitement ran up the back of her neck.

"Good morning, ladies." Colonel Melton called a greeting, sweeping off his plumed hat in a gallant flourish. "Well met, indeed. Lady Devries, Lady Livia. You know Lord Talgarth, of course." He gestured to the other guardsman, who bowed with a similar flourish. "And are you acquainted with Prince Prokov?"

"I don't believe so," Lilly said with a warm smile, her eyes appraising the newcomer with sharp interest. "It's a pleasure, sir."

He bowed and murmured a greeting before turning to Livia. His brilliant blue gaze held her own as he said, "I had the honor of meeting Lady Livia last night . . . how delightful to renew our acquaintance so soon, ma'am."

"Indeed, sir," Livia responded with a neutral smile. But the air had taken on that champagne fizz again and the prickles on the nape of her neck intensified. It was those damnable eyes, she thought. No one had the right to such a dazzling purity of color.

"May we ride with you?" The colonel was turning his horse alongside Lilly even as he asked the polite question. "Tell me, Lady Devries, why you haven't been seen about town for so long. Devries shouldn't keep you all to himself . . . the dog. And I shall tell him so."

Lilly laughed and entered the light bantering flirtation with practiced skill, saying over her shoulder, "Lord Talgarth, there's room for three on the path. I'm sure the prince wishes to further his acquaintance with Lady Livia." She gave Livia an archly conspiratorial smile as she said this.

Livia did her best to ignore the smile, but she couldn't ignore the prince, who had turned his horse to ride beside her. "What a magnificent animal," she said involuntarily as the black tossed his head and set the reins jingling.

"A Cossack horse," he told her. "I brought him with me." He cast a somewhat disparaging eye over her own mount. "Forgive me, but I don't think much of that beast."

Livia gave a rueful shrug. "A livery stable animal . . . what can you expect?"

"Ah . . . indeed." He nodded his comprehension and seemed to dismiss the subject. "How delightfully serendipitous that we should meet in this way. I was intending to call upon you later this morning."

"And now you've been saved the trouble?" Livia questioned with a quirk of her eyebrows.

"I would never consider it a trouble, ma'am," he responded. "A delight, certainly."

"You flatter me, sir." Livia couldn't think of a more original response.

"Never," he said. He lowered his voice and murmured, "I think you must know that I will go to any lengths to spend time in your company." His eyes were full of laughter, his soft voice a throb of invitation.

"With or without the assistance of a well-placed fountain," she said, trying to ignore the invitation but failing lamentably.

"That's better," he said as softly as before. "You are quite beautiful when your eyes laugh."

Livia lost all desire to laugh. She stared at him and then stated, "I have no interest in meaningless and extravagant compliments, Prince Prokov. They may do very well in Russia, but I for one equate restraint with sincerity."

"And why should you imagine I am not sincere?" he asked, apparently unsnubbed.

"You don't know me at all," she said. "And in this country we don't go around making intimate declarations to strangers."

"Well, you'll become accustomed to my ways," he returned with a cheerful smile. "And you may even come to like them. Shall we canter, if that beast of yours can be encouraged to do so?"

He leaned sideways and gave her horse a smart cut on

the flank with his whip. The animal jumped as if it had been stung and lumbered off down the tan in an ungainly resemblance to a canter. Livia was too occupied trying to adapt her seat to the rollicking gait to give vent to her outrage as the prince cantered elegantly beside her. They soon outstripped their companions and once they were out of sight, Alex drew rein and his horse slowed to a walk. Livia's mount, however, continued at the same pace and it took her several tries before she could convince him to slow down.

"How dare you do that?" she demanded furiously, once she had the animal in hand again. "You took me totally by surprise."

"I wished to be private with you," he said, as if it were the most ordinary and reasonable excuse for striking her mount. "And you were in no danger, surprised or not, my dear girl. You can handle a much livelier animal than that plodder."

"That may be true, but you still had no right to do that," she insisted, even as her anger melted away. There was something irresistible about this man's personality. He swept all objections and obstacles before him. If she'd felt bullied in any way, it would have been different, but somehow she didn't.

"Then forgive me?" he asked, reaching out to touch her gloved hand. "Come, don't be angry with me, Livia." He gave her a cajoling smile. "Besides, you know that animal wouldn't have speeded up for any less encouragement than I gave him. Am I forgiven?"

Livia said nothing to that. She glanced over her shoulder and instead observed neutrally, "We seem to have lost the groom in that headlong race."

"Hardly headlong."

She shrugged. "Hardly decorous either. I must go back to Lady Devries before she sends out a search party." She turned her horse and raised her whip in pointed farewell. "Good day, Prince Prokov."

"Allow me to escort you to your friend. It seems the least I can do to make amends," he said, falling in smoothly beside her. "And I would be honored if you would allow me to escort you home. A mere groom, a livery stables groom at that, is hardly adequate escort for a ride through the London streets. Your mount might become startled and bolt with you."

It was too much. Livia went into a peal of laughter. Alex watched her appreciatively, but this time wisdom told him to hold his tongue on further intimate compliments. He was rewarded by her tacit consent to his company back to the others.

"Wherever have you been?" Lilly asked with a note of reproof. "You should never gallop in the park, Livia."

"Lady Livia's horse ran away with her," the prince said solemnly. "She was unable to hold him. I went to her assistance."

"Really," Lilly said, regarding her friend's mount rather doubtfully. "He doesn't look as if he had it in him."

"He doesn't," Livia said. "The prince thinks he's being amusing." She gave him a cool smile. "An unfortunate misapprehension. I think perhaps he does not understand English humor."

"Oh, touché," he murmured, raising a hand in a fencer's gesture that acknowledged a hit.

"Well, no harm done," Colonel Melton said heartily. "Shall we ride on?"

"No, I must return to Cavendish Square," Livia said. "Lady Farnham returned from the country this morning and I must keep her company."

"Then let us go at once," Alex said. "You must not keep the lady waiting another minute." He reached for her bridle to turn the horse on the path. Livia's whip flashed and stung the back of his gloved hand.

He withdrew the hand with a barely stifled gasp and met the blaze of her glare. "Thank you for the offer, sir," she said with deceptive sweetness. "So very kind of you, but I'm very much afraid I have to decline. Do please remain with your friends." She offered her farewells, then turned back to the Stanhope Gate, the groom at her heels.

Alex gave her a minute or two, then made his own excuses and rode after her. He caught up with her before she reached the gate and fell in beside her. She didn't acknowledge his presence, and after a long silence he said, "That was a grave error on my part. Will you forgive me that too?"

She turned to look at him as they reached Piccadilly. "Just who do you think you are?" The question sounded more puzzled than indignant. "I barely know you and yet you are behaving with me as if you have some kind of right . . . as if we'd known each other from the cradle or something."

He gave an elaborate mock shudder. "Oh, no . . . not the innocent intimacy of childhood friends . . . that wouldn't suit me at all."

"It wouldn't suit me either," Livia found herself responding. *And now why was she was chatting with him as naturally as if they had known each other for months and he had never infuriated her for a minute?* She shook her head in irritation, firmly closed her mouth, and didn't open it again until they reached Cavendish Square.

Alex had swung himself down from his horse before the groom had even begun to dismount himself. He reached up a hand to Livia. "Allow me to assist you, ma'am."

"I require no assistance," she said shortly, ignoring the hand. She slipped gracefully from the saddle and smoothed down her skirts. "I give you good day, Prince Prokov."

"I find I'm very thirsty," Alex said somewhat plaintively. "Do you think your butler could furnish me with a glass of water? I hate to impose, but . . ." He touched his throat with an expressive fingertip.

"If you go down to the kitchen door, down the area steps, I'm sure one of the servants will supply your needs," Livia declared. His expression was for once so utterly disconcerted and crestfallen that she couldn't resist a mischievous grin.

"If I'd known how delicious it would be to discompose you, Prince Prokov, I would have tried harder before," she said, setting her foot on the first step to the front door. "Pray come in. I'm sure I can find you something a little more refreshing than plain water."

"You are too kind, ma'am," Alex said dryly. He followed her, reflecting that when it came to Livia Lacey he would do well not to rely absolutely on his customary tactics when turning situations to his advantage. She was adapting to his methods rather more quickly than he was accustomed to. For some reason the reflection didn't annoy him as it might have done; in fact, it brought an inner smile. She would prove a worthy quarry.

Livia banged on the brass knocker with a degree of vigor that surprised her companion. The sound reverberated on the quiet square. "My butler is hard of hearing," she offered in explanation. "And somewhat slow of foot." She banged again.

The door creaked open and Morecombe peered around. "Oh, 'tis you," he said as usual.

"Who else were you expecting, Morecombe?" Livia pushed the door wider to encourage the elderly retainer to step back a little. "Please take Prince Prokov's whip, gloves, hat . . . whatever else he'd like to discard." She stepped past him into the hall and Alex, sensing that he needed to take advantage of the door while it remained open, stepped in smartly behind her.

The old man in a rusty baize apron, most unusual attire for a butler, looked him over. Wordlessly he held out a gnarled hand for the visitor's whip and high-crowned beaver hat, and waited while Alex drew off his fine leather gloves.

"Is Lady Farnham in the parlor, Morecombe?" Livia inquired.

"Not as I know," the retainer said, his gaze flickering once more to the prince.

"Well, maybe you could ask someone to find her and tell her that we have a visitor," Livia suggested. "And perhaps you could bring sherry to the salon?" The questioning inflection was apparent. It was clearly not an instruction.

Morecombe merely grunted and shuffled off towards the kitchen regions, and Alex followed Livia into a large, handsome salon. There was a touch of well-worn shabbiness to the furniture and upholstery, and the colors in the Turkey carpet and the velvet curtains had faded somewhat, but he thought it merely added to the charm of the apartment.

"What an extraordinary servant," he observed. "If that's what he is."

"In a manner of speaking," Livia returned. "He and his wife and her sister, they're twins, were in my relative's service. I call her Aunt Sophia, but I think she was more of a distant cousin . . . anyway, she left me the house, as I explained, but with the proviso that Morecombe and the twins should stay on for as long as they wished." She laughed a little. "They have their eccentricities, certainly, but also their charms. One gets used to them."

"I see." Alex turned as the door opened behind him. A woman entered carrying a tray with a decanter and glasses. She looked to be a little older than Livia, her pale blonde hair plaited in a coronet around a well-shaped head, her brown eyes soft and warm.

"Morecombe said we had a visitor," she said in a pleasantly modulated voice. "I thought it would be quicker to bring the sherry myself." She set the tray on a sideboard.

"Ellie, may I present Prince Prokov," Livia said. "Prince Prokov, this is Lady Farnham, my friend and . . . uh . . . chaperone." She winked at Aurelia, who laughed.

"Purely nominal," Aurelia said, holding out her hand to the visitor. "Prince Prokov, I'm delighted to make your acquaintance."

"The pleasure is all mine, Lady Farnham." He bowed over her hand, raising it to his lips.

"Sherry, Prince." Livia passed him a glass once he'd returned Aurelia's hand. "Or would you really prefer water?" Her thick black eyebrows lifted and there was a hint of mischief in the gray eyes.

He decided to ignore the mischief, at least for the moment. "Sherry will do beautifully, thank you," he said, taking the glass.

He glanced around the salon, observing, "What a pleasant room." He strolled across to the magnificent Adam fireplace, trying to appear as if his interest were merely casual. But he was consumed with the desire to see every inch of this house. He had poured over the plans of the house for years and knew the position of every room, even to the box rooms in the attic. And now, finally, he was here.

He sipped his sherry and looked up at the portrait over the fireplace. A young woman in full court regalia, feathers in her powdered, elaborately coiffed hair, gazed out across the room. Her blue eyes seemed to penetrate every corner, and he could almost fancy that for a moment they saw into his soul.

Chapter Three

So what do you think of him?" Livia asked Aurelia as she returned to the salon ten minutes later, having escorted the prince to the front door.

Aurelia hesitated, choosing her words. "Hard to say, really," she said finally. "He's charming, suave even, and handsome, no two ways about that."

Livia frowned a little. "That sounds like damning with faint praise, Ellie."

"He was only here ten minutes," Aurelia pointed out, rearranging a bowl of heavy-headed chrysanthemums on the sideboard. "Not long enough to form a definitive opinion . . . certainly it wouldn't be fair after such a short time."

Livia sighed a little. "No, you're right, of course. And you're also right that he's charming and good-looking. He's also very determined to get his own way."

"Why? What happened?" Aurelia shot her a shrewd glance over her shoulder as she worked.

Livia shrugged and dropped into an armchair. "Well, first it was dancing with me last night, and then this morning . . ." She told her about the ride. "The strange thing is, Ellie, even while I'm objecting to being somehow manipulated, I don't really seem to mind, deep down. Now, that's very odd, you must admit." ·

"Very odd," her friend agreed. She shook drops of water off her hands. "It sounds to me as if Prince Prokov is pursuing you in a very single-minded fashion." She dried her hands fastidiously on her lace handkerchief. "You must have made a powerful impression on him at the ball last night . . . from the first moment he saw you."

"But that's absurd," Livia said. "A rational man doesn't take one look at a strange woman in a ballroom and decide instantly that he's interested in pursuing her."

"It has been known," Aurelia said, smiling. "Anyway, you seem to be enjoying the game, Liv."

"I suppose I am," Livia agreed. "Anyway, it can't do any harm, and when I'm not enjoying it I shall bring it to an end." She jumped to her feet. "And that reminds me . . . now you're back we can make up a party for the opera and have a small dinner here beforehand. It's time we repaid some of the hospitality, don't you agree?"

"Certainly," Aurelia consented. "And will we be inviting the prince?"

"Why not?" Livia said, with that gleam of mischief in her eye again. "I don't always have to be the mouse . . . I can be the cat as well." She left the salon, her step light and eager.

Aurelia shook her head, a half-smile on her lips but a flicker of doubt in her eyes. Livia had had her share of suitors in the last few months, and Aurelia was certain there had been several offers of marriage, but none Liv had entertained seriously, even though she had always said she wasn't looking for a love match, or a brilliant match, just one comfortable enough to ensure her a respectable establishment and the opportunity to have children. But Aurelia was sure her friend was looking for something more. She was not going to settle for anything or anyone who didn't stir her in some way. It rather seemed as if the mysterious Russian prince had made an impression on her that no one else on the London scene had so far succeeded in doing.

Thoughtfully Aurelia tapped her mouth with her fingertips. Livia was no fool and she was no ingénue. She was quite capable of looking after herself and making her own decisions. Nevertheless, Aurelia decided it could do no harm to investigate the prince's circumstances. Maybe Cornelia's husband, Viscount Bonham, could find out something. Harry had enough contacts all over London, in diplomatic and political circles, as well as the purely social. And he certainly knew how to ask the right questions.

She would write to Cornelia at once, Aurelia decided. Apart from anything else, Nell would want to be kept in the picture.

Unaware of the speculation he had caused in the house in Cavendish Square, Alex rode towards Hyde Park Corner absorbed in his own thoughts. The portrait of the woman over the fireplace filled his internal vision. He had only seen a miniature of her before, and he realized now how little that had done her justice. The intelligent purity of her sapphire gaze as she stared straight out from the large canvas had startled him. The ivory tones of her skin seemed to radiate an inner glow, and her posture, so composed and almost commanding, spoke of an assurance, a self-confidence that he hadn't expected from the bare bones he'd managed to glean about Sophia Lacey from his father.

Not that his taciturn father had told him much about anything, Alex reflected with a familiar stab of resentment that was as much hurt as anger. He'd been given the basic facts about his birth, but none of the emotional connections that would soften those facts. But his father had been dead for seven years and there was little to be gained from nursing a lonely child's resentment. Politics and his service to Czar Alexander had kept him in Russia those long seven years, but finally he had the opportunity to find answers for himself to those questions he really needed to be answered.

He rode into the yard at Tattersalls, the horse brokers at Hyde Park Corner, and dismounted, handing the black to a groom who had come rushing at the sight of a gentleman who was presumably a customer. A man emerged from an outbuilding to one side of a stable block, clad in leather britches and jerkin, a checkered muffler at his neck, a cap pulled low over his forehead. He didn't look like the man who owned and ran the most reputable horse dealership in London, but Alex was not fooled by appearances.

The man greeted his customer with a laconic nod but then turned his attention to Alex's horse, running a professionally assessing gaze over the black. "Magnificent animal," he observed, moving one hand down the gelding's neck while the other stroked the velvety nose. "Are you selling, sir?"

Alex shook his head. "Not for a fortune."

"Pity," the broker said. "I could get you a fortune for him too."

"Doubtless," Alex said. "But I'm buying today, Mr. Tattersall. It *is* Mr. Tattersall?"

The man nodded. "Aye, that it is, sir. What can I do for you?"

Alex explained his needs and Tattersall listened intently, nodding from time to time. "I think I've got just what you're looking for coming onto the block tomorrow. If you like, I'll take a preemptive bid. Have to be sight unseen, though. She's not coming in until the morning."

Alex frowned. It went against the grain, but this man was a prime judge of horseflesh and he wouldn't risk his trade and reputation with a fraudulent claim. "Give me details."

"Right, sir. If you'd like to come into the office."

Alex followed him into the small building that was

stuffy with the heat thrown off by a charcoal brazier. He perched on the end of a deal table and listened to Tattersall's description of the horse. "She'll do," he said with decision at the end of the detailed description. "Deliver her to my stables when you receive her tomorrow." He reached into his pocket for a bank draft.

The broker waved it away. "No need, sir. Settle next quarter day."

Alex shook his head. "No, I like to settle my bills at once."

Tattersall looked at him as if he had descended from the moon. In his wide experience, no gentleman of leisure settled his bills until he had to. However, he accepted the more than sizeable draft on Hoares bank with something approaching a smile on his dour countenance and locked it into a drawer in the table. "If you'll give me the address of the mews, sir, I'll have her delivered bright and early in the morning."

Alex obliged and then left the premises well pleased with his purchase. It was the opening salvo in his siege of castle Livia after the preliminary skirmishes. He thought he had come out of those on the winning side, but he had to admit it was not an open-and-shut conclusion.

He returned to Bruton Street and went straight to his inner sanctum, a small windowless chamber between the salon and his bedchamber. More of a closet than a real room. He lit the oil lamp and opened the desk. There were twelve drawers in the rear of the desk, one for every month of the year, originally intended for the organization of household accounts. These drawers, however, were not used for such a mundane purpose. A tiny gold key opened them all.

Alex took the key from a pocket sewn into the lining of his coat and opened one of the top drawers. Blue sapphires, a small heap of them, winked at him in the low lamplight. He took out a handful and laid them on a soft leather pad on the desktop. They were magnificent stones, perfectly cut and faceted.

Sapphires or diamonds? Which would complement gray eyes the best?

He opened another drawer and took out a handful of diamonds, letting them run through his fingers in a glittering white cascade to form a heap beside the sapphires.

Alex took up a jeweler's magnifying glass and examined each gem in turn, selecting from both piles. Of course he didn't need to buy his way into the house in Cavendish Square, it was legally his anyway. He didn't need to lay siege to Livia Lacey. She had no legal rights to anything.

As soon as he'd received the necessary reports on her from his informants and it seemed she would suit his purposes as well as any other eligible woman, he'd come to London intending to present her with a business proposition that she would have been a fool to reject, given that she was an unmarried lady of no particular fortune. If, however, she refused the offer that conscience obliged him to make, then he would simply take possession of his house and find the wife he needed elsewhere.

But from the moment he'd first laid eyes on her at the Clarington ball he had discovered another and unexpected dimension to the matter: a strange but powerful compulsion to pursue Livia Lacey for reasons quite outside the practical. And if he chose to go about the pursuit in this fashion, well, there was no one to tell him how to spend his own fortune.

He took the gems he'd selected, three sapphires and three diamonds, and dropped them into a small velvet pouch. Rundell and Bridge, the jewelers, would be able to do what he wanted done with them.

He was replacing the other stones in their drawers when he heard the knocker sound. He cursed softly. Like his father, he detested chance visitors, but it seemed to be a commonplace social event in this city. He dropped the pouch into his britches' pocket, locked the drawers of the desk, and tucked the key away, turning casually as Boris opened the door that led into his bedchamber.

"Prince Michael Michaelovitch, Your Highness. In the salon."

"I'll be there immediately." Alex was still in riding dress, hardly suitable attire for town visitors, but Michael would not relish being kept waiting. He went into the salon.

"Michael, such a pleasure." He held out his hand in greeting. "What may I offer you?"

"Vodka, just a tincture," his visitor said, taking the proffered hand. "Pleasant apartments these." He gestured expansively around the room. "Lucky to find them."

"So I gather." Alex went to the sideboard to pour his guest a drink. "But I have a suitable house in mind and will take up residence as soon as possible. Lodgings can't help but be cramped and I like to entertain."

"Ah." His guest nodded sagely as he took the glass. "Yes . . . yes . . . well, one can entertain as well here as Moscow or St. Petersburg, or even Paris, I daresay."

"I confess to a fondness for Paris," Alex said, pouring himself a glass of rather more innocuous madeira.

"Yes, well, who knows. If the czar's friendship with Bonaparte continues to progress, we could all be dancing again in the ballrooms of Paris before long." The prince nodded again with the same sagacity. He tossed back the contents of his glass in one deep swallow and nodded again, this time with approval. "Excellent . . . so what do you think of this business, Alex?"

Alex brought the vodka bottle over to refill his glass. "What aspect of the business exactly, Michael?"

"This business of breaking off diplomatic relations with the Court of St. James, of course," the older man said. "The ambassador told me himself he expects to be recalled any day now. How're we to know what's goin' on over here when we have no one in place? The English are tricky bastards. They lie through their teeth even as they embrace you as their truest ally. Who's supposed to be watchin' this pot? That's what I want to know." He regarded his host ferociously over the lip of his glass.

Alex shrugged easily. "Come on, Michael, you're not here to ask the question. You're here to have your suspicions confirmed . . . yes?"

"So are you here on the czar's business?" The prince cut to the chase.

"And if I am?" Alex took a seat on the sofa and gestured an invitation to the opposing sofa.

His visitor took the seat and glared at him. "You're a soldier, not a diplomat, Alex."

Alex raised his eyebrows. "Oddly enough, my friend, I believe I can do both. And so, it would appear, does our emperor."

"But the English don't know that's why you're here?"

Alex laughed. "Hardly, Michael. That would defeat the purpose. I am a social butterfly, a dilettante with nothing on my mind but cards and dice, flirtation, maybe even a little discreet seduction, the theatre, opera, concerts, balls, and rout parties. A man, in short, with nothing but frivol on his mind . . . and who knows, I may even find myself a nice, respectable English wife. The perfect hostess for all the entertaining that will bring London's social and political elite to my drawing room." His clear blue eyes met his visitor's darker gaze with nothing but amusement. "How would that be for a cover?"

The prince nodded slowly. "It would certainly give you impeccable social credentials. Do you have a contact at court as yet?"

Alex's amusement seemed to deepen. "If I had, *mon ami*, I would not be telling you."

Michael glowered for a second and then threw his head back with a deep rumble of laughter. "No . . . no, of course you wouldn't. Foolish of me to try to catch you out." He drained his glass again and set it down as he rose to his feet. "Well, I won't trespass any further on your time, Alex. Bear in mind that if you need the counsel of an elder statesman, I'm here." He held out his hand.

Alex saw him to the door and closed it softly behind him. He stood in the dimly lit hallway for a minute. So the czar, who supposedly trusted Alexander Prokov as his best friend and most intimate confidant, had put Michael on to watch him. Trust only went so far, apparently.

In truth he couldn't blame the czar. It was a safe assumption that it was the Committee for General Security who'd set the oversight in motion. It didn't make his job any easier, though. Michael was a blustering old fool a lot of the time, which made him hard to second-guess. His loyalty to the emperor was absolute, as was his loyalty to Mother Russia, but for him the two were inextricably intertwined. Czar Alexander *was* Mother Russia and neither could do wrong.

But he had pleasanter matters to occupy him for the rest of the day. Alex called for Boris to fetch his hat and gloves, and a few minutes later he was strolling in the direction of Piccadilly and the business of Rundell and Bridge.

Within the hushed portals of that business a discreet gentleman, on hearing his identity, swiftly ushered him into a paneled chamber behind the shop, where he was introduced to Mr. Bridge, a dignified gentleman in black coat and waistcoat, who rose to greet him from behind a massive desk. "An honor, Prince Prokov. How may we be of service?"

Alex tipped the gems into the palm of his hand and then set them on the pouch on the desk. "I have a design in mind for these," he said without preamble. "But I am also open to suggestions."

The gentleman appraised the gems with one sweeping glance and said almost reverently, "Allow me to fetch our master jeweler, sir." He slipped away as soundlessly as a black wraith and was back in seconds with a tall, impossibly thin man, whose hunched back indicated hours of labor bent over a workbench.

"This is Mr. Arkwright, sir," the first gentleman said. "He is a master craftsman."

Alex acknowledged the new arrival with a nod and gestured to the glittering pile of stones on the desk. "I have in mind a ring and a pendant. If you have paper and pen, Mr. Arkwright, I will sketch the designs I had in mind."

The jeweler regarded Alex's efforts with something akin to respect, then took the pen. "If I might make a suggestion, sir." He made a few adjustments.

"I take it these are for a lady, not . . . how shall I put it . . . not a debutante, sir?" Mr. Bridge murmured. "Sapphires and diamonds, sir . . . not entirely suitable for the very young."

"I am aware of that," Alex said, and then wished he hadn't sounded so dismissive, as Mr. Bridge hummed and huffed apologies for an interminable length of time. "You weren't to know, Mr. Bridge," he said, interrupting the murmur. "But as it happens, the lady is no longer a debutante and is well up to wearing such stones."

"Yes . . . yes, of course, sir. Forgive me . . ."

"Let us dispense with that now, Mr. Bridge," Alex said, waving a hand. "It's a matter of no further concern." He turned back to the jeweler who was weighing the stones. "So, Arkwright, will these stones do?"

"These stones are flawless, sir," Mr. Arkwright said. He glanced up at the customer. "If you had more, I would suggest diamond ear drops with a sapphire center would be an admirable addition to the set."

Alex smiled. "Yes, they would, but I don't wish to run before I can walk, Mr. Arkwright. When the time comes, I will return with that commission."

"Of course, sir. May I take them now?"

"Please." Alex gestured to the stones in invitation. "How long do you think?"·

"A month."

Alex's eyes narrowed, his fair brows drawing together. He *had* to carry the castle before then if he was to keep to his timetable. "Three weeks," he stated.

Mr. Arkwright looked at his employer, who nodded at him. He scooped the gems into the pouch. "Three weeks it shall be, sir."

"Thank you." Alex picked up his hat from the chair

where he'd deposited it on his entrance. "I'll be back three weeks today."

Mr. Arkwright gave him a nodding bow and hurried away. Mr. Bridge bowed more deeply. "Such a pleasure to do business with you, Prince Prokov." He escorted his customer to the street and stood bowing until he'd disappeared into the throng.

Chapter Four

Livia DESCENDED THE STAIRS THE following morning, her eyes on the sheet of vellum she was reading, and then her progress halted. She stared openmouthed at the hall below her and wondered if she'd somehow been transported to the botanic gardens. Flowers of every hue spilled from baskets, were massed in great copper jugs, covering the parquet floor.

"Good Lord, where did all these come from?"

"I'm trying to find out." Aurelia popped up from behind an enormous basket of deep crimson dahlias. "I can't find a card anywhere here. Come and help."

Livia took the last few steps with a skip and a jump and plunged into the tropical garden. The mingled scents were almost overpowering. "There must be some mistake. Who brought them?"

"Some carrier, according to Morecombe." Aurelia shook her head in bemusement. "Of course it didn't occur to him to ask the man anything about the delivery, he just let them pile everything here and went off about his business in usual Morecombe fashion. I found all this when I came down five minutes ago."

Livia gazed around her. She ran distracted hands through her curls. "What are we to do with them?"

"I don't know. Let's find out who they're from first. It might well be a mistake. You start on the right and I'll take the left." Aurelia began a methodical search of the containers.

"This is ridiculous," Livia said after a few futile minutes. *"Morecombe."* She raised her voice and yelled in the general direction of the kitchen regions.

"You'll be lucky," Aurelia observed with a grin. But to her surprise the elderly retainer shuffled into the hall a few minutes later.

"You want summat, m'lady?"

"Yes," Livia said, straightening from a basket of roses. "Did the carrier say anything at all when he unloaded these?"

The butler shook his head. "Nowt that I 'eard, mum. Said as 'ow they were fer Lady Livia Lacey, an' dumped the lot 'ere an' went about 'is business, like any other God-fearing fellow." He turned at the sound of the door knocker and grumbled, "Anyone would think we was a coachin' inn."

Livia exchanged a look with Aurelia as Morecombe plodded to the door and fiddled with the latch before finally opening the door a crack.

"Good morning," a familiar voice said. "Is your mistress within?"

"Seems t'be," Morecombe responded.

"Then would you announce me?" The prince's voice was patient and pleasant.

Livia went to the door. "It's all right, Morecombe." She took the door from him and opened it wide.

Prince Prokov, hat in hand, bowed, the sun catching golden glints in his fair head. His eyes seemed particularly blue this morning, Livia thought somewhat distractedly, and his teeth gleamed very white as he smiled.

"My dear lady, what a great pleasure it is to see you." She did look enchanting, he thought. She wore an informal morning gown of apple-green cambric and her curly hair was rather unruly, as if she'd been trawling her fingers through it, giving her the appearance of dishabille. Her complexion had a delicate pink flush to it as if she'd been exerting herself more than usual.

Livia wasn't sure whether he was teasing her or not. It was a ridiculously flowery greeting, but there was something in his smiling gaze that flustered her a little. She said as firmly as she could, "Good morning, Prince Prokov. You're paying calls rather early . . . unfortunately this is not the most convenient moment for us."

"Oh, I don't mind, please continue with what you were doing," he said blithely. "I won't be in the way, I promise." He took a step up to the door and looked over her shoulder. "Oh, good, the flowers have arrived. Do they please you?"

"*You* sent them?" She stared at him, and then realized that she should have guessed all along. It was just the kind of flamboyant, overwhelming gesture she should have expected from this Russian prince.

"Yes. Didn't you find my card?" He took advantage of her momentary disarmament to step past her into the hall.

"Good morning, Prince Prokov." Aurelia emerged from a garden of hothouse tulips and regarded him with a cool smile and clear mistrust in her steady gaze. "Am I to understand we have you to thank for this . . . this largesse." She made an expansive gesture encompassing the massed blooms behind her.

"I thought they might brighten your day, ma'am," he said with a bow, his eyes searching her expression with a little frown in their depths. "Was I mistaken?"

"We don't mean to sound ungrateful," Livia said quickly, "and indeed they are most beautiful . . . but what are we to do with them all?"

"Arrange them," he suggested. "Isn't that what ladies usually do with flowers?"

"A bunch at a time perhaps," Livia said, unable to keep a chuckle from her voice. It really was absurd. "But not an entire botanical garden. Where did you get them all?"

"I have my sources," he said. "But if they're too much of a nuisance I shall have them taken away at once."

"Oh, no, you mustn't do that," Livia exclaimed. "I don't mean to be ungracious. It's . . . it's just that such a quantity is rather overwhelming."

"Then allow me to help you arrange them." He tossed his hat onto the Jacobean bench by the door and followed it with his cane and gloves. Then he bent and lifted a woven basket of lilies. "Now, where would you like me to take these?"

"In the salon, I think, don't you, Ellie? They have the most wonderful scent." Livia cast a helpless glance towards her friend.

Aurelia accepted the fait accompli. "Yes, they'll look pretty on the console table between the windows," she agreed, telling herself that flowers were a perfectly respectable offering from a gentleman to a lady. It was only the quantity that was the problem here. Somehow such munificence seemed to detract from the general respectability of the gift.

Livia, on the other hand, didn't seem concerned at all, Aurelia noticed. She was laughing and chatting inconsequentially as she directed the prince's labors, arranging banks of flowers on windowsills and tables, her cheeks delicately flushed and her gray eyes glinting with light like sun on the sea. Aurelia sent a swift prayer for Cornelia's rapid return to town. She could do with reinforcements together with a second opinion, and the situation cried out for Harry's investigative contacts.

The house resembled a hothouse when the flowers were finally dispersed throughout the ground floor, the air heavy with their fragrance.

"It's like living in a garden," Livia said with delight

even as Aurelia sneezed. "Oh, dear, do they tickle your nose, Ellie?"

"A little," the other woman admitted, blowing her nose on a lace handkerchief. "But I'm sure I'll get used to it."

"*Lawks-a-mercy.*"

They all turned to the door at the exclamation. Ada, Morecombe's wife, stood staring, her gray hair drawn into a severe bun on the nape of her neck, the greenish cast to her pallor more noticeable than usual. She called over her shoulder, "Our Mavis, would you jest come an' take a look at this lot."

Her sister appeared almost immediately with Morecombe at her back. "Well, I never did," Mavis declared. "I never saw nuthin' like it, not never."

"Eh, an' jest who's goin' t'be waterin' this lot, that's what I've been wantin' to know," Morecombe stated.

"Aye, take all day it will," his wife agreed, her sister nodding vigorously. "If 'n you expects yer dinner on time, mum, ye'll not be lookin' to our Mavis an' me to see t' this lot."

"An' 'tis not my job, neither," Morecombe announced.

"It's quite all right. I'll take care of it myself," Livia said. "With Lady Farnham's help, of course." She shot Aurelia a look of anxious appeal.

"Yes, of course," Aurelia said, trying to contain her laughter at the disapproval on the faces of the three retainers. "Of course we wouldn't expect any of you to take on such a monumental task. But I'm sure Hester can help, and Jemmy can fill watering cans."

"Oh dear," Alex murmured as the trio departed without offering an opinion on the assistance of their juniors. "Somehow the practicalities of such an offering escaped me. Shall I come every morning and water them myself? Would that help?"

"No, of course you shan't," Livia said on a bubble of laughter. "We'll manage even if I'm condemned to wander amongst them with a watering can for the rest of my days. I'm sure I shan't miss attending all the balls and the parties . . . although I confess I am particularly fond of the theatre," she added with a mournful sigh. "It might be difficult to forgo that."

"Absurd woman," Alex accused, thinking once again how much he enjoyed her laughter, even when she was mocking him. He glanced at the long case clock in the corner of the room as it struck ten. "Damn it, but I have to go. An appointment . . ." He hurried to the hall for his cane, hat, and gloves. "Livia, I came to ask you to join me in the park this afternoon. I'll collect you at five o'clock . . . that is the hour for seeing and being seen, is it not?"

"Generally yes," Livia said, following him into the hall. "But has it occurred to you that I might have something else to do this afternoon?"

He drew on a glove and frowned at her. "No . . . do you? Can't you put it off?"

"I might not wish to," she said, on her mettle once again.

His frown deepened. "I'm not very adept at this game of flirtation, ma'am. It has always struck me as pointless. If you don't wish to join me this afternoon, then please say so."

"As it happens, I wasn't flirting," Livia retorted, the sunshine vanished from her eyes. "I don't care to have my mind made up for me by someone else's assumptions. You presume too much, Prince Prokov."

"Ah." He drew on the second glove, smoothing the fine leather over his hand, frowning as he did so. "It is perhaps a failing of mine," he conceded after a minute. "In my culture men tend to make the decisions." He looked across at her then and his teeth flashed in a smile. "I'm willing to learn the English way. Surely you can't resist the opportunity to teach me, ma'am?"

Perhaps she couldn't. Livia debated the question, keeping him waiting for her answer, although his smile didn't waver and that clear blue gaze didn't move from her face. "I've always enjoyed a challenge, sir," she said finally. "We'll see if I'm up to this one."

"I don't doubt it for a minute." He reached for her hand and brought it to his lips, brushing her knuckles with the merest breath of a kiss. "At five o'clock, then."

"Five o'clock." She moved to open the door but he reached over her to lift the latch himself.

"Forgive the observation, ma'am, but isn't there a saying about not keeping a servant and opening one's own doors?"

"The saying you mean goes something like, there's no

point keeping a dog and barking oneself," she said. "And Morecombe and the twins are a law unto themselves. They don't really work for me, they work for the memory of Sophia Lacey, as I think I explained . . . and talking of dogs . . ." She broke off as Tristan and Isolde came hurtling up the steps from the street, a flustered Hester struggling to hold on to their leashes.

"I beg your pardon, mum, but I can't hold 'em," Hester panted as the leash was wrenched from her hand. "I was going to take 'em round to the kitchen."

"That's all right, Hester," Livia said above the yapping of the terriers, who seemed to have decided that Prince Prokov was their new best friend.

He seemed untroubled by their attentions, merely brushing them down as if they were dust balls as they pranced on hind legs at his knees. He said something sharply to them in a language that Livia didn't understand, but the effect was remarkable. They dropped to their haunches and gazed up at him, tongues lolling.

"Whatever did you say?" Livia asked. "Oh, no, what a ridiculous question, they wouldn't have understood you."

"Oh, you'd be surprised," he said carelessly. "The language of animals is universal. It's not the sounds so much as the tone. I could speak to them in Mandarin in the same tone and they'd respond in the same way."

"Could you speak Mandarin?" she asked involuntarily even though she was bristling again at his calm assumption of some supernaturally superior power. *Talk to animals, indeed.*

He gave her a shrewd look, sensing her annoyance. He shook his head, but with a smile. "No, as it happens I don't speak Mandarin. But I do have a way with animals . . . even such unlikely-looking creatures as these." The dogs drooled adoringly as if they knew he was speaking of them.

Livia bent and picked up the dropped leashes. "Don't let me keep you from your engagement, Prince."

"Until this afternoon, Livia." He gave her a brief bow and then strolled down the steps to the street. He turned and raised a hand in farewell and the dogs howled.

"Oh, do be quiet, you fickle creatures." Livia hauled the animals into the hall and kicked the door shut behind her. She bent to release the leads and they skittered across the polished parquet towards a standing copper vase of greenery and roses. Excitedly they scampered around the vase, sniffing, tails in the air, and Livia began to get an ominous premonition.

"Oh, no, you don't," she said, bending to scoop them up. "This may look and smell like a flower garden, my friends, but it is *not*." She carried them to the baize door that led to the kitchen regions, opened it, and sent them through. Yet another complication of Alex Prokov's incarnation as a florist.

She returned to the salon but there was no sign of Aurelia, just the heavy scent of myriad blooms. She ran her to earth in the parlor. "Ah, here you are."

"Yes, I needed some fresh air," Aurelia said, putting down the periodical she was reading. "We managed to keep the flowers out of this room. What an impulsive man he is, Liv. Who would think to do something like that?"

"I don't think Alex Prokov considers it at all odd," Livia said. "It seems to go hand in hand with pushing people into fountains if they're in your way."

"Why do I think you don't really mind his impulses?" Aurelia asked, watching Liv closely as she paced the room.

Livia shrugged. "I don't . . . at least not all the time. They're rather exciting." She stopped pacing and stood by the window, facing Aurelia. She still had that glow about her, Aurelia noticed, still that sunshine sparkle in her eyes. "I'm never bored in his company, Ellie."

"Well, I can certainly see the appeal there," her friend agreed cautiously. "But don't you think we should try to find out more about him?"

"I don't know that I want to," Livia said, surprising herself as she spoke. "I rather like not knowing what's going to happen from one moment to the next. It's not as if I'm contemplating spending the rest of my life with him, Ellie. It's just an interlude. For some reason he's interested in me, and I'm enjoying his interest. What harm can it do?"

"None, I hope." But Aurelia was not completely convinced of that. As long as Liv kept her head, then all would be well, but while Liv was generally levelheaded, she could also go off at a tangent on occasion.

"Anyway, I'm walking with him in the park this afternoon," Livia said, as if that closed the conversation. "May I borrow your brown velvet pelisse, the one with the gray trimming? It goes so well with my gray silk, and at least I won't go blue with cold when the sun goes down."

"Yes, of course," Aurelia said readily. Until Cornelia had broken up the trio by marrying Harry Bonham, the three women had shared clothes and accessories as a matter of necessity. They'd learned that clever adjustments to a limited wardrobe could expand that wardrobe quite considerably. "And you should wear the high-crowned gray velvet hat, and the gray kid gloves."

"Exactly so." Livia nodded her satisfaction. "Now, could you bear to have just one vase of flowers in here? I think those golden dahlias and tawny chrysanthemums would look lovely on the pier table."

"Yes, they would," Aurelia agreed, getting to her feet. "It isn't that I don't love flowers, I do, but . . ."

"In moderation," Livia finished for her. "I'm not sure how much the Russian prince knows about moderation."

Aurelia said hesitantly, "Probably more than he lets on, Liv. I just have the impression that there might be more to him than he's letting us see."

Livia looked at her, her head tilted to one side, her gaze quizzical. "Isn't that true of pretty well everyone, Ellie? If I thought what I'd seen was all there was to see of Alexander Prokov, then I would have no interest in him whatsoever."

"You could be playing with fire."

"I could," Livia agreed. "And if I burn my fingers, it will be with full knowledge."

Aurelia nodded. "Let's hope it doesn't come to that. I must go to Franny. I promised to take her for a walk. Are you in for luncheon?"

Livia grimaced. "Letitia Oglethorpe has inveigled me into a small ladies' luncheon to discuss the latest on-dits."

"For heaven's sake, Liv . . . why did you accept?" Letitia was their bête noire.

"Accidentally," Livia said with a groan. "The invitation was in a pile I was answering and I found I'd accepted it without realizing who it was from. And by then Jemmy had taken it to the post and it was too late . . . I could plead a headache . . ." She brightened momentarily, then sighed. "No, I can't. Not if I'm going to walk in the park with the prince a few hours later. Someone's bound to see me and mention it."

"Well, good luck. I'm glad she didn't invite me."

"She would have done if she'd known you'd be back in town," Livia pointed out. "But you could always just come." Her smile was mischievous. "You know how delighted she'd be to see you . . . and just think of all the questions she'll ask about Nell and Harry."

"No, thank you," Aurelia said firmly. "I'll see you later."

"So, tell us about Prince Prokov, Livia?" Lilly Devries leaned forward in her chair, her eyes bright with curiosity. "A most handsome man, I thought. Where did you meet him?"

"Oh, intrigue," crowed Letitia Oglethorpe. "Is this a new man about town, Livia? I don't know the name."

Livia sighed. She'd guessed this would happen as soon as she'd seen that Lilly was one of the select group of ladies at Letitia's luncheon. "I don't really know anything about him. I met him at the duchess of Clarington's ball the other night and danced once with him," she said, hoping that an assumption of careless indifference to the subject might put them off pursuing it.

No such luck, of course. Letitia had an unfailing nose for sniffing out hidden morsels of gossip. "Well, *is* he handsome?" she demanded. "Handsome *and* rich?"

"I have no idea whether he has money or not," Livia stated a little sharply. "I don't go around asking strangers the state of their financial affairs . . . rather vulgar, I would have thought."

It worked to a certain extent; Letitia pouted and turned her shoulder to Livia, demanding of Lilly instead, "Tell me about him. Where does he come from? How long has he been in town?"

Lilly threw up her hands. "I don't know anything, Letitia, except that he's a Russian prince and *I* at least thought him handsome. But Livia's tastes may run to a different kind of look." She glanced at Livia as she said this.

Livia decided it was probably best to get the subject

over and done with. "He's fair, with blue eyes . . . tall, quite slim, dresses well," she said, counting the points off on her fingers. "I have the impression that he's relatively new to London, but he hasn't confided in me . . . I barely know the man."

"Well, I shall ask Oglethorpe as soon as he comes in," Letitia stated. "I must say, Livia, your lack of curiosity is unnatural. An eligible bachelor arrives in town and solicits your hand for a dance, and you don't have any interest in him at all. It's not natural, is it?" She appealed to the three other women in the salon.

"Not everyone is as inquisitive as you, Letty," a somewhat older woman said, offering Livia a sympathetic smile.

"Maybe so, but I think it's most ungenerous of Livia not to share her opinions," Lady Oglethorpe declared. "Let us go into luncheon." She rose from her chair in a swirl of orange taffeta and tucked her arm into that of Lady Devries. She led the way to the dining room, leaving the remainder of her guests to trail along in her wake.

Livia glanced at the clock as they crossed the hall. It was half past one. Another hour and a half and this torment would be over.

Chapter Five

Aurelia was returning from a walk in the park with Franny when Livia stepped down from the hackney carriage that had brought her back to Cavendish Square.

"Aunt Liv . . . Aunt Liv, we've been in the park," the little girl shouted. "We fed the ducks." She tugged on her mother's hand, prancing on tiptoe in her eagerness to reach Livia.

"How was it?" Aurelia called, as she obeyed her daughter's insistent tugs and hurried across the road, clutching Franny's hand tightly. The child had a habit of shooting off on frolics of her own if not firmly tethered.

"Ghastly," Livia said, pressing her hands to her temples. "It will teach me not to hurry when I'm answering invitations. I can't think how I missed the card. Guess what the main topic of conversation was?" She bent to kiss Franny, whose chattering monologue continued unabated.

"Prince Prokov," Aurelia hazarded.

"Spot on." Livia turned to the steps to the front door. "Are you coming in?"

"Yes, I think I've probably succeeded in tiring Franny sufficiently to take an afternoon nap." Aurelia, still holding Franny firmly by the hand, followed Livia up to the door and they waited the usual interminable time before Morecombe opened the door.

The heady scent of the flowers hit them as they stepped into the hall. "I'm guessing you didn't mention the prince's inordinately extravagant gift," Aurelia said, releasing Franny's hand and picking her way past an ornamental shrub that seemed to have thrown out tendrils, since it was carefully positioned on one side of the front door. Franny, shrieking with delight, ran from one display to another, like a bee sipping nectar.

"You guess right," Livia agreed above the child's excited babble. "Can you imagine what the gossips would make of it?" She shook her head with a grimace.

"If he continues to pay you attention, though, it will get out," Aurelia warned her. "You are prepared for that?"

"Yes, but as long as the attention's within bounds, it'll be no more than the usual gossip," Livia said, making her way to the stairs. "Talking of which, I'd better get ready for our jaunt in the park. That will stir some tongues certainly."

"But it's a perfectly respectable jaunt," Aurelia said with a soft laugh. "Not like the florist's shop. By the way, I left the brown velvet pelisse on your bed."

"Thank you, you're a love." Livia hurried upstairs.

Half an hour later Livia examined her image in the cheval glass in her bedchamber and decided that if she wished to make a favorable impression on the Russian prince, then she was certainly going to succeed. The brown velvet pelisse had a richly luxuriant glow to it that set off her black curls, and the gray fur trimming brought out a faint bluish tint to her gray eyes. The high-crowned gray velvet hat gave her height and an air of elegance, nicely matched by gray buttoned boots and long gray kid gloves.

With a nod of satisfaction she headed downstairs to get Ellie's opinion. "So, will I do?" she asked as she whisked into the parlor.

Aurelia turned from the secretaire, laying down her pen. "Oh, yes," she said at once. "Very soignée, Liv. Very elegant."

"Whom are you writing to?"

"Nell. I was wondering whether she and Harry had decided to come back to London before Christmas. She hadn't made up her mind when I left Ringwood the other day."

"I can't wait to see her . . . well, all of them." Livia perched on the arm of the sofa, arranging her skirts around her. "It seems ages since they eloped and her letters have been few and far between."

"That's the fault of the mail service," Aurelia pointed out. "And if you'd seen Harry's house way up in the Highlands you'd see the difficulties. Isolated is certainly the word for it."

"I suppose so," Livia agreed. "And it's what Harry wanted. Long enough out of the social circuit for the old scandal about his wife's death to die in the gossip mill. His instincts were right. It was on everyone's tongue for a few weeks after he married Nell, but no one ever mentions it now. I doubt it'll rear its head once they're back in town.

"But still," she added reflectively, "six months is a long time . . . the children will have grown out of recognition. Thank goodness Stevie didn't suffer any lasting effects from the kidnapping."

"No, he doesn't really seem to remember much about it at all," Aurelia said. "It was over so quickly, of course, and I think Nigel did try to reassure him throughout the ordeal that it was all going to be all right in the end."

Livia looked a little skeptical. "How is Cousin Nigel these days?"

"A reformed character." Aurelia shook her head. "I don't understand what could have possessed him to gamble so high and get into so much trouble. He's not a fool."

"No, but he's young," Livia said. "And he was running with such a wild, fast set, all much plumper in the pocket than he is. It's hard to acknowledge that you can't keep up."

"True enough," her friend agreed. "Anyway, Nigel's back at Oxford, apparently concentrating so intently on his studies that his tutors are now worried he'll go into a decline. Isn't that absurd?"

Livia laughed and then turned at the sound of the

door knocker. "Ah, that will be my escort to the park." She jumped up. "Everything in order?"

Aurelia looked her over and nodded. "Absolutely perfect. You look enchanting."

"Well, thank you kindly, ma'am." Livia dropped a mock curtsy and went to the door as the knocker sounded again. "I'd better open the door."

She hurried across the hall, waving away Morecombe, who shuffled slowly from the kitchen. "It's all right, Morecombe, I'll get it." She pulled open the front door. "Good afternoon, Prince Prokov."

"Good afternoon, Livia . . . and please would you drop this prince nonsense," he said, sweeping his hat in a flourishing bow. "It grows irksome." He straightened and continued before she could summon the words to respond to this. "Ah, you're not dressed for riding. Enchanting though you look."

"You said nothing about riding," Livia protested, taking in his immaculate buckskin riding britches, pristine white stock, and gleaming boots. "I thought we were going to walk. Besides, I don't have a horse. I didn't send to the livery stables."

"What they provide can't truly be called a horse," he said dismissively. "I have brought you a horse. See for yourself." He gestured to the street behind him.

Livia peered over his shoulder and her eyes widened. A groom stood holding the reins of the magnificent Cossack black, but also those of a dainty silver mare, whose elegant lines bespoke the Thoroughbred. "Oh, what a beautiful animal," she breathed. "A perfect match for the black. Did you bring her from Russia too?"

"No, I bought her yesterday from Tattersalls," he said nonchalantly. "Come down and make her acquaintance."

Livia needed no urging. The mare raised her head, whinnied softly, and gave a well-bred shiver when Livia stroked the silky length of her neck. "Oh, you beauty," Livia said, passing her hand over the velvety nose as the animal nuzzled her palm.

"Yes, I'm pleased with her," Alex said a touch complacently. "How long will it take you to change?"

"Fifteen minutes," Livia said promptly.

"I'll wait here." He watched her run back into the house with a most unladylike haste and smiled to himself, resigned to a long wait. In his experience no lady could change her dress in less than half an hour.

Livia, however, was not cut from the usual cloth. She reemergéd in just under fifteen minutes, drawing on her gloves as she ran down the steps to the street. "There, I wasn't too long, was I?"

"Indeed not," he agreed. "I'm astonished at your speed." He ran an appreciative eye over her figure, clad in a form-fitting dark green riding habit, the jacket adorned with epaulettes and hooked buttons in the manner of a hussar's uniform. Her high-crowned hat sported a debonair curling plume. "Very nice," he murmured. "Very nice indeed."

Livia ignored the comment as she had tried to ignore

the scrutiny, but it pleased her nevertheless. There was something very gratifying about such open approval.

Alex took the reins of the silver from the groom and gave them to Livia, then bent with cupped palm to give her a leg up into the saddle.

She went up easily and settled into the saddle, noticing the fine grain and supple feel of the leather. Fine tack for a fine animal, she reflected, but it didn't surprise her that Alexander Prokov should own only the best. There was something so fastidious about him, it was impossible to imagine him coming into contact with, let alone owning, anything rough or inferior.

"Comfortable?" He ran practiced hands over the girths and stirrup leathers, checking the security and fit of the one and the length of the other.

"Very, thank you." Livia smiled down at him, unable to disguise her delight in her mount or her eagerness to try the mare's paces.

Alex nodded and swung onto his own horse. They rode out of the square, the groom following at a respectful distance on his own mount, a horse that Livia had already noted was also of a higher caliber than the customary mounts allotted to servants.

"You're setting up your stables, then?" she inquired as they turned onto Oxford Street. She checked the mare, who pranced a little at the clatter of iron-wheeled carriages and the bustle of pedestrians and street vendors hawking their wares.

"To a certain extent," he agreed, watching covertly to

see how she handled the horse, who he thought was probably more highly strung than Livia was accustomed to handling, but he saw quickly that his vigilance was unnecessary; her hands were light but firm on the reins, her voice soft in reassurance, and the mare soon quietened. "I have the black, and two pairs of carriage horses."

"And now this beauty," she said, leaning to pat the mare's neck.

"Ah, no, she belongs to you," he said.

Livia sat up abruptly and the suddenly startled mare plunged forward. It took Livia a moment to soothe her before she could say anything in response to such an extraordinary statement. When she was able, she stared at her companion. "Don't be ridiculous."

"There's nothing ridiculous about it," Alex stated. "I bought the horse for you. She's a perfect ride for you. If you don't have your own stables, then I will keep her in mine, and whenever you wish to ride, you will send a message and my groom will bring her to you. It's a matter of utter simplicity."

Livia continued to stare at him. "I think you've run quite mad," she said. "I wouldn't dream of accepting such a gift. Even if it weren't utterly improper I couldn't possibly accept such an overwhelming present . . . oh, it's impossible even to express how insulted I feel."

"*Insulted?*" Alex looked genuinely astounded. "What could be insulting about such a gift? The horse is beautiful, you said so yourself. I thought only to give you pleasure, and it pleases me to see you riding a mount worthy of you."

"How can you *not* understand?" she said, realizing that he really didn't understand the impossibility of what he was proposing. "I don't even know you. We've met twice . . . well, three times now. How do you think it would look?"

"Does it matter how it looks?"

"Now you're being disingenuous," she accused with exasperation. "I have to live in this society. You may play by your own rules, Prince Prokov, but I can't. You may think nothing of such an outrageous proposal, but I assure you everyone else will draw the kind of conclusions that I do not want hanging around my neck. I think it would be best if I returned to Cavendish Square."

She drew rein and attempted to turn the horse back the way they had come. Unfortunately a hackney cab was coming up behind them at a fair clip and the mare, suddenly faced with the cab's horses, shied and threw up her head with an anxious whinny.

Alex leaned over and put a steadying hand on the bridle, drawing the silver mare to one side as the cab bowled past, the cabbie cursing them with colorful vigor.

"Unwise," Alex said calmly. "Never pull up a horse suddenly in the middle of a crowded thoroughfare."

"I know that," Livia stated through clenched teeth. "Take your hand off my bridle."

He didn't do so immediately. "Let's go on to the park,

it'll be much safer to continue this discussion out of the traffic."

It made sense even to a furious Livia. She couldn't simply ride home alone on his horse, and neither could they argue in the middle of Oxford Street. She flicked at her reins in an impatient gesture of acceptance and he removed his hand at once, urging his horse forward.

They rode in silence into Hyde Park and turned their horses onto the tan. It was immediately clear to Livia that they couldn't possibly continue to quarrel here. London's Upper Ten Thousand was out in force on a lovely late September afternoon, carriages bowling by on the broad pavement beside the tan, which was itself busy with riders, pausing to greet friends and acquaintances. Speed was impossible, and it was necessary to acknowledge the waves and greetings that came their way, and throughout she was acutely conscious of the speculative eyes on her horse.

"We can't talk here," she said softly after they'd been riding in silence for a few minutes. "I'm willing to ride once around the park and then I would like you to escort me back to Cavendish Square and we can put this ridiculous episode behind us."

"I fail to see why a gift should come under the category of a ridiculous episode," Alex protested, his voice as soft as hers, his smile unwavering. "Your definition of insult, my dear girl, is vastly different from mine."

"Be that as it may . . . oh . . ." She broke off as a man came riding down the tan towards them. She waved a hand in greeting. "Nick, how are you? I haven't seen you in an age."

"I've been out of town, dear lady," Sir Nicholas Petersham said, drawing rein. He raised his eyebrows as he took in her mount. "What a lovely creature, Liv," he observed appreciatively. "Has the livery stable improved its stock, or are you setting up your own stable?"

"Neither," Livia said swiftly. Nick was an old friend from their earliest days in London and the last thing she wanted was for him to have the wrong idea. "He doesn't belong to me. Prince Prokov has loaned him to me for the afternoon. Are you acquainted with the prince?" She gestured to Alex at her side.

"We met at Brooke's the other night, I believe," Nick said in his easy way. "How d'ye do, Prokov?"

"Well enough, thank you, Sir Nicholas," Alex returned with a nodding bow. "We're enjoying the ride."

"Ah, yes . . . quite." Nick frowned a little. He had the feeling that his presence was unwelcome, at least to Livia's companion. He glanced at Livia, then back at the prince. "Well, I'll leave you to enjoy it then. Must be getting on myself. Any news of Harry and Nell, Liv? Harry's last rather brief communication said they were getting ready to return to London."

"They're in Hampshire at the moment, paying a peace-making visit to the earl," she said. "We're not sure when they'll be back in town." Livia wondered whether to ask Nick to ride with them, and then decided against it. There was something about Prince Prokov's demeanor that seemed to indicate he would not like company, and for some reason she found that something powerfully persuasive.

It was all part and parcel of the man's ability to plough through any obstacle or objection, she reflected with an annoyance that she realized was directed as much at her own inability to resist as at Alex himself. "Call in Cavendish Square, will you, Nick?"

"Of course, ma'am. Tomorrow, if I may?"

"That would be lovely."

He raised a hand in farewell, nodded at Alex, and rode off down the tan, frowning. Something seemed not quite right to him. Livia was strung as tight as a bowstring.

"A good friend of yours, I gather," Alex commented as they resumed their ride.

"Yes," Livia said shortly.

"And do you have many good male friends?" he inquired in a neutral tone.

"What business is that of yours?" Livia bristled.

He turned his head towards her and smiled. "I was wondering if I have many rivals."

"Rivals for *what*?" she demanded, wondering why she was perversely amused by his effrontery.

"For the attention of the most fascinating and attractive woman in London," he returned promptly.

"Fustian," she stated. "I have no patience with these empty and extravagant compliments, Prince Prokov. Any more than I care for your equally extravagant gestures."

"Ah, it must be my Russian blood," he lamented with

a heavy sigh. "We are not a race known for our moderation. It would seem, alas, that such cultural differences are harder to bridge than I imagined."

"I don't believe a word of it," she said roundly. "I don't believe your Russian blood or your so-called Slav temperament have anything whatsoever to do with your behavior. You're playing a game, and for some reason I seem to be the object of that game. But permit me to tell you that your present tactics will not achieve whatever it is you wish to achieve."

He regarded her thoughtfully for a moment or two as they continued to ride. "Then I suppose I had better change them," he said finally. "Would you tell me what tactics *would* work? I learn quickly, you know."

Livia frowned at him, puzzlement and a hint of unease in her clear gray eyes. She was suddenly certain that this was no game. "Why are you pursuing me so purposefully, Alex?"

"I don't seem to be able to help it," he responded. "From the first moment I saw you, I needed . . . wanted . . ." He shrugged with a disarming smile. "Couldn't you simply be flattered and accept the compliment?"

It sounded innocent enough, and she was too honest to deny the strange frisson she got from his attention. And far too honest to deny that it both pleased and flattered her. "Perhaps I can," she said with an attempt at nonchalance. "But I'll accept no more presents . . . not so much as a bunch of flowers."

"That's a pity. I do so like to give presents."

"Oh, now you're making me sound ungracious and mean-spirited," she protested. "Surely you can see the difference between a bunch of flowers and an entire garden, or between a silk scarf and a Thoroughbred horse?"

"Not really. A suitable present is one that suits the recipient and pleases the giver. However, will you at least accept the loan of the mare whenever you wish to ride her?"

His eyes held hers, and there was an unmistakable appeal in their depths that she found irresistible. At this moment he didn't seem arrogant or presumptuous, merely charming and a little vulnerable. If the man liked to give, what right had she to deny him? Firmly she put away the little voice that told her she was being disingenuous.

"Yes," she said. "I would be happy to accept the loan, Alex, and I thank you for it." She leaned forward and stroked the mare's neck. "She is a delight to ride, but I'd love to try her paces somewhere less formal and rigid than Hyde Park."

"Then let us go to Richmond," he said promptly. "The rides there are broad and long and you could give her her head." He urged his black forward as he spoke and the horse broke into a trot.

"Not *now*," Livia exclaimed, realizing that he had every intention of riding off into the sunset in the direction of Richmond Park without a second thought. "It's almost evening."

"Tomorrow morning, then. I'll bring her around at

ten o'clock and we will have all day. We shall take a picnic." He nodded decisively.

Livia looked at him in some exasperation. "You're doing it again, Alex."

"Doing what?"

"Assuming that I have nothing better to do than to fall in with your plans. You heard Sir Nicholas tell me that he would call upon me tomorrow."

"Oh, but that's of little importance," he declared with a dismissive wave of his hand. "If you're not in, he'll leave his card and call another time. Besides, you could write him a note or ask your friend to receive him and explain."

"Aurelia might have other plans too," Livia pointed out aridly.

"Then write him a note or leave one with your butler. I predict a beautiful sunny day tomorrow and we should take advantage of it. One can never be certain of the weather at this time of year," he observed gravely.

"You're incorrigible," Livia said.

"One of my finer qualities," he agreed with a laugh. "Now, what will you name the mare?"

"She's not mine to name," Livia stated.

"I have a poor imagination and I'd probably call her something ordinary like Silver, so you'd do both me and the horse a favor by taking on the task. The naming of a horse is a most important matter."

He was a totally overpowering force, Livia reflected. "I won't argue with that," she said, yielding because the struggle seemed fairly pointless. "But I'll need some time to think about it."

"Then for the present she must remain nameless. Shall we go back to Cavendish Square now or would you like to take another turn?"

"Cavendish Square," Livia said firmly. She felt rather as if she'd been run over by a dray loaded with ale barrels. Prince Prokov seemed to have that effect and she badly needed some time to catch her breath and reflect.

"By all means," he agreed with an amiable smile.

At the house he dismounted and held up a hand to Livia as she slid from the saddle. He held her hand for a moment longer than strictly necessary, then raised it to his lips for a light brush of a kiss. His eyes held hers as he said softly, "Until tomorrow then, Livia."

Livia nodded. "At ten o'clock." She tried to withdraw her hand and for a second his fingers tightened, then with a smile he released her and turned to the steps to escort her up to the door.

Livia felt strange. There had been something in those amazing blue eyes that disturbed her. A hint of ruthlessness, of a determination that didn't quite jibe with his playful-seeming flirtation and the extravagant compliments. He wasn't playing a game, she thought with renewed conviction. There was something deadly serious going on here, and the sooner she found out what it was the better.

Alex knocked vigorously, waited until the door was opened, then bade Livia farewell. And now as he smiled there was no hint of the look that had so chilled her. "I will count the minutes until the morning, my dear Livia."

Livia made no response, merely smiled her own farewell before stepping swiftly through the door into the peaceful sanity of her own hall and a world she understood and could control.

⌥

Alex strolled down the steps and remounted, his expression thoughtful. He glanced up at the house again and frowned. He had so little time in which to storm this citadel. By the time the ambassador was recalled, Prince Prokov needed to be well entrenched in society, accepted not just by London's frivolous bachelors but by the court, the grandes dames and their husbands, by diplomats and politicians. He couldn't be married by then, of course, but eligibly betrothed to an impeccable fiancée with a wedding date in the near future would give him the entrées he needed just as well.

The tactics he had chosen were designed to achieve his goal in the shortest possible time, and his not inconsiderable experience of women had only bolstered his belief that his game plan would succeed. Women tended to succumb to the mix of masterful determination and flattering flirtation. Now, however, he was having doubts. Livia was not like the women he had known hitherto. She had mettle in her makeup. She was a spinster, in her late twenties, and she should be susceptible to the attentions of an eligible suitor; she should be more than eager for marriage. But there must be some reason why such an attractive woman was still single, he reflected. A reason that transcended the customary imperative of a woman of her social position. Of course, she was financially independent . . . *or thought she was.*

And of course he could simply disabuse her of that belief and make his compensatory offer without all the uncertainties and entanglements of courtship. She would be out of her mind to refuse him. But something had happened since he'd met her. It was as if she were spinning a web around him and he was losing sight of his primary objectives. He wanted her, plain and simple, with a desire that if he wasn't careful could consume him. It wasn't only lust, although he certainly felt that when he looked at her, at the high, rounded bosom, the slender waist, and the graceful curve of her hips. He was drawn to the sense that, composed and poised though she was, there was an unruliness beneath that surface, an impulsive mischief that would make her a wonderful partner in bed and out of it. Livia Lacey radiated a curious quicksilver brightness, and she had an edge to her character that she wasn't afraid to use if she felt her sense of integrity was somehow threatened.

He caught himself smiling at the reflection and pulled himself up sharply. He mustn't lose sight of the fact that Livia, properly handled as his wife, could be very useful in the grim business that had brought him to London. If he held on to that fact, then he could keep a rein on this unruly and untidy desire.

He frowned as he continued to look up at the house. That was one objective he would never lose sight of. His mother—the mother he had never known. Who and what was Sophia Lacey? Once his father's lover, certainly—a woman unselfish enough to give up her child because she believed it was in the child's best interests. But what else was she? He was consumed with curiosity, had been since early childhood, with the passionate need to discover the essence of the woman who had given birth to him. Somewhere in the shadows of her house he might find a key to the true nature of his mother. Her faithful retainers would have something to give him. They must have served Sophia long and well for her to take such pains over their future. But he couldn't ask them until his presence in the house was accepted.

Once again he banished reverie and brought himself back to the grim business that had brought him to this point. There was little time to waste. So should he change his tactics with Livia? Or increase the pressure on the assumption that he would eventually wear her down?

It was a decision he needed to make before the jaunt to Richmond in the morning.

"What happened?" Aurelia asked as Livia came into the parlor. "You're in riding dress . . . you weren't when you went out."

"Actually I was," Livia said, flinging herself onto the sofa. "It turned out that Alex had riding in mind, not walking. He brought the most beautiful horse for me to ride." She debated whether to tell Aurelia the truth about the prince's intentions regarding the silver, and decided not to for the moment.

"So you came in and changed?" Aurelia asked with a frown in her eyes. Something wasn't quite right here.

"Precisely," Livia replied airily. "And we're going riding in Richmond Park tomorrow morning. I want to try the mare's paces."

"Oh, I see," Aurelia said, not at all sure that she did.

"If Nick comes to call, will you make my apologies and tell him that I was called away?"

"Yes, of course. Are you expecting him?" She looked closely at Livia.

"I met him in the park. He said something about coming to call," Livia said with a vague gesture. "Nothing definite."

"I see," Aurelia repeated, still not sure that she did. "But if I stay here, who's going to chaperone you on your ride with the prince?"

Livia frowned. "I don't need a chaperone, Ellie. No one will see us, no one need ever know about it."

Aurelia shook her head. "You can't be sure of that, and if you're seen riding alone out of town with the prince, it'll fuel a conflagration of gossip that won't do your reputation any good at all. It's one thing to ride in

Hyde Park under everyone's eye, quite another to seek the seclusion of Richmond."

Livia chewed on her lower lip as she thought. Her friend was right, of course, but a chaperoned, decorous ride was most definitely not the point of tomorrow's excursion. It wasn't that she didn't enjoy Ellie's company, quite the opposite, but not when she wanted the hint of danger, the sense of playing with fire, that seemed to accompany her meetings with Alexander Prokov. It was a realization she'd taken her time acknowledging, she had to admit to herself, but there were no two ways about it. Ordinary decorum and the Russian prince were not compatible, and that excited her and filled her with a heady, almost reckless sense of anticipation. There were any number of men she could ride perfectly pleasantly with in Richmond Park in Ellie's company, but not Alexander Prokov.

She became aware of Aurelia's intent gaze and felt herself flush a little. "I'll take a hackney to Richmond. Even if anyone sees me get in it, they won't know where it's going, and once we're on the road it'll be totally anonymous," she said finally. "I'll meet up with Alex and the horses in the park. Then I'll come back in another hackney after our ride and no one will be the wiser."

"Particularly if you take only the most secluded rides," Aurelia remarked dryly. "The roads least traveled, as it were. I take it that's the point," she added, her eyes narrowed.

"It does seem to be," Livia agreed, her flush deepening a little. "And there's no harm in it, Ellie."

Aurelia shrugged. "If you say so. I'm not your keeper, Liv, and you know what you're doing."

Livia laughed slightly. "Do I? I wonder."

"I'm not about to preach morality, Liv," her friend said with a smile. "Neither of us turned a hair when Harry played Casanova at Nell's window, and if you want to have a liaison with a Russian prince under the trees of Richmond, then I'll merely warn you to be careful of damp grass."

Livia smiled with unconcealed relief. "I don't think it's going to come to that, but a little dalliance is very appealing."

Chapter Six

THE CZAR'S SEAL EMBLAZONED THE message await-ing Alex as he returned to his lodgings. He took up his paper knife and slit the seal, opening the sheet that was covered in the emperor's elegant script.

My dear friend. Alex winced a little at the salutation. The czar had always embraced him as an elder brother . . . except on those occasions when his dignity demanded a degree of reserve . . . those occasions when he considered Alex had overstepped the boundaries of friendship with advice or faintly concealed criticism. Then he was icily imperial and not at all afraid of reminding his *friends* of the precariousness of their position, which depended solely on the degree to which they pleased their emperor. Unlike his grand-mother, Alexander I was not a listener and did not choose to heed advice that went counter to his own convictions . . . convictions that once held were fixed in stone.

Alex sighed a little and returned to the missive. The czar's enthusiasm for his new alliance with Napoleon filled the page, overflowed in superlatives. The promise of this alliance had no limits, it was to lift Russia into the position of world supremacy, side by side with her dearest friend, France. Together they would subjugate Europe and bring England to her knees. They would divide the known world between them. And Prince Prokov, the czar's most trusted and loyal friend, was to help in this worthy aim and he would reap rewards beyond his dreams.

Send us information soon, my dear Alex, about the mood in the English court. Are they disheartened at our new alliance? How will they react when Russia joins Napoleon's continental blockade? What will they do when they can no longer trade with Russia?

And just what will Russia do when England no longer receives her exports? Alex thought, his lip curling. England was Russia's biggest export market for its raw materials. The merchants of St. Petersburg and Moscow would be in a frenzy of rebellion when English ships no longer anchored in their harbors and the warehouses bulged with the goods they could no longer sell. And all because of the orders of that *Corsican parvenu,* as the Dowager Empress described the Emperor Napoleon.

He turned his eyes back to the czar's fluent script. *What plans do the English intend making with Austria? You will discover this in your clever way, my friend. And as to your fears that there may be disaffection among the émi-*

grés in London, have no fear, I have it well under control. I have my spies. Be careful yourself, my friend. No one can be trusted.

Alex read the last sentences carefully, a deep frown corrugating his brow. It sounded like a warning, but why should the czar warn *him*? Was he afraid Alex would run afoul of the disaffected? Or was he afraid of something quite different?

He remembered his visit from Prince Michael Michaelovitch. The old man was certainly devoted to his emperor, but he was not the brightest candle in the chandelier. If the secret police had indeed sent Michael to watch Alex, they had sent a rabbit to watch a fox.

"Will you be dining in tonight, Your Highness?" Boris, his arrival soundless, spoke softly from the door.

Alex shook his head. "No, I'm engaged with a party to the opera." He glanced at the ormolu clock on the mantel. "In fact I'm going to be late as it is. Bring sherry to my chamber while I change, if you please, Boris." He hurried through the door into his inner sanctum and from there into his bedchamber, shrugging out of his riding coat as he went.

Boris appeared within minutes with the sherry decanter and a plate of sweet biscuits. He set the tray on the dresser, and while Alex poured himself a glass, he opened the armoire and took out the black coat, white waistcoat, and knee britches that would be suitable wear for the opera.

The front door knocker sounded as he was helping

his master into the coat. "Who can that be?" Alex muttered. "I'm not in to visitors, Boris."

"No, sir." The manservant glided towards the door to the hall. He opened it and then nodded. "Ah, it is only a messenger, Your Highness. Leo has answered the knock." He stepped into the hall and summoned the bootboy who was just closing the front door. "Bring it here, boy."

"Right away, Mr. Boris, sir." The boy, who was no more than thirteen, scurried across the waxed floor, his boots skidding slightly in his haste. He touched his forelock as he handed Boris a wafer-sealed parchment. "'Tis for His Highness, Mr. Boris, sir."

"One would assume so," the manservant observed without expression as he took the sheet. He glanced over his shoulder. "Shall I send Leo to summon a chair, sir?"

"Yes, I'll be ready in five minutes." Alex frowned slightly as he made a minute adjustment to his starched cravat. "Bring me the message." He held out a hand even as he continued to lean forward towards the mirror, twitching at a fold in the snowy linen.

Satisfied at last, he straightened and took the parchment from Boris. He glanced at the writing. Definitely a feminine hand, although the paper was white and unscented and the pen strokes lacked the flourishes and curlicues so common in female penmanship.

He took up a nail file from a silver dish on the dresser and slit the wafer. He opened up the sheet and took in the contents in one swift appraisal. A smile touched the corners of his mouth. So Lady Livia had a care for her reputation, did she? But not sufficient of a care to propose bringing a chaperone on their ride. Instead, she was proposing what could only be called an assignation. A secret rendezvous no less. It would seem she might have something more in mind than the need to try the mare's paces.

He laughed softly. Livia had made the decision for him. Now was not the moment to change his tactics. If he kept up the pressure, increased the pace even, the citadel would surely fall. Livia Lacey, as he'd hoped, was able and willing to entertain her impulses. Her ready laugh and mischievous sense of humor had entranced him from the first moment and matched something deep in his own personality, a devil-may-care desire to shrug off convention, to pursue one's own course. An unusual quality in a young woman of Livia's position, but a most appealing one. She would be a worthy partner in his enterprise.

"Tell the chairmen to wait," he instructed Boris as he got up from the dresser. "And tell Leo I will have a message for him to deliver to Cavendish Square in a few minutes." He strode into his inner sanctum and sat down to write a reply to Livia.

⚬⚬⚬

"So, does the name Prince Prokov ring any bells, Harry?" Cornelia asked her husband somewhat impatiently. He seemed to be taking an inordinate length of time reading Aurelia's missive.

Harry glanced up at her and gave her a wicked smile. "Maybe . . . maybe not," he teased.

They were in the library of Cornelia's country house, Dagenham Manor. In truth the house belonged to her young son, Stevie, who had inherited the title of Viscount Dagenham and the Dagenham estates on his father's death. But until he came of age and found himself a wife, his mother would continue to consider it her own.

Cornelia leaned over the back of Harry's chair and playfully snatched the vellum from his hand. "I don't know how you could possibly know anything about him, or find out anything. You've been out of touch with your *friends* in the underworld for so long, I'm sure they've forgotten all about you." She moved away from him, her eyes on the letter.

"Oh, unkind," Harry protested with a chuckle. He reached out an arm and caught his wife around the waist, pulling her down onto his knee. "Such a sharp tongue, Nell. I've a mind to tame it." He tipped her backwards, so that her head was against his shoulder, and kissed her smiling mouth.

When at last he raised his head, she was still smiling, but her breath came fast and her cheeks were flushed, her eyes bright with the ready desire that Harry unfailingly aroused. "Well, there's some truth in what I said," she murmured, reaching up a hand to touch his face. "Don't you think it's time we returned to the real world, love?"

"Have you had enough of marital seclusion, then?"

He caught her hand and turned it up, pressing his lips into the palm.

"It's not that," she said. "But I think you're beginning to get restless . . . not bored exactly, but you need your work." She sat up straight and looked at him closely. "Tell me I'm wrong."

He was silent for a moment, then he shook his head. "No, you're right. I do feel an itch now and again."

"Then I think we had better scratch it before it consumes you," she said, jumping up from his knee. "I'll tell Linton that we're leaving for London in the morning. She has plenty of time to get the children ready, although, of course, she'll protest mightily." She moved energetically towards the door.

"Just a minute." Harry stopped her as she put her hand to the latch. "I get the impression you're as anxious to get back into the swim of things as I am, Nell."

She gave him a rueful smile. "In truth, perhaps I am. And I'm very curious to form my own impressions of this prince who's pursuing Liv so ardently. Ellie seems to have reservations, didn't you get that impression?"

"A little, perhaps. But I think she's more concerned about Livia's response to the pursuit."

Cornelia turned her eyes back to the letter. "Perhaps so," she murmured. "Reading between the lines, it sounds as if Livia finds the Russian more than ordinarily attractive and that's what's concerning Ellie. Anyway, do you think you'll be able to find out anything about him from your colleagues at the ministry?"

"I'm sure I can," Harry said confidently. "No Russian émigré in London is going to escape the surveillance of the ministry at the moment, not after Tilsit . . . in fact not before either," he added. "I'll send Eric up to London with a note to Hector warning him that we'll be back in Mount Street by the day after tomorrow."

He stood up and stretched. "With the children, we'll need to make frequent stops on the way tomorrow and break the journey overnight."

Cornelia grimaced. Harry had learned the hard way about the drawbacks of coach journeys with a travel-sick child. "Susannah should be all right if we stop every two hours," she said somewhat tentatively.

He nodded. "Rather what I thought. But I intend to ride and I can take her up with me for a while when the motion of the carriage gets too much for her."

"That's a good notion. I'll do the same, and maybe we can accomplish this journey without too much drama."

"Don't forget to write a note of farewell to the earl," Harry reminded her as she opened the parlor door.

"That will be a pleasure," Cornelia stated. "I'll send it around to Markby Hall this evening." Markby Hall, the seat of the earl of Markby, her first husband's father, was a mere two miles from Dagenham Manor. Cornelia had no love for her ex-father-in-law, who before her marriage to Viscount Bonham had done everything in his power to control her life and that of her son, Stevie, his grandson and heir. Her marriage to Harry had at first enraged him, but somewhere along the line Harry had managed to reconcile him to the changed circumstances.

Cornelia suspected that her husband had promised the old earl that no decisions about his grandson's future would be taken without his knowledge, maybe even his approval. It was a generous offer, and one that Cornelia herself would probably not have made, but in the circumstances she was willing to let sleeping dogs lie and ask no questions as to how Harry had brought about the miracle of reconciliation. Time enough for that if it ever became an issue.

She went up to the nursery, bracing herself for the inevitable storm to come when Linton, the children's nurse, was informed that the nursery was moving to London the next day.

∽∾

Livia woke at dawn, restless with a sense of excitement. She pushed aside the covers and got to her feet, stretching her limbs with a feeling of intense well-being. She went to the window and pulled back the curtains, then opened the casement, kneeling on the window seat to gaze out over the dew-glistening square garden. The sky was streaked with orange and red and the dawn chorus filled the air, which had a crisp tang to it, a foreshadow of autumn.

The city at this hour seemed fresh and clean and new. In an hour or two it would be noisy and dirty, filled with clanging iron wheels, shouting voices, and the reek of manure and human waste, sweat and rotting vegetables, mingling with the fragrance of meat pies and new baked bread.

But for the moment, it seemed to Livia to belong only to her, and the promise it contained was only hers.

Ludicrous fancy, of course, but still one that brought a frisson of excitement tingling along her spine.

She jumped off the window seat and went to the armoire, for the first time in her life wishing she had more than one riding habit. While the one she had was certainly elegant enough, the prince had already seen her wearing it twice. Then she pulled herself up sharply. She and her friends despised such petty considerations and her father, the austere Reverend Lacey, an aristocrat who refused to use his ancestral title and gave the revenues from his family estates in tithe to the church, chose to live as modestly as any country vicar. He had brought up his only child to accept, if not particularly to enjoy, a life of simple comforts, rigorous intellectual pursuits, and relative self-denial.

What he'd say to a Russian prince didn't bear contemplating, Livia thought with a chuckle. Fortunately there was no reason for him ever to juxtapose such an exotic being with his carefully reared vicarage daughter.

She pulled out her riding habit and was wondering what she could do to effect some subtle change to the overall appearance, when a light tap at the door heralded Aurelia's arrival.

"Oh, you're up and about already," Aurelia said cheerfully. "Franny had me up half an hour ago so I thought I'd come and see if you were awake. I was thinking that if you wore my black jacket with your green riding skirt, it would look like a different outfit." She held up the close-fitting black jacket adorned with gold braid. "It would go well, I think."

"A little daring," Livia said. "Green and black and gold . . . but somehow fitting, I believe." A devilish smile danced at the back of her gray eyes. "Will it fit, though? You're rather smaller here"—she passed her hands vaguely over her bosom—"than I am."

"A certain form-fitting tightness can be very fetching," Aurelia responded with a similar gleam of a smile. She laid the coat on the bed. "What time are you meeting your prince?"

"He's hardly mine," Livia protested. "But he said in his note that he would be waiting with the horses at the White Hart at the Richmond Gate at ten o'clock. It's too early for anyone else to be riding for pleasure in the park, so we should be quite safe."

"It'll take you at least an hour by hackney," Aurelia said. "You should leave by nine at the latest."

"I'll leave at nine," Livia agreed. "And if it takes longer, then he must wait for me. A lady's prerogative, after all."

"Certainly." Aurelia nodded. "I think you should wear my black felt hat with the little veil instead of the beaver with the plume. He'll have to be very observant to notice that you're still wearing basically the same habit."

"And if he does notice, so what?" Livia declared stoutly. "The limitations of my wardrobe are no one's business but mine."

"Quite so," averred Aurelia, but with another little smile. "I'll fetch the hat."

⚜

Punctually at nine o'clock, Jemmy jumped down from the hackney he had hailed on the corner of the square and ran up to the front door. "Jarvey says he don't mind going to Richmond, Lady Livia," he declared with satisfaction as he bounced into the hall. "First two I stopped wouldn't go that far."

"Thank you, Jemmy," Livia said with a smile, drawing on her gloves. "I knew you'd manage."

"You'll be quite inconspicuous in a hackney," Aurelia reiterated, adjusting the little veil on her friend's hat. "Apart from the fact that no one's going to see you anyway. It's far too early for most society folk to be out of their beds let alone on horseback in Richmond Park." She stepped back to examine the effect of her adjustment. "Yes, I think that's perfect. You look very elegant."

"Then I am ready to go." Livia leaned forward to kiss Aurelia's cheek. "Thank you, Ellie, you're a rock of support."

"Nonsense," Aurelia scoffed. "You don't need support. Go now and have a wonderful morning. If the mare's as magical as you say, it should be bliss to ride her where you don't have to worry about decorum."

"Indeed," Livia agreed. "That is, after all, the object of the morning's exercise."

"Of course," Aurelia concurred gravely. "Of course it is."

Chapter Seven

A LEX STOOD IN THE STABLE yard of the White Hart, slapping his gloves impatiently into the palm of one hand as he watched the stable clock. It was now just after ten o'clock. *Where was she?*

He'd arrived at the inn by nine, had breakfasted in the tap room, and, until the last few minutes, had been perfectly serene and composed. Now he was seething with impatience, an emotion he had always avoided, believing that haste inevitably led to costly mistakes. He was a past master at waiting with a tranquil mind for the outcome or event he was expecting. So why this morning could he not take his eyes away from the clock?

She would come, he was certain of it. It was a journey of less than an hour on horseback, but in a hackney it would take quite a bit longer. So he rationalized the delay, but he was tapping his booted foot on the cobbles when a hackney turned into the gates to the stable yard at a quarter past ten.

He was aware of a swift surge of anticipation, a prickle of excitement as if at the beginning of a chase. And after all what was he embarking on if not the opening pursuit of a hunt?

He stepped forward to the door as the coachman drew in his horses, and opened it almost before the carriage had come to a complete stop. "Good morning, Livia." He swept off his beaver hat and bowed, the sun glinting off his fair head as he greeted her with a smile, no indication of his earlier impatience in his calm tone. He held out a hand to assist her to alight.

For the entire journey Livia had had the sense that she was taking an irrevocable step into what was for her unknown territory. Several times she had leaned forward to open the window to tell the jarvey to return to Cavendish Square. But each time she'd sat back again, her hands clasped tightly in her lap, her heart beating too swiftly for comfort.

Now she drew a deep breath and returned the greeting, pleased at the steadiness of her voice, as if they were merely meeting casually on the street instead of embarking on some kind of tryst. As always he was immaculately dressed in buckskin britches, shining top boots, a dark gray coat, and a simply tied white linen stock. There was nothing ostentatious, nothing of the dandy, about his appearance, merely a sense of quiet, composed perfection that was almost intimidating, and Livia had a strong desire to see him ruffled, untidy, discomposed, as if it would in some way even the playing field.

She took the offered hand, stepping down to the cobbles, blinking behind her wisp of veil at the sudden brightness of the morning after the dim light in the coach.

"A beautiful morning," she observed, taking back her hand when he seemed disinclined to relinquish it. The banal remark was so at odds with the jumbled emotions of excitement, apprehension, anticipation that swamped her as she looked up at him that she could almost have laughed at herself. Except that she didn't feel in the least like laughing.

"Perfect for riding," he observed in much the same tone.

His tone might have been calm and matter-of-fact, but there was nothing matter-of-fact about his eyes as they swept over her. Their usual brilliant blue had darkened to an almost purple, a deep glow in its depths. She could read impatience, hunger, *lust* in his close scrutiny and a quiver ran through her belly. Suddenly it was as if all pretense, all the conventional delicate maneuvers that obscured true emotions had been stripped away. And she had a fleeting glimpse of the edge on which she teetered.

He spoke again into the moment of charged silence. "Do you wish to refresh yourself in the inn before we set out? I have bespoken a private parlor and there's a maid to attend you."

For some reason this considerate foresight surprised her, but she found its ordinary courtesy immediately reassuring. It brought her back from that edge. "Thank you, yes, I would like that," she said appreciatively.

"Then come with me." He reached out and lifted the little veil, setting it back over the neat black hat that perched at a rakish angle on her dark curls. "That's better, I like to see your eyes." His own were still as penetrating as two beams of blue light as they looked closely at her, seeming to take in every centimeter of her countenance. He gave a little nod, as if of approval, then took her hand and tucked it into his arm to usher her into the inn.

And immediately her sense of reassurance vanished. There was nothing conventional or ordinary about either the scrutiny or his proprietorial manner. How could she possibly insist on a proper formality, or expect a conventional distance between two near strangers, when she had not only agreed to this encounter in the first place, she'd insisted on a secrecy that immediately made it most improper?

Not that Alexander Prokov had ever observed the distances, she reminded herself, not even in the first moments of their initial meeting . . . one that he had carefully and quite ruthlessly engineered. She'd never been under any illusions, so it was a little late now for second thoughts. With a mental shrug she yielded to the greater force and allowed herself to be escorted into the inn.

The parlor was neat and comfortable. There was coffee and bread and butter, a discreetly provided commode behind a worked screen, and a smiling maid.

"How long shall I give you?" Alex asked as he stood in the open doorway, his gaze sweeping the chamber to make sure all was as he'd ordered.

"Fifteen minutes," Livia said.

"I'll be waiting with the horses." He bowed over her hand, said softly, "Don't keep me too long," and left.

Livia drew off her gloves and took the cup of coffee the maid handed her. She sipped gratefully of the revivifying liquid and concentrated on composing herself. No harm would come of this little adventure. No one would know of it; she would have an exhilarating ride in company that she enjoyed. No more and no less. With a nod of determination she slipped behind the screen to make use of the commode.

Alex was standing with both horses, talking with a stranger when Livia reemerged into the sunshine of the yard a quarter of an hour later. He broke off his conversation as Livia came up to them.

"At noon then, Boris."

"Yes, Your Highness." The stranger bowed to Livia. "Good morning, ma'am."

Livia returned the greeting wondering absently what *at noon* could mean. The silver mare whickered softly as she stroked her nose, and her hide rippled with a little shiver as if she were anticipating the prospect of a gallop as eagerly as her rider.

"She's such a beauty," Livia said, putting her foot into Alex's cupped hands so that he could toss her up into the saddle.

"Any further thoughts on a name for her?" he asked, settling into his own saddle on the Cossack black.

"I don't know her well enough as yet," Livia responded, leaning forward to pat the mare's silky neck. "When I've had a chance to ride her properly, then we'll see."

"Then let us go." Alex clicked his tongue and the black pranced forward.

Livia's anxiety had vanished the minute she was in the saddle and now she relaxed, getting the feel of the mare's gait as they moved at a trot towards the entrance to the park. The air smelled crisp and slightly autumnal, but there was some warmth in the sun as they trotted down a wide deserted ride between lines of copper beech trees.

Livia nudged the mare with her heels and the horse threw up her head and broke into a canter. Her stride lengthened as Livia settled into the rhythm. Another nudge and they were galloping down the ride, Livia's wisp of a veil flying up away from her face, the wind cold on her cheeks, her lips parted in a silent cry of exhilaration. She could hear the black behind her, then he was beside her, keeping pace so that they rode neck and neck. She glanced at Alex and he met her gaze, laughing with an exhilaration to match her own.

"Let her go," he shouted above the rush of air that held them in a tunnel, a world of their own.

Livia leaned forward over the mare's neck, reducing the wind resistance, and encouraged her with soft words into her flattened ears. And the horse raced along the broad ride, her stride lengthening, as the black kept pace and eventually drew ahead. For a few minutes Livia let the race continue, but then reined the mare in, inch by inch, knowing that the animal hadn't the chest and heart of the Cossack black. The mare slowed with seeming reluctance to a gentle canter and then fell back into a trot.

Alex drew in his own horse and waited for them to reach him. "You know your horse," he commented. "I knew you and she would be a good match."

"She is gallant," Livia said, leaning to stroke the mare's neck. The animal was not in the least distressed by the mad gallop, indeed seemed eager for another race, tossing her head and sniffing the wind. "What do you call the black?"

"Suleyman."

"Ah, yes, the Magnificent," Livia said with a nod. "Appropriate." She patted the mare's neck again. "This lady, however, is Daphne. A woodland nymph who loved the chase."

"And was ensnared by Apollo's golden arrow." Alex raised his eyebrows. "If I recall the myth correctly, she had no interest in marriage and begged her father to respect her wishes."

"Yes, and he said he wouldn't force it upon her but her beauty would," Livia responded. "But Apollo still needed to set a trap to capture her," she added.

"Indeed," Alex murmured. He glanced sideways at her as they trotted along the ride. "Has anyone attempted to set a trap to catch Lady Livia Lacey?"

Livia looked up sharply. "Why would they need to?"

"Ah . . . forgive me." He raised a hand in disclaimer. "But it is unusual for a woman of your attributes to be single at—"

"At my advanced age," Livia interrupted, an edge to her voice. "As it happens, Prince Prokov, I am single through choice . . . I could see through any trap anyone might wish to set for me . . . and there's absolutely no reason on earth why anyone would wish to set such a trap." She nudged the mare with her heels rather more urgently than she'd intended and the horse leaped forward into a renewed gallop.

Alex watched them go. Another mistake on his part, he reflected ruefully. He couldn't seem to get the note right with this woman. He'd hoped for a lightly amusing exchange that would lead easily into a declaration of his own interest. Instead, he'd sounded like a clumsy blunderer who hadn't a sensitive and articulate word in his vocabulary. He set Suleyman to follow the mare.

Livia heard the black's hooves growing closer and swung her horse onto a smaller, narrower ride through the trees. He would have to slow down to follow her. Perversely, she was aware of a thrill of excitement at the chase, a desire to outwit her pursuer. Impulsively she directed Daphne onto a still narrower ride with low overhanging branches. It would slow Alex even more, if indeed he bothered to follow her. And with another surge of exhilaration she realized that she would be very disappointed if he didn't.

A broad oak tree dominated the head of the path just before it opened into a wide grassy sweep between majestic beech trees. The trunk divided about six feet from the ground from a deep saddle-like fork. An image from her childhood rose unbidden in Livia's mind. There had been a tree with a crotch like that in the New Forest, outside Ringwood, the Hampshire village where she and Nell and Ellie had grown up. During school vacations the three of them had roamed freely in the company of Nell's elder brother, Frederick, and his various school friends, until their parents had variously decided the time had come for their daughters to pursue more ladylike activities. Climbing that ancient oak tree had been one of their greatest pleasures.

Livia glanced briefly over her shoulder. There was no sign of Alex and the black as yet. She drew rein beneath the oak tree and knotted Daphne's reins safely on her neck. She looked up at the fork of the tree, a quick assessing glance that seemed to send her straight back to her childhood. Without further thought she reached up for the branch above the fork and swung her body up off the saddle and into the tree. It was as if her body, her muscles, all remembered exactly what she had done so many times in the past. In the old days she had relied on Frederick or one of his friends to boost her up until she could grab on to the branch. But Daphne's back had done as well.

The mare seemed startled at being suddenly riderless and pawed at the ground, shaking her head, setting the bit jangling. Then she raised her head, her ears pricking at the sound of another horse. The Cossack black appeared on the narrow path.

Alex, bent low over the saddle to avoid the overhanging branches, had been cursing both Livia and his own tactlessness from the moment she and Daphne had disappeared onto this narrow path that barely qualified to be called a ride. Now he raised his head gingerly and his heart leaped into his throat at the sight of the riderless mare. Had Livia been thrown? It was hard to believe, knowing what an experienced rider she was, but maybe she'd been knocked from the saddle by a branch . . . knocked unconscious . . .

"Livia . . . Livia . . ." He shouted at the top of his lungs, startling both horses. There was no response and a film of sweat formed on his brow as his heart beat faster. He rode up to the mare, who had turned on the pathway and was high-stepping towards them. It was then that Alex saw the carefully knotted reins on her neck. They hadn't tied themselves, and it was a task beyond the abilities of an unconscious victim of an overhanging branch.

His eyes narrowed as he scanned the path and the trees to either side. His moment of panic had passed. *Where the hell was she?* Clearly playing some game . . . and he wasn't at all sure how he felt about that. He dismounted and walked slowly forward to where the mare had been standing. As he reached the spot something stung his cheek. He jumped, glancing down. An acorn had fallen to his feet.

"Livia, you devil," he exclaimed, looking up for the first time.

She laughed down at him from her perch in the tree. "I thought I'd forgotten how to climb trees," she said. "It's amazing how the body remembers the old tricks. Not bad for an aging spinster, don't you agree?"

"You know I didn't mean that," he said somewhat uncertainly. He didn't know whether he was amused or angry.

"Maybe so," she said with a chuckle. "But quite frankly I found the urge to puncture your complacence irresistible."

Alex frowned, then suddenly he laughed. "Well, you certainly succeeded, and I probably deserved it. I'd thought you many things, but not a tomboy. Get down now." He reached up for her. "And try not to tear your skirt."

Livia leaned forward, putting her hands on his shoulders, prepared to jump down, but Alex caught her waist and lifted her out of the tree. For a moment he held her above him, looking up at her with a gleam in his eye and a smile curving his mouth. "Scapegrace . . . hoyden," he declared, and set her on the ground.

Damn the man, Livia thought, realizing that by holding her like that he had totally and knowingly taken the advantage away from her. Now she was flustered instead of triumphant.

"Shall we continue our ride?" Alex inquired, leading Daphne over to her. He didn't wait for her answer.

"Allow me," he said smoothly, and once again caught her around the waist and lifted her into the saddle.

Livia said nothing, merely unknotted the reins and nudged the mare onto the wide sweep of grass ahead of them. Alex brought Suleyman up beside them and for a few moments they walked quietly, the horses comfortably companionable. More so than their riders, Livia thought. At the moment there was nothing of the comfortable companion about Prince Alexander Prokov. The very air around them seemed to be crackling with an intense uncertainty. It was most unsettling.

Alex was thinking that if anyone had told him wooing would be this difficult, he would never have believed them. But then he'd never come up against the reality of a Livia Lacey. Combative, intransigent, fiercely independent, she challenged him and his preconceptions at every turn, and for some reason he relished every minute of it.

After a minute he gave up a fruitless train of thought and said, "Shall we try another gallop? Daphne is ready for it."

Livia glanced at him. It seemed a good moment for action to banish tension. "Yes, why not?"

They rode fast through a glade, jumped over a stream, and galloped across a meadow. It occurred to Livia at one point that Alex knew exactly where he was going, but now she was enjoying herself too much to question his lead.

They rode for close to two hours, slowing now and

again to rest the horses, but they said little to each other. Instead a strange kind of companionable silence settled between them. Strange, because it was a silence that Livia associated with her close friends, people with whom such silence spoke of an intimacy that required no conversation. It was hard to remember that just a short time ago she had found his company unsettling to say the least.

Finally, Alex directed them back into the trees and they rode more sedately now into a small copse that led up a hill towards an open-sided pavilion.

"Where are we?" Livia stopped at the top of the hill and looked around. The vista was lovely. Below, the Thames curved among its reaches and islets, and ahead stretched the meadows and woods of Surrey.

"Still in the park," Alex said, dismounting and coming over to her. "Come." He reached up and lifted her down with the same easy informality that somehow this time seemed quite natural.

"Lunchtime," he said with a smile as he set her on her feet, his hands lingering on her waist. Her hat was crooked and her hair was escaping from its confines in an unruly tangle of windswept black curls. A smudge of dust decorated one cheek. He took out a pristine handkerchief and wiped away the smudge before mopping the glow of perspiration that glistened on her forehead.

"I must look like a sad romp," Livia said with a faintly embarrassed smile at these attentions.

He shook his head. "Oh, no . . . far from it," he stated,

and very lightly pressed the tip of her nose with a finger-tip. He turned from her at the sound of a soft footfall behind. "Oh, there you are, Boris. Is everything in order?"

"Indeed, Your Highness."

The man who'd been in the stable yard emerged from the pavilion, a young boy at his heels. "We'll water the horses, sir, and lunch is ready as you ordered. If you'll allow me, ma'am." He took Daphne's reins from Livia's suddenly slack hand.

"Yes, of course," Livia murmured, relinquishing her hold. "Loosen the girth—"

"Of course, ma'am," the man called Boris said, leading the mare away.

"I'm hungry as the proverbial hunter," Alex said, taking Livia's hand. He regarded her gravely. "Can we just be ourselves for a while, Livia? I'm tired of games."

"I didn't realize we were playing any," she responded.

"You were the one playing them as I recall," he retorted, and then shook his head. "No, forget I said that. I did provoke you, although not intentionally." He swung her hand in a sudden gesture of exuberance. "I am a Slav who woos without artifice and I am trying to be a proper Englishman who approaches the dance of courtship with all the right steps. You don't like the steps and I'm incompetent at making them, so may we start afresh?"

Livia frowned. This was the first she'd heard of wooing, although thinking on it, on the things he'd done in the last few days, it seemed a reasonable assumption.

Her skin prickled as if she were standing in a draught and once again she had the sense that she was the object of some deadly serious intent, and she had no idea of its purpose.

She managed to make her tone casual and insouciant as if she hadn't really heard what he'd said. "I'm happy simply to enjoy each other's company and the company of these magnificent horses. I can't tell you how much I've enjoyed riding Daphne this morning."

He looked at her closely, those dual shafts of penetrating blue light, then he shrugged a little before turning towards the pavilion.

She followed him into the pavilion that overlooked a bend in the river. "This is such a pretty view."

"One of the nicest at Richmond," he observed, going over to a square table set in the middle of the pavilion. "Wine?"

Livia turned back from the view and saw the elegant table for the first time. "Yes, thank you." She came closer. "Oh, game pie . . . and strawberries. How do you get strawberries in September?" But then she remembered the hothouse flowers. "Grapes too," she murmured, plucking one from the artistically arranged bunch.

She took the glass of white wine that he gave her and sipped appreciatively.

"I did say we would have a picnic," Alex reminded her as he raised his own glass in a toast.

"It's not quite the ordinary picnic hamper I'd expected," Livia said, responding to the toast. She was on edge, as if at any moment she should expect the unexpected. She turned away from him, gazing out at the view, holding her glass in one hand, her other arm held across her body.

She didn't see him set down his glass but she felt him come up behind her and once again her skin prickled. She could feel his breath on the back of her neck, stirring the unruly tendrils of curls escaping from the pins that before the ride and tree climbing had neatly confined her chignon beneath the little black hat. And then she felt his hands on her shoulders and his lips on her nape in a light brush of a kiss. He reached down for the glass she held, stretching behind him to set it on the table.

Her skin was damp from the morning's exertion and smelled of fresh air and horses, mingled with the scent of lavender in her hair. Alex drew his tongue up the groove in her neck and felt her shudder. He had intended a light, flirtatious kiss but something was happening to him as he held her lithe body close. His hands slid of their own accord around her body to cup the swell of her breasts beneath the tight-fitting jacket. He moved his lips to her ear, nibbling the lobe as his fingers deftly unhooked the little fastenings at the front of her jacket. He felt a quiver of resistance run through her as his hands slid inside the jacket, and then it was gone and her breasts beneath the thin cambric of her shirt filled his hands. Her nipples pressed small and hard into his palms as she leaned back against him, yielding to his touch.

Livia had been afraid of the unexpected, and now she understood that what was happening was entirely to be expected. On some plane of knowledge she had known this would happen. But she hadn't truly known how she would respond, and her response took her breath away. After that one tiny thrill of resistance her body gave itself to the sea of sensation. Her breasts were alive beneath his hands and she wanted his touch on every inch of her skin. His lips had moved to trace the curve of her cheek and she turned her face against his shoulder towards the kiss. His hands pushed the loosened jacket off her shoulders and she felt it slither away from her.

His flat palms slipped down her ribs to her waist, turning her towards him. She lifted her head and for an instant looked into his face, seeing the desire alight in his eyes, knowing that it was reflected in her own. His expression was intent, his mouth firm and yet softened. Livia lifted her arm to come around his neck and pulled him closer to her, her mouth opening hungrily beneath his, her tongue now urgently pursuing its own exploration. His mouth tasted of wine and his sun-warmed, wind-burned skin smelled of earth and leather and the herbs of the linen press.

His body was hard and powerful against her own and as she pressed herself against him she felt his penis stir and stiffen against her belly. It sent a jolt through her loins, a deep trembling in her belly, and her thighs tightened instinctively. Her free hand slid between their bodies and she cupped the hardness pressing against his britches, feeling it twitch and throb against her hand. And she heard his deep intake of breath with a surge of satisfaction.

His hands roughly pulled the shirt from the waistband of her skirt and moved up her back beneath the cambric, tracing the line of her spine. Slowly he raised his head, leaving her mouth, and he took a step away, his hands still on her bare back. He slid his hands around beneath the shirt until they held her breasts, and Livia caught her breath at the shocking intimacy of his touch, at the finger delicately flicking her nipples, bringing them to aching awareness.

She leaned back, offering him her breasts with a low moan, her eyes closing of their own accord. She felt the air cool on her skin as his fingers flew at the tiny pearl buttons and the shirt opened. His mouth took her nipples in turn, his tongue flickering in a butterfly kiss of such delicacy that her body was filled with an exquisite yearning.

Alex drew a deep shuddering breath. He had not meant this to happen and in the far reaches of his mind, where desire did not rule to the exclusion of sense, he knew he had to stop before they were both lost.

With an effort he raised his head, let his hands fall away from her, and stepped back.

Livia was aware of a sharp stab of loss. Her lips were tingling, her body a seething turmoil of arousal. She was hot and cold, her loins full and warm, deep vibrations strumming in her belly, and her heart was racing. She could still feel the imprint of his hands on her bare skin. She looked at him in silence because there were no words.

Alex stroked her cheek with a forefinger, and then fastened her shirt as deftly as he'd unfastened it. "It seems you have the Slav passion in you too, Livia," he murmured, his breathing still ragged, his cheeks flushed, his eyes still dark with the residue of arousal. "Dear God, what I wouldn't give for a bed in a private chamber at this moment." It was spoken barely above a whisper, but the statement held the desperation of lust cut short, and Livia understood it in every fiber of her being.

She moved away from him, turned back to the view that she no longer saw. Her hands were shaking and she pressed them to her cheeks. *How could she have reached the age of twenty-seven without ever experiencing that?* A key had been turned somewhere and the door stood wide open.

And she was damned if it was going to close again.

On that fierce resolution, Livia thrust her shirt back into the waistband of her skirt.

Alex's hand reached over her shoulder, holding her glass of wine. "Drink," he said. And she drank deeply, savoring the flowery taste on her tongue. It hadn't seemed extraordinary a few minutes ago, but now it was quite delightful. Every sensation seemed suddenly enhanced.

"Shall we have lunch, or shall we talk a little first?" he asked, coming around to lean against the low railing of the pavilion, facing her with his back to the view. He sipped from his own glass and watched her over the rim.

"Talk about what?" She heard how stupid it sounded even as the words emerged. She shook her head impatiently. "I didn't say that."

"I understand." He set his glass on the rail and bent to pick up her jacket from the floor of the pavilion. "Put this on before you get cold." He held it for her as she thrust her arms into the sleeves with an almost clumsy haste, and he waited quietly while her fingers fumbled with the hooks. He wanted to help her but he knew that if he touched her again, there would be no turning back. And this was neither the time nor the place for the lovemaking his body cried out for.

Resolutely he pushed himself away from the railing and declared, "Lunch it is. What may I serve you?" He looked at the table. "There's a York ham, a rather splendid game pie, smoked trout, and a dish of savory tartlets . . . oh, and a salad of watercress and dandelion."

"Everything." Livia emerged from her trance, forcing herself to pretend to behave as if what had just happened had not. "A little of everything, if you please." She swallowed the last of her wine and came over to the table, helping herself from the bottle as he arranged morsels delicately on a blue-rimmed plate for her. A heady feeling of liberation surged through her. She would drink this lovely wine, eat this delectable lunch, and let the future take care of itself.

"Sit down." He gestured to a folding canvas chair at one side of the table and set her plate before it.

Livia sat down, spread a snowy napkin on her lap, and took up her fork. She felt most peculiar. As if she'd drunk too much champagne. Not that she'd ever been drunk in her life, but from what she'd heard from the young men of her acquaintance, it resulted, at lease initially, in a state of euphoria where anything seemed possible and the world was bathed in a glorious rosy glow. Which was exactly how she felt at present.

Alex served himself and sat down opposite. From somewhere had come the conviction that straight talking was his best policy with this woman. "So, let us talk." He took a sip from his glass, then said directly, "Will you marry me, Livia?"

Livia stared at him, her fork suspended between plate and mouth. "I beg your pardon?"

"I said, will you marry me, Livia?" He smiled a little ruefully. "It's a proposal. I'm not accustomed to making them, so you must forgive me if it lacks polish."

But you don't lack polish. Never have, never will. Livia heard the little voice of disclaimer in her head. She laid down her fork and cupped her chin in her elbow-propped hands, regarding him across the table. "Why would you wish to marry me, Prince Prokov? And don't give me some disingenuous reason."

He grimaced and shook his head. "Believe me, I have never proposed to a woman before."

"I'm willing to believe that," Livia said. It stood to reason that if the Russian prince had ever offered a woman a legitimate proposal of marriage before now, he'd have been accepted. No suitable woman in her right mind would turn him down.

"But why me? We barely know each other." She felt rather as if this conversation were going on outside herself, that she was floating somewhere above this pavilion watching the scene unfold.

"We know each other a little better now," he pointed out with a quizzically lifted eyebrow.

Livia to her annoyance felt herself blush. "I can hardly deny that," she said. "Not without being a complete hypocrite. But that . . . those moments . . . they're hardly a solid base for marriage."

"I disagree," he said, reaching across the table for her hand. He turned it palm up and ran his finger over the palm. "That kind of compatibility carries its own promise. Without it, I would never contemplate sharing my life with anyone." He paused and then said deliberately, "And I would not offer you a less than honorable proposition, Livia."

She shook her head as if to dispel bewilderment. "I appreciate that, of course, but . . . but . . . there has to be another reason. It's not as if I have a fortune to bring you, or indeed anything of value."

He laughed a little. "I have no need of a fortune, my dear. My father was one of the wealthiest princes in Russia. I inherited vast tracts of land, twenty estates, close to fifty thousand serfs . . . and a lot else besides. Money is of no interest to me at all."

"So what is?" she asked flatly.

He chose his words carefully, treading a delicate path through truth and obfuscation. "I will be frank, although it might do my cause little good." He played with his fork, frowning. "I need . . . no, I want . . . a wife, Livia. And an heir. I'm thirty-six years old and I've played the bachelor long enough. But until I saw you that night at the ball, I had never seen a woman I thought I could spend an amicable life with."

"How on earth could you decide that just from seeing me?" she broke in.

"I couldn't." He shrugged. "But you intrigued me, and you were supposed to dance with that clod, Bellingham, and it seemed a dreadful waste . . . as I said at the time, I believe."

Livia nodded and the champagne fizz buzzed anew in her veins.

"And then when I started to talk with you, I was . . ." Another expressive shrug. "I was disarmed, enchanted, *lost.*" He continued to play with her hand as his direct blue gaze held her own. "I am accustomed to going after what I want, Livia, I admit it freely. And I think I may have gone too quickly for you. Tell me you have no intention ever of entertaining my suit and I will never trouble you again."

It was a gamble, but sometimes a player had to throw down his hand.

Livia slid her hand out from his. She stood up and walked away to the edge of the pavilion, gazing out over the view, her arms crossed over her breasts, hugging her hands in her armpits. She wasn't cold, but she felt the need to enclose herself.

What an impossibly gigantic step. How could she take it? And yet this inconvenient voice in the back of her mind kept chanting, *how could she not?* This man stirred her as no other had ever done. She liked him. Even if she was not ready yet to consider the idea of love, she could not possibly deny desire. She enjoyed his conversation and his company. And when she thought of a future with him her toes curled with excitement, the map unfurled, blank and waiting before her. It wouldn't be what she was used to. It wouldn't be what people expected for her, or of her. But maybe . . . just maybe . . . it was what she wanted, what she'd been waiting for without knowing it. A slice of the unexpected.

She thought of her father. What in the world would he say to a Russian prince asking for his daughter's hand? It didn't bear thinking of. Her shoulders shook with a bubble of suppressed laughter. And yet what could he object to? Prince Prokov was an equal match in every way for the daughter of a reclusive English earl. Perhaps not quite a perfect match for a frugal English vicar's daughter, however.

She turned around. Alex had risen with her, but he hadn't moved away from the table. He stood quietly, his hands resting on the table.

"I need some time," she said simply.

He bowed his head in acknowledgment. "Of course." He picked up a pair of tiny scissors and snipped a branch of grapes off the bunch. "Let us continue our lunch."

Chapter Eight

LIVIA SAT IN THE HIRED post chaise on the return journey to Cavendish Square, her hands clasped lightly in her lap, her head resting against the leather squabs, her eyes closed. She found the dim light, the motion of the carriage, and the regular hoof beats of the sturdy team almost mesmerizing. She was tired, and not just as the result of a day's hard riding. Her brain hurt, she decided. Wrestling with the ramifications of this extraordinary situation would exhaust the mental capacity of Diogenes in his barrel.

But perhaps she was overthinking. What did she *want*? Really want? Marriage, children, yes, always. But she'd turned down three offers for her hand in the last few months, perfectly suitable prospects, but the future they promised had seemed dreary. They were nice enough men, who would each make some woman a good husband, but it seemed as if that was not exactly what Livia wanted.

Had she been, all unknowing, looking for this fizz of danger, the tingling anticipation that accompanied every encounter with the Russian? She still felt it now, a wonderful lingering hum in her veins, a tingle of her skin, and this extraordinary sense of being more truly alive than she had ever been, every physical sense aroused, honed to a sharp edge, and the latter most particularly when she remembered those wild and passionate moments in the pavilion. Her nipples hardened anew just at the thought of his hands on her body.

Did it really matter that she knew so little about him? She would surely have felt some warning signs if he was a *bad* man. A violent man, a brute, a villain . . . no, he was none of those things. Although he was certainly more than the sum of the parts he'd shown her thus far. Was he a liar, a deceiver? How could she possibly know the answer to that? He hadn't told her enough about himself. How could she look for lies when she'd been given no facts to test?

So what did Alex want with this proposal? That was a much harder question to answer. At least it was if she discounted his simple explanation that he needed, and wanted, a wife, a woman who would give him an heir, and that he'd never met anyone he could see in that role before. Which, when she thought about it, was exactly her position with the sexes reversed. In her ideal world she would have a husband and children, and she could certainly imagine Alex as both husband and the father of her children. So if it worked as a reason for her, then why shouldn't it work for him?

Livia sat up and pushed aside the strip of leather that covered the window of the chaise. It was a much more comfortable vehicle than the hackney cab that had driven her to Richmond. Alex had ordered it as soon as they'd returned to the White Hart. One thing she knew for certain about him, he was accustomed to ordering the comforts of life seemingly without reference to cost. He was a rich man.

And just how much did that matter to her? She stared out at the city crowds hurrying through the gathering dusk; link boys already carrying the evening's lighted torches were offering pedestrians their escort, and lamps were appearing in the windows of shops and residences as the carriage bowled along the cobbles.

Livia didn't consider herself a mercenary person; indeed, she'd never been given the opportunity to become so. Creature comforts were important, of course. Good and plentiful food on the table, soft beds, clean sheets, warm fires. But she had never been used to luxury and she could light the fire, make the bed, and cook a simple meal perfectly well herself. Her father refused to keep more than the most basic household staff and his daughter had stepped into the role of housekeeper at the vicarage twelve years ago, at fifteen, after her mother's death. But there was no denying that the luxuries of a post chaise, a beautiful riding horse, fine wine, and a maid bringing morning tea to her bedside every day were more than pleasant. As was the idea of a lavish and elegant wardrobe. On one level she quite enjoyed the ingenious tricks she and her friends had used to give the impression of a varied and modish wardrobe, but she couldn't help thinking that an armoire full of her own clothes that could be replenished as needed would be rather appealing.

Was this something to be ashamed of? Should the Reverend Lord Harford's daughter never give in to such thoughts?

Livia chuckled suddenly. No, she wasn't ashamed of it, and there was no reason to be. Frugality was all very well in its place, and maybe it *was* good for the soul. But sometimes the soul needed a little pampering too.

They turned onto Cavendish Square and the chaise drew to a halt outside the house. The lamps were lit in the hall and a lantern hung above the front door, throwing a welcoming shaft of light over the steps. The liveryman jumped down from his perch at the back of the chaise and opened the door, letting down the footstep.

"This is it, m'lady."

"Yes, thank you." She stepped down and he ran ahead of her to the front door, banging the knocker. "You need to sound it more vigorously," she said as she came up behind him. "My butler is a trifle deaf."

But the door opened rapidly and Aurelia stood in the lighted hallway. "I thought it must be you," she said, her gaze swiftly taking in the liveryman and the chaise at the curb. "You must have had a long ride." Her eyes darted a mischievous question.

"It's a big park," Livia said, stepping into the hall. She offered the liveryman a smiling word of thanks as he pulled the door closed behind her.

"A post chaise, no less," Aurelia remarked. "Rather more comfortable than a smelly hackney."

"Much more comfortable," Livia agreed, going towards the stairs. "I need to change, Ellie. I reek of horseflesh."

"I'll be in the parlor when you come down," her friend said. "I told Morecombe that we would be dining *à deux* in the parlor. I didn't think you had any engagements this evening?" She raised an interrogative eyebrow.

"None that I must honor," Livia said. "And to be honest, I'm dead on my feet, Ellie. I haven't ridden so hard and so long since my last hunt. All this sedate trotting around Hyde Park gets one out of practice." She spoke over her shoulder as she went up the stairs and Aurelia, resigned to hearing no details until later, returned to the parlor.

When Livia came down again, clad in a simple round gown that had seen better days, it was clear she was intending to settle in for a cozy domestic evening. She took the glass of sherry Aurelia handed her and sank with a sigh into a deep faded chintz armchair, stretching her slipper-clad feet to the fire. "This is nice."

"I'm sure it's a pleasant contrast to a day spent in an assignation with a Russian prince," Aurelia responded, taking up her embroidery. "Not all of us have so much excitement."

Livia laughed. "I don't know what to tell you, Ellie."

"Everything, of course," her friend stated. "Well, you could leave out any details about getting grass stains on your riding habit . . ."

"Not grass stains exactly," Livia said with a quick and slightly self-conscious laugh. "But it was a close call, Ellie."

Aurelia regarded her thoughtfully. "I thought you had something of a glow about you," she observed.

Livia pressed her fingers to her cheek as she admitted with a rueful smile, "I've never felt anything like it, love . . . and I have to say, I have every intention of discovering what happens next . . . and sooner rather than later."

Aurelia continued to ply her needle for a moment, then she inquired almost casually, "A general voyage of discovery or one confined to the attentions of Prince Prokov?"

"He asked me to marry him," Livia said in oblique answer as she took a sip of her sherry.

Slowly Aurelia put down her embroidery, her lips pursed in a silent whistle. "He doesn't let the grass grow, does he? What did you say?"

Livia shrugged. "I said I needed some time to think." When Aurelia said nothing, she went on, "I was rather hoping you might help me think, Ellie. I'm bewildered."

"I'm not surprised," the other woman said. "It's rather

sudden. Proposals of marriage don't usually come out of the blue." She was feeling her way, unwilling to say anything that inadvertently might upset Livia, but unsure whether her friend was asking for unconditional support or a truly reasoned discussion of the pros and cons.

"But was it really out of the blue, Ellie? Bellingham's swim, the botanical garden, Daphne——"

"Daphne?"

"Oh, yes, I didn't tell you all there was to tell about the horse." Livia wriggled her toes on the fender and gave her friend a ruefully apologetic smile. "Initially Alex said the horse was mine . . . not a loan at all, but a gift. Of course I told him I couldn't accept it and we had some to-ing and fro-ing over it, and finally I said I would be happy to accept the mare as a loan."

"He wanted to give you a Thoroughbred horse on your second, or maybe third, meeting?" Aurelia asked incredulously.

"He doesn't behave like ordinary people," Livia said, thinking how lame that sounded.

"No, I should say not." Aurelia reached for the decanter and refilled their glasses. "Do you think we should try to find out something about him before you make up your mind?"

"How?"

"Harry."

Livia nodded slowly. If anyone could find out about a mysterious Russian prince on the London scene, it would be Harry. "But he's in Ringwood."

"No, they're on their way back. They should be in London sometime tomorrow." Aurelia got up and went to the secretaire. "A runner delivered a message from Cornelia. They're driving up slowly because of Susannah." She handed the letter to Livia.

Livia read it. "I can't wait to see her," she said, looking up, her eyes suddenly sharp. "And Harry and the children, of course. Have you mentioned Alex to Nell, Ellie?"

Aurelia nodded. "You must have known I would, Liv. Anything that concerns you concerns us all. I wasn't feeling quite capable of supporting you alone."

Livia smiled and shook her head. "It's a somewhat complicated situation, I grant you. And I would welcome Nell's opinion . . . but . . ." She hesitated. "But I'm not sure I want Harry setting his dogs onto Alex, Ellie. It seems rather disloyal. If I'm going to trust him, believe in him, then I have to do it from my own instincts, not because he's been vetted by a member of the British secret service."

"I can see that, but you don't even know who his friends are," Aurelia pointed out. "He must have some . . . some fellow Russians, I would think. Don't you think it would be useful to discover where he stands in the émigré community? Is he in exile for some reason, or is he really just a casual foreign visitor? With the political situation between Russia and England . . ." She shook her head with a frown. "Supposing he's not the dilettante prince he says he is?"

Livia gazed down into her sherry glass. "If—and I

said *if*—I decide to marry him, then I'll marry him for whatever he is, Ellie, and he'll be marrying me for who I am. I can't imagine agreeing to spend the rest of my life with anyone on any other terms."

"And I applaud you for it," Aurelia said. "But what if he wants to take you to live in Russia? Could you really give up everything . . . family, friends . . . the life you know?"

Livia chewed her lip for a minute before she answered. "I would have to, Ellie. I wouldn't marry him without accepting that such a move might be a consequence. If I can't accept that, then obviously I can't marry him . . . but I would hope he'd take my feelings and wishes into consideration too."

Aurelia nodded. There wasn't much more to say on that subject, vitally important though it was. It was something for Livia and her prince to thrash out between them. She hesitated a moment before asking, "Are you talking about the grand passion here, Liv? Is it love . . . or will you settle for a mutually agreeable marriage of convenience?"

Livia grinned suddenly. "I don't know about love as yet, Ellie, but there's certainly lust. And if that's not part of the grand passion I don't know what is. I'm trying to decide if it's sufficient fuel for a marriage of convenience." She paused for a minute, a smile tugging at the corners of her mouth. "And I have to say, Ellie, it would be very convenient to be Princess Prokov."

Aurelia's peal of laughter broke the gravity. "Oh, yes,"

she agreed. "And I can just see your father's face when the prince asks for his daughter's hand in marriage."

Livia grimaced. "I was wondering how he would react myself. He can't refuse permission since I'm well beyond the age of consent, but I wouldn't like him to disapprove, Ellie."

Aurelia's laughter died. Livia and her father were actually very close, for all that the daughter had not embraced the spiritual dictates of frugality and self-abnegation of her parent. It would be devastating for her if the Reverend Lacey refused to officiate at her marriage. "He's never pushed you into making any decision," she pointed out. "He's always let you find your own way."

Livia nodded. "Encouraged me to do so," she agreed. "With the chessboard as example." Her father had taught her to play chess as a four-year-old and had honed her skills until on a good night she could defeat him two out of three games. He had always said logical thinking and the ability to see the consequences at least five moves ahead of the move one was about to make were the skills one needed to navigate a path through life.

But could she apply that lesson to making a decision to marry Alexander Prokov?

"Talk it over with Nell, anyway," Aurelia said. "Even if you don't want Harry to vet him."

Livia nodded. "Three heads as they say . . ."

☙❧

Cornelia arrived in Cavendish Square the following afternoon, on foot and without her children or her husband. She ran up the steps to the door that had been her own for so many months and banged loudly on the lion's-head knocker. Brightly polished, she noticed, just as the steps were well honed.

She waited patiently, ear to the door, listening for the scuffle of Morecombe's carpet slippers across the parquet. At last the door creaked open and the elderly man's face peered around. "Oh, 'tis you," he said, as if she hadn't been gone the entire summer.

"Yes, Morecombe, it's me," she affirmed cheerfully, pushing open the door. "Are the ladies in?"

"Haven't seen 'em go out," he observed. "Reckon they're in t' parlor."

"Thank you, Morecombe." She moved towards the parlor door.

"You want tea, m'lady? Our Ada's made some of 'em spice cakes what you like," the butler said.

Cornelia stopped and turned back. "That would be lovely, Morecombe. I've been dreaming about Ada's spice cakes ever since I left."

He nodded. "Thought as 'ow they might go down a treat, mum." He shuffled off towards the door to the kitchen regions.

Cornelia smiled. It was good to be back. She opened the parlor door and peered around it. "Guess who?"

"Nell." Livia and Aurelia jumped up and rushed to

embrace her. "Oh, it's lovely to see you. We've been waiting in all afternoon," Livia said.

"Yes, you can't imagine how many visitors we've had to turn away so that we'd be alone when you came," Aurelia said, laughing, drawing her into the room. "I'll go and ask Morecombe for tea."

"He's bringing it already," Cornelia said, shrugging out of her pelisse. "And some of our Ada's spice cakes."

"They must have known you were coming," Livia said. "We haven't had spice cakes since you left."

"Well, we've always known the twins have special powers," Aurelia said. "Sit . . . sit, Nell . . . how was the journey? How are the children?"

"How's Harry?" put in Livia, taking her friend's gloves and hat.

"They're all well. Susannah managed the journey without throwing up once and Linton is examining the refurbished nursery quarters in Harry's house on Mount Street with something like approbation, and Stevie's in the mews making the acquaintance of his new pony." Cornelia sank onto the sofa and threw her arms above her head. "Oh, it's just like old times."

"Not quite," Aurelia pointed out quietly.

"No," Cornelia agreed, sitting up straight. "I don't live here anymore, but that doesn't change our friendship." She looked at Livia and Aurelia. "So, tell me what's been happening?"

"You know perfectly well," Livia said. "Ellie told you all about the Russian prince."

"I haven't told her about the latest development," Aurelia said. "About what happened yesterday."

"Ah." Cornelia put her head on one side, looking between them. "So tell me." Morecombe came in with the tea tray at that point and they fell silent. When he'd left Livia explained.

"It would be simple if it was someone we could understand," Cornelia said when Livia had finished her recitation. "Someone who played by the same rules, fitted the same molds as we do, but this Prince Prokov is an exotic. With someone you understood you could say, well, I know what he wants, what he expects, and it either suits me or it doesn't."

"Precisely," Aurelia said.

"But that's what I find irresistible," Livia said slowly. "I don't understand him, I can't predict his next move, and I love it."

"Then I suggest we stop trying to make sense of this and let Liv follow her instincts," Cornelia declared.

"Well, you certainly followed yours," Aurelia said.

"And it's brought me only happiness," Cornelia said softly. She leaned over and touched Livia's hand. "Liv, you know what's right for you. And we'll stand behind you every step of the way."

"Absolutely," Aurelia said, her hand joining Cornelia's. "But let Harry make sure he's unknown to his network."

"It's a simple precaution, Liv," Cornelia said. "We're at war with Russia."

Reluctantly Livia nodded. She hated the whole business of distrusting someone so much that you had to dig into corners looking for bad things. But a thread of common sense told her that she knew so little of this man, it was only common sense to use the tools at her disposal to eliminate at least some of the uncertainties.

Harry found very little. Prince Alexander Prokov was certainly known to Harry's contacts. But he appeared to present no threat. He had no political history, no reason that they could unearth to have fled the Court of St. Petersburg. He was simply a dilettante visitor. A wealthy Russian aristocrat who'd been a protégé of the Empress Catherine. He had known the czar well as a youth, had been an officer in the prestigious Preobrazhensky regiment, but like so many Russian noblemen appeared to have little interest in anything but entertainment.

"I don't know," he said to Cornelia as they lay in bed two days later. "There are no indications that he's anything but what he appears to be. Russians of his social standing spend more time visiting European capitals than they do in St. Petersburg. They're an educated, wealthy, cosmopolitan lot and always have been. He seems uninterested in politics, and I'm told he's well liked among the loose circle of Russian émigrés and equally well liked in the clubs. An affable, easygoing, perfectly gentlemanly member of society. And to all intents and purposes a more than suitable suitor for

Livia . . . in fact, a highly desirable one, I would have said."

He leaned over and kissed her. "I can keep digging if you wish."

Cornelia shook her head. "No, Liv doesn't want that." She turned into his embrace. "She has to make up her own mind." A few minutes later, she said abruptly as if the idea had just come to her, "But if she does marry him, he might take her away, back to Russia."

Harry sighed and stopped what he was doing. "I don't seem to be able to hold your attention tonight," he complained. "Am I boring you?"

"Don't be ridiculous," she said, reaching up a hand to stroke his face as he gazed down at her, an expression of mild irritation in his green eyes. "It was just that the thought came to me and I didn't like it . . . please go on . . . *please*, Harry."

"That's better," he said, and his wife swiftly rediscovered her concentration as she lost interest in anything but the activity at hand.

⌘

Two days later, Harry drew up in his curricle outside White's, tossed the reins to his groom, and strolled into his club intent on a game of Macau. He'd been closeted in his dingy office at the War Ministry for nearly two days, deciphering a particularly troublesome Russian code, and was relishing the prospect of putting his agile brain to work on calculating the odds at cards, an activity that he knew would relax him and clear his head.

"Ah, Harry . . . there you are." A cheerful voice hailed him from a chair in the bow window, and Lord David Foster waved a hand in greeting. "Come and join us. Nick, here, was regaling us with some tall tale about a boar he shot in Bavaria."

"Nick's never been to Bavaria," Harry declared, laughing as he made his way across the elegant salon, taking a glass of madeira from a waiter's tray as he passed. He paused at the table, one hand resting casually on Nicholas Petersham's buckram shoulder. "Have you, Nick?"

"I went in the long vacation once . . ." the other declared with a touch of feigned indignation. "And I'll thank you, Bonham, not to call me a liar."

"Call him out, I should," David said with a lazy grin. "Can't let the insult lie, you know."

"Call Harry out? I'm not mad enough for that," Nick stated. "I'd rather face the boar again."

"No need for that." Harry deposited his long frame in a deep armchair opposite his friends. "I apologize for the calumny, Nick. I had forgotten about that visit. As I recall now, you came back to school with a scar on your calf that you insisted had been caused by the boar's tusk." He shook his head sadly. "Not sure anyone believed you then. You always did have a talent for exaggeration."

Nick laughed. "It's always a mistake to spend time with people who've known you since you were in short coats. And," he added with mock menace, "I could tell some tales of you, Harry, that I'll lay odds you'd not want broadcast."

"I'm sure you could, Nick," Harry said nonchalantly. He uncoiled himself from the depths of his chair. "I've a mind to play Macau, anyone care to join me?"

"No . . . no, I've lost a hundred guineas already today," David said, shaking his head. "I'm intent on drowning my sorrows."

"Nick?"

Nicholas Petersham set down his glass and stood up. "I'll probably regret it, but a hand or two perhaps."

They went off to an inner room, one where the candlelight gave the impression of perpetual night accentuated by the hushed voices of the groom porters calling the odds, the slap of cards on baize, the rattle of dice, the intense silence around the tables as the players made their bets.

A group at a corner table attracted Harry's attention. He'd met two of them briefly, Russian émigrés both. Duke Nicolai Sperskov and Count Constantine Fedorovsky. They had attracted the attention of the English secret service when they'd first arrived in London, as did all foreign visitors who seemed set to stay in the country for some length of time, and Harry had seen their files. They contained nothing of any particular interest. Like other Russian aristocrats, they had no shortage of funds, moved within a wide international social circle, and seemed intent for the most part on the pursuit of pleasure. No different in that respect from their English counterparts moving between the idle entertainments of the London season and the country house circuit.

Duke Nicolai was said to be something of a high-living roué. He enjoyed a lavish lifestyle and entertained a string of mistresses, all sophisticated married ladies with impeccable social connections. There was no hint that he used them for anything more devious than bed sport. No hint of intelligence activity anywhere. Fedorovsky was a rather less expansive character, a good conversationalist with wide-ranging interests, but again the usual investigations had revealed no indications of devious activities.

"D'you know the man playing with Sperskov and Fedorovsky, Nick?" Harry asked, pausing before taking his seat at a Macau table.

Nick raised his quizzing glass and peered across the room. "Oh, what's his name . . . ? I met him at Brooke's and then I came upon him riding with Livia . . . a week or so ago . . . begins with a P . . ." He snapped his fingers. "Prokov, Prince Alexander Prokov, that's it."

"Ah," Harry murmured. "I've seen him around, but I've never been introduced. D'you care to do the honors, Nick?"

Nick, who was about to seat himself at the table, gave his friend a rather pained look of inquiry. "Now?"

"No, when they leave the club . . . I've a mind to bump into them, as it were. Let's go back and talk to David about boar hunting . . . forgive us, gentlemen, I've just remembered a previous engagement." He offered an apologetic smile to the card table's present occupants, who'd been waiting for them to take their seats.

"Whatever you say," Nick agreed amiably, turning away from the table. "What's your interest in the man . . . he's just another Russian aristocrat."

"He seems to have a certain interest in Livia," Harry said. "I'm commissioned by my wife to look him over."

"I thought there was something smoky going on there," Nick declared with an air of triumph. "When I came upon them in the park, Liv was as taut as a drawn bow. And our Russian friend had a damned proprietorial air about him too. If he's making a nuisance of himself to Liv—"

"No . . . no, quite the opposite, I gather," Harry said, waving a soothing hand at his friend.

"Livia returns his interest?" Nick paused in his progress towards the salon.

Harry shrugged. "I'm not in her confidence at this point, Nick. I only obey my wife's instructions."

Nick gave him a disbelieving look, then continued on his way into the next room.

"We've decided to return to the subject of boar hunting," Harry declared to David as he deposited himself in a deep armchair opposite.

"Oh, I thought you were for Macau." David hailed a waiter with a tray of glasses.

"Not any more; Harry decided for his own inscrutable reasons to wait for an opportunity to accost Prince Prokov . . . d'you know him, David?"

"Only to bow to," the other man said. "Seems a pleasant enough fellow."

"So I thought," Nick said darkly, "but it seems he has designs on Livia Lacey."

David sat up abruptly. "Does he indeed? Can we permit that?"

"You don't know the ladies of Cavendish Square very well, David, if you think it has anything to do with you," Harry observed with a chuckle, taking a glass from the waiter's tray. "Or indeed with me, except that Nell demands I make inquiries and what the lady wants the lady gets."

His friends chuckled knowingly and raised their glasses in a silent toast.

It was half an hour later when Alex with his two friends emerged from the card room, all of them blinking a little at the bright daylight after the gentle candlelight in the inner room.

Nick rose from his chair and hailed the three of them. "Come and join us for a glass, Prokov . . . I would make you known to an old friend who's just returned to town from an extended honeymoon in Scotland."

The three Russians approached the group in the bow window; smiles and bows and murmured courtesies were exchanged. Alex was a little puzzled at Petersham's friendliness—it seemed to imply a depth of friendship that didn't exist between them—but he was confident the answer would reveal itself at some point, as indeed it did.

"Been riding again with Lady Livia?" Nick inquired casually. "I've looked out for you in the park, but haven't seen you."

"I haven't had the pleasure of another ride in the park with Lady Livia," Alex said, his eyes narrowing in speculation. He took one of the extra chairs that a watchful waiter had brought over when it was clear the party in the window was going to expand.

"Bring us a bottle of the '97 burgundy, there's a good fellow," Nick instructed the waiter before confiding merrily to Alex, "Harry, here, is married to Livia Lacey's best friend."

"Indeed," Alex said, inclining his head towards Harry. "I thought Lady Farnham filled that position."

Harry smiled. "Lady Farnham and my wife, her sister-in-law, share the honor."

"Ah, I see," Alex said, seeing perfectly. Clearly he was being vetted. Well, he had no objections. After all, he had nothing to hide from these three carefree members of the Upper Ten Thousand, and they were precisely the company he wished to cultivate. He settled down to make himself thoroughly agreeable.

Duke Nicolai, always happy simply to be in good company, particularly when the wine was flowing, sank into an armchair with a sigh of pleasure. Constantine, whose interests ran along rather more intellectual and scientific lines, took a seat a little reluctantly, but was soon diverted by a comment Harry made about Joseph Priestley and the chemical experiments that had led to the discovery of oxygen.

As the second bottle of burgundy was emptied, Harry said expansively, "I have several very fine bottles of the '96 from the same vineyard . . . let's broach one, gentlemen, and see how it compares. It's but a short walk to my house in Mount Street."

"With pleasure, Harry," David said, standing up with just the slightest stagger. "The day's young after all."

"Aye, it's barely three in the afternoon," Nick said. "Come, gentlemen, let's go and sample Bonham's cellar."

Alex agreed with alacrity. He had nothing to lose and everything to gain by charming and disarming Livia's friends.

"Duke Nicolai . . . Count Fedorovsky . . . you'll join us too, of course?" Harry said.

"Oh, yes . . . yes, why not," Nicolai said warmly, pulling on his luxuriant black moustache. "No better way of passing an afternoon than in good company sampling good wine, I always say. Constantine, you've a fine palate . . . what d'you say?"

"I'd be delighted to accept your hospitality, Viscount Bonham," the count said with a formal little bow. "I'm most interested to see your copy of *The History and Present State of Electricity*. Some of Priestley's finest work, I've always thought."

"I'd agree," Harry said. "I've always counted it a great loss to England that the riots drove him to America. His political and theological views were unpopular, but that's no reason to drive a man violently into exile."

"Politics and theology arouse violent passions," Alex observed. "We have only to look at the world around us."

"True enough," Nicolai declared, shaking his head. "But enough seriousness for one day, let's sample that wine."

Alex gave a mental shrug and followed the group out of the club. He was aware that Nicolai had decided the conversation was getting too close to home, but making no mention of world affairs would draw as much suspicion as trumpeting their own cause from the rooftops.

Chapter Nine

CORNELIA WITH AURELIA AND LIVIA entered the Bonhams' house in Mount Street later that afternoon, followed by a footman with an armful of bandboxes.

"Oh, Hector, could you have these taken up to the nursery, please?" Cornelia asked the butler. "Linton will want to check that I've fulfilled all her commissions exactly to specifications." She gave him a conspiratorial smile that he returned with a solemn bow.

"Indeed, my lady, I'll have it seen to straightaway. His lordship is in the library, with some gentlemen," he added.

"Oh, anyone I know?"

"Sir Nicholas and Lord Foster, ma'am, and three other gentlemen who are unknown to me."

"Well, in that case I think we should make them known to us," Cornelia said cheerfully. "Come, ladies." She sailed across the hall in the direction of the library. If Harry was entertaining his two closest friends as well as the strangers, it would be a social visit and he would have no objection to his wife's interruption.

She tapped lightly on the door and opened it immediately, popping her head around. "Good afternoon, gentlemen. I trust we're not interrupting?"

"Not at all, my dear. Bring the rest of you in here," Harry said, a smile lighting his green eyes as it always did at the sight of his wife. "Oh, even better . . . Aurelia and Livia as well."

He rose from his chair and crossed the room, hand extended in greeting. "Come in . . . come in . . . let me introduce my visitors . . . at least," he added with a chuckle, "those who are in need of introduction." He cast a sly glance at Livia as he said this.

Livia caught the glance but was too absorbed in her own extraordinary reaction to the unexpected sight of Alex to pay Harry any attention. He was standing a little behind two men whom she didn't know, his brilliant blue gaze assessing her, a tiny smile lifting the corners of his mouth. Lust, pure and simple, melted her loins, stabbed deep in her belly, set her blood running swiftly. She was aware of sudden color flooding her cheeks as she took an involuntary step towards him, iron filings to his magnet.

Alex moved swiftly away from his companions, his eyes never leaving hers as he came to take her hand. "Livia, I had not looked for such pleasure this afternoon," he murmured, lifting her hand to his lips.

She managed some response but was not at all sure

what she said. She could feel the eyes of her friends watching her and knew she was betraying herself, not to Nell and Ellie, from whom she had no secrets, but to Harry, and to David, and to Nick. *And she couldn't help herself.*

Harry came to the rescue. "I was forgetting you're already acquainted with Prince Prokov, Livia," he lied smoothly. "But Cornelia, allow me to present Prince Prokov. Prokov, my wife, Lady Bonham."

Relieved at the momentary respite, Livia turned to Nick and David, welcoming the distraction of their easy informality. Their curiosity might have been piqued by her reaction to Alex, but they were far too polite and considerate to comment, and instead chatted inconsequentially with her and Aurelia like the old reliable friends they were, and Livia quickly regained her equilibrium.

Lady Bonham was a striking woman, Alex reflected as he bowed to the tall, elegant figure in a walking dress of boldly striped muslin, honey-colored hair confined beneath a close-fitting brown felt hat. "Your servant, ma'am."

"I'm delighted to meet you, Prince Prokov," Cornelia said, offering him her hand with a warm smile that did little to disguise the speculative scrutiny in her eyes. "Livia has spoken of you."

"I am honored," he said. "May I present my compatriots . . ." He turned towards the count and the duke, who were waiting in courteous patience for an introduction to their hostess and her two companions.

Livia examined Alex's friends with covert interest. They were older than Alex, and seemed at first glance to have little in common with him. The count was a rather earnest gentleman, studiously polite, and the duke, unless she was much mistaken, had a definite leer in his pale blue eyes and the genuinely benign if slightly self-satisfied smile of a cream-filled cat. She did her best to concentrate on their conversation, but every inch of her was alive with sensations that had nothing to do with the demands of polite small talk. She could feel Alex's eyes on her whenever he turned his gaze on her. She could hear his voice, every word he spoke, even when he was on the other side of the room.

"A glass of sherry, Livia?" Harry spoke at her shoulder and she jumped.

"Thank you." She took the glass with an automatic smile and he gave her a searching look before turning back to his other guests. Livia addressed the duke, who was savoring his burgundy with an air of deep appreciation. "Have you known Prince Prokov long, Duke Nicolai?"

"Oh, for many years," the duke said, sipping his burgundy. His light blue eyes gleamed in his plump, pink-cheeked countenance and Livia had the unmistakable impression that she was being weighed up, as if he was considering her for some position. His voice lowered and became as mellow as treacle, as he laid a soft white hand on her arm and gave it a meaningful squeeze. "Tell me, dear lady, how do you amuse yourself in town? I'm

sure the young men must be beating down your door."
He winked. "If I were ten years younger, that's where
you would find me."

Laughter welled as Livia realized what he was up to.
This old roué was trying to decide if she was sufficiently
bed-worthy to make outright pursuit worthwhile. She
cast an amused glance in Alex's direction and was rewarded with a comprehending glimmer of a smile.

With a word of excuse, he moved away from Aurelia
and Harry and came over to Livia and the duke. "You
must be glad to have all your friends back in town, Lady
Livia."

"Yes, indeed, Prince. Nell's been away all summer . . .
it's wonderful to have her back. Old friends are irre-
placeable, don't you agree? The duke was saying he's
known you for many years."

"Since I joined the Empress Catherine's household as
a ten-year-old, when the Grand Duke Alexander was
four years old," Alex said. "Duke Nicolai was a young
courtier." He laughed. "It was Nicolai who advanced my
education in certain, shall we say, more worldly subjects."

"Oh, stuff and nonsense," the duke exclaimed. "I
merely ensured that that part of your education was not
neglected, since I doubt the czarina would have seen to
it with the same care she gave to more intellectual subjects. I did the same for the young grand duke when he
was of an age."

"Perhaps I shouldn't be listening to this," Livia demurred, although she was fascinated by this glimpse into Alex's past.

Alex looked at her over the lip of his glass. "I doubt it comes as a surprise to you," he said softly.

To her annoyance, Livia felt her cheeks warm again. She sipped her sherry and asked hastily, "Do you have brothers and sisters, Prince?"

"No," he said. "The closest I had to a brother was the czar. We shared a schoolroom, but there are six years between us."

"Why would you use the past tense?" Livia asked with a stab of interest. "He's still alive. Is he not still as close as a brother to you?"

"He is now the czar, my sovereign," Alex said, his voice taking on a distance. "One does not claim such ties to the czar of all the Russias without being true blood kin."

"I see." Livia frowned. Alex had withdrawn in some way and it was quite clear he didn't wish to pursue the subject. She glanced at Duke Nicolai and saw that he too had become grave, his eyes no longer warm and lascivious, but rather cool and distant. Perhaps there was some unspoken Russian etiquette about discussing their emperor on purely social occasions. She turned with relief to Cornelia, who came up with the wine bottle.

"Do you live in St. Petersburg, Prince Prokov? Or are you a Muscovite?" Cornelia asked as she refilled the men's wineglasses with burgundy.

"Like most Russians I have a foot in both camps," he said. "My family has palaces in both cities."

"Yes, but you wouldn't want to spend much time in Moscow," the duke declared. "None of the elegancies in that city."

"It's a city that treasures the old traditions, Lady Bonham." It was Count Fedorovsky who spoke, turning eagerly from his perusal of Harry's bookshelves. It was a topic that interested him. "St. Petersburg looks towards Europe, the new life, the new world, but Moscow is the national heart of Russia. It stands for our Asiatic past."

"The houses are draughty, the streets filthy and narrow, the aristocrats insular, and the serfs surly," the duke declared with a sweeping gesture. "Its architecture is a tumble-down hotchpotch of wooden houses and collapsing cottages."

"It has a certain energy to it," the count protested with a touch of reproof in his tone. "And its churches are magnificent . . . even the Kremlin, grim fortress though it is, has a grandeur all its own."

"What's your opinion, Prince?" Livia asked, watching Alex as he considered the question. She knew so little about that vast empire, a mere smattering of its chaotic and violent history, and until Alex, she had never met a Russian. It seemed there were many kinds of Russian . . . so what kind was Alexander Prokov?

"I agree with the count," he said lightly. "It has more essential energy and attracts those who prefer to live independently of the intrigues and games of the court of St. Petersburg, where ambition is the ruling spirit. Muscovites enjoy themselves and are untroubled by ambition. But each to his own . . . and I would certainly find it hard to choose if I was obliged to pick one city over the other as my only domicile."

"But you are not thinking of returning to Russia in the near future, Prince Prokov?" Cornelia said, with just a hint of a questioning inflection.

"None of us are, ma'am," Alex stated with a careless shrug. "While Europe is engulfed in war, and Napoleon looks fair to rule the entire continent within a year or so, discretion seems the better part of valor. For as long as your delightful country will give us hospitality, my friends and I are committed to these shores." He looked deliberately at Livia as he said this and she gave an infinitesimal nod, grateful for a piece of information that he had understood she needed.

Count Fedorovsky glanced at his fob watch and stated, "Well, I think we've trespassed on your hospitality long enough, Lady Bonham . . . and we've certainly drunk more than our fair share of your husband's excellent burgundy." He bowed formally to Cornelia and to Livia, then took himself across the room to make his farewells to his host and the remainder of the party.

"Yes . . . yes . . . of course, Constantine's quite right," the duke said, sounding rather reluctant. "We mustn't outstay our welcome."

"Indeed, Duke, you couldn't possibly do so," Cornelia responded with a hostess's aplomb.

He laughed and kissed her hand. "Too kind, dear lady . . . too kind . . . Lady Livia, honored to have made your acquaintance." He kissed Livia's hand in turn, and then followed his compatriot across the room to his host.

Alex bowed to Cornelia, murmured his thanks, aware as before of her close scrutiny.

"I'm sure we shall see you again soon, Prince Prokov," Cornelia said, offering her hand.

"I would be honored, ma'am." He bowed again over her hand and turned to look for Livia. She had withdrawn a little apart into a shallow window embrasure and he went over to her. He took her hand between both of his in a warm, firm clasp and his brilliant gaze swept her countenance. He said softly, "May I call upon you?"

Livia knew he was asking if she had an answer for him. And she knew that she had. She nodded. "Yes . . ." And then involuntarily, almost under her breath, she added, "Please." Immediately she saw the light intensify in those piercing blue eyes.

He smiled and raised her hand to his lips. "Soon," he promised.

Livia wondered rather wryly if she should have kept him guessing right up to the moment he renewed his proposal. The Letitia Oglethorpes of this world would certainly have done so. But she could see no point at all in prevaricating, and the game of hard-to-get had never appealed. She had made up her mind, and that was all there was to it. All that remained now was to formalize the business.

The following morning Alex went about his preparations. He visited the jeweler's, and then paid a lengthier visit to a lawyer in Threadneedle Street.

The lawyer, John Masters, Esquire, greeted his visitor with a low bow. "An honor, Prince Prokov . . . and how may I be of service, sir?"

"I wish you to examine these papers and make certain that all is clear and in order," Alex stated, dropping a sheaf of documents fastened with a red ribbon on the desk. Then he strolled to the window and stood, hands clasped behind his back, looking down on the street.

The lawyer resumed his seat behind the massive mahogany desk and reverently untied the ribbon. The seal of the house of Prokov was stamped upon every sheet. He read in silence, glancing up once or twice at his visitor's averted back. A look of distress crossed his rubicund countenance as he came to the end. He coughed into his hand and returned to the first page again.

"I don't quite understand . . ." he murmured, flipping through the documents again as if in search of a missing sheet.

"What don't you understand?" Alex swung away from the window, looking at him with a frown. "As I understand it's perfectly clear."

"Yes . . . yes . . . it is . . . but . . ." The lawyer came to a stammering stop and looked helplessly at him. "Prince Prokov, I understood that the house on Cavendish Square belonged to Lady Livia Lacey. It was left to her in her relative's will. I have a copy of the will . . . let me fetch it." He pushed back his chair with a noisy scrape on the wooden floor.

"Don't trouble yourself," Alex said, waving him back. "That document was drawn up in error, as you can see." He gestured to the sheets. "The house on Cavendish Square was given to Sophia Lacey by my father for use in her lifetime only. It was not and was never intended to be a gift."

Masters picked up the sheets again, his expression one of acute dismay. "I understand, Prince Prokov . . . but . . . but . . . surely you cannot mean to evict Lady Livia?"

"No, I don't mean to do that," Alex said. "But since you were the executor of the late Lady Sophia's will, I wished to apprise you of the true state of affairs. I want this muddle cleared up once and for all."

"I see . . . but if you don't intend to evict Lady Livia, will you expect her to pay rent if she wishes to continue living there?" Masters took off his horn-rimmed spectacles and rubbed his eyes. "I know something of Lady Livia's affairs and I'm certain that a fair-market rent will be beyond her financial capacity."

Alex shook his head. "I have no intention of charging the lady rent, and my present intention most certainly does *not* involve eviction."

"So . . . so, sir, may I inquire what is your present intention?" Masters asked blankly.

"I have every hope that the lady will agree to become my wife," Alex stated. "In which case the issue will be moot. All I wish of you at this point, Masters, is a signed declaration that you have examined the papers and found them in order and that these documents take precedence over Lady Sophia's will, which was drawn up in error. I can only assume Lady Sophia misunderstood the nature of the gift my father made her, or . . ." He shrugged. "Or perhaps in the intervening years she forgot the finer points. Either way, it is immaterial."

"I see," Masters said, although he didn't see at all. He had grown rather fond in an avuncular fashion of Lady Livia and there was something about his visitor's manner that made him uneasy. But then, he was Russian and they were a peculiar race, as everyone knew. If Lady Livia was prepared to marry him, he couldn't be all bad.

"And at the same time, you may draw up the marriage contracts," Alex continued calmly. "They will specify that the house on Cavendish Square will become the marital home for as long as my wife and I remain in London."

"And is Lady Livia to be apprised of the true owner-ship of the house, sir?"

"That's an issue that need not concern you, Masters." Alex drew on his gloves.

"I see," Masters said again. "And . . . and with the marriage contracts . . . is there to be some provision made for Lady Livia? For her personal expenses? I am unsure how such matters are conducted in your country, Prince, but it is customary in England for a husband to settle something on his wife on their marriage and to make provision for a quarterly allowance . . ." He let the sentence fade away with a helpless little shrug.

Alex reached across the desk and picked up the lawyer's quill. He dipped it into the inkwell and wrote some figures on a sheet of paper. "There, that should be enough for you to work with." He spun the paper across the desk to the startled lawyer, then picked up his high-crowned beaver hat from the chair.

"You may send the declaration and the marriage contracts without delay to my lodgings on Bruton Street. I give you good day, Masters."

Masters was for a moment too absorbed in the figures on the paper to respond and only when the prince repeated his farewell did he look up, his expression both startled and bemused.

"Oh . . . I beg your pardon, Prince Prokov . . . just looking at this . . . very generous, I may say . . . yes, indeed, very generous. Uh . . . good day to you, sir . . . a pleasure to serve you, sir." Hastily he came out from behind the desk to bow his visitor out of the room and down the stairs to the street.

He returned uneasily to his desk. The late Prince Prokov's will left his entire estate to his son, Alexander Prokov. And a considerable estate it was too. There was no explanation at all of why he had left Sophia Lacey the use of his property in Cavendish Square in the first place.

When Masters had known Lady Sophia, she'd been an elderly recluse with a sharp mind and an even sharper tongue. And a hint of a scandalous past. But such hints tended to accompany unmarried ladies of means. Except that her means had been more figment than fact. She had lived to all appearances very well in her youth and middle years, but frugally in her later years, and the paucity of her estate on her death explained why. There were no debts, though. No creditors banging on the doors. Unless you counted Prince Prokov as a creditor, come to call in his loan.

It was all very rum, Masters decided. But it was not his business to question or speculate, merely to do what he'd been employed to do.

Chapter Ten

LIVIA WAS NOT AT HOME when Alex first called in Cavendish Square the following day. Morecombe held the door open barely a crack until the visitor identified himself, then he opened it a shade wider and stood for a minute staring with rheumy eyes at the prince. Then he shook his head irritably as if to dispel cobwebs and informed the visitor, "If 'tis the ladies y'are after, they've gone out. Took the babby."

"Do you know where they went?" Alex inquired civilly.

"No," Morecombe stated flatly, and began to close the door.

Alex put his foot in the crack. "Do you happen to know when they'll be back?"

"Dunno that neither," Morecombe responded. Then he seemed to reconsider when the foot remained in the door. "They've the babby wi 'em so they'll not be out beyond teatime, I reckon."

"Thank you." Alex removed his foot and the door closed smartly. He shook his head, wondering just what he was going to do about the problem of Morecombe when he took possession of the house. Sophia's will stipulated that her three retainers had the right to remain in service in Cavendish Square until they decided to accept a small pension and retire. Livia had honored the request and he supposed he would do the same.

It would seem that Morecombe and the mysterious twins had known Sophia Lacey very well, had certainly looked after her in her declining years well enough for her to ensure their future after her death. Servants in general knew a lot more about their employers than those employers either realized or cared to admit, Alex reflected.

At some point, once he'd won the old man's confidence, if indeed such a miracle was possible, he would talk to Morecombe about Sophia. As always, Alex hungered for information about his mother, not the basic facts, not the hard reality that Alex's father had imparted, but something about the woman herself. Who she really was . . . how she thought . . . what was important to her . . . the emotional aspects of the mother he had never known. Whether the reclusive Morecombe would let him in on any of these secrets was another question, but he would have to try.

But for now Livia was his most pressing concern. After their conversation at the Bonhams', that soft *please* that he guessed had slipped unbidden from between those delectable lips, he had been hard-pressed not to yield to naked impulse and come banging on her door within the hour, but a cooler head had prevailed, as it had to, and the business with the lawyer had had to be settled. And there was, of course, the small matter of the ring. A man couldn't propose without a ring. He brushed the pocket of his coat, feeling the square shape of the ring box. With that, at least, he knew he was on solid ground. It was a most exquisite piece.

But now he was left in a wash of anticlimax. The lady was not in and he would have to try again. He walked back down to the street and set off in the direction of Wigmore Street. As he reached the corner of the square he saw the three women with the three children coming towards him, deep in animated conversation. They hadn't seen him and he was debating whether to step back out of sight around the corner and wait until Livia was alone to meet up with her when she looked up and it was too late.

She raised a hand in greeting and he walked quickly towards the little party. She met his smile with one of her own that he couldn't quite interpret. It seemed a little hesitant, a little questioning, and he felt a jolt of alarm. Had she changed her mind?

"Livia . . . Lady Farnham . . . Lady Bonham." He bowed, hat in hand, aware that Livia's friends were both regarding him with deceptively casual smiles of their own, as if they knew something that he did not. His alarm increased and he glanced at Livia, who met his eyes with a glimmer in her own that was so full of lustful mischief he nearly laughed aloud. She was teasing him. He was not accustomed to being teased and it surprised him that he was amused rather than annoyed. Or perhaps it was simply relief that he felt.

"Were you coming to call upon us, sir?" Aurelia inquired, grabbing at Franny, who had seen something of interest in the gutter and was diving forward for further investigation.

"I was just coming disconsolate from your door, ma'am," he responded, hiding his amusement as he bent to pick up the shiny object that had caught Franny's eye. "Is this what you were looking for, *ma petite*?"

Franny took the button and polished it against the sleeve of her pelisse. "It's a jewel."

"No it's not. You don't find jewels in the street," Stevie scoffed. "Let me see." He reached for it.

Franny opened her mouth on an incipient yell of protest and Cornelia said swiftly, "It's Franny's, Stevie, she found it."

"There's 'nother one," Susannah shouted, wriggling away from her mother to hurl herself on the treasure. "It's *my* treasure."

"Oh, Lord," Cornelia said, raising her eyes to heaven as Stevie lunged, grabbing at his small sister's clenched fist.

"Look over here, Stevie . . . there are two more in the gutter." Alex took the boy's hand and firmly directed him towards the new find.

"These are bigger," Stevie said with satisfaction, kneeling in the gutter to gather up the shiny paste shoe buckles. "They're better than buttons."

"No, they're not," Franny cried. "They're not, are they, Mama? Man . . . man, find some more big ones." She pointed imperiously at Alex.

"Franny, don't be rude," Aurelia chided. "I'm sorry, Prince Prokov."

He laughed. "Don't be. I have some experience with importunate children, and they don't trouble me in the least. I enjoy their spirit." He glanced around his feet. "I'm afraid we're out of luck, though." He shook his head and mused, "One can't help wondering what activity led to the wholesale loss of buttons and shoe buckles."

"Particularly in the august surroundings of Cavendish Square," Livia said with a chuckle. "Oh, wait a minute . . . here's another button." She swooped on it and held it up. "Now, if Stevie gives a buckle to Franny, and I give him this button, everyone has equal shares." Excluding Susannah, of course, but she seemed perfectly content with her one piece of treasure.

"It's only fair, Stevie," Cornelia said. "Don't you think Harry would say so?"

The invocation of his stepfather gave the child pause. He nibbled his lip, considering the issue. "He'd probably say I ought to give it to Franny because she's a girl and smaller than me," he said finally, handing over one of his buckles.

"Bravo," Livia applauded. "And here is the other button." She handed it to him. "You are a perfect gentleman, Lord Dagenham."

Stevie beamed.

"I'd better take these two home, before anything else crops up," Cornelia said. "Come now, Stevie, we have to go home. Susannah's tired." Her daughter, in confirmation, abruptly sat down on the pavement. Sighing, Cornelia bent and lifted her onto her hip.

"I thought you were coming for tea," Livia said, wondering at her own perversity. The last thing she wanted was the planned tea party. Not with Alex in front of her, his eyes caressing her, his smile warming her with the promise of what was to come. Her rational self told her he was a most attractive man, but it wasn't her rational self that was thrumming like a plucked harp string when his gaze fell upon her. It was her body, responding to lust, pure and simple.

Cornelia gave her a look of total disbelief. This was no place for either herself or Aurelia, not to mention squabbling children. "I hadn't realized the time," she stated. "Susannah is really tired and Linton will be cross as two sticks if I don't get them home before four o'clock. It'll take me hours to placate her."

"I want to go with Stevie," Franny stated. "We want to look at our jewels but we can't do it here in case we drop them."

Aurelia smoothly picked up her cue. "In that case, we'll go back with Aunt Nell and you can have tea in the nursery with Stevie and Susannah."

Livia said nothing and Alex merely bowed his farewells as the women and children turned and walked away in the opposite direction.

"Your friends are discreet," he observed, turning to look at her, the smile vanished, his gaze intent as if he would read her mind. "They are in your confidence, I assume."

"Yes," she agreed simply.

So they would know the decision she had come to. He inclined his head in acknowledgment and offered her his arm. "Then may I escort you home?"

"Thank you." Livia took his arm. A shiver went through her and she knew he felt it. He turned to look at her, his eyes narrowed, a glow in their depths that brought an involuntary smile, curving her mouth. He felt as she did, and that was as reassuring as it was exciting. Somehow, out of the blue, this thing had come upon them, and it made her toes curl and her skin ripple.

For once the front door opened promptly at her knock. Young Jemmy offered a salute with a tugged forelock. "Mr. Morecombe's with the pullets, m'lady."

"Pullets?" Livia gazed at him in astonishment. "What pullets?"

"Some our Mavis bought," the boy informed her. "They'll be good layers, she says, but they're so small we 'ave to keep 'em in a hat in the kitchen by the range, otherwise they'll get cold and die on us."

"Whose hat?" Livia heard herself ask, aware even as she did so of what a non sequitur it must've seemed to her suave companion. But somehow to her it seemed a perfectly natural question given the oddities of the domestic arrangements of this household.

"'Tis a fur one, mum," Jemmy said. "An old one of our Ada's. An' our Mavis says as 'ow you've got a muff that'll do if the 'at's not big enough."

"I do," Livia agreed. "Tell her to send Hester to fetch it if she needs it. Hester knows where it is." She glanced up at Alex and saw he was looking bewildered as well as amused. The frisson between them was fizzling now like a damp firework rather than an electric charge.

"You want me to bring summat, m'lady?" Jemmy asked as Livia moved towards the parlor.

Livia stopped. "What would you like, Alex? Tea, sherry, wine . . . ?"

"Nothing at the moment," Alex said firmly. He took Livia's hand, drawing her in front of him. "We have some urgent business ahead and I don't wish for any interruptions." He waved his free hand at Jemmy with a gesture of dismissal. "We'll ring if we need anything."

Livia nodded, relieved that he'd taken charge even if it was in her own house. She obeyed the slight pressure in the small of her back urging her forward and led the way into the parlor.

Alex looked around the cheerfully shabby room. "I haven't been in here."

"No, it's our private parlor, we don't show it to the public," Livia said with a tiny but expressive shrug.

"Then I'm honored." He drew off his gloves and laid

them with his hat and cane on a chair by the door.

Livia was playing with her own gloves and made no attempt to remove her own hat. Partly, she was aware, because it suited her, the creamy straw framing her face and setting off the cluster of dark curls escaping beneath. The dark green silk ribbons tied beneath her chin gave her a rather winsome air, or so Aurelia had said. Livia was not entirely sure that winsome was a quality that would appeal to Prince Prokov, but judging by the way he was looking at her, it didn't seem to trouble him at the moment.

Her knees were not behaving like themselves; they seemed to have lost all sinew and were showing a lamentable tendency to buckle. "Won't you sit down?" She indicated the sofa and dropped onto a stiff-backed tapestry side chair before her legs gave way.

"Not just yet," he said. He crossed the room and reached again for her hands, pulling her to her feet. He slid his hands up her arms to rest on her shoulders and looked steadily into her upturned face.

His eyes seemed to swallow her whole; she felt as if she was drowning in the intensity of his scrutiny. Her tongue touched her dry lips and she took a tremulous breath.

"Well?" he asked softly. "Give me my answer, Livia." He released her shoulders, moving his hands to the swell of her backside, drawing her hard up against him.

Livia drew another breath as her lower body seemed to soften and moisten, as if in counterpoint to the muscular hardness of his. Her skin felt flushed and feverish.

"Yes," she murmured, lifting a hand to touch his mouth, her fingertip tracing the full, sensual curve of his lips. A tiny smile touched her own mouth and she said firmly, "I will marry you, Alex."

He caught her wrist, turning her hand up to press a kiss into the palm. "You have made me the happiest man," he said simply. "I've been in an agony since we last met, telling myself that I hadn't misunderstood you, and yet I didn't dare count on it."

He gave her a rueful smile. "I am not usually prey to such racking uncertainties, but I couldn't imagine what I would do if you said no." He tipped her chin with his finger and kissed the corner of her mouth, then drew back, examining her with an expression that warmed Livia to her core. It was as if he were gazing upon a rare and precious treasure.

"What do you see?" she murmured, her eyes languorous as muscle and sinew seemed to melt beneath his gaze.

"You," he said, his voice low, his eyes heavy with passion. "Just you. And I am on fire to possess every inch of you, Livia. I have never wanted a woman as powerfully as I want you."

Livia shivered. She seemed to be losing touch with herself as her blood surged in response to his words.

With a muttered oath, Alex untied the ribbons of her hat and lifted it off her head. He tossed it roughly aside and took her face between his hands, holding her fast as he brought his mouth to hers, his tongue demanding entrance until she parted her lips and his tongue invaded the warm, moist cavern of her mouth.

She pressed her lower body against him, feeling the hard bulge of his penis rising against her belly as she kissed him greedily, fascinated at how his mouth was both soft and yet pliable, dry and yet moist. Their tongues fenced and danced and she gloried in the taste of his mouth, the velvety inner softness of his cheeks, the smoothness of his teeth. Her hands caressed his back, her fingers digging with sudden urgency into the muscles of his backside, as her body ran riot with sensations for which she had no name.

And when at last he moved his mouth from hers and she could draw breath again, her heart was racing, her skin on fire, her lips swollen and kiss-reddened. He still held her face between his palms and now he kissed her eyelids, a featherlike brush that tickled even as it delighted. Then he straightened and stepped back, his breathing ragged.

"Ah, Livia . . . Livia" was all he said as he looked at her.

Livia merely nodded helplessly. For the moment she had no words.

Alex reached into his pocket and drew out a small box. He opened it and worldlessly took her left hand. He slipped the ring onto her finger. "Do you like it, love? If you wish to change it in any way, you have just to say."

Livia looked at her hand and her mouth formed a

round O of surprise and delight. She lifted her hand to the fading light from the window and gazed awestruck at the sapphire and diamond ring. "It's quite beautiful, Alex . . . I've never seen anything so exquisite." She turned her hand this way and that so that the light caught the sparkling facets of the jewels. "Is it an heirloom?"

He shook his head. "The stones have been in the family vault for generations, but I designed the ring myself and had it made up for you."

That surprised her. No craftsman could produce such a beautiful setting in a mere two days. She stared at him. "*Before* I had agreed to marry you?"

He shrugged with a touch of self-deprecation. "What can I say . . . I'm an optimist."

Livia shook her head in astonishment. He was the most amazing man, and she was feeling far too happy and rather fuzzy around the edges to question such extraordinary assurance.

"I assume I must ask your father for permission to marry you," Alex said. "Your father is still alive? Or is there some other guardian?"

"My father is still alive," Livia said, raising her eyes reluctantly from her wondering examination of the ring. "But if he were not, there would be no one you would need to ask. I am of an age and an independence that allows me to make my own decisions."

"Of course," he said smoothly, hearing the hint of challenge in her voice. Livia Lacey had managed her own affairs for too long to yield to another hand on the wheel. "Then must I ask him?"

Livia nodded decisively. After the wild abandonment of the last minutes it was a welcome relief to deal with practical issues that grounded her in reality again. "Oh, yes. I love my father dearly and we must do this right."

"Then we will get down to the practicalities. But before we do, I think, if you have any in your cellars, we should drink some champagne . . ." He looked around. "Is there a bell?"

"There is, but there's little point ringing it," Livia said, pointing to a faded bell rope half hidden by the curtain at the window. "I'll go to the kitchen."

"Let's try. That youngster seemed quick on his feet." He tugged vigorously twice. "While we wait, tell me about the parent I must charm."

Miraculously, Morecombe opened the door within a few minutes. If she hadn't known better, she'd almost have suspected he was waiting outside.

"You want summat, mum?"

"Do we have any champagne, Morecombe?" Livia asked. "I have a sudden desire for a glass."

He seemed to consider this for a moment, his gaze moving slowly between herself and the prince, then he nodded. "Oh, aye, reckon we do. You want I should bring it?"

"Please," she said, avoiding looking at Alex, who wore a dumbfounded expression.

"Aye . . . an' 'ow many glasses shall it be?"

"Two, please," Livia said.

He nodded, cast another glance in Alex's direction, and shuffled out, closing the door behind him.

"I don't know how you have the patience," Alex observed. "I've never come across a servant like him."

"As I told you once . . . I'm honoring Sophia Lacey's memory," Livia responded. "Anyway, once you learn his ways, Morecombe is perfectly easy to manage. Now, let me tell you about my father, the Reverend Lacey, earl of Harford. There are some idiosyncrasies you should know about before you meet him."

Alex listened intently, and he decided that regardless of Livia's vaunted independence, he had better make damn sure he won the approval of her parent. She described the man and his idiosyncrasies with such tender amusement and occasional flashes of loving exasperation that he had felt a most unlooked-for prickle of envy as he thought of his relationship with his own father.

He left Cavendish Square an hour later, still thinking about that austere man who had governed his growing. He could see himself as a small boy anxiously reciting his lessons to his father, watching for a sign of approval. He had never expected warmth or more than a firm handshake from his parent but he had eagerly sought approval. Sometimes it was withheld for no reason that the child could understand, until he grew older and then understood what his father's reticence had been telling him. He must learn to stand up for himself. His own approval of himself was all that was necessary for him to fulfill the destiny he'd been born to.

It was not a bad lesson for life, he thought now. And his father had certainly been a living example of its precept. He had devoted his life to his country and to his motherless son. Alex knew that his father had left his mother and brought their child back to Russia for the child's benefit. He, the child, had not always acknowledged the benefit, he had to admit, but he had never questioned that his father's motives had been unselfish. He didn't know what kind of relationship his father had had with the mother of his child, the subject was taboo, but he knew that his father had made the only choice he had thought possible. And Alex now enjoyed the fruits of that choice.

And he had also inherited its burdens, he reflected. His father's patriotism had been all-powerful, and Alex had learned that lesson well. He too was governed by the same all-consuming imperative. An imperative that had led him here, to these London streets, and to the wonderful prospect of Livia Lacey in his bed.

His step quickened at the thought and his body stirred with arousal as he remembered the feel of her softness against him, remembered the passionate eagerness of her responses. He had come on this mission in search of a wife to facilitate his work, but he had not expected the search to end in such glorious promise. He and Livia would deal very well together.

The lights of a tavern beckoned down a side street and

Alex found his steps moving towards the yellow glow and the sound of laughter, raised voices, the banging of tankards on deal tables. He pushed through the door into the warm fug reeking of tobacco and stale beer.

A few eyes were turned towards him, but then the ale drinkers returned to the serious business of the evening. What interest had they in an effete aristocrat in his buckskin britches, silky coat, and high-starched cravat? He didn't look like a man to be easily robbed, therefore he was best left alone.

Alex strode to the ale counter and spun a copper coin. "Ale."

The landlord set a tankard under the tap and filled it. He set the tankard on the counter with a slap, palming the coin at the same time, and turned immediately to another customer.

Alex took the tankard to a secluded corner and sat on the stained bench. He drank deeply and welcomed his anonymity, the sense that for these few minutes he was in a different world, one that had no knowledge of the world he usually inhabited. No one here in this noisy, crowded taproom knew or gave a damn who he was or what governed him. It was unaccustomed luxury for a brief while to indulge only in the present, to revel in the thought of what he had just achieved without reference to the underlying reasons for it. At this moment, he thought only of the joy of Livia Lacey, of the promise of the wedding night to come, of the life that lay ahead for them, if the gods smiled.

He looked up abruptly at a breath of warmth beside him. A woman stood there, skirt slightly kilted, ripe bosom peeping over her bodice. "You look lonely, sir." She set two tankards of ale on the bench between them. "Drink with me."

Alex hid his annoyance at the interruption. The last thing he wanted at this juncture in his lustful and triumphant reflections was the company of a whore. He laid a silver sixpence on the bench as he stood up. "My thanks for the offer." He gave her a courtly bow and strode through the noisy throng to the door.

The woman picked up the coin and tucked it into her bosom. That was a gentleman for you. She'd have charged him less for half an hour upstairs and no holds barred.

∞

Livia stood alone in the parlor, gazing rapt at the ring on her finger. She had never possessed anything like it. Her father would disapprove of this starstruck worship of mammon, but he wasn't here to see it, so for the moment she would indulge herself. She held out her hand and examined the jewels in the glow of the newly lit lamps. They were magnificent, even someone as inexperienced as she could tell that just by the size and the glow. But she knew that it wasn't just the ring that filled her with this delight. It was the thought of what it meant—what it promised—that made her want to dance around the room.

She started as she heard Aurelia's voice in the hall.

And then Cornelia's. Livia jumped up as the parlor door opened.

Cornelia came in. "We left the children in Linton's hands," she said, her eyes narrowing as she examined Livia's flushed countenance.

"We thought a quiet evening alone might be in order?" There was a question in Aurelia's statement as she followed her sister-in-law into the room.

"Yes," Livia agreed, trying to compose herself. "We can finish the champagne."

Her friends exchanged looks. "So, it's champagne, is it, Nell?" Aurelia said with a wink. "Good news, do you think?"

"Either that or we're drowning our sorrows," Cornelia said. "But somehow I doubt that."

"We need two more glasses," Livia said, not troubling to enter this debate. "I'll fetch them."

"No, I'll do it." Aurelia was still in the hall. "I'll get them from the dining room cabinet."

Cornelia wasted no further time. "So?"

Livia extended her hand. "I can't wear it in public until it's official, but . . ."

Cornelia took her hand and examined the ring. "Our Russian prince knows his jewels," she observed. "I wonder if it's an heirloom."

Livia shook her head. "No, he had it specially made."

"Not in the last two days?" Cornelia exclaimed.

"No," Livia agreed. "Some time ago . . . he says he's an optimist." She shrugged and couldn't help what she was sure was a somewhat fatuous grin. She turned as Aurelia came in holding two champagne glasses upside down by the stems between her fingers.

"What do you think, Ellie?" Livia extended her hand.

Aurelia set down the glasses and examined the ring with an unladylike whistle. "Beautiful," she breathed. "Magnificent. So, love, I assume it's settled?"

Livia poured champagne. "Father has to approve."

"Of course." The other women nodded their comprehension. "Is your prince going down to Ringwood?"

"In a couple of days . . . but I'm going to go tomorrow. I need to talk to Father first. I couldn't possibly spring Alex upon him."

"No," Cornelia agreed with a choke of laughter. "No, Liv, you could not possibly spring Prince Alexander Prokov on the Reverend Lacey."

Chapter Eleven

THE REVEREND LACEY WAS IN his study, wrestling with Sunday's sermon, and didn't hear the bustle of arrival late the following evening. In general, as long as matters progressed with a degree of order and custom, he took little notice of his surroundings. And when his study door was opened without so much as an alerting knock he looked up from his paper with an air of startled annoyance.

Livia had pushed just her head around the door so as to minimize the disturbance. "Shall I go away again?" she asked with a smile.

"Good God, come in, Livia," her father demanded, pushing his spectacles up onto his broad white forehead. "Why didn't you tell me you were coming, child?"

"Well, I didn't know I was until I did," Livia said, coming fully into the familiar room, closing the door at her back.

"What's that supposed to mean?" her father demanded. "I'm always telling you to be precise in your speech. The English language is the richest in the world and you do it no honor by employing such ridiculous, nonsensical phrasing." But despite the irascibility of his tone, his faded gray eyes were filled with pleasure as he came around the desk and opened his arms to her.

He held her in a tight embrace for a moment or two, then stood back and put his hands on her shoulders. "Let me look at you." The youthful brightness of his eyes might have faded somewhat, but the sharpness of observation and intellect was far from blunted.

"Is something amiss, Livia?"

She shook her head. "No, quite the opposite. But I don't want to disturb you in the middle of working. I'll go and get some supper and come back in an hour. It's been a long day."

"You came from London in one day?"

"In a post chaise," she said. "We changed horses every hour so we were able to make good speed."

Her father frowned. "That must have cost a pretty penny."

Livia made no mention of the fact that it was not her own purse that had funded the expensive travel. Instead she responded calmly, "Probably no more than putting up for the night in a coaching inn, and I'd have had to bring a maid with me if I did that, so I think it was a cost-effective luxury on the whole."

He seemed to consider this, then he shook his head. "Well, maybe . . . maybe. Go and get some food inside you and come back in an hour to tell me what brings you home in such impetuous haste."

Livia left him and made her way to the kitchen, where Martha, the village woman who had stepped in as housekeeper when Livia went up to London, was stirring a pot of soup on the range.

"There's cabbage and potato soup, Lady Liv, and a morsel of chicken pie left from the reverend's dinner," she said. "Will that do? Or shall I boil you a couple of eggs?"

"No, soup and pie will be perfect, thank you, Martha." Livia pulled out a chair and sat at the long kitchen table. "How's he been?"

"Well enough." Martha ladled soup into an earthenware bowl and set it before Livia. "His joints bother him when there's damp in the air, and he will fuss if I light a fire in his study. Not until—"

"October twentieth," Livia chimed in with a chuckle. "I never understood what was so magical about that date. No fires after March thirtieth and none before October twentieth. Only six inches of snow on the ground could change his mind." She dipped her spoon in her soup. "But otherwise he's keeping well?"

"Oh, aye." Martha sliced a loaf of barley bread and passed Livia a piece on the end of the knife. "He's so busy with his books and papers, he barely gets to bed of a night, but he's well enough in himself." She went into the pantry to fetch the pie, talking as she did so. "He misses you, though, Lady Liv. Not that he'd ever say as much."

She backed out of the pantry with a pie dish that she

set on the table. "Will I pop this in the bread oven for a minute or two? Just to warm it through."

Livia nodded, her mouth full of bread and soup. It seemed strange to be sitting here in her father's kitchen eating this good homely food, chatting with Martha just like her life before Cavendish Square. Before her head was turned by duchesses and rout balls, card parties and the opera.

Had these last months changed her in any fundamental way? She glanced across at Martha, who was sliding the pie into the brick chamber in the hearth where the bread was baked. Martha wasn't behaving as if Livia were any different from the young woman who had cheerfully helped her peel oranges for marmalade and stew damsons for jam.

What on earth would Martha say to Princess Prokov?

"So what brings you home so sudden like, Lady Liv?" Martha sat down at the table, wiping her hands on the apron. "Nothing bad, I trust."

"No, nothing bad." Livia wiped out her soup bowl with the last of her bread. "Is there a bottle of that elderflower wine around, Martha? I quite fancy a drop."

Martha chuckled and looked at her shrewdly. "You always did like that. I think we've one bottle of the last batch left." She got up rather heavily and went back to the pantry. "Aye, here it is." She brought out a dusty bottle and wiped it on her apron.

"You'll join me in a glass," Livia said, getting up to put her soup bowl in the sink.

"If you like," the other woman said placidly. She put the bottle on the table. "You open it and I'll dish up your pie." She busied herself at the bread oven, asking casually, "So is it a celebration, then?"

"Well, I hope so," Livia answered, pouring wine into two thick squat tumblers. "I hope to be getting married, Martha."

"Why, mercy me." Martha turned from the oven, the pie in her hand, her face wreathed in smiles. "Well, that's the best news I've heard in many a month, m'dear. And who's the lucky man?" She put the pie down in front of Livia and picked up her tumbler.

"Alexander Prokov," Livia told her, digging a fork into the steaming fragrant dish in front of her.

"Sounds foreign," Martha observed, sitting down again. "But I daresay there's lots of 'em around in London town."

"There do seem to be," Livia said casually. "He'll be arriving the day after tomorrow, to talk to Father. I think we can put him up in the blue room, if we air it out tomorrow."

"So he'll be staying, then?"

"He will, if my father agrees," Livia said. "If we're betrothed, there's no reason why he shouldn't stay under my father's roof."

"No," Martha said. "Well, here's to you, m'dear. Long life and happiness." She raised her glass in a toast. "And I'm sure you'll be able to talk the reverend around to the idea of a foreigner."

Livia's eyebrow flickered. Martha didn't sound completely convinced. But her father was a sophisticated, highly educated man of the world. He wasn't going to hold an unreasoning prejudice against a foreign suitor for his daughter's hand.

She was hard-pressed to hide her anxiety, however, when she returned to his study. He was standing in front of the empty grate, hands sunk deep into the pockets of his britches that Livia couldn't help but notice were somewhat shiny and threadbare. Of course he had as little interest in clothes as he did in the delicacies of the table. Her heart lurched a little at the contrast between her father and the immaculate Prince Prokov.

"So, what have you to tell me, my dear?" His gaze was sharp beneath his bushy eyebrows. "Or shall I guess?"

"Could you?" She perched on the arm of a chair.

"I can think of only a few reasons why you would come home without warning," he said. "Either some disgrace has befallen you, or the financial independence Sophia Lacey left you has somehow disappeared, or you have decided to get married and thought to do me the courtesy of informing me of it before the rest of the world."

"You would never be the last to know such a thing," she said quietly, hurt that he should even have imagined she could be so neglectful. "You're right that I wish to be married, and that I'm here to tell you about it before Alex comes to you himself."

"Alex?" he murmured. "Alex . . . ?"

"Alexander, Prince Prokov," she said, watching his expression.

It didn't change. "A Russian . . . interesting, particularly with the present state of the world's affairs. So, tell me all about him, Livia." He turned to a side table on which reposed a decanter. "I think this calls for something in the nature of a toast. Will you join me in a glass of cognac, my dear?"

Livia was unsure of the wisdom of cognac on top of elderflower wine, but she decided a little Dutch courage would not come amiss. "Thank you." She took the cut-glass goblet he handed her and began her story.

When she had finished, the vicar merely nodded and sipped his cognac in silence for what seemed to her an interminable length of time. At last she said, "Do I have your blessing, Father?"

He looked at her over his glass. "It has long been my dearest wish that you would find the right man . . . one you can love and respect in equal measure, and who will return those feelings."

He took a sip from his glass and looked at her closely. "However, while you have told me who this man is, or at least what you know of him, which, my dear, strikes me as lamentably little, you have not told me that you love him, that your life will not be complete without him."

Livia gazed down into the contents of her goblet. "I am not very experienced in these things, Father. But I do know that I am ready for marriage and I want this to happen, that what I feel for this man is unlike any feeling I've had before, and that he shares those feelings. I think there is a difference between being *in* love and loving someone. I am *in* love with Alex. I don't know how else to describe it. And I hope and trust that that will grow into just plain love in the fullness of time."

Her father nodded slowly. "A good answer, my dear. You are certainly old enough to know your own mind in these matters. But I would not be a responsible parent if I didn't point out that you both seem to have come to this momentous decision in a very short time." He raised his eyebrows interrogatively.

"I suppose it does look like that," Livia said. "But in truth, Father, I feel as if I've known him for much, much longer. I agreed to let Harry look into his background because I knew you'd have reservations . . . but, there's nothing there. I've met a couple of his compatriots . . . they seem perfectly respectable . . . and he moves in the best circles. I don't know much about his English mother . . . I rather got the impression that she died when he was born . . ." She paused, wondering how she'd formed that impression. She couldn't remember whether Alex had actually told her that.

"But anyway," she continued, dismissing a somewhat irrelevant issue, "Alex has been presented at the queen's drawing room, so he must have an impeccable social background. And besides, he was educated at the czarina's court, a companion to her grandson." She extended her hands, palm up in a gesture of helplessness. "I don't know what else one needs to know."

"His character, perhaps?" her father said mildly.

"Do you not trust my judgment?"

The Reverend Lacey had always encouraged his daughter to challenge him if she felt he was wrong, and now he smiled a little. "I trust your judgment, Livia. But passion can sometimes obscure clarity. By your own admission, you're *in* love with this man. Can you be certain you know *who* it is that you're in love with?"

"Certain enough to satisfy me," she stated.

"And he's not intending to spirit you away to Russia the minute the knot is tied?"

"He says not, and I believe him."

He said nothing for a long moment, his faded gray eyes fixed upon her in quiet contemplation, then he shook his head briskly. "Well, at least I needn't worry about how you'll get your bread . . . these Russian aristocrats have unimaginable wealth, all amassed on the backs of slaves . . . or serfs as they call them."

His mouth twisted with disdain. "The feudal system is an abomination, Livia, and I can't like the idea that you'll be its beneficiary, however much your happiness might depend on this marriage."

Livia's heart sank. Surely he wouldn't refuse her his blessing simply because of a principled objection to a society that had been in existence for centuries. "Alex couldn't change the system," she said, hearing how lame it sounded.

"He could free his serfs, and pay them a living wage to work his lands," the Reverend Lacey declared. Then he sighed. "But you're right. I can't lay the blame for generations of abuse at the door of one young man. And, who knows, maybe he'll come to see things my way. So be it, my dear. Send Prince Prokov to me, and I will do whatever it is a father does in these circumstances. Have you a wedding date in mind? I must enter it into the church calendar."

"The Saturday before Christmas," Livia said, tears starting behind her eyes as relief swept through her, so powerfully that she realized only then how anxious she had been about this interview. Whether her father liked Alex or not on meeting him, he would not now withhold from her his blessing or his approval.

"The Saturday before Christmas, then. So be it." He came over to her and tipped her chin, kissing her lightly on the cheek. "You will be a most beautiful bride, my dear. Remind me to give you your mother's jewels. There are some rather fine pearls, as I recall. They will look very well with your hair and your complexion."

❧

Two days later, Alex was making his way to the mews to collect his horse for the journey into Hampshire when he realized that he was being followed again. He couldn't see anyone immediately suspicious on the pavement either behind or on the opposite side of the street, but every nerve in his body had sprung to full alert. He'd had too much experience in the army not to trust this gut instinct for danger.

He slowed his step, paused to brush a speck from his sleeve, glanced around. A man opposite had stopped and was looking up at the façade of a double-fronted mansion with every appearance of fascination. He wouldn't be alone, Alex knew. He started to walk again, and this time picked up the sound of even footsteps some way behind him. The man opposite had begun to walk again, swinging his cane idly. These watchers had been around for over a week now. They seemed to pick him up the minute he left his house.

So whose were they? Agents of the English secret service? Had he fallen under suspicion just because of the political rift between Russia and England? He would swear he had not made a false move since his arrival. None of them had. Nicolai played the disarming roué to perfection, easy enough for him since it was all too close to his natural character anyway. Fedorovsky carried his role as somewhat distracted scholar to perfection for the same reasons. And the same applied to the rest of their small band of revolutionaries. Only Tatarinov was different, but he didn't mix in the same circles, and as far as Alex was aware, he kept very much to himself.

Alex quickened his step and turned into the mews, but instead of collecting his horse, he took a small gate that led into a narrow side street lined with silversmiths. It would take them a while to realize that he wasn't going to emerge from the mews on horseback.

He glanced casually behind him and saw that for the moment the street was empty. He stepped swiftly through a doorway into the dark interior of the shop.

The silversmith bustled out from a back room, smiling expectantly. "What can I do for you, my lord?"

"I was looking for a sugar caster," Alex said, stepping sideways so that he could look through the door to the street without being seen.

The silversmith was moving around behind him, arranging a selection of the required object on the long deal counter at the rear of the shop. Alex saw the man who had been on the opposite side of the previous street enter the empty side street through the gate. Alex gave him full marks for quick thinking. It confirmed his gut suspicion that he was being followed, but by the same token it meant that his follower knew that his quarry was aware of the surveillance. But the game was growing tedious anyway, Alex reflected. The man started to walk quickly, stopping at each shop door to peer inside.

Alex moved to the counter. He picked up a plain silver sugar caster and said, "I'll take this one, but hold it for me. I'll leave this on account." He opened a billfold and took out twenty guineas. "Is there a back way out of here?"

"Aye, m'lord." The silversmith looked rather dazed at the speed of this transaction. He pointed to the door at the rear. "When will you be back for the caster, sir?"

"In a week or so," Alex threw over his shoulder as he moved swiftly to the door. "Keep this transaction to yourself, man, and I'll add twenty guineas on top of the full purchase price." He stepped through the door into the silversmith's workshop and out through another door into a small yard with a noisome outhouse and a chicken coop. Another gate led into another, narrower lane.

Alex stepped into the lane and took a minute to get his bearings. London was riddled with these passageways and alleys. They all connected in sometimes mysterious fashion, but it was very easy to get lost in them. This lane he guessed doubled back to the street of the silversmiths. He walked towards the point where the lane opened out and saw that he'd been right. He peered around and saw no one. Had they given up?

He waited patiently, and then a man appeared at the head of the street. A very familiar figure. *Tatarinov.* Just what was *he* doing here? Following the followers? And if so, why?

Alex stepped out into the street of the silversmiths and began to stroll towards Tatarinov. The Russian saw him and for an instant seemed to hesitate. Then he raised a hand in greeting and continued towards the prince.

"Good morning, Prince Prokov. Buying silver, are you?" he inquired, his hard, sharp eyes scrutinizing Alex.

"As it happens," Alex said. "A gift."

Tatarinov nodded. "Well, I must be on my way. Don't let me keep you."

"No," Alex said coolly. "By the way, Tatarinov, have you noticed any unusual company on the street in the last half hour?"

His companion's eyes narrowed. "What kind of unusual company?"

Alex shrugged. "It behooves one to be a little watchful these days, and I have the sense that a couple of people are taking an unwarranted interest in my movements."

"The English or our own people?" Tatarinov asked.

"I wish I knew," Alex replied. "Well, I have business out of town for a few days, so I'll bid you farewell."

"Godspeed, Prince." Tatarinov bowed and watched Alex until he'd turned out of the street towards the mews.

Alex's horse was saddled and ready for him in the mews. His groom held the reins of the Cossack black and his own mount, with Alex's portmanteau fastened to the back of his saddle. The black pranced on the cobbles as Alex approached.

"He's impatient, Your Highness," the groom said in oblique reproach.

"Yes, I'm sorry to have kept you waiting." Alex swung into the saddle. "Let us ride."

They arrived in the village of Ringwood late afternoon the following day. Alex inquired at the inn, a modest establishment on the village green, for directions to the vicarage. He left his tired horse at the inn in the charge of his equally weary groom and strolled through the village to the vicarage.

It was a square, stone, slate-roofed house next to the church, set in a small but well-tended garden, a pair of iron gates standing open between stone gate posts. He stood in the gateway, looking up at the house. Livia had clearly not been exaggerating when she'd told him of her aristocratic father's loathing of ostentation. This modest property was most unlike the usual residence of an earl.

An upstairs casement flew open and Livia's curly head appeared. She raised a hand in greeting and then vanished.

Alex walked up the path to the front door, which opened as he reached it. Livia stood smiling.

"You made good time," she observed, offering her hand, wondering why she felt suddenly shy and hesitant. She realized that it was one thing to meet him, to respond to him in the drawing rooms of London, where she was independent, a grown woman who controlled her own destiny and could give rein to the turmoil of sensation aroused just by being in the same room with him. Quite another here, in her childhood home, with her father in his study not twenty feet away.

Alex found her momentary awkwardness endearing, and he could make a fairly accurate guess at its cause. He took her hand between both of his and brought it to his lips, murmuring huskily, "It's been four days . . . and every minute a torment."

The tactic worked. Livia went into a peal of laughter, her strange moment of shyness banished. "You're still doing it, Alex. Such flowery extravagance will never persuade me of your ardor."

"Then perhaps this will." He was laughing even as he

pulled her hard into his embrace. He pushed up her chin and the laughter died in his bright blue gaze. The sensual glow that never failed to arouse her took its place, and he murmured almost to himself, "God, how I've missed you." He kissed her hard and she leaned into him, no longer aware of her surroundings, conscious only of the scent of his skin, his hair, the taste of his mouth, the hard length of him against her own softness.

Finally he moved his mouth from hers, lingering for a moment on the tip of her nose before he straightened, smiling down at her flushed countenance, her languorous eyes. "Oh, dear," he said. "We had best be a little careful. I would not like to fall foul of your father."

"No," she agreed, straightening her crumpled bodice, reaching up to tuck a loose curl into its pins. "After all my hard work, that would never do."

"Hard work?"

"He doesn't approve of the feudal system," she explained with an apologetic shrug. "But I don't think he'll bring it up until he knows you better."

"Actually, I would quite enjoy discussing it," he said. "Believe it or not, my dear girl, I'm not blind to its faults . . . but other than that subject, will this be an uncomfortable interview?"

"No," Livia said. "He's looking forward to meeting you." She took his hand. "I just feel a little strange myself. It's hard to explain . . . but I'm not the same person here that I am in London. You'll understand if I don't seem to—"

"I will understand." He laid a finger over her mouth, stopping her hesitant words. "My love, I already understand. It's almost impossible to go back to one's childhood home without somehow reverting to certain assumptions and aspects of that time."

"Oh, yes, that's it exactly," Livia said, relieved at the speed of his comprehension. "Russians aren't that different from us, it would seem."

He laughed again. "No, I think certain kinds of human experience are translatable across cultures. Particularly those of childhood . . . so shall we beard the lion in his den?"

"Yes," she agreed, filled with an immeasurable sense of relief and anticipation. She stepped back into the hall. "Come in."

He followed her, casting his eye over the simplicity of the square hall, the austere oak staircase, the leaded casements. The sconces were pewter, an oak bench stood by the door, a plain pier table with a pewter plate was against the wall, the wooden floorboards were uncarpeted. Apart from a copper jug of silvery honesty on a windowsill, there was not a flourish or furbelow in sight.

"It's a vicarage," Livia reminded him with a smile, having little difficulty reading his mind as his gaze roamed. "My father collects souls, not luxuries."

"Of course," he agreed smoothly. He looked at Livia, a quizzical gleam in his eye. "I'm just wondering if this apple has fallen far from the tree."

Livia looked puzzled, then her expression cleared.

"Oh, my dress, you mean. I don't embrace my father's frugality. But while I'm under his roof, I do nothing to offend it."

She brushed at the drab fawn gown. "I was helping Martha prepare dinner." She reached behind her to untie her apron. "The dress is an old one that's been lurking in my wardrobe."

"Ah." He nodded gravely. "Perhaps it's time to give it to some worthy cause."

Livia chuckled. "You may be right. It probably came from a worthy cause in the first place."

Alex reached out to reposition a hairpin that was coming loose from the knot on top of her head. "Will your father impose his frugality on the wedding?"

"Good heavens no," Livia said cheerfully. "Even the Reverend Lacey acknowledges that there's a time and place for everything. He won't stint on the wedding and then he'll donate the equivalent to whatever cause he deems fit. Now, give me your hat and gloves and I'll take you to meet him."

Alex followed as she led the way to the vicar's study at the rear of the house. He was both curious to meet the man who had shaped Livia and fearfully anxious, afraid that he wouldn't meet with approval. The feeling took him right back to his childhood and he had to struggle to regain his balance as Livia knocked, then opened the door. "Alex is here, Father."

"Then bring him in." Reverend Lacey rose from his desk and came out from behind it, hand outstretched in welcome. His gaze was as shrewd as his handshake was firm when he greeted his future son-in-law.

"I'll leave you two alone, then," Livia said once introductions had been made.

"I hardly think that's necessary," her father said. "Repetition is a waste of time, and since this business concerns you most nearly, I can't think why you shouldn't be a part of the conversation from the beginning." He gestured to the prince. "You have no objections to my daughter's presence, I trust."

Alex shook his head hastily. He couldn't imagine objecting to any decision of the Reverend Lacey's. However unusual it might be for Livia to be present at the conventional interview between her suitor and her father, it wasn't for him to point it out.

"No, indeed not, sir, not a one."

"Then take a seat, and let us begin." The vicar returned to his own chair behind the desk. "Livia tells me she would like to be married the weekend before Christmas. That seems to suit my calendar. I trust it suits yours?" He looked over at Alex, who, after a moment's debate, had chosen an armless, tapestry-covered chair over the more comfortable leather sofa, into a corner of which Livia was now ensconced.

"I am at your service, sir," Alex said. "And entirely at Livia's disposal, in this and all matters."

The vicar regarded him a shade sardonically. "Not entirely the best recipe for a successful marriage, if you don't mind my saying so. It won't do for either party to ride roughshod over the other." He took off his spectacles and wiped them on his handkerchief.

"That wasn't quite what I was implying, sir," Alex said. "I merely wished to convey a spirit of consensual decision making."

The vicar chuckled. "Ah, yes, consensual decision making. Nicely put. So, that's agreed then. The wedding will take place the Saturday before Christmas in my church. The details I will leave in Livia's capable hands, and I suggest you do the same. Now . . ."

He replaced his spectacles and leaned over the desk, hands clasped in front of him. "To the serious questions."

"Ah, yes." Alex stood up, reaching into his waistcoat. "Settlements. I have drawn up these contracts, sir." He laid a sheaf of papers on the desk. "As you will see, I have made provision for a quarterly allowance for Livia that I trust you will consider generous, and provision for any children. You will see on the last page a statement of my own fortune, which I trust you will find satisfactory." He returned to his seat and sat quietly, legs crossed at the ankles, watching his future father-in-law peruse the documents.

Livia remained curled in the corner of the sofa, intensely interested in the contents of the documents but curbing her curiosity until her father had finished. She could see from his noncommittal expression that he was prepared to say nothing about his principled objections to the source of the wealth that would benefit his daughter, and she knew the effort it cost him. But she also knew that nothing would get past that fierce intelligence. If there was anything remotely unclear or doubtful in the legal statements, he would pick it up.

Finally, he looked up, tidying the documents in front of him. "This all seems perfectly satisfactory," he said. "However, one thing interests me. You specify that the marital home should be Livia's house in Cavendish Square. Isn't that somewhat unusual for a man in your position, Prince Prokov? To move into his wife's property?"

Nothing in Alex's expression gave an inkling of his thoughts. "It seemed a practical step, sir. I rent lodgings in London at present, and I had been intending to buy a property when one suitable came on the market. However, as you must be aware, such opportunities are few and far between, and the house in Cavendish Square is a very fine property."

He paused, then said, "I am not asking for a dowry, Lord Harford, and I will settle on Livia sufficient funds to keep her in comfort in the event of my death. The house in Cavendish Square will kill two birds with one stone. It will serve as a dowry that would of course revert to Livia on my death, and for the present will save me the time and expense of buying a suitable house."

Lord Harford nodded slowly. "I applaud your reasoning. Why buy another property when there's a perfectly suitable one to hand." He looked across at his daughter. "What think you, Livia? Are you willing to offer your house as your contribution to the marriage settlements?"

"I would be very happy to continue living in Cavendish Square," Livia said. "I can't see why in all reason I should have the slightest objection." And she didn't think she had. But a niggle of unease disturbed her. The house was hers. Oh, she was willing to share it with her friends, but she had developed an extraordinarily strong bond with it. Whether it was because of the spirit of Sophia Lacey, who seemed to inhabit every nook and cranny, or just the fact that the house had rescued her from a drab future, she didn't know. But she wasn't sure how she felt about joint ownership. In fact, it wouldn't even be joint ownership. She would be bringing it into the marriage, and like all marital property it would legally belong to her husband unless he predeceased her.

But that was a selfish and nonsensical reaction. If her father considered that Alex was being more than generous with his settlements, surely she could share the one thing she had with a good grace? And be glad she had something to contribute to this marriage.

"Of course, any refurbishments that you wish to do, Livia, will be entirely your business," Alex said, watching her face, puzzled by the reluctance he could read there. *What did the house mean to her?* "I won't interfere in any way."

Livia thought of what needed to be done to the old house. She had barely touched the surface of neglect in the months since she'd inherited it. Sophia's legacy of five thousand guineas hadn't gone very far, but with money and imagination the house *could* be magnificent again. She could imagine the pleasure she would have restoring it to its former glory. It was a mouthwatering prospect.

"It does need some work," she said. "But I don't believe it could be ready by Christmas."

"Oh, you'd be surprised," Alex said, suddenly brisk. "I'll bring an architect to talk with you, and when decisions have been made we'll leave the business in his hands while you prepare for the wedding."

"One further point, Prince Prokov?" The vicar was frowning. "I'm an old man, and I'd be sorry to lose my daughter. I understand that you are intent on remaining in England for the duration of the war, at least."

"Yes, sir, that is so. While Europe is at war, I can safely promise that I intend to remain in London for the foreseeable future. When peace comes, who knows?" He shrugged expressively. "But I will make no decision without consulting Livia."

The vicar's frown deepened and his eyes were shadowed. "Damnable war . . . there's no peace in sight. Indeed it's hard to envisage the circumstances that would allow for it. Fools, greedy, godless fools, the lot of them."

It was an extraordinarily vehement speech from the normally mild-mannered man of God, and Livia sat up in surprise. "It can't go on forever," she protested softly.

Alex looked at her, and his own expression was now bleak, no sign of the easygoing, untroubled dilettante she was used to. "Your father's right, Livia. There's no end in sight."

Not unless he and his associates could hasten it along. But the step they would have to take filled them all with misgivings even as they knew they would be following in the ancient traditions of their land and society.

How many despots and idiots had been assassinated in the long history of the bloody murk that was Mother Russia?

Too many to count. And if necessary there would be one more.

Livia, watching his face, shivered as if she was in a draught and looked over her shoulder, expecting to see an open window. But no breeze stirred the curtains at the firmly closed casement.

Chapter Twelve

THE AUDIENCE CHAMBER IN THE Hermitage Palace in St. Petersburg was chilly, and it wasn't just the temperature. The atmosphere, as always at the czar's rare receptions, was as cold as the waters of the River Neva that flowed beneath the palace windows. The line of diplomats stood rigidly at attention, staring straight ahead across to the line of Grand Dukes and Duchesses facing them. The silence was heavy as the czar in his emblazoned imperial uniform, his sumptuously clad mother on his arm, his more somberly dressed wife walking alone a few paces behind, progressed slowly between the lines, offering only a silent nod until they reached the French ambassador, General de Caulaincourt.

Czar Alexander stopped in front of the general. The Empress Mother and her daughter-in-law halted. Alexander smiled a thin smile. "Good evening, Ambassador. I trust you are well."

"Yes, indeed, thank you, sir." The general bowed

stiffly. "And honored to be here. I trust your majesties will grace my reception at the embassy next week."

"If time permits us to indulge in such frivolity, Ambassador, we shall be pleased to attend." The thin smile flickered again and the emperor and his ladies passed on down the line. At the end of the line they passed through double doors flung open by liveried footmen, and within the audience chamber there was a collective shuffle of relief.

"Thank God that's over," muttered a senior French diplomat to his ambassador. "Give me a reception at the Empress Mother's palace any day. Now, there's a lady who knows there's more due to the monarchy than dreary exercises in protocol."

Caulaincourt looked sour. "The empress lives in grand style, certainly . . . but she can afford to do so," he added grimly, his voice barely above a whisper. "Soon I'll be forced to sell my shirt. These damn Russians are so haughty, they're all smiles and sugary compliments as they grab anything you offer, and then turn around and spit in your face."

His companion nodded in sympathy. It was well known that the ambassador, in his attempts to win over hostile Russian society, was close to bankrupting himself with the lavishness of his hospitality. "They certainly don't care for us," he said in the same low voice. One could never be sure who was listening in the halls and antechambers of the palaces of St. Petersburg.

The ambassador frowned and murmured, "I tell you, Alain, I grow tired of wasting time and money on such ingratitude. They'll never be reconciled to us, to Bonaparte . . . and quite frankly I fear for the czar. This is not a ruling class that tolerates despotic sovereigns who don't please them." He drew a finger across his throat in an expressive gesture. "I don't know whether Alexander understands the precipice he's on. I doubt he even listens to the whispers."

༺∞༻

Alexander, at this moment, was wearily but courteously listening to his mother. "I trust you will not be attending Caulaincourt's reception," she declared. "The man's as much a parvenu as the emperor he serves."

"His lineage is impeccable, madam," her son pointed out mildly.

"Which is more than you can say for the Corsican," the lady stated, accepting the correction with a vaguely dismissive gesture. "You are in danger of becoming a lackey of Napoleon's, Alexander. And I don't know whether you realize it."

Alexander sighed. "Of course I respect your opinion, madam. But in this I must follow my own way. Alliance with the French will bring our country honor and glory."

"Oh, the Corsican has bewitched you," the Dowager Empress stated disgustedly. "Do you not hear what everyone's saying? They're saying that Napoleon runs the affairs of Russia as if it was a French province and you, its emperor, are in reality no more than a provincial prefect."

"They may say what they please," Alexander said, still patiently. "But I am czar of all the Russias, madam, and I will rule as I see fit."

The Empress Mother took an angry turn around the room, her richly embroidered taffeta skirts swishing around her ankles with the impatience of her stride. "And what of the plots against you?" She spun back to face him. "Can you ignore those, Alexander? Think of your father . . . would you have the same fate befall you?"

Her son shook his head with a faint smile. "I know that people are plotting. I know about the intrigues, both here and overseas, England in particular, and I am not afraid of them. I have my own plots, my own intrigues, madam, which I believe are more than a match for my enemies."

His mother looked at him, her eyes suddenly narrowed. "Prokov is in London," she said. "Are you relying on him to nip sedition over there in the bud?"

"Can you think of anyone better qualified, madam? A better friend? A cleverer, wiser friend?"

The empress frowned in thought. "No," she conceded after a minute. "If there is an assassination plot originating in London, Alex will discover it."

"Exactly," the czar said with a decisive nod. "And Arakcheyev's secret police will deal discreetly with the plotters." His smile widened and he said, "Have faith, Madam Mother. There'll be no palace revolution either. I have ears to the ground everywhere. I know what's said, and I know what's planned. But rest assured, at present there are only grumbles . . . no assassination plots in the wind."

The Dowager Empress said only, "I hope you're right, my son."

❦

"Stand still, Lady Livia." The dressmaker fussed through her mouthful of pins. "I'm sure I had the waist measurement perfect last week, but now it seems too loose."

"I'm too excited to eat," Livia offered apologetically, casting a pleading glance towards Aurelia and Cornelia, who were critically watching the proceedings in Livia's borrowed bedchamber in Mount Street. Livia and Aurelia had moved out of Cavendish Square, which was crawling with painters, builders, and the like, and taken up residence with the Bonhams until the wedding. "You'd think I'd be too old to be excited, wouldn't you?"

Aurelia shook her head with a smile. "You're getting married, love."

"And more to the point, you're lusting after the groom," Cornelia put in with a ribald chuckle. "It's enough to make anyone excited."

"Now, now, ladies," the seamstress protested, but only mildly. Miss Claire had been dressing the three women since they'd first arrived in London and was used to their free and easy manners.

"It may be indecorous, Claire, but it's God's own

truth," Cornelia said with another chuckle. "In two weeks, our virgin friend will be initiated into the joys of the marital bed."

"Oh, do be quiet, Nell." It was Livia who protested this time, her cheeks a little pink. "Now, tell me what you think of the gown?" She put her hands on her waist and examined her reflection in the long glass.

"It's beautiful," Cornelia said, serious again. "That old ivory really looks enchanting on you. It complements your hair and eyes beautifully."

"I love the embroidery," Livia said, smoothing the skirts with a loving hand. "It's so incredibly delicate."

"Exquisite," Aurelia agreed. "And the fine wool and silk blend should keep you from freezing to death in the church."

"Yes, a practical but necessary consideration, Lady Livia," the seamstress said, tucking and pinning the full puff sleeves that finished just above the elbow. "The long gloves should keep your arms and hands warm enough, although, of course, you'll have to take the left one off for the ring." She turned aside to pick up the embroidered veil that hung over a chair. "Let us see the full effect now." She lifted it high and dropped it lightly over Livia's head, arranging the folds down her back.

"Lovely," she pronounced. "Don't you think so, ladies?"

Livia turned to her friends, a question in her gray eyes. They both smiled at her, and Aurelia blinked away an inconvenient tear. Her own wedding day came back to her in a flood of memory . . . her nervousness, the uncertainty she felt about the step she was taking, her sudden panic that she didn't really know the man she was marrying, even though he was her best friend's brother and they had grown up in the same village. How different it had been for her. Livia was in love. With the best will in the world, Aurelia could not say she had been in love on her wedding day.

Oh, she'd grown to love her husband. They'd become easy together, good friends, quiet lovers. But there was no grand passion. No sweeping desire. No sense that the world was tumbling about her ears, the way Livia described her feelings. Livia was radiant, and the radiance increased with every moment she spent with her fiancé.

Livia said suddenly, "Oh, is that the time? I have to go. I arranged to meet the decorator at the house." She lifted the veil from her head. "There's so much to do and I have to be in Ringwood by Friday at the latest. I'll need at least a week to finalize preparations." She handed the veil to Cornelia and turned her back for Claire to unfasten the dress. "I'll see you both at dinner this evening."

"I just hope Harry finishes whatever's been occupying him upstairs," Cornelia said with a rueful grimace. "He's closeted in his attic office. Something was delivered from the ministry this morning and he disappeared upstairs with it. There's no knowing when he'll reappear. Hosting a dinner party comes rather low on my husband's priorities in these situations."

Her friends nodded their comprehension. Viscount

Bonham's cryptology work for the War Ministry frequently took him out of social circulation for days at a time. Since he didn't like his work to be generally known, Cornelia was growing adept at finding excuses for his absences when they conflicted with social engagements.

"Will you be able to explain things to Alex, Liv? If Harry doesn't appear," she asked rather tentatively, unsure how Livia would take the need to keep the truth from her fiancé.

"Of course," Livia said cheerfully. "Harry's business is not mine to reveal. We can simply use his usual excuse. A family emergency with one of his many sisters or their offspring has taken him out of town."

Her friends laughed with her, remembering how Harry had so often explained his sudden disappearances in such fashion. He was quite shameless about roping in his large extended family to bolster his excuses.

"That's settled, then. Dinner at eight." Cornelia headed for the door.

Livia dressed again quickly and hurried downstairs. Harry's butler was in the hall as she crossed to the front door. "Will you be taking the dogs, Lady Livia?" he inquired.

Livia stopped and sighed. "I wasn't going to, Hector. Are they being a nuisance again?"

"They seem to have something against the butcher, ma'am, and since the butcher is very important to Lord Bonham's chef, particularly when he's preparing for a large party, it tends to cause an upset in the kitchen when he brings the choice cuts for Monsieur Armand's approval and the dogs attack him. No one can hear themselves think for the noise, ma'am," he added apologetically. "And if Monsieur Armand becomes upset, then dinner tends to suffer."

"And of course the butcher is coming this afternoon," Livia said with another sigh. "I'll take them with me, Hector. I'm walking to Cavendish Square anyway."

Hector looked relieved. "I'll fetch them myself, Lady Livia."

He returned in a very few minutes with the two pink Lakeland terriers prancing and skittering on the marble floor. Livia looked at them with disfavor. "I do not understand how two such ridiculous bits of fluff could cause so much havoc," she scolded.

For answer, they jumped up at her, tails wagging furiously, eyes bright with adoration, tongues lolling. "Oh, come on then," she said, taking their leads from the butler, who hurried to open the front door for her. "Thank you, Hector."

"Thank *you*, my lady," the butler said, closing the door gently behind her.

It was a cold December afternoon and Livia walked swiftly, the dogs prancing at her heels. When she reached Cavendish Square she stopped outside the house and looked up at the façade. The gleaming windows threw back sunlight and the front door stood open despite the cold as workmen hurried in and out. Alex had been right. An amazing amount of work could be achieved in a short space of time. At least with the aid of a bottomless purse and the right influence. Alex, it seemed, had both.

It had occurred to her to wonder how he'd acquired the influence in the short time he'd been in London, but when she'd asked he'd just laughed and said it was always possible to get what one wanted if one was determined. And Prince Prokov was certainly that.

The thought brought a smile to her lips as she went up the steps to the house, moving aside to let a pair of workmen carrying trestles get past her. The dogs barked indignantly and sprang at the men.

Livia dragged the animals into the hall and into the parlor. It had been finished first and was now a blissful haven amid the chaos. She released their leads and looked around with satisfaction. This was her private room. Fresh paint and new upholstery had updated it without destroying its essential character. She had kept the faded Turkey carpet, and most of the furniture, re-placing only the broken-down sofas and a chair with a wobbly leg. It was here that she felt the spirit of Sophia Lacey most strongly.

A discreet knock at the door heralded the appearance of the decorator. "I have the swatches you asked for, Lady Livia." He stepped back, holding his samples up high as Tristan and Isolde came at him in a yapping rush.

A sharp command sounded from behind him and in-stantly the dogs sat back on their haunches, tongues lolling. Alex stepped past the decorator. "I'm assuming you had no choice but to bring them," he said to Livia, the light in his eyes as he looked at her contradicting the slight exasperation in his tone.

"No, it was the butcher, you see," she said, feeling the fire start deep inside her, the glow spreading up from her loins to her lips.

"I'm not sure that I do," he said, "but never mind." He took her hand and kissed it, then leaned forward and kissed her cheek. The decorator's presence dictated a discreet salutation, but even so he felt her stir beneath the cool brush of his lips and he was aware of the deep, masculine satisfaction in knowing how easily he could ignite her passion to meet his own flare of desire. Just the lightest touch of his lips on her skin was enough these days to bring his body to a peak of lust, and he could read its match in the smoky depths of her gray gaze.

Resolutely he turned to the decorator. "Have you completed your consultation with Lady Livia?"

"Not as yet, Prince Prokov." The decorator looked a little uncomfortable. "I was about to show her ladyship the swatches for your bedchamber."

"Oh, in that case, I'll take a walk around the house and see how the work's getting on."

"By the way, there's something I most particularly wish to show you . . . in the dining room," Livia said, a rather wicked gleam partnering the lingering desire in her eyes. "I'll be finished here in about fifteen minutes. But just tell me what you think of this for the bed curtains. It's rather handsome, I think." She indicated a swatch of turquoise silk embossed with silver medallions.

Alex examined it solemnly for a minute, and then said, "My dear, I'm sure your instincts are impeccable in such matters. I leave it entirely in your hands. But don't be long, I'm anxious to see this dining room mystery." The words were perfectly straightforward, but his voice stroked her with promise and the look in his eyes spoke of another anxiety altogether.

Livia had never been cursed with a tendency to blush until she'd met Alexander Prokov, but now with the slightest inflection of his voice, a little flicker of blue fire in his eyes, he could bring a rush of color to her cheeks. And the damned man knew it. He never lost an opportunity to put her out of countenance.

"I'd welcome your opinion on the wall hangings in the salon," she said, turning her attention sedulously to the swatches on the table. "I think the pale gold complements the straw-colored upholstery, but there was also an apple green that might be even prettier. Do go and look."

"At your command, ma'am." He clicked his heels and offered a formal bow that gently mocked her confusion and left the parlor. He closed the door behind him and then stood in the hall, looking around, letting the feel of the house settle around him.

It was only his second visit since his engagement to Livia, and the first occasion had been with the architect. He had said very little himself, offering few opinions, since it was clear that Livia had plenty of her own and she and the architect seemed very much of a mind about most issues. She displayed a sensitivity to the house that transcended a mere interest in beautifying a piece of property, and he thought it explained her strange and visible reluctance to agree to the clause in the marriage settlements that in essence gave him the house.

He was now quite determined that she should never know that the house had never belonged to her. It would be an unnecessary hurt and he needed no such overt acknowledgment from anyone but the lawyers. But his blood stirred anew as he looked around the handsome hall with its lovely proportions, the elegant curved horseshoe staircase, the frescoed ceiling, the beautiful parquet beneath his feet. All his life he had lived in palaces, and by contrast this was a rather modest house, but it had been his parents' house and as such held a fascination for him so deep it was intrinsic to his soul.

He strolled across the hall towards the open front door, wondering if his followers were still there. Even though they had to know now that he was aware of the surveillance, they still persevered. They must know that if indeed he had anything to hide, he would be extra careful not to give anything away now that he was alerted to their presence. Nevertheless, they'd picked him up again as soon as he'd left his house this afternoon. He was getting so used to them these days, he'd probably miss them if they dropped their surveillance, he reflected with a sardonic smile. But he still didn't know whose side they were on. Not that it mattered as long as he kept up his vigilance.

He stepped through the door onto the top step and looked around. No sign of anyone suspicious, but a man opposite was diligently shoveling horse manure from the street into a bucket. Not an unusual sight in these well-traveled streets, but there was something awkward about the way the man swung the shovel. He didn't look as if he was accustomed to the task.

Alex shrugged. It was no business of his if his shadow spent a malodorous hour or so up to his elbows in steaming dung. He turned to go back inside when a movement in the square caught his attention. He looked back sharply. A head showed for an instant above a gap in the privet hedge behind the garden railings. And then it was gone. Alex frowned, pulling uneasily at his chin. Unless he was much mistaken, it had been Tatarinov. What business could he have in the square garden? He debated crossing to the garden to find out, but he heard the sound of Livia's quick footsteps in the hall behind him. Confronting Tatarinov would have to wait. He stepped back into the hall.

"Ah, there you are," Livia said as she accompanied the decorator to the front door. "Did you look at the wallpaper in the salon?"

"Not as yet," Alex said, tucking Tatarinov away in another compartment of his mind. "Shall we look now?"

"Yes, let's." The dogs skittered around her ankles as

Livia went into the salon, where the paper hangers were very busy. "Oh, dear," she said. "I do hope you like the gold. I think it's too late now to change it for the green."

"It would appear so," Alex agreed. "But fortunately, my dear, I find the gold perfectly agreeable." He looked down in pained exasperation as the terriers, for reasons known only to themselves, broke into a symphony of yapping, alternately pressing their bellies to the floor, tails thumping, and dancing up to his feet, before prancing back.

Seeing that they were not finding favor with the object of this adoration, Livia gathered up their leads, reining them in against her legs. "Do be quiet," she said, trying to make herself heard above the racket.

Alex plucked at the knees of his doeskin britches and squatted on his heels. He spoke to the dogs in a low stream of words that Livia guessed was Russian. It worked as it always did and they fell silent.

"You know, those dogs will have to be taught some manners if they're going to share a roof with me," he observed, rising smoothly and brushing off his britches.

"You could try," Livia said with a laugh, "but I wouldn't give much for your chances."

"Then they will have to go," he stated. "Now, what were you going to show me?"

Livia was momentarily startled. It hadn't sounded as if he was in jest. Indeed, he had seemed deadly serious for a second. Then she shrugged it off.

"In the dining room. But we'll need a stepladder. We could borrow that one." She gestured to one of the painter's ladders at present unoccupied.

"This is certainly mysterious," Alex said, lifting the ladder easily. "Lead on."

Livia led the way into the dining room, where the furniture was shrouded in dust sheets, and the walls half painted. "We did some work in here when we first moved in," she informed Alex. "Really just a cleanup and a touch-up coat of paint." She didn't add that it was all she could afford at the time.

"However, while we were doing it we noticed something very interesting." She stopped in the middle of the room and pointed up to the ceiling. "Take a look at the fresco." Laughter danced in her voice and she stepped back as he set up the ladder.

Alex, with a somewhat suspicious air, went up the ladder. He leaned his head back and stared up at the delicate painting on the ceiling. "Good God."

"Isn't it marvelously wicked?" Livia chortled from below. "Why would a respectable spinster lady like Sophia Lacey have such shocking artwork above her dining table?"

Alex was unaware how tightly he was holding the top struts of the stepladder as he stared up at the lascivious scene until he felt a tingling in his hands. He released his hold, flexing his fingers, unable to find words for a moment. His mother had commissioned this? Or was it his parents? Something they'd enjoyed, a private piece of sensual mischief? He couldn't imagine his father having anything to do with such a thing. And yet . . . and yet what did he know of his father? Nothing beyond an austere distance, and an unshakeable sense of patriotic duty on whose altar he had sacrificed whatever relationship he had had with Sophia Lacey. The Czarina Catherine had demanded her subject's return and Prince Prokov had obeyed. At least, that was what he'd told his son. Bare bones of a story that had to have had some emotional meat.

"Are you all right?" Livia sounded anxious. "Doesn't it amuse you?"

He found his voice again. "Yes . . . yes, of course it does. It's extraordinary. A Roman orgy, no less." He managed a light laugh as he descended the ladder. "I suspect most people would paint it over."

"That would be sacrilege," Livia said, genuinely shocked. "It's a beautiful thing, even if it is a little lewd. And besides, I feel as if this house is only on loan to me, or rather entrusted to me . . . I think that's what I mean. I must honor its character, otherwise I suspect it will do something very nasty to me." She laughed as if mocking herself, but Alex had the feeling she was deadly serious.

"I'm sure you're right," he said easily, folding up the ladder. "Are there any more of those kinds of hidden delights?"

"Not really," she said, following him back to the salon, where he replaced the ladder. "Just a few funny little things in the kitchen, a suspect jelly mold, and a very salacious piece of scrimshaw . . . still, it made us all wonder."

"As it well might," he said, still trying to absorb this new dimension of his unknown mother. "However, talking of the kitchen . . . where are the ancients while all this renovation is going on?"

Livia had no difficulty interpreting the question. "Oh, they and the house cat are happily grumbling away in their own quarters," she told him, hauling back on the dogs, who were sniffing paint buckets. "They won't let the workmen into their own apartments, so I'm leaving them alone. They'll come back to work when everything's completed."

"Ah, yes." Alex stroked his chin with a forefinger. "Maybe this is a good moment to talk about that. Shall we go back into the parlor?"

Livia felt a stab of unease, but she acceded with a nod and led the way back to the parlor, releasing the dogs, who collapsed breathily before the empty hearth. She shivered in the December chill. "We could light a fire in here. I'll fetch coals from the kitchen."

"*No,*" he said more sharply than he'd intended. He softened his voice, trying for a lightly amused tone. "Livia, dear girl, what's appropriate in a country vicarage is not appropriate behavior for the mistress of a London house."

Livia was not placated. "You may have a point . . . but there's no one else to light a fire . . . unless, of course, you would care to do the honors, Prince Prokov?"

He decided not to rise to the unmistakable challenge.

She'd made it all too clear over their short acquaintance that she didn't respond too well to an authoritarian manner. "I think we can suffer the chill for a few minutes." His smile was conciliatory.

He shrugged out of his coat. "Here, wrap this around you." He draped it around her shoulders, drawing it tight under her throat so that her face was lifted towards him. "So fierce," he said softly. "Let me see what I can do about that."

Chapter Thirteen

ALEX KISSED HER, GENTLY AT first and then with increasing pressure, feeling her swaying into him as she lost the hard sinews of determination and annoyance. And he could hear his own blood beating in his ears as he held her, ran his hands over the supple curves of her body beneath his coat. Her scent intoxicated him as it always did, a mélange of rosewater, lavender, and beneath it all the purely female hint of arousal.

She had never made any attempt to hide her desire, and the honesty of her responses, her unself-conscious lack of inhibition, was a spur to his own desire, so much so that in these weeks of their betrothal he had been hard-pressed to hold himself back from tipping them both over the edge. Now was one of those moments.

Livia was no longer cold. Her skin was warm, glowing with heat from the blood racing in her veins. She reached against him, her mouth pressed to his, trying in some way to absorb him within her own shape. Her hands caressed his ears, palmed his cheeks, fingers tugged playfully on his earlobes, and she felt him hard against her, his penis pressing into her belly, and the sensation sent waves of shocking need through her loins, tightening her thighs. She heard her own inarticulate moan as his hands dug into the hard muscle of her backside, and her thighs parted without volition.

And without volition she fell back onto the sofa, his coat falling away from her, her legs sprawled in wanton invitation as he came down with her, his mouth still locked against hers. One hand roughly pushed up her skirt, flattened over her silk-stockinged thigh. His tongue pushed deep into her mouth as he continued to draw up her skirt. She felt the air, chill on her thighs above her garters, and her hips lifted to his probing fingers. A shiver ran from her scalp to her toes, her scalp tightening, her toes curling, as a wave of sensation more powerful than any she had yet experienced rocked her. His palm flattened, sliding between her thighs, spreading them further, and a charge like a lightning bolt jolted her loins and the pit of her stomach at an invasion so deep and so intimate that for a bare instant she tightened her thighs against the intrusion. And then she felt his fingers part her, slide within her body, moving within her, and the instant of resistance vanished and from somewhere way above her she heard her own ecstatic cry as a wave of delight flooded her to her core.

Alex held her against him until her breathing slowed. She opened her eyes slowly, looking up into his face as he held himself above her. "What was that?" she murmured.

He laughed softly. "A little taste of what's to come, my love." Reluctantly, he pushed himself back and stood up, looking down at her flushed face, her swollen lips, her gray eyes dark and heavy with fulfilled passion. "Damn . . . I hadn't intended that to happen . . . not yet, at least." He shook his head, painfully aware of his own acute physical discomfort. "But you're so beautiful, Livia, and so passionate . . ."

Livia pushed down her skirt and sat up. She was still shaky but filled with a glorious languor. Now she knew what it was she'd been waiting for these long, frustrating, tantalizing weeks of desire. And she was certain that that, wonderful though it had been, was the mere tip of the iceberg in this business of lovemaking.

She looked at him wordlessly for a moment as the slow realization came to her that Alex had taken nothing for himself from those delicious pleasure-filled moments. If he had been as frustrated as she had before, he must be in agony now. But she could give back. Now, more than anything else, she needed to touch his body as he had touched hers.

She stood and reached for him, whispering, "Let me give you the same, Alex?"

Her hand brushed the mound of his erect penis beneath his britches and he groaned. Swiftly she unfastened his britches and pushed them off his hips. She clasped his penis, enclosing it in the warmth of her palm, and instinctively moved her hand up and down the shaft, a finger dancing over the moist tip. She seemed to know exactly what to do, and it felt so wonderfully right.

Alex stood with his head thrown back, his eyes closed, and Livia watched his expression as she continued to touch and to stroke, aware of a delicious feeling of satisfaction that she could give this much pleasure. And at the last, when he cried out as she had done, she reveled in a wondrous glow of triumph, not taking her eyes from his transported face.

At last, Alex came back to himself. His eyes opened again as he fumbled with his britches. "Dear God, Livia, where did you learn that?" he murmured.

"I don't know," she said with a delighted little chuckle. "It just came to me. It just felt right."

He pulled her hard against him again. "Oh, it was certainly that," he said into her tumbled curls. "And I don't know how I'm going to wait for another two weeks before I can have the rest of you."

Livia chuckled again. "Why do we have to wait?"

He sighed and tucked a stray curl into a loosened pin. "Because I want to love you at leisure. And I don't want to be worrying that someone might barge in on us," he added, casting a speaking glance towards the door. "Besides, anticipation is the most powerful aphrodisiac, my sweet."

He ran his finger over her mouth. "We have a lifetime

to indulge passion, to learn each other, to know each other in every possible way. It's torment to wait, but a perversely sweet torment nevertheless."

He took her hand and kissed her fingers, taking each one into his mouth in a slow, lascivious stroke of his tongue that made her nipples peak anew, prickling against the bodice of her gown.

"My father would approve," Livia said, trying to ground herself again.

"How so?"

"Deferred gratification," she responded. "It's his credo. Assuming, of course, that gratification is appropriate in the first place."

Alex thought of the dining room fresco and wondered again what that could tell him about Sophia Lacey and by extension perhaps himself. Would some knowledge of Livia's parents tell him anything about her? "And does he think sexual gratification is appropriate, do you think?"

Livia considered the question. "Yes, I believe so," she said. "He may be a country vicar, but he's also a brilliant scholar and like most such he considers all subjects worthy of consideration. And he considers taboos to be the refuge of a small mind, so . . ." She shrugged a little. "I don't believe he would disapprove of the gratification of passion."

"What of your mother . . . their relationship?" He tried to hide his intense curiosity.

"I have no idea how they were behind the bedroom

door," Livia said. "But as I remember, they were friends, companions, both intellectual and familial. I think it would be hard to have such a depth of shared feeling if there wasn't some passionate love to underpin it."

She shook her head. "Why are we being so serious, Alex?" But even as she asked the question she knew the answer. They knew so little about each other . . . oh, they knew the basic facts, but very little of what made them as they were. And these were the conversations that teased out the little facts that would finally create the picture. But it would only be a completed canvas long after they'd taken the step to the altar.

Alex said with a laugh, "To distract ourselves, my love."

"I suppose so," she agreed. "Didn't you tell me once that you never knew your mother?"

"I might have done," he said carefully. "Since it's true."

"Dying in childbirth is so tragic," Livia said. "And for your father . . . it must have been dreadful. To be left with a baby to bring up all alone. Did he every remarry?"

"No." Alex shook his head. He didn't think he'd ever actually said his mother had died giving birth to him, but it seemed easier to leave Livia with that assumption.

He reached for her hands again and pulled her in against him, but this time he held her lightly. "There will be plenty of time for questions and explorations, Livia. But I do want to talk about your ancient retainers."

"What about them?" Unease prickled again.

"I understand we can't turn them off," he said carefully. "But a generous pension would surely satisfy them."

"No," Livia declared. "Sophia's will states absolutely that they are to leave this service only when they choose."

"Have you asked them about that?" He was treading carefully, aware that Livia had the same proprietorial feelings towards the retainers as she did towards the house itself.

"It isn't necessary," she said. "They know the terms of the will and when they're ready to go they'll say so."

"I understand," he repeated. "But surely you must see, Livia, that once we're married, Morecombe cannot be the doorkeeper, let alone butler, in the household of the Prince and Princess Prokov?" He opened his hands in a gesture that could have been mistaken for supplication.

Livia did not make that mistake. "What do you suggest?"

Alex heard the edge to the question and debated whether to push the issue now or have it out when they were married and Livia would have to accept that Morecombe and the twins were his employees and potential pensioners. But honesty insisted that he continue.

"There would be no reason for them to leave the house if they didn't wish to vacate their quarters," he said reasonably. "But their duties could be curtailed quite drastically without offending them, I would have thought."

Livia realized that physical passion was a truly

ephemeral sensation. "Quite apart from going against the spirit of Sophia's will, such a move would make them feel useless and unwanted. This is as much their house, Alex, as it is mine, and their claim precedes mine, quite frankly."

Her voice rose a fraction. "I can't and *won't* have them put out to grass. Quite apart from how they rallied around when Nell and Ellie and I arrived, with three squalling children and an outraged nurse in tow, the twins are the most wonderful cooks."

She folded her arms, once again aware of the chill in the room. "I'm sure we can dissuade Morecombe from answering the door. I don't think he'll see that as a demotion since he doesn't like doing it anyway, but everything else he does . . ."

She shook her head vigorously. "No, Alex. The twins continue to reign in the kitchen and Morecombe does what he chooses to do. That's the way it has to be."

"I have an excellent cook myself," Alex pressed mildly. "His father was Russian, and he was trained in France. I don't think he would take kindly to working under the supervision of two old ladies."

"Then he must learn." Livia realized that they'd reached some kind of line. And this was no time to be taking up definitive confrontational positions. She said quickly, "I'm sure I can persuade Morecombe to give up his responsibilities for answering the door, but I can't tell him he's no longer butler."

She offered a conciliatory smile. "I have to get back to

Mount Street to change for dinner. But surely these are things we can discuss later, Alex. It will all fall into place when we start to live here together. Everything will be in a state of flux, and everyone's role will have to be re-designed. Who knows, maybe Morecombe and the twins will decide to leave of their own accord once they realize how things have changed."

Livia fervently hoped for such a resolution, but doubted that it would be that simple. Morecombe, Ada, and Mavis were as much fixtures of the house in Cavendish Square as the dining room fresco.

Obviously this was a battle to be fought another day, Alex decided. Since it was inconceivable that he should lose it, nothing would be gained by a premature confrontation. He was not yet master of this particular household. And, in truth, he had no wish to distress his mother's old retainers. He was very interested in listening to their reminiscences, and they certainly wouldn't be open for a comfortable chat if they thought he was out to dispossess them. It would be possible to make incremental changes in their roles in the household once the new regime was established.

"I'm sure you're right," he said easily.

He opened the parlor door and Tristan and Isolde raced between his legs towards the spurious freedom of the hall. "Perhaps Morecombe could take sole responsibility for those creatures," he suggested, with what he hoped was a note of ironic humor.

"He gives the impression that they annoy him too,"

Livia said, responding in what she hoped was the same tone. "But actually he seems to like them and it seems to be mutual."

"Then perhaps we've solved two problems with one solution," Alex said, escorting her down to the street. "Let me take you back to Mount Street."

❧

Alex saw Livia into the house and left, blowing her a kiss with the promise that he would see her at dinner. Then he set off at a brisk walk towards Piccadilly. He picked up a hackney and directed the jarvey to Half Moon Street and Tatarinov's lodgings.

He paid off the hackney and stood in the narrow street contemplating the tall house where Tatarinov had two small rooms. The man had no interest in the trappings of wealth and lived a very different life from that of the rest of their little band of conspirators. But then he was cut from a different cloth, Alex reflected, raising his hand to the knocker.

Tatarinov had presented himself to Constantine Fedorovsky on the latter's journey to London. He had impeccable credentials, letters of recommendation that were sent directly by the small group of revolutionaries controlling the flow of information from St. Petersburg. His competence was unquestionable and for all the roughness of his manners, Alex and his fellows had accepted him in their number with gratitude rather than suspicion. Now Alex was not so sure.

He banged the knocker again and after a minute the door opened a crack. A young maidservant peered around. "Yes, sir?"

"Is Monsieur Tatarinov at home?" Alex asked politely.

"Aye, sir. Shall I tell him who's come?"

"No, just show me in." Alex pushed the door wide and stepped into a narrow hall. "Where will I find him?"

"Second door on the landing, sir." She pointed up the stairs towards the darkened upper reaches of the house.

Alex nodded his thanks and took the stairs two at a time. He knocked sharply on the indicated door and waited, watching the tiny eyehole set close to the top of the door. There was no sound from within, but he saw an eye at the peephole, and then a key grated in the lock and the door opened.

"What brings you here, Prince?" Tatarinov asked, surveying his visitor without expression.

Alex moved the silver knob of his cane between finger and thumb. The seemingly ordinary accessory became a lethal sword stick with the right pressure on the spring mounted in the knob. He didn't think he would need it, but it was as well to be prepared.

"I came to ask you what took you to Cavendish Square this afternoon," he replied easily. "I am aware I have some followers, but I hadn't thought to number you among them, Tatarinov."

"Ah." The other man nodded. "You'd best come in." He stepped back, holding the door wide.

Alex stepped into a parlor where a fire of sea coal

belched noxious fumes and the light came from three tallow candles on the mantel.

"Not quite what you're used to, eh, Prince?" Tatarinov stated with a short laugh. "Not all revolutionaries are feather-bedded aristocrats." He went to the table and picked up a vodka bottle, filling two squat tumblers. "Drink with me." He held one out to his visitor.

Alex debated returning a sharp answer to the somewhat derisive comment and then decided to ignore it. He took the glass and drained the contents in one swallow. Tatarinov nodded his approval and followed suit, then he refilled both glasses and set the bottle back on the table.

"So, you've caught their surveillance, then?"

"I'm aware I'm being watched, but I don't know who by," Alex said. He kept his hand still on the knob of his cane, his eyes never leaving Tatarinov. "I'm hoping you'll tell me since you seem to be a part of the surveillance."

"Aye, well, 'tis Arakcheyev's men," the other man told him. "They don't have anything to go on, but they've been told to keep an eye on every Russian in town, follow 'em for a couple of weeks. They don't suspect you of anything at present. I've put their minds at rest on that score. They think I'm one of 'em who's also watching you all for Arakcheyev. If I tell 'em nothing's going on, they'll believe me. You should lose your shadows by Christmas and they'll watch someone else for a while."

It made sense. Alex was well acquainted with the dreaded head of the czar's Committee for General Security. Arakcheyev had the czar's absolute trust and he would be excessively diligent when it came to rooting out threats to his sovereign's safety on any continent. It was typical of his methods that he would suspect everyone initially and take them off his list only when he was certain they were innocent.

"So, are you working for Arakcheyev also?" he asked, tossing back the contents of his glass.

"He thinks so," Tatarinov said with a shrug. "Way I look at it, I'm most useful to you if I keep in with them."

"Indeed," Alex agreed. He wasn't sure whether he could believe this man or not. He gave the impression of open honesty, of having nothing to hide, but if he was clever enough to play the double agent here, then he was also clever enough to deceive the conspirators.

"Why are you interested in deposing the czar, Tatarinov?" he asked.

The Russian turned and spat onto the coals in the grate. "Not for the same reasons as you, Prince. I don't come from your palace world of privilege. Me and mine have worked the land for the gentry, and died doing it. Alexander has sworn to keep the old system . . . he won't consider reforms, and the people have had enough. The peasants will turn on him and his like eventually, you mark my words. The time may not be now, but when it comes the streets will run with blood."

A cold finger ran up Alex's spine at the conviction in the man's voice. It was true that the injustices in his homeland were many, and it was true that there were grumbles in the villages, but there always had been and the landed gentry put down any hint of rebellion with the savagery of the knout.

He couldn't deny Tatarinov's accusations. But they put his mind at rest about the man's true allegiance. His motives were different, but none the less powerful for that, and the end was the same.

"I'd appreciate it if you could keep me informed of anything that you might hear in your double role," Alex said, setting down his glass. "It would be as well for two of us to share the knowledge."

"As you say, Prince," Tatarinov agreed. "I hear all sorts of tidbits, and I'll be the first to know if Arakcheyev suspects anything concrete."

"That's a comfort," Alex said somewhat dryly. He didn't need reminding that this was a dangerous business they were on, but the danger was somehow now made manifest. He turned to the door. "I'll leave you now. Keep me informed."

"Aye, I'll do that," Tatarinov said. "And, by the bye . . . Viscount Bonham . . . husband to your fiancée's friend . . ."

Alex paused, his hand on the latch. "Yes, what of him?"

"He does something hush-hush for the War Ministry here," Tatarinov said. "Not sure what, but you'd best watch yourself around him."

Alex raised his eyebrows. "Interesting," he commented. "I'll be on my guard." He waved a hand in farewell and went down the stairs, letting himself out into the cold street.

Strangely enough, the information didn't surprise him particularly. He had had the measure of Harry Bonham for some weeks now, and had only respect for him. He had suspected that the man probably had interests outside the general run of sport and pleasure. Nevertheless, it was an unnerving piece of information and he would have to watch his step around Cornelia as much as her husband.

That said, he would far rather fall foul of the British secret service than Arakcheyev's men.

Had the czar anything to do with this surveillance, or was it only at the instigation of Arakcheyev? On the whole, Alex thought it probably the latter. The czar might go so far as to ask an elder statesman like Prince Michael Michaelovitch to keep an eye out for his unofficial ambassador just in case he got himself into deep water and couldn't swim out of it, but it would be prompted more by concern that Alex should accomplish his task for Russia efficiently than by a suspicion that he might be up to no good. Arakcheyev, on the other hand, looked after his master and even the czar's most trusted advisors would not be given a free pass.

Oh well, worries for another day, he decided. If he didn't hurry he'd be late for the Bonham's dinner party.

Chapter Fourteen

THERE WAS A LIGHT DUSTING of snow on the ground when Livia walked up the aisle of her father's church on the Saturday before Christmas, attended by her two matrons of honor. Alex stood at the altar, Viscount Bonham beside him.

It had been agreed among his peers after Tatarinov's information about the viscount that the less they came into contact with Bonham as a group the less risk they would run. Livia had expressed surprise and dismay that he was inviting no one of his own to the wedding, but she'd accepted the fib that only Duke Nicolai and Count Fedorovsky were sufficiently close to him to warrant an invitation, and unfortunately they both had long-standing invitations to spend Christmas elsewhere.

It was a useful fabrication. He didn't want Livia getting too friendly with his own people. A man who was playing both ends against the middle needed to keep the separate strands of his life well apart lest the spark that would be ignited if they touched turn into a conflagration that would engulf them all.

Now, as he watched Livia's steady progress towards him and their shared future, he thought how far he had come in this relationship from the early days when he had seen her as his passport to an easy social acceptance in her world. Now it wouldn't matter if she could bring him nothing. He wanted her for herself, for that lively sense of humor, that delicious bubble of laughter, for the way her eyes turned smoky with passion and her body melted into his. He had never met a woman like her and he wanted to marry her, to keep her safe, to love her and be loved by her.

But he also knew that he was deceiving her, that the entire bedrock of this marriage was based on deception, and he could do nothing to alter that. The die was cast, and he had to maintain the deception if he was to protect her. Only thus could she continue living the life she was used to, a life now enhanced by her married status, by her title, and by his wealth. It was a forgivable deception, surely. He had only to keep her safe from the other side of his world, even as she played an unwitting part in it. A fair exchange?

As she reached him, Livia smiled through the gauzy transparency of her veil. He looked unusually tense, she thought. It was as monumental a step for him as it was for her.

She had not a single misgiving. It had surprised her, but she had woken up that morning happy and full of excitement. Maybe it was a wildly impractical thing to do, to join one's life with a near stranger simply because it *felt* right . . . simply because just thinking of him made her heart sing and her blood surge. But she could not imagine doing anything different. She could not imagine how she could ever have made a different decision. And here on the steps of the altar she still couldn't.

As she smiled through her veil, he smiled back and she could feel the tension slide from him. Perhaps he'd been afraid *she* was having second thoughts.

And then the organ music faded and the Reverend Lacey began to speak, his sonorous tones ringing through the old raftered church. Wintry sunlight bathed the congregation in color as it poured through the stained-glass windows.

Towards the end of the service Livia gave her bouquet of white roses to Cornelia and drew off her left glove. Alex slipped the slender gold band on her finger, his fingers tightening over hers as he held her hand for a minute. And it was done.

The vicar pronounced them man and wife, stepped forward again, and raised his daughter's veil. "You may kiss the bride."

Alex's mouth whispered over hers and Livia was aware of a seething elation. Today her life was really beginning. And even though she knew it was naïve to believe it, she could see only a path strewn with roses. Naïve, yes, but so what? This was her wedding day.

They emerged from the church to the clamor of

church bells and the applause of the crowd gathered in the churchyard. It seemed the entire parish had turned out to celebrate the wedding of their vicar's daughter. Rice showered the bridal couple as they stood for a moment arm in arm in front of the church doors. The dazzle of the sun on snow made Livia blink and her eyes water.

It seemed to be having a similar effect on her friends, she noticed. Their eyes were definitely a little blurred. A gust of wind blew her veil across her face and it was Alex who lifted it aside, tucking it back behind her ears.

"I think we had better get out of the wind before you take flight," he murmured, and was rewarded with a soft chuckle.

The vicar's pony and trap, decorated with white ribbons in honor of the occasion, waited in the lane beyond the lych-gate, and they walked down the path through the cheering crowd and another rice storm. Alex handed Livia into the trap, lifting her train in after her, arranging it in a puddle at her feet, then he climbed nimbly up beside her.

"I've a mind to be alone with my bride," he said softly, lightly caressing her cheek with a fingertip. He turned to the boy holding the horse. "Give me the reins. I'll drive, you may walk."

"Right y'are, m'lord." The youth jumped down. "I'll run ahead." He set off at a rapid trot.

Alex clicked his tongue at the stolid pony between the traces and the trap moved slowly down the lane to the vicarage, the rest of the wedding party following on foot.

"I wish I could have provided my own conveyance," Alex stated. "This is the most undashing equipage." He flicked the reins, trying to encourage the pony to increase its pace. "Now, my curricle, on the other hand—"

"Would have been very dashing," Livia finished for him, glad for this light and inconsequential chatter. She was feeling suddenly and for the first time overwhelmed, as if she'd been living in some champagne bubble that reality had finally penetrated.

"My father would not have let me leave his roof for my wedding in anything but his own transport," she explained with a little laugh. "He can be rather old-fashioned on occasion."

"Well, when we *do* leave his roof later it will be in much more elegant style," Alex promised.

Livia turned to look at him, and the bubble enclosed her again. Her heart did a little skip of pleasure and anticipation. His fair hair shone in the sun, shot through with little coppery glints, and his profile, dominated by the long, straight nose, was as commanding as it was attractive. Aware of her gaze, he turned his full face towards her, an inquiring smile on his well-shaped mouth, and the full force of those blue eyes once again engulfed her in a hot flood of desire.

"Where *are* we going later?" she blurted, her mind a riot of sensual images, of feather beds and tangled limbs.

"Wait and see," he said, as he had done every time she'd asked the question. "You won't be disappointed, I promise."

"Oh, no," she said softly. "I know I won't be disappointed, Alex."

The double meaning was not lost on him. His eyes narrowed, his lips moved in the semblance of a kiss, but he said nothing further.

The stable boy was already waiting for them when Alex drew rein outside the vicarage. Alex jumped down and lifted his bride to the ground, holding her in the air for a moment. "Two hours," he stated firmly. "Not a moment longer, wife of mine. I want you all to myself, and if I must carry you off across my saddle, then I give you fair warning, I shall do so."

"That could be amusing," Livia said with a grin. "But it would probably shock people. Besides . . ." She was serious again. "We must stay for at least a couple of hours. People have been so kind, it would be rude to abandon them too soon." She took his hand to lead him into the house.

Martha, who had stayed in the church just long enough to see Livia married, was already in the dining room supervising a troop of village girls arranging platters of food on the table. She flung her hands up when Livia came in and hurried to embrace her. "Congratulations, m'dear. What a lovely ceremony . . . and the vicar seemed so happy." She patted Livia's cheeks, her eyes misty. "Such a beautiful bride."

Belatedly she remembered the bridegroom, who stood beside Livia. Somewhat self-consciously she dropped a curtsy. "Congratulations, m'lord . . . uh . . . Your Highness. I wish you very happy, and I'm sure you will be with this angel beside you." She wiped her eyes on the corner of her apron.

Alex thanked her gravely, unsure if he would ever grow used to the informality of English servants, who in so many cases seemed to consider themselves family friends, and were treated as such. There were no such confusions in a feudal society. Serfs knew their place in the hierarchy. And the system bred the Tatarinovs of its world, he reflected a shade grimly.

"Liv . . . Alex . . . oh, there you are." Aurelia came into the dining room. "Come and greet your guests, *Princess Prokov.*"

An hour later Livia was beginning to feel her husband's impatience as a palpable force. It was a small wedding and only the closest of her London friends had been invited. Alex was comfortable enough with Nick and David and Harry, and of course with her father, but none of the local gentry, the squire, the gentlemen farmers seemed to know what to make of this exotic foreigner. They stumbled through a few sentences about the weather, or the local hunting, then fell into an uncomfortable silence. Alex tried hard, she had to admit. He talked farming with the farmers, horses with the squire, but nothing would really draw them out.

"My dear child, your poor husband is a fish out of water." The vicar spoke softly as he came up beside her. "I think you should put him out of his misery as soon as decently possible." He took an appreciative sip of the claret in his glass. "I must say, it's a real pleasure to drink a fine wine once in a while." His eyes held a twinkle of self-mockery.

"You could drink it every night of the week if you so chose," she said, laughing.

"But I wouldn't enjoy it so much," he observed. "The good things of life should be savored in small doses." He laid a hand on her arm, his expression now grave. "Come into the study with me."

"Of course." She went with him into his study, where the quiet was almost startling after the buzz of voices, the chink of glasses, the constant rattle of silverware. "Is something the matter, Father?"

"Not at all," he said, leaning against his desk. "And you needn't worry, child, I'm not about to embarrass us both by giving you a parental talk on the subject of your wedding night; you have your friends for that. And I'm sure they're a lot more qualified than I." His smile was dry.

"However, I will say this. I am here, always. Should you ever need advice, support of any kind, you must promise me now that you will come to me. I have set aside a small trust fund for you to be released in the event of anything . . ." He paused. "Anything untoward happening."

"Untoward?" She frowned. "Like what, Father?"

He shook his head with a touch of impatience. "I don't know. But this is a foreign union, a journey you're embarking upon that's unfamiliar to us all, Livia. Alex is Russian, a man from a vastly different culture. He will have expectations that will probably take you by surprise. I believe you have the strength of mind, the fortitude, to face those challenges with humor, with a willingness to make concessions, but without compromising your own values. However, if anything arises that troubles you, then remember that you are not alone."

Livia stared at him, taken aback by the idea that her father, who had just married her in his own church, was now expressing deep-seated doubts about her new husband, about this union that he had just blessed. "Do you not like Alex, Father?" she stammered after a minute.

He shook his head again vigorously. "I like him well enough, child. He's a sophisticated, cultured, highly educated man. But it's inevitable that he plays by different rules, and it's inevitable that you will clash. I would be doing you no service if I promised you only roses in your path. There will be thorns . . . there are always thorns, but these might be sharper and more unexpected than those we're accustomed to."

He pushed himself away from his desk and took her shoulders, smiling down into her stricken countenance. "No need for such a worried look, my dear. I have every confidence that you two will make a splendidly matched couple. But I don't expect there to be no fireworks, and neither should you."

He kissed her forehead. "I pray that you and Alex will have as much happiness in your life together as your dear mother and I had in ours. And more than that I could not wish for anyone."

Reassured, Livia kissed him, holding him tightly for a few minutes, startlingly conscious now of how a phase of her life was behind her. Even though she had had her superficial independence these last months in London, she had still been first and foremost a daughter. Women were always defined by their primary relationship to the men in their lives. Now her husband was that primary relationship, and she was a wife.

In essence, what difference did it make? In the ordinary scheme of things a woman exchanged a father for a husband. So why did that suddenly make her feel diminished in some way?

A soft knock came at the door. "Livia?" It was Alex's voice.

"Come in, Alex," the vicar called, stepping back from his daughter. He smiled warmly at Alex as he came into the room. "We were just having a family chat, but I'll give you back your wife now."

"Thank you, sir." Alex held out a hand to Livia, but his eyes were questioning as he looked at her, noting the pallor that had not been there before, and the slight uncertainty in her eyes. Just what had the Reverend Lacey been saying?

"If you're ready to leave, Aurelia and Cornelia are waiting to help you change," he said, giving her a reassuring smile and a quick squeeze of her fingers.

"Yes, it's high time you two got on with your lives," Reverend Lacey declared briskly. "Go and change, Livia." He shooed her from the room.

"Ah, there you are." Aurelia and Cornelia were waiting at the bottom of the staircase. "Alex is getting impatient."

"You can't really blame him," Cornelia said. "These people must be as alien to him as the man in the moon." She looked at Livia sharply. "Is something the matter, Liv?"

Livia shook her head. "No, of course not . . . what could be? Let's go upstairs." She hurried ahead of her friends up to her bedchamber.

Cornelia exchanged a look with Aurelia, who shrugged her own perplexity, and they followed Livia.

"Was the vicar giving you the obligatory pre-nuptial-night words of advice, Liv?" Cornelia asked casually as she helped Livia unfasten her gown.

"Not exactly," Livia said, her voice muffled in the folds of her dress as she lifted it over her head. "He said you two were better suited for that particular talk, and probably more knowledgeable than he is anyway."

Aurelia chuckled as she hung the wedding gown reverently in the linen press. "Any questions then, Liv? We're more than ready to oblige with answers."

"No," Livia declared, stepping into a driving skirt of dark red broadcloth. "Most of it I know already, and I'm rather assuming that any other questions I might have will be answered empirically in the very near future. Thank you anyway." She fastened the catch at the waist and smoothed the skirt down over her hips.

"It's to be assumed your prince will know what he's doing?" Cornelia said with a mischievous smile as she held the matching jacket for Livia.

Livia thrust her arms into the sleeves. "I am certainly

making that assumption," she responded, her attempt at a lofty tone collapsing on a choke of laughter. "What an absurd conversation."

"At least it made you laugh," Cornelia said. "So, what did your father say to trouble you, Liv?"

"What makes you think he said anything to trouble me?" Livia demanded. She fastened the tiny buttons of braided black silk down the front of the jacket, lifting her chin as she struggled with the topmost button on the high collar.

"Oh, for goodness sake, Liv, we know you too well."

Livia sighed. "It was just a dose of reality, that's all. And I didn't really want to hear it. I like living in my bubble at the moment, and I don't want it burst."

"And is it burst?" Aurelia asked, watching her face.

Livia considered, then shook her head, the glint returning to her gray eyes. "No," she said definitely. "No, it isn't. I am so hungry for him, my dears, that I could swallow him whole."

She laughed as the exhilaration returned in full measure. "I am in a turmoil of lasciviousness and I can barely keep my hands off him. If we don't get away from here soon I shall do or say something that will shock the old biddies downstairs to their collective core."

Her friends exchanged a relieved glance at this return of the old Livia.

"Do you think this is as elegant as we thought it was?" Livia surveyed her image in the long glass.

"Without question," Aurelia said firmly. "It fits you like a glove."

Livia put her hands at her waist and considered with her head on one side. Aurelia was right. She could almost have been poured into the jacket that nipped her waist and clung to the swell of her hips and bosom. "It's a good color."

"With your coloring you could never go wrong with red," Cornelia agreed. She lifted the matching hat from its stand, smoothing the black plume. "Do you know where Alex is taking you?"

"No, he still won't tell me." Livia set the hat on top of her crown of dusky curls. The brim curled up on one side, and the black plume on the other swept to her shoulder. "There." She gave the hat a final pat. "That's as good as it gets."

She turned away from the mirror and smiled at her friends. "Wish me luck."

"All the luck in the world, love." Cornelia embraced her tightly, then moved aside for Aurelia.

Livia clung to them both for a long moment, then straightened, putting back her shoulders with a decisive gesture. "Let's go."

Alex came to the foot of the stairs as the three women came down. He reached for Livia when she was still five steps up, catching her around the waist and swinging her down beside him. "At last," he said. "I was about to come in search." He took her hand and led her through the crowd of guests and outside into the bright and frosty late afternoon.

His curricle stood at the gate, a groom holding the bridles of a handsome pair of match bays who were tossing their heads and shifting their hooves, their breath steaming in the cold air.

"We'd better not be going far," Livia muttered with a shiver.

"Indeed, Prokov, an open carriage in the middle of December." The vicar sounded disapproving as he bent to kiss his daughter good-bye.

"Don't worry, sir. There's a lap robe and a hot brick for Livia's feet," Alex said with cheerful insouciance. He lifted his bride without ceremony into the carriage, shook hands briefly with his father-in-law, and jumped up beside her.

It was apparent to all and sundry that this bridegroom was very anxious to be away with his bride.

Alex took up the reins. "Let go their heads, Jake."

The groom released the bridles and eagerly the horses started forward. The lad jumped up behind as the carriage went past him and took his place on the board at the rear of the curricle, balancing easily as Alex dropped his hands and the horses obediently increased their pace.

"Warm enough, sweeting?"

Livia felt a prickle of pleasure at the first endearment he had ever used. She murmured her assent, snuggling into the fur lap robe as she looked up at the sky where the evening star had just appeared.

Chapter Fifteen

LIVIA WASN'T SURE HOW LONG they drove down country lanes beneath a clear and increasingly star-filled sky. She was warm as toast in her fur wrap and her feet were blissfully cozy. Alex drove in silence, but the hint of a smile played over his fine mouth and every now and again he would look sideways as if to check that she was still there, and then the smile would broaden and his eyes would glitter as if reflecting the starlight.

Livia was content with the silence. She was both tired and not tired, inhabiting a quiet world of anticipation until Alex turned the horses onto a narrow lane that threaded through a thicket of birch and beech towards the lights of a cottage in a clearing ahead.

She sat up. "Are we here . . . where are we?"

"Journey's end," Alex said, drawing rein on a gravel sweep in front of the cottage. Actually, Livia realized, it was a lot more than a cottage. A substantial brick lodge with a slate roof, smoke curling from two chimneys, yellow light showing from behind diamond-paned windows. There were thatched outhouses and stables to one side, and all around the ancient trees of the New Forest.

"Whose house is this?" she asked, wondering exactly where in the forest they were, and how Alex, a stranger to this part of the world, could so unerringly have found his way here.

"Mine," he said calmly, jumping down from the curricle. "Or rather yours. Come, madam wife?" He reached up and lifted her from the carriage.

Livia put her arms around his neck as he held her and rested her head on his shoulder. Her tiredness had vanished. Very soon now, finally, she would be making love with this extraordinary, generous, impulsive man. She smiled dreamily at him in the moonlight. "When did you buy a house in the New Forest?"

He leaned down and kissed the corner of her mouth, cradling her tightly. "I didn't buy it myself, my agent found it and acquired it for me," he replied. "I thought you might appreciate having a place in a countryside you know well, and that's also quite close to your father. It's a wedding present, my love."

Livia was stunned. She knew how much he enjoyed giving presents, the more extravagant the better pleased he was, but this was such a thoughtful, such a *caring* present. While she struggled to find words the front door opened, releasing a flood of golden lamplight across the gravel.

"Ah, and here's Boris," Alex said. He strode with her

to the open door. "You must meet Boris, my major-domo. You will find that he runs an admirably smooth household and you may safely leave all tedious domestic details in his more than capable hands."

"Put me down, then," Livia whispered.

"No," he said with a chuckle. "Not until I can put you where I want you . . ." His eyes narrowed and his lips curved in a suggestive smile. "I imagine you can guess where that is."

She felt herself blush as her body responded to the soft promise in his voice. She couldn't begin to offer a dignified greeting to the stately black-suited gentleman, who, seeming not to notice his new mistress's present position, bowed low and said in faintly accented English, "Congratulations, Princess Prokov."

"Thank you, Boris," she managed to murmur. She raised her head from Alex's shoulder and looked around the square, well-appointed hall. Stone-flagged floor, paneled walls, silver sconces. The staircase was a curving sweep of shallow steps that led up to a galleried landing.

Alex's eyes followed hers upwards and he chuckled. "Yes, we're wasting time."

"Everything is arranged as you ordered, Prince," Boris said with another bow.

"Good." Alex nodded with ill-concealed impatience. He turned to the stairs and strode up them, holding Livia tightly against him.

She could feel his heart beating fast against her breast and her own speeded in response. At the head of the stairs Alex strode around the gallery and stopped at a door. "Lift the latch, love, my hands are full."

Livia leaned sideways and lifted the latch. Alex kicked the door open and carried his burden within, kicking it shut behind him. He carried her to the bed, leaned down, and deposited her with a little thump in the middle of the coverlet. Then he stood looking down at her, his brilliant blue gaze burning as his eyes ran over her supine figure.

Livia licked suddenly dry lips. She felt the now familiar tightening in her belly, the pulsing in her loins, but there was something else too. A tiny tremor of apprehension blossomed deep within her as she felt the intent purpose in his gaze. In a short while her body would no longer belong to herself. Alex would possess her in every sense, and while she longed for it, she also now feared it.

"There's nothing to be afraid of, Livia," Alex said softly, reading the spark of uncertainty in her wide gray eyes as she looked up at him. He reached down and pulled her into a sitting position. "You can't make love in a hat." It was a sufficiently prosaic observation to break the intensity for a moment, and the spark of apprehension became a mere flicker and then died. Alex unpinned her hat from her curls and tossed it with a flick of his wrist onto a nearby chair. His eyes were hooded, his mouth a soft curve as he leaned over and began to take the pins from her hair, releasing the knot of curls to cascade to her shoulders. He ran his hands through the dark mass, a look of total concentration on his face.

"How I've been longing to do this since I first laid

eyes on you." He slipped his hand beneath the fall of her hair to palm her scalp, and then with aching slowness he brought his mouth to hers.

A tremor ran through her, a slow, spreading warmth, and she leaned into him, her lips parting beneath his as his tongue demanded entrance. And now that there was no need for restraint, Livia felt herself slipping away from the center of the self that she knew. She was aware only of her body. Her nipples burned against the fine lawn of her chemise beneath the tight-fitting jacket as her tongue joined in the dance with his, her own hands pushing up beneath the fair hair, feeling the shape of his head with renewed delight.

Alex drew his head back slowly, still clasping her neck. He looked at her face, framed in her tousled curls, the gray eyes heavy and languorous with passion, her lips kiss-reddened. "Stay right there, don't move."

He eased his dark silk coat off his shoulders, without taking his eyes off her. He unfastened his white silk cravat and tossed it to join his coat on the chest at the foot of the bed. His waistcoat followed, and as Livia watched in breathless suspense he unbuttoned the tiny studs of his white shirt.

Livia had felt the muscular power in his chest and shoulders, she had inhaled the warm fragrance of his skin, but nothing had prepared her for the sight of his naked torso. He turned to throw the shirt onto the chest and the muscles rippled down his long, lean back. When he turned towards her again, she gazed in delight at the narrow waist, the trail of dark hair disappearing into the waistband of his britches, and a gleam of amusement showed for a moment in his luminous eyes as they watched her expression.

Methodically, and without apparent haste, he took off his shoes and stockings. His fingers went to the buttons of his britches and Livia moistened her lips again. He stepped out of his britches and once again gave her his back as he put them with his other clothes on the chest.

Livia had glimpsed his sex before when she had pleasured him, but she hadn't really absorbed the sight. Now she drank in his back view, his firm buttocks, the slim hips, the long, muscular thighs, and the hard calves. And when he turned slowly to the bed again her eyes lingered on his concave belly and the erect flesh that rose from a curly nest of black hair.

Clothed, the prince was a most elegant figure. Naked, he was utterly magnificent. She held out her arms to him and he leaned over her, cupping her chin in the palm of his hand, bringing his mouth to hers. "Do I please you, my love?" he murmured.

"Oh, yes . . . oh, most definitely," Livia responded in a whisper. She stroked the smooth roundness of his bare shoulder, ran her hand down his arm, exploring the feel of his hard biceps. Prince Prokov was a man-about-town, an excellent dancer, an accomplished horseman, but he had the hard, athletic body of a man who knew how to wield a sword, a man who had known combat. Of course, Livia knew he had been a soldier, but until this moment, she had thought of his military service as more ceremonial than anything else. Feeling his strength beneath her hand as she explored his body, she knew how mistaken she had been.

"I think it's time to even the score," he said softly, taking her hand away from his hip, where it had been tracing the sharp, jutting bone of his pelvis. "I would look at you now, my love."

Bringing one knee onto the bed, he began to unfasten the braided buttons of her jacket.

He worked quickly and slipped the unbuttoned jacket off her shoulders. Her breasts swelled softly above the lacy bodice of her chemise and her nipples were hard and dark beneath the thin material. Alex slid a finger inside the neckline of the chemise, reaching down to the erect crown of her breast.

He slipped the straps of the chemise off her sloping shoulders and bared the opalescent mounds of her breasts. His hands cupped their fullness and his tongue traced a moist path over them, flicking insistently at her nipples. Livia gave a little gasp and he raised his head swiftly, but saw only a wondrous glow in her eyes.

He kissed the hollow of her throat as he found the hooks of her skirt. They flew apart with the ease of temptation and he half lifted her off the bed, holding her against him as he pushed the material away from her to gather in a heap at her ankles. "Lie back and let me rid you of these boots."

She obeyed, falling back on the bed, lifting her legs so

that he could unbutton her boots. He tossed them aside and then leaned over her again, letting his flat palm roam over her body, her warmed skin a pearly pink beneath the filmy fabric of her chemise. His flat palm stroked over her belly, pressing the white silk against her skin, molding her body with the fine material. Slowly now he ran his hand up beneath her chemise, palming the roundness of her knees, sliding up her silk-stockinged thighs. When he reached her lace-trimmed garters, he smiled.

"I think I need to see what I'm doing now," he murmured. He took the hem of the garment and drew it up over her thighs. Her skin leaped, and the secret recesses of her body moistened in anticipation of his touch. He unfastened her garters and unrolled her silk stockings inch by inch.

Livia was acutely aware that a mere strip of lawn kept her from complete nakedness. Her chemise was down to her waist and up to the apex of her thighs, and the air on her bared skin was a seductive, sensual breath. "Lift up," he instructed softly, patting her hip. She lifted her hips and he drew the last filmy shreds of covering away from her.

And then he spoke and his words shocked her. "Stand up," he commanded quietly. "It's time to dress you."

She stared at him, uncomprehending, and he took her hands and drew her upright and off the bed. "What are you doing?" she demanded.

"I'll show you," he said. "Stand still for me and let me

look at you properly." He took a step back, running a long, lascivious look from her head to her toes. "Mmm," he murmured. "It doesn't really need any improvement, but one or two minor additions might add a little spice. Close your eyes now."

Livia was too stunned and bewildered to argue. She simply closed her eyes and waited, standing naked in the middle of the chamber. She heard him moving around, opening something, and then felt him come back to her.

"Keep your eyes closed." His fingers were in her hair, threading something into her curls. Her eyelids fluttered and he said again, "Keep them shut. I haven't finished yet."

She felt something cold and heavy go around her neck and her hands fluttered up to feel what it was. But he seized them swiftly. "Not yet."

Something circled first one wrist and then the other, and then she felt a pinch on both her earlobes. "What are you doing?" she whispered.

"In a minute," he responded. He put his hands on her shoulders and moved her forward. "All right, now you can open your eyes."

Livia's eyes flew open and her mouth opened at the same time. She gazed at her image in the long cheval glass. Stark naked in the soft lamplight, but adorned with bloodred rubies. A three-stranded collar circled her neck, a silver fillet studded with the gems twined in her curls, two ruby studs glowed in her ears, and her wrists were banded with two strands apiece.

"Dear God," she murmured, awed by her image. "I look like a pagan sacrifice."

Alex laughed. "They really do suit you. I debated between diamonds and rubies, but I think that red fire is wonderful with your hair and eyes." He stood behind her, sliding his hands around her, holding her breasts on his palms. "Now watch," he said.

Livia gazed into the mirror as he began to touch her again, his hands moving over her body. She saw her nipples peak anew beneath a flickering fingertip, and saw her skin take on a soft glow as arousal built once more. Her legs shifted on the richly hued carpet as his hands cupped her pubic mound, and she leaned back against him with a soft moan. His fingers parted the curly tangle covering her sex and she saw her eyes open wide in sudden surprised delight when his knowing touch found the little nub of flesh that hardened instantly beneath his caress. It was both shockingly decadent and intensely exciting to watch her own arousal as she stood naked but for the rubies glowing against her white skin. Her eyes were heavy, her countenance somehow soft, her parted lips red and moist.

Her buttocks and thighs tensed as the coil wound ever tighter and his touch grew more insistent, bringing her to a climax of delight that was even more powerful than the first time. She leaned back against him, her pelvis thrust forward towards the mirror, her legs opened for him. She could see the moisture gleaming on her thighs, the rosy pink of her sex, and she let her head fall back onto his shoulder and gave herself to the pulsing glory that filled her.

Alex held her up as her knees buckled. He slid a hand beneath her knees and lifted her, carrying her swiftly to the bed. He laid her down, urgently now, his touch no longer delicate as he knelt astride her and lifted her bottom on the shelf of his palms. With one thrust he drove into her still pulsating body, moist and ready for him. His entrance was smooth, her body unresisting.

Livia gazed up at him, still lost in those moments of glory, but she was aware that her body was on the brink of something else, something even more wonderful. On the periphery of her mind she realized she had expected pain, but there was none. A sense of fullness, of something opening deep inside her, and then only this delightful fluid rhythm.

Alex kissed her eyelids, the corners of her mouth, easing ever deeper within as her body opened for him. And only when he felt her tighten around him, saw the tears of joy start in her eyes, did he give in to his own need. He drove hard and fast and she threw her arms up over her head in a glorious abandonment to sheer delight, her hips rising with his every thrust until it was over, and they collapsed in a sweat-soaked tangle of limbs.

Alex rolled onto the bed beside her, one arm flung over his eyes, his heart bounding against his ribs. His other hand rested on Livia's belly. He laughed softly and turned his head to look at her. "So, my pagan sacrifice, all bedecked in rubies, how did it feel to be laid upon the altar of love?"

"Wonderful," she whispered, stroking his damp hair away from his brow. "And I thank you."

He propped himself on one elbow and looked down at her, slipping one finger into the ruby collar encircling her throat. "You may thank me for your wedding present, if you like, but not for the loving," he said softly. "That was a shared gift."

"Then I thank you for the rubies," Livia said, holding up an arm to examine the bracelet. "I think I shall wear them every time we make love. It might not be as good if I take them off."

"I doubt that," he said with a laugh. "In my experience it can only get better. But it would please me if you keep them on for the time being."

"Certainly, my prince." She rolled against him, settling her head in the damp hollow of his shoulder. "But now I'm very sleepy for some reason."

"It's the usual effect," he said, moving his hand down her turned flank, coming to rest on the swell of her hips. "Sleep, then."

He lay listening to her breathing become slow and even as she slid into sleep. And at last he felt he could answer the question he had posed to himself at the altar that morning. Was he offering her a fair exchange? Most definitely.

∽◈∽

Livia lay watching Alex through half-closed eyes. He was standing by the frost-glazed window, naked, beautifully so, and quite unaware of her covert observation. It was morning but the winter light was dim, obscured by the frost on the windowpanes, and the room was lit by the fire and a branched candelabrum on the bedside table.

Alex seemed to be looking at something outside, his hands braced on the frames at either side of the window. She had grown accustomed to his naked body in the last few days, but she still gazed greedily at the long sweep of his back, the ripple of muscle in the broad shoulders, the taut muscular buttocks, the slim thighs.

"What are you looking at?"

He turned from the casement as she'd hoped he would and she drank in the sight of him, her eyes lingering on his flat stomach, the broad chest and tapering hips. His sex was for the moment quiescent, nestled in the thick tangle of dark hair at the base of his belly, and she smiled a little thinking how quickly she could arouse it to upstanding life.

"I might ask you the same question," he said with amusement. "Do I still please you, ma'am?"

"You know you do." She hitched herself onto one elbow. "Come closer, there's one little adjustment I would make to the scenery."

He obliged, coming to stand beside the bed, his hands resting on his hips as he looked down at her. His penis stirred and when Livia reached a lazy hand to enclose it the shaft sprang to life instantly at her touch. She chuckled with satisfaction. "Much better."

"Have a little pity, my dear girl, I've barely had time to recover from the last marathon," he protested without much conviction. "I appear to have taken a wanton to wife."

"You have only yourself to blame," Livia murmured, increasing the pressure of her stroking caresses. "You're too expert a teacher in the arts of loving, my prince." She edged sideways on the bed so that her head was on a level with the part of his anatomy that held her interest, and delicately flicked his penis with the tip of her tongue. The candlelight caught the rubies at her throat and set the studs in her ears afire.

Alex tried to resist the teasing play but failed miserably. With a low groan of submission he came down on the bed beside her. "After this, you insatiable wanton, you are getting up out of that bed. I don't think you've put your feet to the floor once in the last three days."

Livia laughed delightedly and rolled on top of him. "I feel like doing it this way," she declared, straddling his hips, running her hands over his concave belly, a fingertip tickling his navel. Her braceleted wrists flashed fire. She pushed her fingers through the cluster of gold hair on his chest and played with his nipples before lowering her mouth to his, taking control of the kiss, nibbling on his lips, demanding entrance with her tongue.

Alex held her hips firmly as she kissed him deeply, and when she guided him inside her open, welcoming body he moved his hand to touch her at the exquisitely sensitive point of their fusion. Her body bucked with the jolt of sensation and she bit her lip, leaning back to hold her ankles as she moved her hips in a circle around him.

She wanted it to last but the fever of passion was too high and greedily she reached for the heights, giving herself to the knowing touch of his fingers until she fell through the bottom of the world with a cry of triumph.

Alex pulled her down on top of him, holding her tightly, their sweat mingling as the pulsing aftermath of shared climax slowed and ceased. He reached down and patted her bottom. "It's time to get up now, my love, and reenter the world. There are things to do."

Livia groaned and rolled sideways onto the bed. "I need to sleep again. Such an extremity of pleasure exhausts me."

"Then sleep for a few moments." Alex swung himself out of bed, enviably energized after that bout of activity. "I'm going to order a bath and a late breakfast."

But Livia had closed her eyes and was already drifting into the trancelike sleep that always followed their lovemaking.

Alex shook his head in mock exasperation and pulled on a brocade dressing gown as he went to the door. He opened it and called for Boris, who appeared on the landing in a very few moments.

"Yes, Your Highness?"

"A bath, in fact two baths. One for the princess in here, and one for me in my dressing room. Send the maid up to attend to the princess; you may assist me. Oh, and tell the cook to prepare breakfast. We'll take it in the dining room."

"Yes, sir." Boris turned back to the stairs to execute his commissions. It had been three days since his master had brought his bride to the lodge, and in those three days neither of them had set foot outside the bedchamber.

"Oh, and Boris . . . ?"

"Sir?"

"What did the messenger bring?" Alex had been watching the stranger's arrival from the window before he'd been so pleasantly interrupted by Livia.

"A verbal message, sir, from London. To be delivered only to Your Highness. He's refreshing himself in the kitchen until you should be ready to receive him."

Alex nodded and returned to the bedchamber. Livia was still asleep in the tangle of bedclothes, the rich glow of the gems a strange contrast to the tumbled bed and the abandoned sprawl of her limbs. He watched her sleep for a moment or two, smiling to himself. What an extraordinarily passionate woman she was. He'd suspected some unusual depths but nothing like what she'd revealed in the last three days. He was a very lucky man, he decided, reluctantly turning away from the sleeper and heading into the adjoining dressing room.

It had a bed for those nights when the master of the house came home the worse for wear and out of consideration for his lady's sensibilities did not sleep in the marital bed. Or for those nights when the lady chose to sleep alone. Such occasions, he was resolved, would be few and far between in his own marriage.

A knock on the corridor door heralded the arrival of a manservant with a steaming ewer of hot water that he set on the dresser beside the bowl. He hung an armful of fresh towels on the rack. "Bath's on its way, m'lord. Will I sharpen the razor?" He gestured to the strop that hung on the wall.

"Yes, please." Alex went to the window that looked out on a small garden white with hoarfrost. His mind returned to the messenger. Only two people knew where he was at present. Michael Michaelovitch and the rough-and-ready Tatarinov. Michael knew in case there were messages from the czar. Alexander Prokov was his emperor's servant and must be accessible at all times. Tatarinov knew in case an emergency arose with the small group of plotters and Alex needed to be informed. Two strings to the same bow. But which string had loosed which arrow now?

Well, he would find out soon enough, but not until he'd washed away the residue of sex and sleep and tangled sheets.

Boris came in, a troop of servants bearing a porcelain hip bath and jugs of hot water, and Alex concentrated on the pleasures of hot water.

Livia, next door, awoke dreamily at the sound of pouring water. She sat up, blinking in the bright light of sun and frost. A maid whom she'd never seen before was filling a hip bath before the fire, another hanging towels on a rack in front of the fire to warm. Lavender and verbena scented the air and Livia realized suddenly how sleep-sodden and rank with pleasure she must be. She thrust aside the coverlet and swung her legs to the ground.

"Lord, how I need that bath." She stretched, pushing her tangled hair away from her face, wondering what kind of madness had kept her enthralled in this chamber for three whole days, oblivious of the ordinary needs of ordinary life. She shook her head in mystification and stood up.

"The water's just right, m'lady, if you'd like to step in," one of the maids said.

"Thank you." She reached up to untwine the ruby-studded fillet from her hair and laid it reverently on the dresser before unclasping the necklace. Both maids were staring at her in wide-eyed astonishment as she divested herself of the rubies, and she could hardly blame them. She knew well enough what an extraordinary sight it made. "What's your name?" she asked, sliding the bracelets onto the table and turning back to the bath.

"Doris, ma'am . . . and this be Ethel."

"Doris . . . Ethel . . ." Livia nodded in greeting and stepped into the tub. She was accustomed to seeing to her own ablutions, but today she made no objections as the two maids washed her hair, rinsed it in vinegar to give luster to the dark curls, handed her the verbena-scented soap, and sprinkled lavender oil into the water. When she was ready to get out Doris held up a warmed towel and Ethel took another to dry her hair. It was all rather pleasant, Livia thought. This life of a princess.

"What gown will you wear, m'lady?" Doris had opened the armoire and was examining its contents.

"Gown?" Livia realized with a shock that she had no idea what the armoire contained apart from the red driving habit she'd worn here. She didn't remember packing a portmanteau before leaving the vicarage. Perhaps that could be excused, but surely Ellie or Nell would have reminded her. But maybe they'd done it for her. Wrapping the towel securely around her, she stepped over to the armoire. No familiar garments met her eye.

"This one's pretty, m'lady." Doris drew out a checked muslin.

"It certainly is," Livia agreed, appreciating the elegant cut. "But unfortunately it's not mine."

"Yes, it is." Alex appeared in the doorway to the dressing room, dressed himself now in riding britches and top boots. "Your friends and some seamstress, a Miss Claire, they tell me, put the wardrobe together for you." He came into the room. "Another wedding present. I think . . . at least, I hope, you will find everything to your liking. I thought Aurelia and Cornelia would know your tastes."

How many wedding presents did this extraordinary husband of hers consider enough? At some point she would feel at a disadvantage if this outpouring of largesse went on for much longer. "It's true, they would," she said, turning to him with a rueful smile. "But . . . forgive me, Alex, I think you've given me enough."

"Why?" He took her hands, swinging them gently. "I am your husband, am I not allowed now to give you presents?"

"Oh, yes . . . yes, of course you are," she said with a flood of warmth. He obviously couldn't be reformed. She stood on tiptoe to kiss him. "You are the most generous man. Let's see what we have here." She turned and dived into the armoire to examine its contents for herself. "Oh, I love velvet." She drew out a dressing gown of rich tawny velvet. "I could wear this."

"No," he said firmly. "This evening, yes. But it's the middle of the morning, sweeting, and I would have you dressed. Wear the checked muslin." He leaned in and kissed her. "Come downstairs for breakfast when you're ready."

He strode from the room before she could waylay him and went rapidly downstairs, making his way directly to the kitchen. The man he'd seen ride in earlier was sitting at the table, eating his way through a platter of sirloin.

He jumped to his feet at the prince's appearance, wiping his mouth with the back of his hand. "Your pardon, Highness." He spoke in Russian.

"I'm sorry to disturb your breakfast," Alex said pleasantly. "Walk with me outside." He strode to the kitchen door, opening it onto the beautiful but frigid morning.

The man followed him into the kitchen yard. Alex walked away from the house and through a small gate into a deserted pasture. Frost crackled beneath his boots.

"Give me your message."

The man looked around, tightening his muffler around his neck against the cold, and blew on his hands before speaking in Russian. "I'm to tell you that our little father is preparing to leave his nest. He is sending his army against Finland and then on to occupy Sweden. It is said he will accompany the army on its initial foray." He had to walk quickly to keep up with the prince, who was striding around the perimeter of the meadow.

Only Tatarinov would have sent such a message, and it was typical of the man that he would not risk committing his words to paper, even though on the surface they seemed innocuous enough. But only on the surface. If the czar was going out with the army, even though he would not lead his troops on the battlefield, then he would be accessible, vulnerable to an accident. Much more so than in the palaces of St. Petersburg. Tatarinov was telling him that if they were going to act, then this was the opportunity.

Alex turned back to the house, the man at his heels.

"Is there an answer, Highness?" The man was half running to keep up with him.

"No," Alex said. There would be nothing to connect him to this messenger or to the message. "Return to your master as soon as you're fed and rested. You have no further business here."

He walked back into the kitchen without giving the messenger another glance. He could not afford the slightest taint. He would put no words of his in another's mouth, there was no knowing whose ears they'd find.

"Everything in order, Highness?" Boris turned from the Welsh dresser where he was arranging silver chargers.

"Yes, but I have new instructions for you," Alex said.

Livia was coming down the stairs as he emerged from the kitchen into the hall. She was wearing the muslin checked in pink and gray squares, a darker pink ribbon confining the material beneath her breasts. Her hair was loose, still a little damp, and as a result curlier than usual. Lavender and verbena scented the air around her.

"How wonderful it is to feel so fresh," she said, jumping down the last two steps. "After such a rank and tumbling orgy." She flung her arms around him and kissed his neck. "Oh, and you smell of frost and lemon. Lovely. Which way to the dining room? I'm famished."

"This way." How he loved this innocent exuberance, the natural warmth of her nature. And sometimes it sent a cold shiver through his heart at how easily such openness could be hurt. He put an arm over her shoulders and ushered her into the dining parlor.

"Oh, what a pretty room," Livia declared, going to the big bay window that overlooked the gravel sweep at the front of the house. "Just where are we in the Forest?"

"I believe it's called Sway," he said. "Come and sit down, Livia, before I faint away from lack of sustenance."

She laughed. "More of your dramatic exaggeration."

She took the chair he held out for her. "What do we have?"

Alex went to the sideboard and lifted the lids of the chafing dishes. "Eggs, bacon, mushrooms, kidneys. But also caviar, pickled herring, smoked trout, and meat dumplings. What may I bring you?"

"Would you mind dreadfully if I just ate what I'm used to, just for this morning?" she asked. "It's just that I'm so hungry I don't think I'm ready to branch out yet."

He laughed and began to spoon food onto a plate. "You may eat whatever you please, dear girl. Boris will always provide for me. But one day, I recommend you try the caviar."

"I've only had it once or twice, and I think I liked it," Livia said a little doubtfully. "But I'm not sure about breakfast."

"Try that." He set a laden plate in front of her and returned to the sideboard to help himself.

Livia poured coffee for them both and then attacked her breakfast. She glanced once in astonishment at the plate Alex brought to the table, wondering how on earth anyone could eat pickled herring at the best of times, let alone first thing in the morning. But she would get used to it, she supposed, watching as he sliced a loaf of black bread and piled it with herring.

"You would prefer this, I'm sure," Alex said, catching her glance. He passed her a rack of wheat toast. "Don't worry, my dear, I don't expect you to turn Russian overnight. I'd like you to try some of our delicacies once in a while, but only in the interests of experiment."

"Oh, I'm well aware of the advantages of trying Russian delicacies once in a while," she said with a mischievous up-from-under look. "One of them I find particularly delicious . . . a little salty . . . a little—"

"*Enough*," he stated, his dancing eyes belying the ferocity of his tone. "If you continue in this incorrigible fashion, I'll not be able to take you into polite society. You're supposed to be a vicar's daughter."

"I am a vicar's daughter," Livia said, spreading jam on her toast. "But I don't have to be a prude as part of the bargain."

"That you are most definitely not," he said. "But, my love, I think it's time to bring this interlude to a close. Are you ready to return to London?"

Livia looked at him curiously. "It's rather sudden, isn't it?"

He gave an easy shrug. "I'm anxious to see how the work on the house has progressed. The architect promised it would all be finished two days ago, but you can't be sure unless you're there to crack the whip . . . so . . . ?" He raised an eyebrow in query.

Livia chewed her toast. Returning to London need not bring the idyll to an end. And in all truth, she knew they couldn't continue to live as they had been for the last three days. And in truth she was eager to see her house, to see it in its finished state. And in truth she was more than eager to start her married life in good earnest.

"When do you wish to leave?"

"Would noon be too soon?"

Livia nearly dropped her fork. "But it's already eleven o'clock. How could we possibly be ready to leave in an hour? There's packing to do and—"

"Boris is already taking care of those details," Alex said calmly, spearing a fillet of smoked trout. He squeezed lemon on it, seemingly quite unperturbed by the host of details that loomed in front of Livia. "If we change horses every hour we'll be in Cavendish Square before midnight."

He looked up from his plate. "In Russia, my dear, we're accustomed to moving entire households on a whim and at the drop of a bonnet. Boris knows exactly what to do and he'll be waiting for us when we arrive."

"Oh." She couldn't come up with a more expansive comment.

"So, can you be ready by noon?"

Livia opened her hands in a gesture of acceptance. "I don't see why not," she said. If a Russian could do it, she could.

Chapter Sixteen

THEY ARRIVED IN CAVENDISH SQUARE late that night, changing horses every hour. The post chaise carrying Boris, the cook, and the maid, Ethel, with the luggage piled on its roof, had started ahead of them and when, at close to midnight, Livia climbed stiffly out of the chaise, Boris, as Alex had promised, opened the front door to them. In order to make such good time they too must have changed horses at least every hour, Livia reflected, and unlike herself and Alex could not have stopped to stretch their legs and take refreshment at the various changing posts. She couldn't help reflecting on the expense of such a hasty journey, taken on what seemed like a mere whim. But then she was her father's daughter when all was said and done.

"Your bedchamber is prepared, Princess, and Ethel is waiting for you." Despite his long journey and the lateness of the hour, Boris was as immaculate and dignified as ever.

"Thank you," she responded with automatic courtesy, but her eyes swept the hall, noting the changes, all changes she had authorized, but somehow the house felt alien. It was too perfect.

Castigating herself for being nonsensical, Livia walked into the salon. It was gorgeous, absolute perfection. The portrait of Sophia Lacey had been cleaned and stood out above the mantelpiece, her blue eyes dominating the room.

Livia walked back into the hall and across to the dining room. It was the same there. Perfect, beautiful, too much so. Until she looked up at the fresco and her sense of humor returned. Nothing had really changed. The neglected old lady in Cavendish Square had been beautified, that was all. The essential spirit of the house was still there.

"Is something wrong?" Alex spoke quietly behind her. He had been watching her, a puzzled frown in his eye.

"No, no, nothing at all," she said. "I'm just not used to seeing the house so radiantly flawless. It doesn't feel lived in at all, more like a museum." She shrugged out of her pelisse. "Let's go into my parlor."

Alex followed her into the parlor and watched as she looked around almost warily and then visibly relaxed. This room, at least, was exactly as she had left it, and it welcomed her with a fire in the hearth and lit lamps.

"Where are Morecombe and the twins?" She asked the question casually, but she realized that what was missing in the welcome of this house were its ancient retainers.

"In their apartments I expect; it's very late." He went over to the console table, where a trio of decanters stood. "Boris knows I enjoy a glass of port at the end of the evening." He lifted one of the decanters. "Will you join me?"

"Yes, please," Livia said. "But why would Boris put port for you in *my* parlor?"

He turned in surprise. "Do you object?"

"I don't know," she said candidly. "This is my house, my parlor . . . it feels strange having someone else order things in it. You have the library as your particular room. I supposed I assumed that Boris would arrange things there to your liking . . . I didn't think he'd come in here . . . somehow," she finished with a rather feeble shrug. It sounded so grudging and ungrateful, and she was neither of those things, but she couldn't lose this strange sense of violation.

She wanted Morecombe and the twins to make everything seem normal, but of course it was far too late for them to be up. They'd be in their usual places in the morning, and once she'd had a good night's sleep she'd stop feeling so strange. Or so Livia told herself.

Alex poured port and handed her a glass before responding. "I'm sorry if Boris trod on your toes, Livia. He was only following my orders. I had not thought any part of this house would be barred to me."

"But it's not," she said, taking the glass. "Indeed, it's not, Alex. Of course you're welcome in this room any time you wish, it's just that it's always been mine . . . mine and Ellie's and Nell's," she added miserably. "I need time to get used to the idea that things have changed."

"Used to the idea of being married?" He raised his eyebrows.

"No, not that. Used to the idea of sharing my house with you," she stated flatly. "You and your servants. It feels strange, but I will grow accustomed to it, Alex." She put a hand on his arm. "Forgive me, it sounds irrational, and indeed I can't explain . . . just give me a few days, *please,* love."

"Of course," he said, placing a hand over hers as it tightened anxiously on his arm. "I hadn't realized the house meant so much to you." He had, of course, but he hadn't expected this resistance, hadn't expected her to see him as an invader. "Go up to bed now. You're tired. We'll sort all this out in the morning."

Livia felt a sudden chill. "Are you not coming to bed too?"

"I'll follow shortly, but I have a few things to attend to first." He tipped her chin with a forefinger. "Have no fear, sweeting. You'll not sleep without me." He kissed the corner of her mouth, then took the empty glass from her. "Go now, it's been a long day. Ethel is waiting for you."

And where were Hester and Jemmy? Daisy, of course, was at Mount Street with Aurelia and Franny, but why did she have this feeling of being in someone else's house? Accepting someone else's hospitality? She had left Morecombe and the twins, Jemmy and Hester with the dogs . . . and where were they? Why hadn't they hurled themselves at her in a barking frenzy when she'd walked through the door?

"What have you done with Tristan and Isolde?" she demanded, suddenly afraid of the answer.

"I instructed Boris to bed them down in the mews for tonight," Alex told her. "I couldn't endure their yapping . . . not after such a long journey. You may let them in tomorrow, Livia. Bear with me, please." His eyes were grave, but there was a flicker in them that Livia recognized from once before. A hint of flint, of resolution. It had chilled her the first time she'd seen it, and it had the same effect now.

But she was too tired to deal with confrontation tonight. The dogs would be quite safe and comfortable in the mews. In the morning she would be renewed and she would tackle these issues before they became too contentious.

"I'll go up, then. You'll come soon?" She turned to the door.

"Quite soon."

Alone, Alex drank his port and swore softly. *What had upset her so much?* The house had been refurbished exactly according to Livia's instructions. She'd made all the decisions and to a large extent supervised the work. But perhaps it was inevitable that she'd have a proprietorial feeling for the house. Unfortunately so did he, and he needed to establish his position, draw the lines in the sand immediately, otherwise matters would become very confused.

He refilled his glass and made his way to the salon. The elegant room settled around him as he stood in the double doorway. Sophia Lacey's amazing blue eyes looked directly at him. He raised his glass in a silent toast and an equally silent promise. *One of these days he would learn her secrets.* He was convinced that the house would have something to tell him. There was too much of Sophia's spirit in its very fabric for it not to reveal something of the kind of woman she was.

"I'll lock up for the night, sir?" Boris spoke softly behind him.

"Oh, yes . . . do so, thank you." Alex turned away from the searching eyes. "Did you talk to the old man?"

"He was already abed when we arrived, sir. He came out in his nightshirt waving a blunderbuss as soon as I'd opened the front door." Boris looked a trifle pained at the memory of this reception. "And those noisy terriers too." He shook his head. "But the old man didn't fuss once he knew the princess was on her way here. He went back to bed."

"And the terriers are in the mews?"

"Aye, sir. Quite snug they are. The lad Jemmy took them off, says he'll sleep there with them."

"Good. The princess is very fond of them, she wouldn't want them upset and uncomfortable. Good night then, Boris." He nodded a farewell and took his glass into the library, which Livia had designated as his own private apartment.

It was a pleasant room dominated by a massive oak

desk, on which were laid invitingly a leather blotting pad, a tray of quills, a fine leather inkpot. Floor-to-ceiling bookshelves were filled with volumes that Livia had told him she and her friends hadn't had a chance to examine. In fact, this particular apartment had been left in its original neglect until the recent renovation. Heavy velvet curtains now hung at the long windows that looked onto the small walled garden at the rear of the house, and matching velvet cushions were scattered with apparent randomness on the leather chairs and sofa. A small fire burned in the grate, and fresh candles glowed from the wall sconces.

In the short time he'd had before their arrival Boris had somehow managed to make it seem as if the house's inhabitants had merely been out for the evening.

Alex went to the desk, the one piece of furniture he had chosen carefully for himself. He'd supervised its installation one afternoon after Livia had gone down to Ringwood to prepare for their wedding. One side of the desk held a series of small drawers and one key opened them all. He took the key from his inside pocket and sat down in the leather desk chair. He opened the top drawer. At first sight it was empty, but when he reached inside and pressed a small spring the back of the drawer slid back to reveal a hidden space.

Alex took out the velvet pouches it contained and poured the contents on the blotter. Each drawer revealed its hidden space and the contents of the pouches glittered on the desk as he sorted through them, reassuring himself that the treasure was intact. The work that had brought him to London was an expensive proposition.

He replaced the gems in their pouches and locked them away again, then he leaned back in his chair, staring into the fire. The czar had told him after the Treaty of Tilsit that Bonaparte had suggested to him that he should turn his territorial ambitions towards the Baltic. What had Bonaparte said exactly? Something about the lovely ladies of St. Petersburg must not hear from their palaces the cannons of the Swedes. Something along those lines, and it had certainly galvanized the Russian emperor into this foray against the Swedish province of Finland.

A victory over the Swedes would be as cold and barren a triumph as the country itself, Alex thought with a flicker of derision. If the czar thought such a victory would appease his detractors in St. Petersburg, he was very much mistaken. And for those who were prepared to go further than mere talk of revolt, it would provide opportunity.

He drummed his fingers on the desk for a minute, lost in thought. Then he pushed back his chair and rose wearily to his feet. He snuffed the candles and left the library. Boris had left an oil lamp lit on the hall table together with a carrying candle. Alex lit the latter before turning out the lamp and trod softly up the stairs, the light throwing his shadow on the wall ahead of him.

He went first into his own bedchamber, where fresh candles burned on the mantelpiece and a fire glowed in the hearth. Livia had given much thought to the redecorating of this apartment and the blue and silver bed hangings were certainly handsome. He set his carrying candle on the mantel and stood still, absorbing the atmosphere of the room.

His father, as the master of the house, would surely have occupied this chamber. Was there a hint of that austere and distant man? Some breath of his spirit lurking in the shadows? And just how had that vibrant woman in the salon connected with the lean aesthete that Alex had known?

Had they made love in this room? Tumbled in the great canopied bed? Laughed and tickled and teased?

Alex shook his head impatiently. The father that he knew could not possibly have indulged in such lusty romping. And the woman who had a lewd fresco above her dining room table surely couldn't have found anything to please her in the stiff arms of his father.

He undressed and put on a brocade dressing gown, then softly opened the door that led into his wife's bedchamber. A candle was guttering on the night table and the ashy embers of the fire threw off a little warmth. But Livia was a small, motionless shape buried in the feather mattress beneath a thick quilted coverlet.

He trod softly to the bed and stood for a moment listening to her deep, even breathing. She was sound asleep, her lashes dark half-moons on her faintly flushed cheeks, and he thought she looked much younger in sleep. He wouldn't risk waking her. He turned away and went back to his own room, but he left the adjoining door ajar.

He awoke in the morning to whispering caresses, his body stirring beneath the coverlets under unmistakable stimulation. He lay still, trying to keep his breathing even as if he was still asleep, while Livia worked her magic. She chuckled softly and murmured indistinctly, "Don't pretend to be asleep, my prince."

He pushed a hand beneath the covers and twined his fingers in the curls spread across his belly. "Come up before you suffocate."

"I'm unlikely to do that," she responded in the same muffled tones. "And I'm enjoying myself. Unless I much mistake the matter, so are you."

"Indubitably," he agreed, and ceased his halfhearted protest.

"By the way, you broke your promise," Livia declared as she emerged rumpled and flushed from her exertions in the warm dark of the bedclothes. "Why did you sleep in here last night?"

"Oh, my love, you were sleeping so soundly," he said, seizing her under the arms and pulling her up so that she lay across his chest. "I was afraid to wake you."

"I doubt you would have done," she said, kissing the point of his chin. "But I wouldn't have minded anyway."

"Maybe not." He took her face in his hands, pushing his fingers into the tangle of her hair. "I'll not make the same mistake again."

"You had better not if you value your pleasure," she declared, kissing the corner of his mouth.

"Is that a threat, madam?" He rolled her onto her back beside him. "I don't take kindly to threats." He moved over her, propping himself on his elbows as he looked down at her countenance. Light danced in her eyes and she stretched her arms above her head, grasping the bed rail.

"Do your worst, my prince."

"You might regret that invitation," he said, pushing her thighs apart with his knee.

"Oh, I doubt that," she murmured.

∞

Livia was still in a lighthearted mood when she came downstairs, dressed for the day, an hour later. She headed directly to the kitchen, intent on finding Morecombe and the twins, and pushed open the door onto a scene that bore little or no resemblance to the kitchen she was used to.

Alex's cook was at the range, stirring pots; two minions were chopping vegetables; an unknown scullery maid was scrubbing pots at the deep sink. Of Morecombe, Ada, and Mavis there was no sign.

Livia had not formally met the cook. There hadn't been the opportunity in the lodge. They had not starved themselves in their three days of seclusion, however, so she'd eaten his food, and she certainly had no complaints. Although privately she considered Ada and Mavis to be at least as accomplished if not more so.

"Good morning," she said loudly when it seemed

that no one was going to pay her any attention. And then she remembered that Alex had said the cook was half French and half Russian, so perhaps he didn't speak English. "*Bonjour,*" she said.

The cook turned from his stirring and looked at her as if he couldn't believe his eyes. "*Bonjour, princesse,*" he said after a second's hesitation. There was a distinct question mark to the greeting and Livia began to feel unwelcome in her own kitchen. Before she could say anything further, however, Boris came into the kitchen behind her. He looked about as flustered as the unflappable Boris could ever look and she guessed he had come running at the possibility of a disturbance to his smoothly run household.

"Princess, good morning," he said, bowing low. "How may I help you?"

"You can tell me where I'll find my staff," she said, keeping her tone moderate. Boris would have been obeying his master's orders, he didn't act unilaterally.

"They're keeping to their apartments, Your Highness," he said. "As I understand it, Morecombe and the women feel that they should take orders only from you."

"I see." Livia could feel her temper rising. "Did you perhaps presume to give them orders this morning, Boris?"

"I am the majordomo, Princess," he said, seemingly unperturbed by the flash in her eye. "It is my job to see to the running of the household and the ordering of the staff."

"Not in this instance, Boris," she said crisply. "More-combe, Ada, and Mavis are not subject to your authority. I want that understood right now."

"I would need to talk to Prince Prokov—"

"That will not be necessary," she interrupted him. "I will talk to him myself." She turned on her heel. At the door she said, "I would like my dogs returned to the house, please. And I am assuming that Hester and Jemmy are still employed under this roof?"

"The lad's with the dogs, madam. The girl's working with the laundress."

Livia could see nothing to complain about there, at least not at the moment; there were bigger battles to fight and at least they hadn't been turned off. "See that Jemmy brings my dogs back without delay," she said, and left the kitchen.

In the hall she paused. Where was Alex likely to be? He hadn't said he was going out this morning, so she made her way to the library and opened the door. "Alex, are you here? I need to talk to you." She came into the room and then stopped. "Oh, I'm sorry, I didn't realize you had a visitor."

Alex felt a stab of irritation. He was not accustomed to being walked in upon without so much as a knock. But he controlled his annoyance and said pleasantly, "My dear, may I introduce Paul Tatarinov. Tatarinov, my wife, Princess Prokov."

Livia offered the nod of a bow. Instinctively she didn't care for the man. He had a rough edge to him. His clothes were fine enough, but they sat ill on his bulky frame. His lips moved in the semblance of a smile as he bowed to her, revealing crooked and yellowing teeth. The skin of his hands looked chapped and rough. He was the very antithesis of her husband, so elegant in an olive-green coat, dove-gray britches, an emerald pin in his immaculately tied snowy cravat. His hands as her body knew full well were smooth as silk.

"When you have a moment, I'd like to talk to you," she said, and slipped quietly from the room. She had seen the flash of irritation in his eyes even though it had been quickly disguised.

He had the right to expect his privacy, she acknowledged, going into the parlor. She would grow accustomed to the idea that not every room in the house was hers to enter at will, but it galled her nevertheless. She reached for the bell pull to ask for coffee and then hesitated. Who would answer the bell?

With sudden decision, she stalked out of the parlor and made her way to the back stairs. Morecombe, his wife, and her sister had a small apartment tucked away on the second floor. She and her friends had never ventured anywhere near it before; it had always seemed sacrosanct. But now she had no qualms. She knocked vigorously on the door.

"Who be there?" Morecombe's voice rasped from within.

"It's me, Morecombe. Lady Livia."

The door opened the merest crack. "Oh, 'tis you," he

said as he always did when he opened a door to her. His rheumy old eyes were suspicious, however, and he kept the opening at a mere crack.

"May I come in?" she asked.

"Oh, let the lass in, Morecombe." Ada took the door and pulled it wide. "Come you in. We've a need to talk to you."

"Yes, I can understand that," Livia said, stepping into the room. It was a parlor, hot as Hades, with a huge fire blazing up the chimney. A lug pole hung over the fire with a kettle hooked to it. The room was crammed with pieces of furniture, knickknacks, overstuffed cushions, and china figurines. It was such an unlikely space to be inhabited by the angular, pallid twins and the monosyllabic Morecombe that she was taken aback.

"What a pleasant room," she managed finally.

"Looks like you could do with a cup o' tea," Mavis said from a shadowy corner where she'd been sitting with Puss, the house cat, who jumped up from her lap with an indignant yowl as she stood up, brushing off her apron.

"Thank you," Livia said gratefully. She bent to stroke the cat who was now twisting herself around her ankles. "How are you, Puss?"

"She's right enough," Ada said shortly, going to a Welsh dresser and taking down cups from the hooks. Mavis was pouring water from the kettle into a pot.

"I'm sorry," Livia said, "but I don't know what you've been told . . . what's happened since I left."

"We're not wanted no more," Morecombe declared.

"That Boris fellow told me straight, not an hour past. Too old, not suited to the new master's way . . . out to grass. That's us."

"And it ain't right, Lady Livia," Ada said. "Lady Sophia, she made it all clear in that will of 'ers. We was to stay an' work as long as it suited us."

"Yes, I know." Livia perched on a chair. "Thank you, Mavis." She took the offered cup. "I haven't had a chance to talk to Prince Prokov as yet, but I will straighten it out, I promise." She sipped the tea.

"Well, I'm not cookin' along a that Frenchie," Ada declared. "'Tis my kitchen. Always 'as been . . . mine an' our Mavis's."

"Aye," Mavis agreed. "'Twas good enow fer Lady Sophia, I reckon 'tis good enow for the likes o' some foreigner."

And that foreigner happens to be my husband. But Livia held her tongue. "I don't think my husband fully understands the situation . . . the history . . ." she said. "I'll talk with him as soon as he's free and I'm sure we can sort this out to everyone's satisfaction." She finished her tea and set the cup on the table. "Are Jemmy and Hester all right?"

"Oh, aye, daft as brushes, the pair of 'em," Morecombe said, rumbling from his chair, where he was blowing on the tea in his cup. "Don't know up from down. They do as they're told."

"Well, that's good then." Livia stood up. "We'll discuss this when I've talked to my husband. I'm sure it's just a misunderstanding."

"I doubt that," Mavis said. "But if you can sort it, lass, we'll be right glad." She gave one of her rare smiles. "An' 'ow's the babbies doin'? That young Stevie's all right now?"

"Oh, yes, they're all well," Livia said. "And Stevie doesn't seem to remember anything about his ordeal."

"Well, thanks be." Ada went to open the door for her. "We'll hear from you later, then?"

"Yes, of course." Livia managed a smile that she hoped was reassuring and turned back to the main part of the house. She was angry and also confused. How could Alex have given such orders without consulting her? They hadn't even discussed the disposition of their various servants. He'd agreed that they needed to, but it seemed he'd acted unilaterally anyway.

Well, it had to stop.

She was halfway down the stairs to the hall when an ecstatic frenzy of yapping came from the kitchen and then Tristan and Isolde burst into the hall. They hurled themselves at the stairs and raced up to her, nearly knocking her over. She sat on the stairs rather than risk falling and let them climb into her lap. They curled and licked in a frenzy of welcome.

Alex heard the noise from the library and sighed. Tatarinov looked startled.

"My wife's dogs," Alex explained. "They haven't seen her in a while."

"Oh." His visitor didn't look as if he found the explanation reasonable. "Nevertheless, I must congratulate you on your arrangement." He swept an arm in a gesture that encompassed the room. "A wife and such a house . . . and all so easily and expeditiously accomplished. It's an honor to work with you, Prince Prokov. I have no doubt that we shall succeed in our endeavors." Tatarinov rose from his chair. "I'll be about our business, then. The others need to know that you're back in town."

"Word will get around soon enough." Alex got up from behind his desk. "But you might hasten it along."

"Of course. And your army contact will be easy to reach."

"Good. Have you sufficient funds for the present?"

"For the present," Tatarinov said.

Alex nodded. "Come to me when you're in need." His role as paymaster was the easiest of his many roles in this hydra-headed business. He frowned suddenly. "What news of Arakcheyev's surveillance? I'll lay odds no one was watching me while I was in the country. Have they given up yet?"

The other man shrugged. "As far as you're concerned, yes. Michael Michaelovitch vouches for you."

Alex whistled softly. "I knew Michael was looking to make sure I was diligent in the czar's service, but I didn't think he would actually be in contact with Arakcheyev's secret police."

Tatarinov nodded. "I don't think he likes getting his soft white hands dirty with such company, quite frankly, but he's under orders from the czar to cooperate with the police, and he's nothing if not an obedient subject."

This last was accompanied by a derisive curl of his lip.

Alex nodded. "That's certainly true. I'll keep him sweet, then. It'll be easy enough to keep him convinced that I'm doing my assigned task for the czar. Are they watching any of the others?"

Another shrug and Tatarinov said, "Sperskov interested them for a while. His fondness for the ladies is thought to be rather suspect, but I don't think they seriously think he's anything more than a libertine. And he's certainly doing his best to reinforce that assumption. As for the others . . . they're keeping an eye on them, but I don't think there's much to worry about, at least at the moment. But if that changes, you'll be the first to know, Prince."

"That is indeed a comfort." Alex pulled the bell rope for Boris.

The dogs renewed their frantic barking as Boris escorted the visitor across the hall to the front door. Frowning, Alex went into the hall. Livia was sitting on the stairs halfway down, smothered in wriggling dogs. She was holding them securely, however, as they struggled to free themselves.

"Livia, for God's sake, get off the stairs. It's so indecorous. And do try to quieten those damn dogs."

Livia stood up, tucking a terrier under each arm. "You and I need to talk, Alexander Prokov."

To Alex's puzzlement she was radiating outrage as she came down the stairs, still clutching Tristan and Isolde. Her voice was cold and the soft contours of her countenance had hardened in some way. The sensual lover of the dawn was gone as surely as the night that had ushered it in.

"Whatever's the matter?" he asked.

"You know quite well," she declared. "Shall we go into the library or the parlor?"

He shook his head. "I don't mind in the least. Since I have no idea what this is all about, I'll leave it to you to choose the most suitable venue."

Livia looked at him sharply. Could he genuinely be unaware of what was upsetting her? She turned to the parlor, opened the door, and sent the dogs into the room, closing the door firmly behind them. "We'll talk in the library."

"As you please," he said with a courteous bow. "Please . . ." He gestured she should precede him.

Livia stalked into the room, the flounce of her green crepe morning gown swirling at her ankles. She turned to face him as he closed the door quietly. "I understood we had agreed to discuss the disposition of the staff," she said without preamble. "And yet I find that on your instructions Boris has told *my* people that their services are no longer required. They're too old to fit into the new regime." Her voice shook a little as her outrage grew. "You didn't have the elementary courtesy even to *pretend* to consult me."

"Oh, dear," Alex murmured. "If Boris did indeed say such a thing to Morecombe, and I am by no means convinced he did, then he was exceeding my instructions. I assumed it would come much better from you."

"You expect me to turn off Sophia's servants?" She stared at him. "But I explained to you, Alex, that I would not go against Sophia's will."

He sighed. "I don't expect you to turn them off, exactly. But I do expect you to find some satisfactory compromise that will enable them to stay on here if they wish but that will keep them from interfering in the work of my household."

"*Your* household?" She took a deep breath, trying to hold on to a temper that she rarely lost. "And what of mine, Alex? I am the mistress of this house."

"Certainly you are," he agreed calmly. "But I am its master. And as such the head of this household."

Livia closed her eyes on a shuddering breath. She forced herself to remember her father's words . . . his warning, she now knew it to have been. Nothing would be gained by an undignified war of words. "Tell me," she said after a moment, her voice deceptively calm. "Just so that I am prepared in future incidents. In your country is it customary for a husband to ride roughshod over his wife?"

A flicker of amusement crossed his eyes. "Well, actually, my love, it is both customary and expected. Indeed the Russian church itself lays down very explicit rules on how a man should chastise a recalcitrant wife."

"Don't be absurd," she said somewhat uncertainly.

"It's true," he averred, the amusement now open on his face. "But I am only half Russian so I'm only half inclined to follow such precepts."

"I don't find any of this amusing," Livia stated. "I can't imagine why you're laughing."

"I'm laughing because you're so angry and I am very, very sure that it would do neither of us any good for me to become angry too." He held out his hands to her. "Come, Livia, let's see if we can't find a compromise here."

She hesitated, but a little voice of common sense told her that to refuse the olive branch would achieve nothing. She knew some things, wonderful things, about this man who was her husband, but there were still acres of ignorance to conquer before she could say she knew him well. It was inevitable that she would discover things about Alexander Prokov that didn't sit well with her. But if she couldn't change them, then she would have to learn to live with them. Or she wouldn't be able to live with him. And quite apart from the fact that it was a little late for that, she couldn't now imagine life without him.

"Come," he repeated, still holding out his hands, his gaze quiet but resolved. "Cry peace, and we'll see what we can do to sort this out."

She took his hands. "Peace, then," she agreed. "But on two conditions that are not negotiable. I'll not accept that Morecombe and the twins have outlived their usefulness. And they have said they'll not take orders from anyone but me. By which I believe they mean they won't take orders from Boris."

Alex raised his eyebrows. "Will they take orders from me?"

Livia shook her head. "I don't know. Probably. But that's not the issue."

"No, it's not." He released her hands and steepled his fingers against his mouth, frowning at her. "I doubt my cook will share his kitchen."

She gave a short laugh. "He won't have to. Ada and Mavis are adamant that they'll not share *theirs*."

"I am having certain difficulty finding the spirit of compromise here," he said, and now there was an edge to his voice. "I'm doing my best and you're not helping me, Livia."

She folded her arms, accepting that he spoke only the truth. Her tone was more moderate as she said, "We're talking about people, Alex. People with feelings. It doesn't seem right to discuss them as if they were mere pawns on a chessboard. Is that how you treat servants in Russia?"

"Our servants are serfs," he said. "And I admit on occasion they are treated very badly. But I do accept that things run differently elsewhere. So, as a first step I suggest you talk to Morecombe and the twins and see if they have their own ideas as to how to manage this dilemma."

"And if between us we can come up with a suitable compromise you'll support it?" she asked cautiously.

"If indeed it *is* suitable for all concerned, then I will certainly do so."

"And if Boris proves hard to convince?"

"If you can convince *me* that any objections he may

have are unfounded, then of course I will support you."

Livia considered this. He was putting the onus squarely on her shoulders, but at least he was willing to consider her point of view, something she'd seriously doubted at the beginning of this interview. "Very well," she said, and then added her own olive branch. "I do hate to quarrel, Alex . . . with *anyone*. But it's particularly unpleasant to quarrel with you."

He inclined his head in acceptance of what could be construed as an apology. He smiled and drew her into his embrace. "I didn't realize what a fiery creature you are."

She sighed, resting her head on his shoulder. "I'm not really. Oh, dear, what a tangle. It would have been so much simpler if we'd moved into *your* house, then I wouldn't feel torn in this way."

Alex said nothing to this.

Chapter Seventeen

LIVIA UNFURLED HER OSTRICH-FEATHER fan that matched the ostrich feathers in her hair and sighed with boredom. The antechamber to the Great Drawing Room in St. James's Palace was crowded and hot, the air so thick with perfume and sweltering bodies that it was almost impossible to take a deep breath. Outside it was a chilly February afternoon, but in here it was as hot as a tropical rain forest. Wheels of candles blazed from the frescoed, gilded ceiling, the long windows were all tight shut, and massive log fires blazed from the fireplaces at either end of the chamber.

Her overheated discomfort was augmented by her elaborate court gown of heavy embroidered cream damask, and the ridiculous coiffure of nodding ostrich feathers that such occasions dictated.

"It won't be long now," Alex said, but without too much conviction.

Livia grimaced, glancing longingly towards the great

double doors to the Drawing Room itself. They were manned on either side by two flunkeys in gold livery. Every half hour the doors would open and the set of newly presented debutantes with their sponsors would emerge and a majordomo would call out the names of the next group due for presentation to the queen.

She was a little long in the tooth for this ritual, Livia reflected with another grimace. If her mother had lived, she would almost certainly have presented her daughter herself once she reached debutante age, but Lord Harford, while he would have cheerfully acceded to his wife's demand for the ritual protocol, saw no reason to encourage Livia to have a coming-out season if she wasn't particularly interested. And she hadn't been. But now, newly married as she was, she had little choice but to go through the ceremony if she and her husband were to have any real social position in society. There were many important events in the social calendar that only a properly presented debutante could attend.

"It's ridiculous," Livia muttered. "I don't know why you insisted we go through this, Alex. I don't mind being excluded from the royal box."

He looked at her, mild exasperation in his blue eyes. "You're my wife. *I* do not wish to be excluded from anything simply because you choose not to do what everyone else has done. It'll be over soon and you'll never need to endure it again."

Livia sighed again, but she could see his point. She

glanced around. "Oh, there's Nell, thank goodness for that." She raised a fan, waving it vigorously above the heads around her.

"Careful," Alex warned as she jumped a little, standing on tiptoe, waving at Nell above the crowd. Her three-foot train swirled around the pedestal of a little gilt table, and just in time Livia twitched it aside.

Alex seemed serene and untroubled, although he had to be as hot as she was, Livia thought. He looked particularly elegant in the formal court dress of black silk knee britches, white waistcoat, long-tailed black coat, and diamond-buckled shoes. His high, starched linen cravat was not even wilting the tiniest little bit despite the moist and heavy atmosphere. Like every other man in the antechamber, he wore a dress sword.

"Oh, here you are." Cornelia, deftly maneuvering her own elaborate hooped gown through the crowd, finally arrived at her side. "Isn't this positively ghastly?"

"Appalling," Livia agreed, kissing her friend's cheek. "I was beginning to think maybe you'd managed to find an excuse not to attend."

"I'm your sponsor, remember? I have to be here." Cornelia fanned herself vigorously. "Good afternoon, Alex." She gave him a friendly smile.

He bowed, returning the smile. "Your servant, Lady Dagenham."

"Where's Harry?" Livia peered across the throng.

"He's escorting his aunt." Cornelia chuckled. "No easy feat. The duchess's skirts must be six feet across . . .

ah, there they are." She waved her fan to attract her husband's attention.

Harry eased his great aunt, the duchess of Gracechurch, through the crowd towards them. Livia's eyes widened at the extraordinary sight. Her Grace was dressed in a vast hooped skirt with side panniers. Her towering coiffure was an elaborately curled and pomaded white wig from which four ostrich feathers waved precariously. A short and somewhat stoutish lady at the best of times, this afternoon she resembled a squat galleon under full sail.

She raised her lorgnette and subjected Livia to an intent scrutiny. "Can't think why you weren't presented at the proper time," she stated. "Your mother married Harford, didn't she? Perfectly respectable connection, in fact more than respectable. The Harfords came over with the Conqueror, I believe." She shook her head and Livia and Cornelia held their breath, afraid the entire edifice would come tumbling down. Miraculously, it stayed put.

Livia started to protest that her mother had only failed to do her maternal duty because she'd died before she could, but the duchess swept aside her polite protestations. "Harford turned himself into a churchman, I heard. Strange thing to do . . . all very right and proper for a younger son, but he was the oldest, heir to the earldom . . . not at all the thing. If everyone went around ignoring their duty, the world would come to an end." She nodded decisively.

"Yes, Your Grace," Livia murmured. She had met Harry's formidable aunt often enough to know it was better to let her say her piece. Defense and protestations got one nowhere.

"So, you've married some foreigner, I understand," the duchess announced, raising her lorgnette again. "So where is he?"

"You'll find me right here, ma'am." Alex stepped forward and bowed low, one hand resting on the hilt of his sword. "Prince Alexander Prokov at your service." He regarded her calmly while she examined him.

Finally she dropped her lorgnette. "Russian, eh? Aren't we at war with you?"

"Yes," Alex agreed simply.

It seemed to throw the lady off course. She stared at him for another minute or so, then turned to Harry. "Fetch me some negus, nephew. I'm parched. It's hot as Hades in here."

"At once, ma'am." Harry winked at Alex and turned to look for a footman bearing glasses of refreshment.

A stir went through the crowd as the double doors opened and a group of ladies and gentlemen came out of the Drawing Room, looking for the most part relieved that the ordeal was done. The majordomo read a list of names from a scroll. "Her Majesty will receive Princess Prokov and Viscountess Bonham," he intoned towards the end of the list.

"Thank God for that," Cornelia muttered. "Ready, Liv?"

"Yes," Livia said. "I just hope I don't trip over the train and fall flat on my face."

"Of course you won't," Cornelia said bracingly.

Livia merely raised her eyebrows and cast a speaking look at her husband, who smiled and fell in behind her as she followed Cornelia to the double doors.

Queen Charlotte was enthroned at the far end of the Great Drawing Room, a seemingly endless expanse of carpet between the double doors and her throne. The Prince Regent sat beside his mother, looking bored, one leg crossed casually over the other, his plump and florid countenance resting on his hand, elbow propped on the gilded arm of his throne.

Livia concentrated on her steps as she approached the royal presence. She had to keep her head up, her eyes on the queen, her posture straight as a ramrod, even while she managed her flowing skirts and train. Cornelia walked just a little ahead of her, in exactly the same manner. When they reached the throne, Her Majesty was pleased to offer a small smile.

Cornelia curtsied low and said clearly as she straightened, "Your Majesty, may I present the Princess Alexander Prokov, the daughter of Lord and Lady Harford."

"We shall be pleased to welcome the princess," the queen declared regally. Cornelia stepped aside and Livia took the necessary three steps forward. She curtsied to her knees and remained thus until the queen rose from her throne and bent to kiss her forehead.

Only then was she free to rise, make her curtsy to

Prinny, who acknowledged it with a nod. She curtsied once more deeply to the queen and then walked backwards out of the royal presence to join Cornelia, praying that she wouldn't catch her foot on her train as she held it to one side, praying that the ostrich feathers wouldn't droop over her eyes and blind her.

Once her backward journey was accomplished without disaster, she relaxed a little, watching Alex make his low bow to the queen. He'd already been formally presented at court some months earlier, but a man must support his wife. Men had it so much easier, she thought, in this as in so many other things. They might have to manage a ceremonial sword, but a bow was much simpler to accomplish than a full curtsy, and you could walk backwards in knee britches a lot more easily than with a three-foot train and a full skirt. But at least it was over.

In the antechamber she took a glass of negus from a footman. She would have preferred a glass of iced champagne to this warm wine and sugared water, but since the one was not on offer, she would have to make do.

"That wasn't so bad," Alex said, coming up behind her. "And now you'll never have to do it again."

"If it hadn't been for you, I wouldn't have had to do it at all," she stated, but she was smiling.

"Oh, Livia, are *you* here?" Letitia Oglethorpe materialized in a purple sarcenet gown, dripping with diamonds. Livia, who was fairly well bedecked herself, blinked at the dazzle flashing off Letitia's tiara.

"Oh, my dear, have you just been presented?" Letitia

exclaimed, taking in the cool color of Livia's gown, the color of a debutante. "Goodness me . . . how quaint to be presented at your age."

"So what brings you to the Queen's Drawing Room, Letitia?" Livia inquired, ignoring all the previous comments.

"Oh, I'm sponsoring Oglethorpe's dear little niece," Letitia said, gesturing to a small, pale, brown-haired girl, who looked utterly terrified, and far too young for her regalia. "Agnes, Lady Livia . . . oh, my goodness, I was forgetting. You're married, aren't you, my dear? A quiet wedding is so easy to forget . . . you didn't invite *anyone*." She tapped Livia's arm reprovingly with her closed fan. "I won't tell you how offended we all were. So where's this husband of yours? He's a foreigner, I gather." Her eyes were sharp with curiosity now, mingling with the habitual malice.

"Allow me to present my husband, Prince Prokov." Livia indicated Alex, who was standing just behind her. He bowed, his face expressionless as he murmured, "Your servant, ma'am."

Livia knew that Letitia was perfectly well aware of whom she'd married, and was dying with curiosity.

"Oh, my goodness," Letitia trilled, bowing to Alex. "A prince, no less. Why, Livia, you have done surprisingly well for yourself." She simpered, fluttering her eyelashes at Alex. "Why, goodness me, my dear, you'll take precedence over all of us."

"I doubt that, Letitia," Livia said smoothly. "I'm sure

you're aware that Russian princes are ten a penny in their own country. Isn't that so, Alex?"

Cornelia was buried behind her handkerchief, her shoulders shaking.

Alex bowed again, this time to his wife. "As you say, madam wife. The title is a mere bagatelle." His eyes were dancing. It was quite clear that Livia was more than a match for this odious woman and he was happy to offer what assistance he could to the performance.

"Yes, indeed," Livia said with a negligent shrug. "And it is rather vulgar, I think, to make much of such things. I'm sure you agree, Letitia."

Letitia's eyes narrowed. "So, will we be losing you to the barbarous steppes then, my dear Livia?" She gave an artful little shudder. "I hear it's a savage and barbaric country . . . is that not so, Prince Prokov?"

"In parts," he agreed. "But you would find little difference in the manners and general conduct at the court of St. Petersburg from those here."

"Oh, then you disappoint me," Livia said swiftly. "I find the manners here sometimes quite tiresome." She smiled at Letitia. "If you'll excuse me, Letitia, I see Lady Sefton. I must pay my respects."

"Allow me, my dear." Alex offered his arm. "Cornelia, may I escort you to your husband?" He offered his other arm and the three of them left Letitia to her own reflections.

"What an unpleasant woman," Alex observed.

"An understatement," Cornelia said. "I can handle

Harry's aunt, for all that she's abominably rude, but Letitia . . . it's the malice, I think. The duchess isn't at all malicious, she just speaks her mind."

"I like to think that Sophia Lacey was rather similar," Livia said with a little smile. "Not one to mince her words."

"What makes you think that?" Alex inquired.

"Oh, I don't know, really. Something about that portrait over the fireplace that gives me that impression . . ."

"Not to mention the dining room fresco and the jelly mold," Cornelia said with a chuckle. "Oh, there's Maria Lennox waving to us, Liv. I wanted to ask her about that orchestra she employed for her ball last season. I was thinking I might use them myself."

"When are you giving a ball?" Livia asked with interest, as they weaved their way through the throng towards Maria and the small group of women around her.

"In April, probably," her friend said. "Harry seems to think that since we didn't invite anyone to our wedding we should throw some kind of introductory celebration."

"Doesn't sound like Harry at all," Livia observed.

Cornelia laughed. "No, I know it doesn't. I suspect his great-aunt has something to do with it. She said something about how we need to avoid giving the impression that our marriage was a hole-in-the-corner affair . . . in the light of the old scandal, you know."

Livia nodded her understanding. Harry's first wife had died in rather awkward circumstances and the scandal had hung over him for a long time. It was one reason why he and Nell had eloped . . . that and the need to present the earl of Markby with a fait accompli before he could interfere in Cornelia's guardianship of her children.

They reached the small group of chattering women and Livia's attention was immediately taken up with the kisses and exclamations of congratulation on her marriage. When she could extricate herself, she looked around for Alex. There was no sign of him anywhere. Perhaps he'd gone for some fresh air. She gave a mental shrug and returned her attention to the question she had just been asked.

Alex was in fact standing in a small alcove, partially concealed by a heavy velvet curtain, listening intently to the conversation between two unseen gentlemen on the other side of the curtain.

"So Count Nesselrode is in Paris, making contact with Talleyrand?"

"Aye, we intercepted two of Nesselrode's letters to the czar, containing information given to him by Talleyrand." The speaker gave a short laugh. "According to Bonham, who deciphered them, Nesselrode refers to Talleyrand as *my cousin Henry.*"

"Also *handsome Leander.*" A third voice, which Alex recognized as belonging to Harry Bonham, joined the conversation. Harry sounded amused. "Fouché is known as Natasha, and our dear friend the czar rejoices in the code name Louise."

"So it would seem that Talleyrand is betraying his own

emperor," one of the men mused. "The old fox was always a tricky character. The czar would be a fool to trust him or the information he's sending his way. No one ever knows which side Talleyrand is really playing on."

"Oh, Talleyrand plays only on his own side, Eversham," Harry declared. "That's all anyone needs to know about the man . . . ah, if you'll excuse me, gentlemen, my wife appears ready to leave . . . and not a moment too soon, I might add."

He strolled away, followed shortly by the other two. Only then did Alex step out of the alcove. That had been a worthwhile piece of eavesdropping, he thought. The czar would be interested to know that his secret correspondence with young Nesselrode was being intercepted by the British. It would be a piece of information that would shore up his own credentials as the czar's clandestine eyes and ears in London.

∼∞∼

There were three men gathered in the small room behind the taproom in the Duke of Gloucester tavern in Long Acre. The air was thick with smoke from their pipes, mingling with the reek of sea coal in the small fireplace.

"We know for a fact that Prokov has the emperor's writ," one of the men said in almost musing tones. He was short and stocky, with a rather brutal mouth and a head of iron-gray hair.

"Yes, without question, Sergei," affirmed Prince

Michael Michaelovitch, tossing off the clear contents of his glass with an expert twist of his wrist. "And he's cleverly placed himself in the perfect position to accomplish his task. A wife who's seen everywhere about town, a mansion in Cavendish Square, and his wife's friends give him the entrées into the political and diplomatic echelons of society. He's becoming more English than the English these days, no one would suspect him of spying for the emperor. Don't you agree, Igor?"

"But he also entertains Sperskov and the like," Igor remarked. He was of the same breed as Sergei, with the shoulders of a prize fighter and a luxuriant pair of whiskers. Beside them Prince Michael, pink-cheeked, white-haired, with an air of breeding and benevolence suited to an elder statesman, seemed as rare and delicate as an orchid.

"We have to assume that he's also keeping an eye on them. He'll inform the czar of anything untoward among that group," the prince said. "But I doubt there's anything . . . they're social butterflies, no more than that."

"I wouldn't be too sure," Sergei responded with a dour shake of his head. "The talk of revolution even in the palaces of St. Petersburg is ever more open. People don't even bother to whisper behind their hands these days."

"Well, it's hard to see what they can achieve from London. The czar's well out of their reach," the prince declared. "And I have faith in Prokov . . . as does the emperor."

He pushed back his stool and stood up. "If you'll excuse me, gentlemen, I have an engagement with a rather lovely demimondaine in the piazza." He smiled complacently. "Say what you will, the ladies of this town have a certain refinement, and these bagnios, as they call their houses of pleasure, are most welcoming." He nodded amiably, picked up his beaver hat, and strolled out of the room, swinging his cane with a jaunty air.

"Old fool," Igor said, leaning sideways to spit into the coals. They hissed and foul-smelling smoke billowed into the room.

"He may be an old fool, Igor, but he has the ear of Arakcheyev," Sergei said. "And that's one man you offend at your peril."

Igor nodded grimly and refilled his glass from the squat bottle. Their master would stop at no brutality to achieve his ends. He controlled the secret service as efficiently and savagely as he controlled the army. And if he deemed Prince Michaelovitch worthy of the task of keeping an eye on the doings of émigrés in London, then his minions would do well to keep their opinions to themselves.

"Well, Tatarinov has an entrée with Sperskov and his group," Igor said. "Although how he's managed to gain their trust I don't know. A diamond in the rough, that one. Another Arakcheyev, I would say. I wouldn't want to cross him on a dark street on a moonless night."

"No," agreed Sergei. "Have you ever seen him with a knife?" He shook his head in wonder. "I watched him carve a man into tiny pieces in Moscow once. They thought he was a spy for Napoleon." He gave a short laugh. "How times have changed. Napoleon's spies are now feted, not dismembered."

"Ours not to reason why, my friend." Igor stood up. "I've a mind to find a whore in the piazza . . . nothing as refined as a demimondaine for the likes of me, of course . . ." His laugh was sardonic. "But there are plenty of eager women behind the pillars willing to lift their skirts for a sixpence. Coming, Sergei?"

"Why not?" Sergei stood up, slipping the vodka bottle into the capacious pocket of his coat.

The two men seemed to slide from the room and into the taproom. They left the tavern itself as indistinguishable as a pair of shadows, and the tavern's patrons barely noticed their passing.

⌘

Alex dismounted from his horse outside the house, tossed the reins to his groom, and strolled up the steps. A light tap on the knocker was all it took to bring Boris, who opened the door with a low bow.

"Good afternoon, Your Highness." He took the prince's hat and whip.

"Thank you, Boris. Is Princess Prokov in?"

"I believe the princess is in the library, sir."

"Alone?"

"Yes, sir. I believe so."

Alex nodded and started to walk away, then he paused. "How are things working out, Boris?"

"You mean with Morecombe and the women, Prince?" Boris's expression became frozen and his voice flattened.

"Yes, that's what I mean," Alex said dryly.

"As well as you might expect, sir." Boris brushed at the brim of the hat with an air of concentration. "I have no jurisdiction there, so I don't inquire into their activities."

Alex pursed his lips, wishing he hadn't asked. Even after more than a month the household was still in a state of armed truce and he was well aware that Boris considered he had been betrayed. On the other hand, Alex had to admit that the twins performed culinary miracles in their own kitchen, which had been created in a previously unused scullery, and the cook grudgingly accepted that if his employers wanted traditional English dishes once in a while, then someone should prepare them, and it certainly wasn't going to be him. He had no interest in the likes of Yorkshire pudding, spice cakes, creamed turnips, scalloped oysters, apple pie, or sponge cake.

Morecombe and Boris, however, were another matter. Alex had endeavored to win the confidence of his mother's elderly retainer, but Morecombe had been impervious to all his efforts. He clearly didn't regard the master of the house with any more respect than he accorded Boris, the interloper. It was frustrating, but there was little Alex could do about it if the man refused to unbend. However, neither was he about to encourage Boris to voice his own complaints about Morecombe.

He nodded vaguely at his majordomo and went in search of his wife, well aware of Boris fulminating in hurt silence behind him.

He went into the library and at first couldn't see Livia. Then he heard her. "Oh, Alex, there you are. You won't believe what I've found." Her voice bubbled with laughter and the ladder she was on in order to reach the top shelves wobbled alarmingly as she twisted in his direction.

He loved that bubble in her voice. He looked up into her laughing face as she perched on the top step, her eyes shining with mischievous glee. "What have you found, Livia?" Prudently he put a steadying hand on the ladder.

"It's another of Aunt Sophia's surprises," she said. "Only look at these books, Alex. They're all on the top shelves, presumably to keep them from accidental discovery, but they're so wonderfully wicked. I'll pass some of them down to you."

She began to pull volumes from the shelf, leaning down to put them in his outstretched free hand. "They're all in French, but they seem to have come from Oriental originals. I can't really take them in properly up here, it's too wobbly."

"Then come down," Alex instructed as he took the volumes one by one, dropping them onto a chair beside the ladder. He put his hands on her ankles, steadying her as she came down backwards. "What possessed you to go up there?"

"I was curious," Livia said as he lifted her down the

last rungs. "We didn't do anything to this room when we first arrived and it was so dusty and dirty and uninviting that we never bothered to take a look at the books. I was at a loose end this afternoon so I thought I'd have a look."

She turned in his arms, laughing up at him. "How I wish I'd known Aunt Sophia."

"She must have been an unusual woman," he said, looking over her head, aware of a deep pang of loss. Every day he spent in this house it grew stronger, and with every surprise revelation it grew harder to bear. And the hardest thing to bear was his longing to share it with Livia, and the deadening knowledge that he couldn't, not without revealing things about himself that would hurt her and, more pragmatically, make his business in London much harder to complete.

"You're not disapproving, are you?" Livia said, feeling the change in him as he held her lightly. "You're not a prude, Alexander Prokov."

She leaned back against his encircling arm, looking up into his face. "Or have you been hiding that side of yourself from me?" Her gray eyes were still full of laughter but there was a flicker of uncertainty beneath.

He shook his head. "No, I am not a prude. I couldn't be married to you if I were. Although I have to admit I didn't know I wanted a shameless hussy for a wife until I had one."

Mischievously she played a drum roll on his chest with her fists. "Come and look at them with me." She twisted away from him and gathered up the books in her arms, depositing herself on the sofa. "Come and sit beside me."

Alex obeyed. He whistled soundlessly as they turned the pages, which he had to admit were definitely arousing. Livia glanced sideways at him, and her eyes were suddenly heavy and languorous. "Do you think that's possible?" she murmured, her tongue touching her lips as she examined an illustration. "It looks painful."

"No," he said, giving the idea apparently serious consideration, even though his eyes were dancing. "I don't think it need be." He kissed the corner of her mouth. "Would you care to try, madam?"

She nodded and he got up and went to the door, turning the key.

❦

"I don't know whether that was successful or not," Livia gasped half an hour later, lying sprawled on the floor.

"It might have been more so if you hadn't found it so amusing," Alex said, straightening her contorted limbs. "It's extremely difficult to make love to a woman who's convulsed with laughter. An elementary fact of life that seems to have escaped you."

"I'm sorry," she said, pulling his head down to hers. "But it was ticklish. Do you think Aunt Sophia ever did it like that?"

Not with my father, Alex thought, the idea effectively

dowsing his amusement once again. He raised his head and sat up.

"I wonder how many lovers she had." Livia stretched out on the rug, one hand resting languidly on his bare thigh. "She can't have been a chaste spinster all her life. If I could summon the courage I'd ask Morecombe . . . or perhaps the twins. But they're so reticent about the past. Of course, it was a different era. Thirty years ago . . ."

"It certainly was." Alex stood up quickly. "I can't spend the entire afternoon dallying with you, Livia." He began to put on his clothes.

She sat up reluctantly. "What else must you do?"

"I'm expecting some guests," he said, bending to gather up the books. "Get dressed now."

Livia rose to her feet. There was a strange chill suddenly. She hadn't done anything to offend him, she was certain of it. They'd just made love, however unorthodox the method, but in general such activity generated a wonderful sense of connection between them. But now he seemed to have distanced himself from her.

"Is something wrong, Alex?" She scrambled into her clothes, uncaring how disheveled she might look.

"No, of course not. How could there be?" He was on the ladder replacing the books on the topmost shelf.

"You tell me," she murmured sotto voce, fastening the buttons on her bodice.

The door knocker sounded and Alex frowned. "My guests," he said shortly. He came down the ladder. "My dear girl, you're buttoned up all wrong." He brushed aside her hands and swiftly fastened her gown. He ran his hands through her hair, trying to comb it into some semblance of tidiness. "Anyone looking at you would know exactly what you've been doing."

"You were doing it too," she reminded him, thrusting her bare feet into her slippers, tucking her stockings into her hands. "I'm sorry if you're embarrassed, Alex, I'll go out through the garden and your guests will never see me." She made no attempt to hide her annoyance. It wasn't as if they weren't husband and wife.

"That might be for the best," he said, moving to the door to unlock it. "I don't think anyone should see you holding your stockings in that shameless fashion." A hint of his customary warmth had returned to his eyes and his voice, but Livia was not reassured.

She shook her head and hurried to the French doors that opened onto the garden. "Never fear, I'm going now. Enjoy your guests." Before he could say anything she opened the doors and slipped out into the frigid afternoon.

Alex took half a step in her direction and then turned back as Boris knocked at the door and came in. "Visitors, Your Highness. Duke Sperskov—"

"Yes, yes," Alex said more brusquely than he intended. "I was expecting them." He moved past Boris, extending his hand. "Come in, gentlemen."

∞

Livia reentered the house through the kitchen and went up to her bedchamber. She was troubled. Every now and again in the two months they had been in London this strange thing happened to Alex, his mood would shatter and he would withdraw. She shrugged it off much of the time, but this afternoon was the first time it had happened at such a moment of intimacy.

Did it have anything to do with the visitors he was expecting? For some reason she was never invited to the library when he had visitors. Even though she was slightly acquainted with Duke Nicolai Sperskov and Count Fedorovsky after their meeting at the Bonhams' all those months ago, Alex never included her in their visits. If she happened to pass them in the hall, they always greeted her with impeccable courtesy, just as they did if they met at a social event, but that was as far as it went. And after the one occasion when she had disturbed Alex with the rough-looking Russian, whose name she couldn't now remember, even when she was sure he was alone in the library, she always knocked and waited for his permission to enter.

Presumably, keeping wives separate from their husbands' friends was another strange Russian custom. But it only seemed to apply to *his* Russian friends. He was a very different man with the English and the French royalist émigrés who had fled to England after the revolution. A charming and attentive husband, an impeccable host, and an equally delightful guest.

All in all, her husband was something of a puzzle, Livia decided. And she was in no mood to sit at home and brood on the puzzle. She would visit Nell and Ellie in Mount Street. They'd be highly amused at this latest evidence of Sophia Lacey's proclivities.

She rang for Ethel and then went to the armoire to select an afternoon gown. "Ethel, would you run down and ask Morecombe to summon the barouche for me?" she said as the maid came in. "Jemmy can drive me to Mount Street." She laid a gown of striped muslin on the bed and unbuttoned the sadly mistreated dress she was wearing.

Jemmy jumped down from the box of the barouche as Livia came out of the house. The dogs, who were sitting on the box proud as peacocks, their feathery tails fluffed, ears pricked, let loose a crescendo of excited barks when they saw her.

"Yes . . . yes, I'm delighted to see you too," she said, stroking their heads as Jemmy held the carriage door for her.

"Where to, m'lady?"

"Mount Street, please." She climbed in and Tristan and Isolde clambered into the back to sit beside her, tails wagging, tongues hanging out. "How are you managing with the dogs, Jemmy?"

"Oh, we gets along very well, ma'am," he said, solicitously arranging the lap robe over her knees. "I like the company, if truth be told."

Well, that at least had been a potential problem easily resolved, Livia thought. Alex seemed willing to tolerate them if they weren't permanently underfoot.

Her friends were in Cornelia's sitting room with their children when Livia arrived in Mount Street, the dogs running in front of her. They were as at home here as in Cavendish Square, and the children adored them.

"Liv, what a lovely surprise." Cornelia embraced her warmly. "We're having tea."

"Lovely," Livia said, kissing Aurelia. She greeted the children, but they were too busy playing with the dogs to respond with more than a monosyllable.

She cast aside her muff and shrugged out of the fur-trimmed spencer, tossing it over an ottoman. "So, how have you both been?" She sank into the corner of a chintz sofa and with an appreciative smile took the cup Cornelia offered.

"Well enough. What of you, Princess Prokov?" Aurelia regarded her with a quizzical smile.

"Oh, well enough," she responded carelessly, taking a macaroon from the plate of sweet biscuits.

"You still have a very satisfied glow about you," Cornelia observed with amusement. "A little love in the afternoon, perhaps? I do believe I'm jealous." She heaved a mock sigh. "Ah, the first flush of love, there's nothing like it for the complexion."

"And I suppose that's a thing of the past for you?" Livia retorted, not troubling to deny her friend's accurate statement.

"Well, I've been married for almost a year now, and you know it's really not fashionable to live in one's husband's pocket," Cornelia said solemnly. "The gloss does wear off eventually."

"Oh, nonsense," Aurelia said, laughing. "You and Harry are as head over heels in love as you ever were, and you're so smug about it, Nell, don't deny it."

"I won't," Cornelia said with a grin.

"Well, there's little fear that I'll be living in my husband's pocket," Livia said, dipping her macaroon in her tea.

Her friends looked at her sharply. "Is something the matter, Liv?" Aurelia asked.

She shook her head. "No, it's just that I'm having to learn Russian ways. Russian men do seem to expect to rule the roost. In fact Alex told me so himself, although he was making a joke of it . . . or at least, I think . . . I *hope* . . . he was," she added.

"You didn't mind when he managed things before you married him," Aurelia said, a worried frown creasing her brow. "Is this different?"

"A little," Livia conceded. She hadn't intended to be having this discussion, but she should have known she would end up confiding in her friends. "Before, it was amusing and rather exciting, the way he swept obstacles from his path, doing exactly what he wanted and somehow persuading everyone else, me in particular, that it was what they wanted too. I liked it then, only now . . ."

She chewed her lip. "It's one thing to be swept off your feet in the game of courtship, quite another to feel that your wishes *have* to come second simply because it's a husband's prerogative to take precedence."

Cornelia's frown was a fair replica of Aurelia's. "Alex doesn't bully you?"

"No . . . no, of course not," Livia denied vehemently. "He's charming and funny and gentle, but just adamant about certain things. It's as if he couldn't imagine doing anything differently from the way it's always been done in his experience."

"Well, he does come from a different culture," Aurelia said. "It's inevitable that his experience would be different from yours. Is he willing to compromise?"

"Up to a point," Livia said, feeling suddenly disloyal. "It's nothing serious, really it isn't. I was just a little put out this afternoon."

She set down her teacup, intending to close the conversation, but found herself confiding the other thing that puzzled her. "It's odd, but he never invites me to join them when his Russian friends come to visit. I meet them at other social events, just to bow to anyway, so it would seem natural that he would include me, even briefly, when they come to the house. But he never does. Why would that be?"

"Perhaps they only speak in Russian," Aurelia suggested. "Perhaps it's a part of his world that he thinks you won't understand. Men are just as bad as women when it comes to closing ranks. Look at their clubs. I mean a woman daren't even be seen in St. James's Street."

"True enough." Livia nodded. "Although I don't

think it has anything to do with language. He told me once that only peasants speak Russian, at court everyone speaks French or English. But you're right. I'm making a mountain out of a molehill. It's probably just like an extended port-and-brandy postdinner gathering, with the women safely out of earshot over the teacups." There was some sense to such an explanation and it would have to satisfy her.

"But you don't have any regrets about this marriage?" Cornelia asked, leaning towards Livia anxiously.

"No, none at all." Livia shook her head vigorously. "I love being married to him. These are just little niggles, and I'm probably being childish letting them upset me."

Chapter Eighteen

⚬

LIVIA LEFT SOON AFTER, GOING out into the frigid February dusk, hoping that Jemmy had remembered to warm up the brick again while he was waiting in the Mount Street kitchens. He had and she snuggled into the lap rug, settling her feet on the brick, the dogs on her lap for an added layer of warmth.

Somehow, confiding in her friends hadn't brought her the relief it should have done. She was still uneasy about something, and she was having difficulty putting it into words. It was something to do with the glimpses of a different Alex that she'd caught once or twice. A touch of flint that hardened his eyes into a diamond brightness; a feeling of ruthlessness, of determination about him quite at odds with the generally easygoing, genial public face of Prince Prokov, and totally at odds with the lover whose slightest touch made her blood sing.

But then, as she was always telling herself, she had a lot to learn about the man who was her husband. So why didn't that realization ease her vague perturbation? Did it have something to do with the formless inkling that she had somehow been the object of that ruthless determination?

Had that relentless pursuit and courtship been stimulated by something other than the headlong tumble into lust and love that she'd believed in? The unthinking passion that had swept her along with it on a glorious tide of emotional turmoil?

It was ridiculous to entertain these doubts about her husband, ridiculous and disloyal, Livia told herself as the carriage turned into Cavendish Square. She had no evidence of deception. He had never treated her with anything but loving tenderness. And she was in the mood for a little of that now, she decided firmly.

She stepped out of the barouche and went into the house, hoping that Alex had not gone out or if he was in, was no longer with his friends. The library door stood open but the room was empty. "Has Prince Prokov gone out, Boris?"

"I don't believe so, Princess." The majordomo spoke tonelessly.

"Do you know where he is?"

"Above stairs, I believe, my lady." He didn't meet her eye, speaking to some point over her head, but Livia had long decided she wasn't going to attempt to conciliate him, so she thanked him pleasantly and headed for the stairs.

Perhaps Alex was dressing for the evening. She couldn't

remember his saying anything about going out for the evening, but his plans could have changed after his afternoon with his compatriots.

She went up to her own bedchamber and stopped on the threshold in surprise. Alex in a brocade robe was lounging on her bed, ankles crossed, hands behind his head, a picture of relaxation.

"Ah, there you are, madam wife," he said somewhat plaintively. "I've been waiting for you for hours." A lazy smile curved his mouth and his blue gaze was positively lascivious as it drifted over her. "I had it in mind to further the education that we began this afternoon, but when I came hot foot in search of you, you weren't anywhere to be found." His tone was mock plaintive, but his gaze burned with a quite different emotion.

Livia's body responded as it always did to the sensual promise in his eyes. She unpinned her hat, trying to make her movements tantalizingly slow. "I was in Mount Street," she said, carefully laying her hat on the dresser before unbuttoning her pelisse.

"I know," he said. He crooked a finger at her in invitation. "Come here, wife of mine."

Livia pursed her lips, as if she needed to think about whether she would or not. She remained standing at the dresser, regarding him with narrowed eyes.

"Must I come and fetch you?" Alex swung himself off the bed and took a purposeful step towards her. Livia gave a feigned squeal of fright and darted behind a chair.

His eyes gleamed. "Ah, so that's the way it's to be, is

it?" He lunged for her and she pushed the chair towards him, slowing him down as she dived behind the daybed. She watched him warily, her eyes dancing with mischief.

Alex set the chair straight again and surveyed her thoughtfully. Her cheeks were pink, her gray eyes aglow with anticipatory excitement. He took a step towards her and she grabbed a cushion from the daybed and tossed it at him. He caught it with one hand and threw it aside.

Livia backed away and, laughing, he stalked her around the room, effortlessly catching the series of missiles she threw at him to impede his progress. There was nowhere really for her to go, but the game made her blood run hot and swift, and her pulses race. She tried to sidestep and found herself backed into a corner.

"Now where are you going?" he teased, putting his hands on the wall on either side of her.

Livia didn't answer. She ducked suddenly beneath his arm, surprising him, and nearly made it to freedom, but he moved swiftly, catching her around the waist, swinging her against him. He held her tightly, one hand pushing up her chin. "Got you," he declared with satisfaction.

"So it would seem," Livia agreed, catching her breath, gazing up at him.

"I have a great need for you," he said softly, running his free hand over the swell of her breasts, down to the curve of her hip.

"Then you must win me, sir," she said, her eyes narrowing as an idea came to her.

"And how must I do that?" he inquired, more than willing to play her game. Livia was nothing if not playfully inventive when it came to lovemaking.

"By playing chess with me," she stated. "Russians are expert at the game, but so, I should tell you, am I. I have been wanting to play with you since we first met, but somehow the opportunity never arose."

Alex looked a little taken aback. "Must we . . . right at this moment?"

"Yes," she said firmly, reaching up to kiss the corner of his mouth. "Trust me, you *will* enjoy it."

He took her face between his hands and kissed her hard, his tongue driving deep into her mouth in a statement of clear possession. Then he released her. "That's a promise," he said softly, "to be redeemed very soon."

Livia grinned. "I'll make sure that it is, my prince." She went across the room to the secretaire and dropped the leather desktop. She drew out a chessboard and a box. "Now, where shall we set it up? . . . Here, I think." She put the heavy board on a low table in front of the fire. "If you win, then I will be your slave for the evening . . . on the other hand, should I happen to prevail . . ." Her gaze sparked sensual mischief.

He pulled at his chin, appearing to consider the offer, and the atmosphere grew taut with anticipation. "An interesting proposition," he said finally. "And not one any self-respecting Russian could refuse. Set it up, madam wife."

An hour later he was beginning to wonder quite what

he'd let himself in for. He surveyed his side of the board. Something of a wreck, really. The ranks of his lost pieces far exceeded those remaining on the board. He considered himself to be a more than passable player, but Livia played like a demon.

"Just where did you learn to play like this?" he inquired, watching her as she considered her next move.

"My father taught me," she told him. "The chessboard is his metaphor for life." She looked up with a quick smile. "Always look before you leap, and always consider the consequences of the consequences of your actions." Her hand hovered over her bishop.

"He was a mathematician at university, a senior wrangler at Cambridge before he turned to theology. He used chess as a means of relaxation from mathematical calculations," she expanded, moving her bishop to Queen Four. "Check."

Alex sighed. "So it is." He frowned over his options. They appeared rather limited. "Well, looking ahead to the consequences of my last move, I see only mate in three in my future."

Livia chuckled. "That's what I see too." She was sitting cross-legged on the floor in front of the table, now wrapped in her favorite dressing gown of rich tawny velvet, her bare feet peeping beneath the hem. Her hair was loose on her shoulders. "Will you resign, sir? Or play it out?"

Alex, who was also sitting on the floor, leaned forward and toppled his king with a forefinger. Then he leaned back against the chair behind him and regarded her with a smile. "The next move, I believe, madam, is yours."

She nodded slowly. "Ah, yes, so it is. I have won a slave for the night." She closed her eyes in thought. Then she opened them with a groan of frustration. "The trouble is I can't think of anything I want you to do that you don't already do," she wailed.

Alex threw back his head and laughed. "What a failure of imagination, my love. Most unusual for you." He uncurled himself from the floor and stood up. "Perhaps my task should be to stimulate that imagination."

Bending, he caught her under the arms and lifted her to her feet, pushing up her chin with his palm before kissing her. He moved his lips to the tip of her nose and then to her eyelids, a kiss that was a mere whisper over the paper-thin lids. He nibbled her earlobes and then grasped her face firmly between both hands and kissed her ear, his tongue snaking around the exquisitely sensitive, shell-like whorls. She squirmed in laughing protest at a caress that he knew full well would send her into paroxysms of pleasure even as she struggled to resist.

At last he released her face, his hands moving instead to the tie of her robe. "I can perform my task better if we get rid of this." He pushed it off her shoulders and bent to kiss the pulse at the base of her throat, his hands globing her breasts, running down her rib cage, thumbs pressing into the points of her hipbones. He straightened, still holding her hips, and regarded her flushed countenance with a tiny smile.

"Will you allow me to perform my task in my own way, mistress mine? Or do you have any specific instructions?"

"No," she said, catching her bottom lip between her teeth. "No, I don't. I believe you're more than able to fashion your own."

He nodded slowly, his eyes narrowing, the tiny smile still playing over his lips. "I am yours to command." He tossed his own robe aside. Naked, he looked at her with a little frown of concentration. Then he nodded and smiled as if coming to some satisfactory decision.

"Wait there." He went into his adjoining bedchamber and returned twisting a length of silk between his hands.

Livia was on fire with anticipation, her loins melting, her body thrumming. She had no idea what he was going to do. He came up behind her and tied the strip of silk over her eyes.

"There now," he murmured. "Trust me and I promise you, you will experience everything twice as intensely."

Livia swallowed, her vision a mere red mist behind the soft blindfold. Her bare skin prickled, expecting something, anything . . . she didn't know what. He lifted her and carried her to the bed, setting her down in the middle. She lay still, gazing up into the blindfold, hearing him move around the room, open a drawer.

And then she felt him come back to the bed. The feather mattress took his weight, and he whispered, "This game we play without words, sweeting." And then something soft brushed her cheek, traced the curve of her mouth. It tickled a little but in a manner she found only delightful. It flickered across her ear, tracing the shape of it, and she gave a tiny gasp at the sweetness of the pleasure. And then the sensation shifted to her throat, the soft flicker against the fast-beating pulse, before the soft brush slid slowly down to her breasts. A light, tantalizing stroke outlined her nipples, bringing them to burning peaks of awareness, and the familiar languorous delight began to build deep in her belly.

She felt the brushing strokes across her abdomen, dipping into her navel, moving lower over the white, rippling skin of her belly. She felt his hand part her thighs, gently inexorable, and her breath stopped in her throat. Anticipation of the next touch, of where and when it would come, was now so intense as to be almost painful.

The feathery touch trailed upwards over the smooth skin of her inner thighs and she shuddered with pleasure. It inscribed circles, smaller and smaller on the tender flesh of her thighs, moving ever upwards, closer and closer to the center of joy. And then it stopped, and, as the waiting seemed to stretch into infinity, tears of anticipatory delight dampened the silk of her blindfold and the deepest recesses of her body throbbed with expectation.

And then, when she had begun to fear it would never happen, when she had almost ceased to expect it, she felt it again, a light, brushing caress on her sex, and she thrummed like a plucked lute. His fingers opened her, parting her center for the soft and most intimate caress with this strange instrument of pleasure that he wielded with such exquisite and knowing artistry. And she was lost, mindless and sensate, a body that existed only for this explosion of pleasure in this blind and silent world.

Alex covered her mouth with his, gathering her against him as he slid into her tender opened body with the pulsing throb of his own arousal. She tightened her inner muscles around him and he stifled his moan of pleasure against her mouth. She held him tight within her as her body began to climb again up to the peak of joy, and the instant she hovered on its brink he drew her legs up onto his shoulders, so that he could penetrate deep to her very core, and this time he didn't muffle his exultant cry as the world shattered into silver shards of delight, and Livia cried out with him.

He stayed within her for long moments as the fragments of themselves came together again, and when at last he felt her stir beneath him, he loosened the silk over her eyes and drew it away.

She gazed up at him, blinking in the sudden light, feeling strange and disoriented after the pleasure-filled, self-enclosed darkness. He kissed the corner of her mouth and the tip of her nose, then gently disengaged, rolling onto the bed beside her.

"What were you using?" she murmured, her voice sounding strange after such a long silence.

He smiled and showed her the little badger's hairbrush that she used to apply powdered rouge on the rare occasions she thought her complexion needed a little assistance.

"Oh," was all she could think to say.

"Rest a while," he said, propping himself on one elbow, his other hand tracing the curve of her flank. "The night is barely begun."

Livia thought, particularly after the last hour, that she had experienced all there was to experience in the business of lovemaking, or at least everything that was possible outside of the more esoteric poses illustrated in Sophia's books. She now learned that she had not. Thus far in their union Alex had merely shown her the tip of the iceberg when it came to his knowledge of the world of sensual delight. As the hours passed, he withheld his own release, concentrating only on bringing her again and again to the crest. His mouth and tongue found every nook and cranny of her body in a dance of arousal, and she was lost in a turmoil of sensation. Again and again he held her on the edge of dissolution until she could bear it no longer, and only then would he touch her, a flick of his tongue, a nuzzle of his lips, a stroke of a finger, and she would once more fall into the void, where all sense of herself as distinct from pure sensation did not exist.

The candles were guttering, the fire a glow of embers when at last Alex allowed himself to climax for the second time. He held her tightly against him as his climax shuddered within her and he felt the velvety sheath of her body pulse around him in one last orgasmic convulsion.

Livia's legs fell from around his waist, her arms fell

onto the bed, and she was aware of nothing. Alex moved slowly to disengage, easing himself onto the bed beside her. Her eyelids fluttered and she smiled weakly. "I went somewhere."

"*La petite morte*," he said softly, too exhausted to kiss her but managing a flutter of a hand against her thigh. "It happens occasionally, when a climax has been particularly intense."

Livia closed her eyes again. When she next opened them, Alex was no longer beside her. She struggled onto an elbow and saw that the fire had been fed and was now blazing. Fresh candles were in the candlesticks, although none were close enough to the bed to disturb her sleep. The door to Alex's chamber stood ajar.

"Where are you?" she called.

"Here." He appeared in the doorway, smiling as he retied the girdle of his robe. "Are you hungry? We've had no dinner."

"Oh, no, so we haven't." She struggled up against the pillows, acutely aware of her body. Of the stickiness between her legs, a slight soreness there, a faint, deep ache in her muscles, muscles she hadn't known she had. And she was famished.

"The house will be asleep."

Alex shook his head. "This particular slave is wide awake. I will go and forage, madam."

"I would really like some hot water," Livia said. "But I think you've played your part for one night, so I'll come and fetch it myself."

He shook his head. "No, you won't. You'll stay right here and I'll be back soon." He left the room and Livia fell back on the bed, not at all sure that she was even capable of doing something so energetic as fetching water.

Alex returned in a few moments with a steaming jug. He poured water into the basin and beckoned to her. "My last task."

Livia climbed off the bed and crossed to him on slightly wobbly legs. "Don't start anything, Alex," she pleaded, trying to take the washcloth from him. "I cannot endure any more tonight."

"I'm not sure I can either," he said. "Be still now." He passed the washcloth over her body, leaving not an inch of skin untouched, but with a swift efficiency that would have been appropriate for a nursemaid. He handed her a towel and bent to pick up her discarded robe. "Put this on and I'll go down for our supper."

Livia did as he said and then slumped into a chair by the fire, smiling to herself at the chessboard that was still set up in the endgame. It wasn't possible for a man to be such a wonderfully inventive and unselfish lover and also a deceiver.

Alex returned with a laden tray that he set on the dresser. "Hot food was beyond my capabilities at three in the morning, but there's a cold chicken, vegetables in aspic, one of Ada's game pies, a little salmon mousse, and that amazing pudding that Mavis makes with the crispy meringue. Carve the chicken while I fetch the wine." He disappeared again.

Livia had carved the chicken and served up a little of everything else onto the two plates when Alex returned with a bottle of burgundy and two glasses.

She cleared away the chessboard and sat down on the floor again as he brought the glasses over and set them on the low table. "I didn't know how hungry I was."

"It's hungry work, lovemaking," he observed. "Thirsty too." He drank deeply of his wine and forked a piece of chicken. "By the way, I'd like us to host a dinner in the next couple of weeks."

It was such a non sequitur, such an extraordinary change of subject and mood after their play that Livia took a minute to absorb the statement. "Of course. When?" she responded, trying to hide her surprise and slight dismay that he could so easily move from the glories of the bed to such a mundane topic. It was the first time such an initiative had come from Alex. He always seemed more than happy to go along with whatever hospitality she arranged, or invitation she had accepted for them both, but otherwise, except when they spent time alone together like tonight, he had his own social circle as she had hers. Society would have looked askance at anything else.

"How soon can it be done?" He took a bite of a piece of game pie.

"Not for several weeks," she said. "Even if the invitations went out tomorrow, we have to accept that people have prior engagements. How many guests are you thinking of?"

"Not many . . . six couples only." He leaned back against the chair with a sigh of repletion.

"Close friends?" She sipped her wine, wondering if at last she was going to become properly acquainted with his Russian associates.

"Not really . . . let's just say that they're people I'd like to know better."

So much for that hope. "Who are they?"

"I've made a list." Alex got up from the floor and went into the adjoining bedchamber, reemerging with a sheet of paper. He let it flutter into Livia's lap before settling on the floor again and attacking the meringue.

Livia read the list of names. She was barely acquainted with most of them but she knew they were all on the fringes of the government. The only one who was really familiar made her wrinkle her nose. "I loathe Eversham, Alex," she said. "He's a pompous, bullying ass and his poor little mouse of a wife puts a damper on any dinner table."

"Nevertheless, I would like you to invite them," he said.

His tone was perfectly warm and pleasant but still Livia heard the hint of steel, and despite the evening's play, all her earlier misgivings arose in full flood. "Why?" she ventured.

He raised his eyes from his plate and it was there just for a second . . . that diamond-bright flint. "Sweeting, I have an interest in Lord Eversham's opinions."

"But he's a politician . . . I thought you said you weren't interested in politics?"

"If you recall, I said I wasn't interested in the process, but I did enjoy stimulating discussions."

"And these others . . . they will provide stimulating discussion?" She flicked almost derisively at the sheet of names.

"I hope so," he responded easily.

"More stimulating than Harry . . . or Nick . . . or David?"

"Harry I grant you, but Petersham and Foster are more interested in the gaming tables than the political arena," he said. "Although I enjoy their company on the right occasion. But there's a time and a place for everything, my sweet. So will you oblige me in this?"

"Yes, of course," she said swiftly. It was a simple enough request, it just seemed an odd time for him to be making it. "But I'd like to invite a few other couples just to dilute the brew."

"No." He shook his head. "Just these. That's all I need you to do."

Livia looked at him in frowning silence for a moment. The only reason anyone would want to invite such a group would be to further some political ambition, but Alex couldn't possibly have such an ambition. Maybe in his own country, but hardly in this one.

Oh, well. She gave a mental shrug. She could endure one boring evening with good grace if it would please her husband. He certainly went out of his way to please her. The reflection brought a dancing smile to her eyes.

"Then so be it. The only problem I can see is how to

divide the menu between your cook and the twins." She tapped the sheet again. "These people will enjoy the twins' rather more familiar culinary skills, and probably be a little suspicious of your cook."

"Boris will see to all the arrangements once you've issued the invitations. The twins will have no part in this dinner," he stated. "Come, let's to bed." He held out his hand to her over the table and pulled her to her feet. "My bed, I think. Yours is rather tumbled."

❧

Livia slept the sleep of exhaustion, but when she awoke in the morning it was with a renewed sense of unease that at first she couldn't put a name to. The curtains were drawn securely around the bed and she could hear Alex talking to Boris in the room beyond her enclosed space. They were not talking in English. She had a sudden memory from their first meeting when he'd told her he was fluent in many languages except Russian. He spoke to the dogs in Russian on occasion but she'd somehow assumed he only had a few phrases. She'd never heard him use it as fluently as he was now. And if it wasn't Russian he was speaking now, what was it? Certainly not French. Why weren't they speaking English anyway? Boris was fluent in the language.

They didn't want her to understand them. It was the only explanation that came to mind. But what possible conversation could Alex be having with his majordomo that she shouldn't hear? Perhaps it was something of personal concern to Boris, she decided. It was reasonable that he shouldn't want her to know his personal business. It wasn't as if they were exactly bosom friends.

She lay back and closed her eyes, letting the sounds wash over her, but even so there was something disturbing about the alien words, and she didn't like the feeling of deliberate exclusion. And now she realized that it was by no means the first time she'd felt it since her marriage.

When Alex drew back the curtains with a vigorous rattle, her eyes shot open. "Has Boris gone?"

"Yes, it's all clear." He came to the bed and bent to kiss her. "Good morning, my love. You slept well."

"Yes, like the dead," she agreed. "Was that Russian you were speaking? I thought you didn't speak it."

"I don't speak it very often," he said casually. "And rarely through choice."

"Why did you choose to speak it just then?" She tried to make the question sound merely casual.

"What an inquisitive creature you are this morning. Why would you wish to know?" He was smiling, but there was a speculative look in his penetrating blue gaze.

"No reason. I'm sure your conversations with Boris are no business of mine," Livia said.

"Boris would certainly agree with you," he said smoothly. "Are you getting up now?"

That seemed to be the end of that little discussion. "Yes." She pushed aside the covers. "What are your plans this morning?" She stood up and stretched, the air cool on her naked body.

Alex looked at her appreciatively, then he shook his head and reached for her discarded dressing gown. "Put this on, for pity's sake. You're too tempting and I'm too busy to yield to temptation this morning."

Livia made a mock moue of disappointment. "Too busy doing what?"

"People to see, places to go," he said with a vague gesture, heading for the door. "Don't forget those invitations. Boris will have them delivered as soon as they're written."

"How could I forget?" she muttered. "I still don't know why you want to condemn us to an evening of unconscionable boredom."

If Alex heard, he made no sign, and the door closed behind him.

Livia went through to her own chamber. Someone had been in and cleared away the night's supper dishes. The bed was made with clean linen and the fire relit. As she pulled the bell rope for Ethel she wondered with a suppressed chuckle if the disheveled state of the room had provoked some ribald talk below stairs.

She was going downstairs to her parlor a short while later when the front door knocker sounded. It was too early for social calls and no tradesman would come to the front door. Instinctively she stopped on the stairs, then moved back up them until she was out of sight around the curve of the staircase but had a clear view of the hall. Why she was behaving in this fashion she had no idea. It was her house when all was said and done, but for some reason in these last weeks she seemed to have become secretive, watchful, and she realized now that it was based on the same feeling she'd had that morning in Alex's bed. A feeling that there were things going on that were being kept from her.

She had always been so open in her responses, lying was foreign to her, and as far as she knew no one had ever deliberately lied to her in her entire life. Her father certainly had never kept anything from her or told her less than the truth. In her childhood he had encouraged her curiosity and generally answered her questions fully. On the rare occasions when he chose not to he had always told her the reason. But now she sometimes had the impression that she was living on the periphery of a world that operated by different rules, rules she was not to know. It was a world that ran on parallel lines to the one she did know and understand. The one that contained a loving husband, a vibrant circle of friends, a familiar round of pleasurable activities.

She was beginning to wonder if she was losing her grip on reality, as she hid on the stairs and peered down into the hall. Boris had opened the door and a swift exchange in Russian took place between him and the visitor, who stepped into the hall.

Livia recognized the man as the rough-looking visitor she had met briefly in the library when she'd gone to confront Alex about Morecombe and the twins. How long ago that seemed now. Boris escorted the man to the library and showed him in, leaving the door slightly ajar as he returned to the kitchen.

Livia moved swiftly down the stairs. She crossed the hall and pushed open the library door. "Oh, forgive me, I didn't realize anyone was in here," she lied with a smile, closing the door behind her. "We've met before, I believe." She held out her hand.

"Paul Tatarinov, Princess," he said, taking her hand in a brief clasp. "I am here to speak with your husband." He had a pronounced accent.

"I believe he's not at home at present," she said.

"I will wait," he stated.

"Of course. Please, do sit down. What may I offer you?" She gestured to the decanters on the sideboard.

"Nothing, thank you, Princess." He didn't accept her offer of a seat, but continued to stand awkwardly in the middle of the room.

Livia sat down, arranging her skirts around her. "So, have you been in London long, sir?"

"A few months, Princess." He spoke curtly.

"I see." She smiled sweetly. "And how long have you known my husband?"

He glared down at his shoes.

"Did you know him in Russia?" she inquired, still with the sweet smile.

"No."

A very unforthcoming gentleman, Livia thought. But the iron had entered her soul and she was determined to get something out of him. "So you met him in London, then? Are there many Russian émigrés here, do you know, Monsieur Tatarinov? I should call you *monsieur*?

Or is there some other title you prefer?" The smile was sewn to her lips and she didn't take her eyes off him.

"That is correct, Princess."

"And how many of you are there in London?" she pressed.

"A few," he responded.

She nodded. "I have met one or two. I imagine you spend much time together. It must be comforting to be in the company of your compatriots . . . I'm sure my husband finds it so."

That seemed to get his attention. He looked up at her sharply, his eyes hooded, his mouth hard, but before he could say anything the door opened and Alex entered the library. The expression that flashed across his face chilled Livia as nothing else had done, but then it was gone so quickly she couldn't be certain she'd seen it. But she knew she had.

"Ah, my dear, I see you're entertaining my guest." His tone was pleasant enough, but there was no warmth in his inscrutable gaze.

"Monsieur Tatarinov wished to wait for you," she said, getting up from the chair. "We were passing the time together . . . chatting about his experiences in London."

"I see." Alex held the door open. "Well, if you'll excuse us now . . ."

There was nothing for it but to make as dignified an exit as she could. Livia inclined her head in acceptance and turned to Tatarinov, extending her hand again. "I've so enjoyed our talk, monsieur. But I'll leave you with my husband now."

He took her hand and bowed with a click of his heels. Livia walked to the door, which Alex still held. She glanced up at him as she passed him, but his face was expressionless and his gaze cool as he bowed her from the room.

Alex closed the door and stood with his back to it for a minute. "I don't want my wife having anything to do with you," he stated.

Tatarinov shrugged. "I didn't invite the princess's company. What does she know?"

"Nothing, of course." He strode to the sideboard. "Vodka?"

"Aye. She asked a lot of sharp questions . . . seems uncommonly interested in your compatriots. I'd swear she suspected something." He took the glass from his host and drained its contents in one swallow.

"Don't be ridiculous, there's nothing for her to suspect," Alex said, pouring sherry for himself. But he was deeply uneasy. It was highly dangerous for her to blunder around asking questions, particularly of a man like Tatarinov. Somehow he was going to have to nip this hazardous curiosity in the bud.

Chapter Nineteen

Livia heard Tatarinov leave as she finished inscribing an invitation. Her pen paused, hovering over the engraved card, and despite herself her heart speeded with a touch of apprehension. She had no reason to be apprehensive; entertaining her husband's visitors was a perfectly ordinary courtesy from any lady of the house. And while the look Alex had worn when he saw her with Tatarinov had certainly chilled her, it hadn't been anger so much as dismay. Dismay and just the touch of alarm in the blue depths.

Had he gone out with his visitor or would he come in search of her? Resolutely she returned her attention to the invitations, and when the parlor door opened behind her she did not immediately turn around.

"So, what did you think of my visitor?" Alex inquired, deceptively casual.

"Oh, it's you," she said, laying down her pen and glancing over her shoulder.

"Who else would it be?" he demanded. He was leaning his shoulders against the door at his back, his arms casually folded, his expression as inscrutable as before.

Livia shrugged. "A strange man for you to keep company with, I would have thought," she observed. "He lacks polish."

"That is certainly true," Alex agreed amiably. "And as such is not fit company for my wife."

"But you invite him to the house," she pointed out. "How could he not be fit company?"

"I suppose if I simply say that he is not, you would not be satisfied with that?"

"I was not brought up to accept unilateral statements as reasons for doing anything," she said, regarding him quietly, although her body was wound tight as a coiled spring.

"Ah, the disadvantages of a wife who had her education at the hands of a mathematician." It was an attempt at levity that did not succeed.

"I have met some of your other Russian friends," Livia said, "and while I haven't spent much time in their company, I'd have to be blind and deaf not to recognize that they and Monsieur Tatarinov are cut from very different cloth."

"Perspicacious of you." He didn't move from his position at the door.

Impasse, it would seem. She nibbled the tip of her quill, watching him, waiting.

After a minute Alex said, "It seems we have come up

against a cultural fence, Livia. It may be customary in this society for a wife to entertain her husband's friends in his absence, it is not the custom in *my* society. I do not care to make my friends uncomfortable when they're under my roof. Does *that* make sense as a reason?"

"It's a very useful reason," she observed. "It seems to me the different culture argument can be trotted out in any circumstances to explain why things have to be done the way you dictate. But by the same token it could be used to explain why I expect things to be done as I'm accustomed. And I'm accustomed to greeting visitors to *my* house." It was the gentlest of emphasis but she saw his eyes flash.

"Be that as it may, in this instance, Livia, I will prevail. Tatarinov, as you rightly say, is not fit company for you. The fact that *I* enjoy his company is neither here nor there. I have many friends who would not be considered suitable society for my wife. And I'll lay odds any of your male friends would tell you the same story. Do you think Bonham, for instance, has no acquaintances that he would not introduce to Cornelia?"

"I have no idea," Livia said. Now she'd started, she was not going to give up. "But we're not talking about Harry, we're talking about you and the people who come into this house whom I am not even supposed to greet as their hostess. You don't really socialize with them, Alex. You don't play cards or invite them to dinner. You spend an hour closeted in the library and then they leave. Of course I'm curious. Do they have wives?"

"Not here," Alex said. "If they had it would be different. Then it would be appropriate for us to meet them in company. But Russian men without their wives are uncomfortable in the company of other men's wives." He was lying through his teeth but growing desperate. He couldn't simply issue an order and expect it to be obeyed. Not with this woman. But neither could he risk another encounter like this morning's.

"So what do you talk about when they visit?" Livia asked.

"We drink vodka and talk of Mother Russia," he told her.

"If you miss your country so much, why did you leave it?" Livia's curiosity was now in full flood and she didn't stop to think that if he hadn't left it, she wouldn't be married to him.

"I'm half English, I wanted to experience that half," he said with an easy shrug. "Now, can we stop the inquisition, please? It grows tedious." His voice was sharp, and his eyes cool.

"I'm sorry, I didn't realize it was an inquisition," she said. "But I know so little about you and each day we're together my ignorance grows rather than lessens. Is it so wrong of me to want to understand the man who's my husband?"

It was time for conciliation. "No, sweeting, of course it's not." He crossed the room and took her hands, drawing her to her feet. "It works both ways, you know. I am learning about you little by little, but there's still a large part of my wife hidden from me." He traced the shape of her mouth with his thumb.

"I don't hide myself from you," Livia protested, although she felt herself soften, the hard lines of her determination blurring under the caress and the warmth in his eyes. It was so much more comfortable to have back this aspect of her husband.

"You don't have to," he said. "Until a few months ago I didn't know you existed. Those years made you who you are now . . . I would learn more of them. But it takes time, my love." There was a note of appeal in his voice now. "Allow us to take the time we need. Nothing will be gained by haste."

And there it was. She could not persist without seeming petulant, and grudging, and ungracious. And Livia knew she was none of those things.

"I'm not trying to hurry anything," she said with a feeble attempt at a smile. "But I've never liked puzzles that have no answer, Alex."

He shook his head as if in exasperation and said, "Very well, I will give you an answer, but then you must promise to leave the subject alone, and to follow my wishes as far as these men are concerned. Can we agree?"

"Yes."

"Many of the émigrés left Russia penniless. In some cases they left their estates, their fortunes, everything they owned. In other cases, everything they owned was confiscated by the czar. I help them financially. But they're proud men and they would hate the idea that I had shared that knowledge with you."

"I see." Livia could think of nothing else to say. It was such a simple answer to the puzzle and one she could well understand. Of course he wouldn't wish to expose his countrymen's financial need to someone outside that circle, someone who knew nothing of what they had gone through to find themselves in penury. And of course they'd be awkward in her company when they were here for a handout from her husband.

"Can we leave this now, once and for all?" Alex asked, hating himself for his lies, and yet how else could he manage her? And they weren't entirely lies, he comforted himself. He was certainly a paymaster.

"Yes, let's leave it," Livia agreed. "And I'll forget we ever had this conversation. Your friends, if that's what you call them, will be safe from any encounter with me."

Alex sent a quick prayer of gratitude heavenwards, even as he wondered what problem would next raise its head.

"Do you have plans for this morning?" he asked. "Or would you care to ride in the park?"

A ride would blow away the cobwebs and any lingering dissatisfaction with the morning's resolution, Livia reflected. "Yes, let's do that." She tossed her quill on the secretaire. "I'll finish these when we get back."

His eyes went to the invitations. "How close are you to finishing them?"

"Just two left."

"Do them quickly, then, and I'll give them to Boris to deliver."

Livia frowned. "They'll keep until this afternoon."

"I think they need to go out as soon as possible," he said, picking up the quill. "Come, sit down again. It won't take a minute."

Livia gave a mental shrug. She couldn't see why it was a matter of such urgency, but the sooner it was done the better. She sat down and took the quill he dipped in the inkwell for her.

Livia went upstairs, wondering yet again why he was so anxious to entertain these particular guests. If he wanted to talk politics, why didn't he invite the men to dinner at one of his clubs? She gave another mental shrug and told herself yet again that a tedious evening was a small enough sacrifice to make for her husband.

⚬⚬⚬

The evening, however, produced enough interesting questions to leaven the tedium. Initially it was everything she had dreaded, the conversation alternating between vapid and hectoring. Alex appeared unmoved by either tone. He was a charming and attentive host, keeping his guests plied with wine and not blinking an eye when Lord Eversham demanded, "So, what's this emperor of yours up to, Prokov? Damned fool, if you ask me."

"I fear you're not alone in that opinion, sir." Alex leaned forward to refill the man's glass.

"No . . . no, indeed not," Lord Carmarthon declared, raising his heavy head from his plate. "Excellent turbot, this . . . I congratulate you on your cook, Princess Prokov."

Livia smiled her thanks. It *was* good, but Ada or Mavis could have done as well.

"Whole government's up in arms, I tell you," Carmarthon declared. "Not about the turbot, of course." He laughed as if at a significant witticism. "No . . . no . . . this business of invading Finland. Now what's that all about, Prokov?"

"I'm guessing it's at Napoleon's instigation," Alex said smoothly.

"Well that's what the prime minister says," the earl of Flintock declared. "Says your emperor Alexander's led by the nose and if we leave him to stew in his own juice he'll see which side his bread's buttered."

"Create merry mayhem in the meantime, though," Carmarthon muttered through a mouthful of salsify.

"Napoleon won't let him get his hands on Poland, that's what this is about," Eversham pronounced. "That's the word in government. Boney's keeping Alexander's sticky fingers off Poland."

Alex nodded and gestured to Boris to refill glasses. Livia, following the example of the other women at the table, added little to the conversation. But she was intrigued by it nevertheless. Alex's guests were heaping scorn on a man who was not only his sovereign but a man he'd known from a shared schoolroom, and he offered no defense. Instead his comments seemed to draw them further into criticism.

She signaled to Boris to bring in the second course and turned to answer a soft and somewhat inane question from Lady Carmarthon. Not that she could blame the woman for inanity at this particular gathering, it would be impossible to conduct an intelligent conversation while the men boomed their opinions and their words became slurred as the wine in their glasses disappeared.

"There'll be another conference between them, you mark my words," Eversham said. "The prime minister's convinced of it. Alexander will grow tired of being Boney's vassal and he'll start to make demands . . . and when that happens, the fat really will be·in the fire."

"An interesting opinion," Alex murmured. "Does your government have any real reason to expect such a thing?"

"Oh, yes . . . we have our intelligence." Carmarthon tapped the side of his nose suggestively. "We have every expectation that Alexander will come running back to the fold once the wolf roars. He'll seek another alliance with us, no question."

"There are those in high places who have a different view." One of the guests who had been listening in attentive silence spoke up. He was the only man apart from his host who was not the worse for wear. "They say Alexander is only pretending to friendship with Boney . . . lulling him into a sense of security. I understand you know the czar well, Prokov, how does that sit with you?"

"It may be," Alex said lightly. "But I couldn't say. I knew the czar well at one point, but we've had our differences recently . . . my emperor doesn't take kindly to criticism." He sipped his wine, his expression bland, but everyone around the table understood the implicit message. Prince Prokov was in exile, voluntary or otherwise, because he had fallen foul of his sovereign.

Livia, who thought she knew better, was puzzled. It was clear to her now that Alex had had an ulterior motive for this dinner party with these particular guests. But she couldn't work out exactly what he was up to.

Boris and two of his minions set out the second course. Livia had had no part in the ordering of this meal, as she would have done if it had been prepared by her own staff, but she could find nothing to object to in the menu. The Rhenish cream, the savoy cake, and the anchovy toast all found favor with her guests, as did the champagne that replaced the burgundy, which had accompanied the first course.

"Of course, with Napoleon putting his relatives on all the thrones of Europe, it's perhaps understandable that the czar would like to add King of Poland to his own crown," Alex said, deftly steering the conversation back to the original subject. After a while he caught Livia's eye and gave her an infinitesimal nod.

Livia accepted the signal that it was time for the ladies to withdraw and rose to her feet. The gentlemen stood up politely as the ladies left the dining room; then the serious drinking of the evening could take place. The decanter of port circulated and the men relaxed in their chairs, loosening neckties, leaning elbows on the table, following their host's conversational lead.

Livia endured the tedium of the teacups in the drawing room, listening to the chatter about children, the complaints about servants, the discussions of the latest fashions. Several times she tried to introduce a livelier topic but her guests didn't seem to know what to do with it, and she came to the conclusion that they were so unaccustomed to taking part in any subject outside the domestic realm that they believed anything else belonged to the realm of husbands and was thus beyond them.

Fortunately for her sanity the gentlemen joined them after a relatively short period. Alex came over to her where she sat in front of the tea tray. He bent to take a cup from her and murmured, "I tried not to leave you too long."

Livia passed a cup to the servant who stood at her elbow. "Take that to Lord Eversham, please." She glanced up at Alex from beneath her lowered eyelids and whispered, "I'd have been heading for Bedlam had you waited much longer. This is torment."

He nodded gravely as if she had said something of great import and strolled over to a sofa where three ladies sat side by side like sparrows on a clothesline. Livia had no idea what he said, but suddenly they were on their feet.

"My lord, I think we must be on our way," Lady Carmarthon said, with a flutter of her fan. She glanced sympathetically towards Livia.

"Yes, indeed, Eversham," that gentleman's lady agreed, with her own sympathetic look at Livia. "Such a pleasant evening, Princess Prokov . . . Prince Prokov. So kind of you to invite us." She came over to Livia and whispered, "My dear, how wretched for you."

Livia rose to her feet and responded with the wan smile that seemed appropriate in the circumstances. *What on earth had Alex said?* She shot him an inquiring look that drew only a solicitous smile in return.

"Yes, you poor dear, I know how dreadful these things can be," Lady Eversham murmured, taking her hostess's hand and patting it. "I trust it will pass soon."

"You are too kind," Livia murmured. *What was supposed to be the matter with her? Should she press her fingers to her temples, double over with a stomachache, dab at her eyes with her handkerchief?* She settled for fanning herself languidly and keeping the wan smile in place.

Alex escorted their guests to the door as soon as Boris reported that their carriages awaited, and Livia, acceding to the universal wish that she not disturb herself unnecessarily, remained in the drawing room with the teacups.

Alex returned after a very few minutes, looking remarkably pleased with himself, Livia thought.

"You look very smug," she declared. "What's the matter with me? I didn't know what symptoms to play up."

"You did very well," he said with a grin. "I thought I

should do something to give you a reprieve, since you endured the tedium with such a brave face."

"Yes, but what did you say?" She looked at him a little suspiciously. There was something about that grin.

"I merely hinted that you were a little under the weather, a touch of migraine, only to be expected in the circumstances . . ."

"You implied that I was pregnant?" She stared at him.

"Either that or very much not so," he said airily. "They could draw their own conclusions. But I have noticed that ladies, particularly those with the sensibilities of our guests, tend to respond to female complaints with instant sympathy."

He laughed at her speechless indignation. "My dear girl, only an earthquake otherwise would have dragged their husbands away before they'd had recourse to my cognac. Their ladies needed to be sufficiently engaged with your complaint to overcome for once their overbearing husbands."

Livia could see his point and her mouth curved in a reluctant smile. "Well, it was outrageously indecorous of you, but I'm grateful for the reprieve, however you managed it. But what was the evening about, Alex?" She was serious now, watching him closely. "You had something in mind, but I don't understand what. I understood you to be a friend of the czar's and yet you implied that you were his enemy."

He didn't answer immediately, instead pouring himself a glass of cognac. "May I pour one for you?"

"No, thank you," she said with a touch of impatience. "I just want an explanation for why I've spent the last four hours in that company. What were you doing?"

"I was interested in their views," he said. "I heard them talking in the club a few weeks ago and it interested me." He turned back from the sideboard, his goblet in his hand. "I do on occasion feel rather far away from my home, my dear, and sometimes it's a pleasure to talk about it."

Livia frowned. "That's all. You're homesick and so you invited them so that you could talk about Russia and the czar?"

"In a nutshell." He sipped his cognac.

"But why those men in particular?"

"It so happens that they all have a finger in the pie of foreign affairs," he told her. "They're not particularly important members of your prime minister's team, but I was interested in their views and thought they would be more forthcoming in a social setting."

It was a perfectly reasonable explanation, and yet something niggled at the back of Livia's mind. "Why did you let them believe that you and the czar are at outs?"

"To a certain extent we are," he said simply. *And it was only the truth.*

"Did he send you into exile?"

He shook his head. "No, no, we're not that badly at outs. But I felt it might be wise to absent myself from St. Petersburg for the duration of this war." He smiled rather ruefully. "Slavs tend to be hotheaded, Livia, and our royal courts can be dangerous places when a particular faction gets the wind beneath its wings."

"You thought you were in danger?"

Again he shook his head. "Not really, but I felt a change of scene would be beneficial." He came over to the sofa and sat beside her. "Are you satisfied, sweeting?"

"Of course," Livia said. How could she not be? But she wasn't. There was a ring of truth but the tune was off-key. "I think I'll go to bed. Are you coming?"

"In a short while. I have some correspondence to catch up with." He leaned sideways and kissed the corner of her mouth. "Thank you, my sweet, for putting up with my whim."

"What's one tedious evening in the scheme of things?" she said lightly, rising to her feet. "Wake me." She blew him a kiss as she left the drawing room.

Alex stayed where he was for a while, sipping his cognac. The explanation he'd given her had been close enough to the truth that it should have satisfied her. But he had the unmistakable impression that she was not convinced.

He got up with a sigh. It would have been easier all around if Sophia Lacey had named as her heir some nice mousy lady with an amenable disposition and a somewhat blunted intelligence. He glanced up at the portrait over the mantelpiece and raised his glass in a toast. Absurd to imagine that that vibrant, strong-featured woman could have chosen as her heir any woman who fitted his description. But why exactly had she chosen Livia Lacey?

He made his way to the library, thinking about this. Livia had said once that she'd been told Sophia wanted to leave the house to a woman who bore her name. Even if she didn't know her, even if the kinship was as vague as Livia implied that it was. But why?

He sat down at his desk and dipped the quill in the inkpot, but for a moment he didn't attempt to put pen to paper as he gazed into the middle distance. Sophia's own child could not be named in her will. She shared no name with her own child. Could she have wanted to choose an heir who had a named connection with her, however tenuous? A female heir, someone who could not possibly remind her of the son she had given up?

His gaze went to the top shelves of the bookcase and he shook his head in defeat. Whatever mental gymnastics he put himself through, he could not reconcile the idea of a woman who possessed such texts with the father whom he had known.

He put pen to paper and realized that the ink had dried on the nib during his cogitations. He had little interest in writing his dispatch to St. Petersburg tonight, but it needed to be done while the ideas were still fresh. Diversionary tactics were complicated enough without a faulty memory.

⸙

Livia awoke the next morning with the now familiar sense of unease. She lay gazing up at the embroidered tester that portrayed a rather wonderfully erotic copy of a Fragonard painting. It had been part of the original furnishings of the house and she had come to like it so much that she had had it cleaned and repaired in the renovations. Another little piece of the puzzle that was Aunt Sophia. How many lovers had she enjoyed in this bed, gazing up at that richly sensuous scene?

Alex stirred beside her and as always came awake in an instant, clear-eyed and coherent, with none of the cobwebby tendrils of dreams and sleep that always plagued Livia for a few moments on waking. "Good morning, my love."

"Good morning." She stretched indolently and turned her head on the pillow for his kiss. "It's raining." The relentless drumming on the windowpanes was loud in the room.

Alex sat up. His gaze flicked upwards, as it always did in this bed, to the tester. And his thoughts were very similar to his wife's. "That's a nuisance, I was engaged to ride with some friends." He pushed aside the covers and stood up, rubbing the back of his neck. "What are your plans for the day?"

"A lunch party, but I think I'll make my excuses." Livia hitched herself up against the pillows, enjoying the sight of her naked husband. "Will you ring for Ethel?"

He did so, came back to the bed to kiss her again, then went into the adjoining chamber to ring for Boris, who, despite his elevation to majordomo, continued to serve as the prince's valet. He sharpened the razor on the strop and handed it reverently to his master, draping a warm towel around his neck.

Alex dipped the razor in the water. The dispatch he had written the previous night needed to be sent by the clandestine courier service, but he intended that it should also come to the notice of Prince Michael Michaelovitch before it went on its way. A nice piece of deflection that would cover tracks most effectively. How best to do that?

He was still considering his options when he went down to breakfast and found a message from Tatarinov beside his plate. It was oblique but clear enough to Alex. *Contact has been made.*

Alex helped himself to a dish of creamed herring and poured a tankard of ale. Livia never joined him for breakfast; she maintained that his choice of diet in the morning turned her stomach. He considered her preferred menu of coddled eggs, bread and butter, and strong tea to be equally repulsive, but fortunately it was not a bone of contention. There were enough of those already, incipient for the moment certainly, but lurking, a layer of complexity beneath the apparently smooth surface of their marriage.

His wife was puzzled, confused. She was uneasy. Alex knew that. But he also knew he couldn't give her the answers that would solve her problem. He needed her, needed the framework of this marriage within which to work, and he could not risk jeopardizing that framework.

Contact had been made with their agent in the army. The man had the funds to act. Now he needed the opportunity. *And the courage.* He would be unlikely to survive.

Alex buttered a piece of black bread, wondering what kind of man it was who sent another man to his death while staying warm and safe at home.

Should he call this off . . . go and take care of it himself? The opportunity would present itself to him quite easily. But of course he couldn't. He was the man who organized, arranged, and paid.

And he had a wife. Which brought him full circle. He would have to leave her in England and he couldn't do that. It would leave her unprotected, and his personal protection was all he had to give her. A more personal involvement would endanger her even more than she was already endangered.

Most of the time he succeeded in ignoring the danger she was in by concentrating on the conviction that such a consideration was secondary to the vital business that had brought them together. His father had instilled in him the belief that there was no higher motive, no greater goal for a man, than patriotism. No sacrifice was too much for one's country. But did he have the right to involve in his own patriotic struggle someone for whom the issue had no relevance?

Alex got up from the table with Tatarinov's message and went into the library. He sat down and wrote a warm invitation to Prince Michael Michaelovitch.

Chapter Twenty

THE RAIN SHOWED NO SIGNS of lessening through-out the morning. Livia debated excusing herself from her luncheon party and then decided against it. For some reason she was restless and the weather didn't help. Alex, undeterred by the wet, had gone to his club, and the prospect of staying alone with only a book for company, listening to the rain beating against the windows, seemed a poor prospect.

"Morecombe, I'll take the berlin to Berkeley Square this morning," Livia instructed as she crossed the hall on her way upstairs to change. "It'll keep the rain off."

"Oh, aye," he said, and wandered away towards the kitchen regions.

Livia, unperturbed by this monosyllabic response, continued upstairs, knowing that Morecombe would send Jemmy to fetch the coachman, and indeed when she came down to the hall a little later Morecombe was standing sentinel at the front door.

"Coach is 'ere." He struggled with the bolts and eventually pulled open the door.

Livia put up her umbrella and ran down to the street, where Jemmy held the carriage door open for her. "Nasty day, m'lady."

"That it is," she agreed, handing him the umbrella as she climbed into the gloomy and somewhat dank interior of the ancient coach. Slow and lumbering it might be when compared with the barouche, but at least it had a roof.

The rain had not diminished when she left Betsy Ormond's house in Berkeley Square a couple of hours later.

"That's such a wonderfully eccentric coach, Livia," Betsy observed, accompanying her guests to the front door.

"Maybe, but it's also very practical in this weather," Livia said cheerfully. "May I take anyone else up?"

"If you don't mind dropping me in Albermarle Street, my dear, I'd be grateful," an elderly lady said, winding an extremely long fur boa around her neck and then tucking her hands into her muff. "Hargreaves has the carriage this morning, and I was going to send a man for a hackney, but I'd much prefer to travel in such delightful style."

"I'll be glad of your company, Lady Hargreaves," Livia said. "Ah, here's Jemmy with the umbrella."

Jemmy ran up the steps with the umbrella raised to shelter the women the short distance from the door to the carriage. "Tell the coachman we'll be going to Albermarle Street first," Livia instructed as she stood back to give her passenger precedence into the carriage. She climbed in after her, careful not to step upon the trailing boa, and Jemmy closed the door.

"So, my dear, how's married life?" her companion inquired, leaning forward eagerly, eyes bright at the prospect of a confidential chat.

"Well enough, I thank you," Livia said, unsure as always quite how to respond to such inquiries, unless they came from Nell or Ellie.

"No happy event on the horizon as yet?" the lady asked. "Oh, impertinent of me, I know, my dear, but forgive an old woman's curiosity."

"Not as yet," Livia said, hoping that would put an end to the topic.

"Ah, well, it can take a while," Lady Hargreaves said comfortably. "So long as that husband of yours is patient."

Livia simply smiled a response. Her companion leaned forward again. "It's amazing what you've done with Sophia Lacey's house . . . I was only saying to Hargreaves just the other day how she'd barely recognize it now. It was such a pity that in the last years she became so reclusive. Quite the gadabout she was in her youth, and even later when with all the goodwill in the world one had to admit she'd passed her prime."

"How well did you know her?" Livia tried to conceal the extent of her interest.

"Oh, not well, my dear. She was fifteen years older than I . . . we moved in different sets." She gave a small laugh. "My mama would not permit me to mix with Sophia's circle."

"Oh, why not?"

"She had a reputation, my dear." Another chuckle punctuated the confidence. "There was always talk wherever Sophia went . . . men around her like bees at the nectar, and her door knocker was never still with the parade of gentlemen calling upon her. None of us gals was ever permitted to get too close . . . always whisked away at the most interesting moments."

"Was there ever a scandal?"

Lady Hargreaves shook her head. "There was always talk, but I never knew any details. Whatever it was happened when Sophia was very young, long before I knew her . . . some mad love affair, I daresay, but no one would ever talk of it openly."

She sighed. "I admit I always envied her . . . such excitement . . . to be considered not respectable always seemed so dashing to us poor conventional debutantes. Ah, Albermarle Street. Thank you so much for the lift, Livia dear."

"My pleasure, ma'am."

"I did enjoy our little chat," the lady said, enfolding herself in the fur boa again as she edged out of the carriage. "Give my regards to that handsome husband of yours . . . I've often thought I've met him somewhere before . . . nonsense, of course . . . quite impossible, but sometimes there's an unmistakable impression." She shook her head. "I'm becoming a foolish old woman.

Good-bye, my dear, good-bye." Waving merrily, she gathered up the trailing fur and went up to her own front door.

Livia chuckled. She liked Lady Hargreaves, as did Nell and Ellie. The ladies of that generation were in general a lot less silly than those of their own and on occasion had a refreshing candor about subjects that modern society considered taboo. She'd confirmed Livia's suspicions about Sophia Lacey rather than offered any new insights, but nevertheless, what little she'd said had whetted Livia's perennial curiosity about her benefactress.

The carriage drew up outside the house in Cavendish Square and Livia hurried out of the rain into the lamplit hall. "Is my husband in, Boris?" she asked as she unbuttoned her pelisse.

"He has a visitor, Princess. In the library."

"Ah." Livia nodded. Off-limits, in other words. She went to the stairs, hurrying up to her chamber to take off her hat and pelisse. Alex was occupied, it was still raining, and a book by the fire seemed no more appealing than it had that morning. On the other hand, the memory of the conversation in the carriage was still very fresh in her mind. On impulse she picked up the oil lamp that was already lit on her dresser and made her way up the narrow staircase to the attic.

She'd only been up here once since she'd taken up residence in Cavendish Square. It had been dirty and dusty, full of shrouded shapes, trunks, and boxes, and as she stood on the threshold, holding the lantern high, she reflected that, unsurprisingly, things had not improved. Something scurried across the floor in a dark angled corner. Rats . . . mice . . . squirrels?

Livia was not squeamish about livestock, however. She hung the lantern on a hook suspended from the steeply gabled ceiling and a pool of light illuminated the central part of the attic. The corners remained in shadow. Four round windows under the eaves were obscured by a lacy tracing of cobwebs, but there was little enough light outside anyway, so they made little difference.

Livia looked around, wondering where to start. Dust-covered shapes that were obviously discarded furniture were of no interest. If there were treasures up here she would be very surprised. It was the trunks and boxes that intrigued her.

She was struggling with the catches of an iron-bound chest, which seemed to have rusted in place, when she heard her name. It was Cornelia's voice from the floor below.

"Liv . . . Liv, where are you?"

"Up here, in the attic," she called back, scrambling to her feet, brushing the dust and dirt off her cambric skirt.

"What on earth are you doing up here?" Cornelia appeared at the head of the stairs. She looked around with interest. "It's filthy."

"I don't suppose it's been cleared out in years," Livia said, regretting that she hadn't thought to change into something old. "Is Ellie with you?"

"Yes, she's downstairs talking to the twins. Franny has

been pestering her for days for some of those ginger-bread men that our Mavis bakes, so she's asking her to make some."

"That'll please Mavis," Livia said somewhat absently. "I don't really know where to start."

"I think the question is why would you want to start in the first place?" Cornelia said. "God knows what's up here."

"That's exactly the point," Livia told her. "There could be anything." She gestured expansively at their surroundings.

"Liv . . . Nell . . . are you up here?" Aurelia's quick step sounded on the stairs and she emerged into the attic. "What on earth are you doing?"

"My question exactly," Cornelia said. "If you want to go through all this stuff, why don't you get the servants to carry it downstairs so that we can look at it in a civilized manner?"

"No, that's too much trouble. I'm happy enough up here, but you don't have to stay."

"Oh, yes, we do," Aurelia stated firmly. "Having braved the rain to visit you, we're not going to turn tail." She bent over the chest that Livia had been wrestling with. "These locks need to be pried loose. There must be something up here, like a crowbar or something." She looked around.

"Try this." Cornelia picked up a thin metal file from a gate-legged table with one leg missing.

"Let me try." Livia took it from her and knelt in the

dust again, prying the locks up with the end of the file. It took a few minutes but finally they sprang loose. "Now, what have we here?" She lifted the lid and sneezed as a cloud of dust rose from the interior of the chest. .

"It looks like old clothes." Cornelia peered over her shoulder.

Livia lifted out the top layer of heavily embroidered gold taffeta. "Heavens, it's a ball gown of some sort." She shook out the folds. "It would have had a hoop underneath with panniers and suchlike."

"I do believe it's the same gown that Sophia's wearing in the portrait in the drawing room," she said. "Oh, it's full of moths . . . what a pity."

"I'm going to look in those boxes over there." Cornelia went over to a pile of boxes under the eaves. "Do you want to help, Ellie?"

"I want to investigate that trunk over there," Aurelia said, now as caught up in the project as her friends.

Livia lifted out the layers of clothes in the chest, fascinated by the elaborate designs, the yards and yards of material. In these clothes Sophia would have worn powdered hair and strategically placed beauty patches on her face. As she sorted through the clothes Livia felt a strange connection with the woman who had worn them; it was almost as if Sophia's spirit were lurking in these dusty, moth-eaten folds.

Ridiculous fancy, of course, but one she rather liked. She buried deeper in the chest and her fingers closed around something that was not cloth.

"What's this?" She lifted it out. "Oh, it's a writing case, I think." She got to her feet and carried the case to the rickety table. "It's locked. I wonder where the key could be."

"Probably still in the chest," Cornelia suggested, sitting back on her heels.

Livia went to look. She took everything out, shaking out the folds of material while a veritable dust storm enveloped her, but there was no key.

"You can probably break the lock with that file," Aurelia suggested, still burrowing in the trunk. "There's some lovely cashmere in here, and a beautiful mantilla. What a waste to leave them for the moths."

But Livia was too absorbed in her task to pay attention. She pushed the file into the lock and tried twisting it, then wrenching it. Brute force would ruin the writing case, but since it had been moldering in the attic for heaven only knew how long, it hardly mattered. Finally the lock gave way and she opened the case.

Packets of letters tied with blue ribbon lay neatly stacked inside. She picked up one packet, untied the ribbon, and picked up the top sheet. The paper was yellowing and the seal on the back was broken, but it was of thick, heavily embossed red wax. She put the edges together and saw the initials AP.

"What have you found?" Cornelia asked, glancing over her shoulder.

"Letters, packets of them." Carefully Livia opened up the sheet, afraid it would disintegrate. The ink had faded somewhat but the writing was strong and masculine. The letter began:

> *My heart, it has been so long since I heard from you. I have not smiled since I left you and doubt I will ever do so again. I love you too much ever to find peace or laughter or even rest again. Sometimes I conjure up the image of the ordinary everyday things around you. Simple objects like the fork that you use, the pillow for your head, the little silver box where you keep your rings, your handkerchief with the embroidered initials. And then I see you again, feel you in my arms, inhale the sweet fragrance of your skin . . .*

Livia read on, feeling like a trespasser, an eavesdropper, and yet unable to stop herself. It ended simply. *Yours unto death, A.* And then, at the bottom, engraved on the paper, was the name *Prince Alexis Prokov.*

Livia stared at it, uncomprehending. It didn't make sense and for a lunatic moment she thought the letter had to be from Alex. But of course it wasn't. How strange, she thought disjointedly, that Sophia had also known a man called Alexis Prokov.

"What is it, Liv? You look as if you've seen a ghost." Cornelia came over to her.

"I have," Livia said. She handed the letter to Cornelia and opened another sheet. The same name engraved on the bottom, the same initials, the same outpouring of love and sorrow.

"What does it mean?" Aurelia asked, reading over Cornelia's shoulder. "Who is this Alexis Prokov?"

"I have no idea," Livia said, opening letters feverishly now, scanning them with hungry eyes.

Cornelia exchanged a worried glance with Aurelia, then she said gently, "Liv, I don't see how it could be pure coincidence."

Livia looked up from the letter she was reading. "No," she agreed, a deep frown between her brows. "No, I don't see how it could be." She looked in the writing case. "There are dozens of them in here, they must cover several years, I would have thought."

"Are any of them dated?" Aurelia asked.

"None so far. Here, you take some and have a look." She handed them a packet each and then continued with her own. The three of them read in concentrated silence, each moved by the deep emotion the letters revealed.

"I wish I could read Sophia's side of the correspondence," Livia said at last, folding the final letter carefully into its creases. "They clearly loved each other with a grand passion." She stood frowning, her fingers steepled at her mouth. "But they never married. I wonder why not."

"Perhaps he was already married," Aurelia suggested, tying the ribbon again around her own packet of letters.

"Perhaps." Livia dropped the packet back into the writing case. "But just what relation was Prince Alexis Prokov to Prince Alexander Prokov?"

"A distant relative?" offered Cornelia, but without much conviction. Something was seriously awry here.

Livia shook her head. "I don't think so," she said, then added slowly, "I think I had better get it from the horse's mouth, don't you?"

"Yes," Aurelia agreed. "And I think we should leave you to do that, Liv."

"Unless you want us to stay?" Cornelia added.

"No, but thank you. I need some time to think this through before I talk to Alex." Livia was surprised at how cool, how calm she felt . . . how distant from emotion.

"We'll go now." Cornelia kissed her. "Send for us at once if you need us."

"Yes, promise," Aurelia insisted, hugging her.

"I promise." Livia smiled vaguely at them. "But it won't be necessary. I'm sure Alex will be as intrigued by this extraordinary revelation as I am."

"Yes, of course." Her friends went swiftly to the stairs. "Don't come down with us," Cornelia said. "We'll call tomorrow."

Livia made no attempt to follow them. She stood motionless in the attic for a long time, staring at the dusty cobwebs. It couldn't be a coincidence. A man bearing Alex's name had been Sophia Lacey's lover. Was that what had brought Alex to this house? Did it have something to do with the single-minded way he had pursued her?

But how or why would that be? Sophia was dead, and it was to be assumed her lover was too. Abruptly she shook her head as if she could somehow dismiss her fears. Nothing was to be gained by fruitless speculation. If Alex had answers to her questions, then he must give them to her.

Livia gathered up the writing case, unhooked the lantern, and left the attic. She went first to her bedchamber and put the case on her dresser, then she went in search of Morecombe.

She found him in the twins' kitchen, drinking tea in a rocker by the range. The scent of gingerbread was rich and heavy in the air. "Did Lady Farnham take the gingerbread for Franny?" she asked.

"Aye, come for it a minute or two past," Mavis said, rolling pastry on the pine table.

"You wants summat, m'lady?" Morecombe inquired, making a half-move to get to his feet.

"No . . . no, I just wanted to ask you all something." Livia traced a pattern in the flour on the table with a fingertip. "How long were you in Lady Sophia's service?"

The three of them seemed to consider the question at some length. "'Twas just 'afore the Regatta on the Thames," Ada said finally, adding a pinch of salt to the simmering contents of a cauldron. "Remember that, Morecombe? Oh, what a day that was, all them boats on the river. Pretty as a picture."

"Oh, aye, Lady Sophia give us the day off," Mavis remembered. "She looked right pretty herself, had a seat up there in the grandstand with all the toffs."

"What year was that?" Livia asked, brushing the flour off her finger.

"Oh . . . don't rightly know . . ." Morecombe muttered.

"Seventy-five," Mavis stated. "'Twas the year I got my fox bonnet."

"You've the right of it, our Mavis," Ada agreed. "Seventy-five, that was it. We started in with Lady Sophia in January. Lady Sophia was with that Austrian chap . . . you know the one, Mavis?"

"The one with the moustaches," Mavis said with a reminiscent chuckle.

"Eh, that's enow," Morecombe growled from his rocker. "What's past is past."

The twins seemed to remember Livia's presence and with a quick glance in her direction fell silent.

"Don't mind me," Livia said. "I'd love to hear all your memories of Lady Sophia."

"Well, as to that, we'll mind our tongues, ma'am," Ada declared. "She was a fine lady, and never hurt a soul in her life."

"But she knew how to enjoy herself," her sister said with a chuckle. "And she never turned a hair when others did too."

Livia decided it would be prudent to beat a retreat before something was said that the speaker would later regret. If they'd joined Sophia's service in 1775, they hadn't known Alexis Prokov. Alex had been born several years earlier and as far as she knew had been in Russia with his father from the moment of his birth. Although, what was truth anymore?

"Well, I'll leave you to your work. Prince Prokov is very fond of that veal and ham pie, Ada. Maybe you could make one for lunch one day next week."

"Aye," Ada agreed without expansion.

Livia left them and made her way to the hall, where Boris was as usual in attendance. "Is my husband still with his visitor, Boris?"

"No, Princess. Prince Michaelovitch left half an hour ago."

"Thank you. Would you ask Prince Prokov to come up to my bedchamber?" Livia moved to the staircase. "At his convenience, of course."

Boris bowed and went towards the library.

Alex was contemplating the success of his little play that afternoon. It had been so simple, but then Prince Michael was a simple man. When he'd been left alone with the dispatch to the emperor lying openly on his host's desk, it hadn't occurred to him to question the convenience, or Prokov's apparent carelessness. Alex, ostensibly fetching a particularly fine claret for his guest, had watched through a crack in the adjoining door as Prince Michael had devoured the contents of the dispatch. Alex thought he understood why the fearsome Arakcheyev employed such a naïve tool as Michael. The man never suspected manipulation or deception and was so obviously proud of the work he thought he was doing, he could be set to follow any scent, as implicitly obedient to instinct as any bloodhound.

But now Michael would be able to report to his masters that Prince Prokov was fulfilling his task as the emperor's eyes and ears in exemplary fashion.

Boris's knock disturbed his moment of self-congratulation. "Yes?" He looked up, half expecting and more than half hoping to see Livia's smiling mouth and sparkling gray eyes. He concealed his disappointment with an interrogative eyebrow. "Yes, Boris?"

"Princess Prokov, sir, requests that you attend her in her bedchamber when it's convenient," Boris intoned.

"Thank you." He nodded dismissal and the majordomo backed out. What was Livia up to? She never gave Boris her messages. If she had something to say to him she came in and said it, or stuck her head around the library door and asked him to join her in the parlor. Why would she use Boris to pass on an invitation to her bedchamber?

Well, there was only one way to find the answer. He dropped wax onto the dispatch and impressed his signet ring, then he tucked the missive into his waistcoat. Later he would deliver it himself to the clandestine poste restante at the Black Cock in Dean Street.

He went into the hall. "We'll need the carriage at eight o'clock, Boris. My wife and I are going to the theatre."

"Yes, Prince." Boris bowed. "You'll be dining in, I understand."

"Yes, before the theatre." Alex mounted the stairs and knocked on the door to Livia's bedchamber.

He entered at her invitation. "I've been puzzling

about why my wife in the middle of the afternoon would summon me to her bedroom," he teased. Then his expression changed as he saw her face. She was very pale, her eyes strained.

"Is something wrong, love? Are you unwell?" He crossed quickly to where she sat at the dresser.

"No, I'm not unwell," she said. "As to something being wrong . . . to tell you the truth, Alex, I don't know. But perhaps you do." She passed a hand over her eyes, suddenly both weary and rather frightened. Her earlier calm had vanished as the reality of the letters had finally taken hold.

He took her hands, looking down at her, and now he saw the fear. "What is it?"

"These." She pulled her hands free and gestured to the writing case. "I don't understand them."

"What are they?"

"Letters I found in the attic. Read them for yourself."

Alex took up the top packet, untied the ribbon, and carefully unfolded the yellowing paper. He read in silence while Livia sat on the dresser stool, watching his face in the mirror.

After a while he picked up the remaining packets and went to sit on the bed. He said nothing as he opened each sheet and read systematically. Livia remained where she was, looking at his reflection in the mirror. She could read nothing in his expression, which had become once more inscrutable.

Alex was stunned. His father had written these. His

father had been capable of so much passion . . . so much feeling. The cold, distant, emotionless, duty-bound parent that Alex had known had once been *this* writer. And nowhere in the letters was there mention of himself, of the child of the woman he was writing to. Had she never asked after him? Had she not cared what became of him?

He went back through the letters, for the moment oblivious of Livia, searching for something he might have missed, a glancing reference even. But there was nothing. It seemed that as far as Sophia Lacey was concerned, her son had never existed.

But the passion between herself and his father, that was so real it almost scorched his fingers as they turned the pages.

He looked up at last, holding the final letter between his hands. "Astonishing," he said. "I would never have believed it possible."

"Believed what possible?" She turned on her stool to look at him. Her voice was flat and distant.

"That my father was capable of writing such things." He shook his head, his mouth twisted.

"Alexis Prokov was your father?" The same flat voice.

"Yes . . . and Sophia Lacey was my mother."

"I see." But she didn't. Not yet. "No, I don't see," she said, sounding stronger now. "I don't understand anything, Alex. Why did they not marry? Was your father married already?"

"No," he told her. "He never married either, and now I understand why." He tapped the letter in his lap. "And he never gave me a real reason why my mother was will-ing to let him take me and carry on with her life as if I'd never existed." He gave a short laugh. "As a boy I some-how assumed it was my fault, I wasn't loveable enough."

"I could feel sorry for that child," Livia said slowly. "But I see only the man now, and I know he has lied to me. As far as I can see, my marriage is a farce, a per-formance for some audience I know nothing of. You came after me for some reason that it's clear to me now had nothing whatsoever to do with the person that I am. I'm owed an explanation for that."

Alex sighed. "Yes," he agreed. "I believe you are." He could give her half an answer at least. "I came to London on a secret mission for the czar. He withdrew his ambas-sador from the court of St. James's last November and since then it's been imperative that he have eyes and ears here." He shrugged. "I am those eyes and ears."

"And that explains dinner party discussions about Russia and all those closeted visitors, I suppose."

"Yes."

"But why did you have to find a wife?"

She'd believe no comforting lies, Alex knew. It was better to cut deep once and then stitch the wound quickly.

"For an extra layer of protection," he said. "A ready-made social position, a hostess, a normal, ordinary ap-pearance that no one would question."

"But why me? Why would you choose me to use? There are any number of unattached women in society who would have been delighted to accept what you were offering." Her voice was cold now.

Alex got off the bed and came over to her. He put his hands on her shoulders, gazing down into her eyes. She looked as if she'd received some dreadful wound, he thought, and his heart ached. "My love, you must believe that it's been many, many months since I thought of you as anything but the woman I love."

"Why me?" she repeated, her nostrils flaring slightly. "You came after me like a terrier after a rat. I ask again, *why me*?" She twitched her shoulders impatiently as if to rid herself of an irritating itch.

He let his hands fall from her shoulders. "This house," he said. "My mother did not actually own it, although she clearly thought she did. My father gave it to her for use in her lifetime only."

Livia stared at him. "Are you saying she had no right to leave it to me?"

"Yes," he said simply. "I came to London intending to claim my property. This house was listed as a part of my father's estates . . . estates to which I am the sole heir."

"So why didn't you simply take it, then?" she demanded harshly. "I presume you have legal documents proving your ownership; why didn't you evict me with the full permission of the law?"

"That was certainly one of my options . . . until I met you," he responded. "But that night at the Clarington's ball . . ." He shrugged, trying to smile. "From the moment I saw you, Livia, I was lost. I realized that by choosing you for my wife, I could have the house too."

"What an admirable conservation of energy," she said with a cynical twist to her mouth. "Two birds with one stone, as they say."

"I probably deserve that," he said, pushing a hand through his hair in a gesture of frustration. "I didn't intend it to sound quite so brutal."

She didn't respond and he tried once more. "You must believe that such considerations soon became irrelevant. You *must* believe that, Livia." His gaze intensified as he tried to convince her of that truth, but he could see from the blankness of her own stare that he was getting nowhere.

"Would you go away now?" Livia turned back to face the mirror, but she could barely recognize the image looking back at her. She stayed like that until she heard the door close behind him, then she dropped her head onto her folded arms and allowed the tears to come.

Chapter Twenty-one

I GOT YOUR MESSAGE . . . WHAT'S SO hellfire important that you had to drag me away from a woman?" Sergei grumbled as he came into the smoke-filled chamber. "A good woman too. Got an arse on her like a carthorse . . . and by God, does she know how to use it." Blackened teeth showed in a lascivious grin as he drew an obscene diagram in the air.

"A communication from Arakcheyev. It says they've picked up a suspicious character in Nystad." The man called Igor took a swig from the vodka bottle and passed it over to his compatriot. There were no refinements in the dingy lodging above the pie shop in Cheap Street.

Sergei drank in his turn and wiped his mouth with the back of his hand before passing back the bottle. "What did they get out of him?"

"Not much at present. He's a member of the imperial guard and he'll be hard to break, but he has gold on him, English gold. We're to pick up Sperskov. Softer meat . . . we're to find out what he knows of the gold."

He took another swig. "Sperskov or Fedorovsky. Arakcheyev says either will do. Whichever one we can pick up without too much fuss."

Sergei laughed. "Sperskov's more of a fool than the other one. Full of ideals, that one. And I know just how to snare him. He has a little love nest in Half Moon Street . . . married lady, so he doesn't stay with her all night. I'll pick him up as he slips out. Where should we take him? No good here, it's a noisy business and there's too many people around."

"There's a place on the river. A warehouse of sorts in Botolph Lane, you can't miss it, it's at the end and there's only river rats to hear." Igor spat onto the stinking sea coal in the grate. "They'll not care one way or the other."

"You want me to bring him there?"

"Yes, but not until after midnight."

"Then I'll go back to my whore for an hour. She still owes me a few moves." Sergei went to the door, pausing with his hand on the latch. "You'll do the business? Or you want me to?"

"We'll both do it. I've no objection to spilling a drop or two of aristocratic blood." Igor laughed derisively. "I'm not squeamish."

Sergei shrugged. "It makes no difference to me. I'll have the stomach for it after another hour with my girl and a good capon her dame has roasting."

"After midnight, then." Igor took up the bottle, reflecting that for the work ahead tonight he needed vodka rather than roast capon in his belly.

❧

Duke Nicolai Sperskov stepped into the street, closing the discreet green door of the house in Half Moon Street behind him. He adjusted the set of his hat and set off towards Piccadilly. There was a spring to his step and he swung his cane in jaunty fashion as he passed the mouth of a narrow alley. He had no warning. One minute he was breathing the frosty air of a wet February night, feeling well satisfied by the evening's pleasures, and the next he was suffocating in the smothering folds of a horse blanket.

He was half carried, half dragged a few feet even as he cursed and swore and fought against his silent assailant. He was bundled up into a carriage and fell onto the floor, the door slamming shut behind him. The vehicle lurched forward and he struggled to free himself from the swaddling cloth. A boot landed in his stomach and he choked, gasping, curling over the pain. And still not a word had been spoken by his assailant.

❧

Alex listened outside the door to Livia's bedroom. He could hear nothing, but Boris had said she hadn't left her chamber all evening. He raised his hand and knocked gently. No response. For once he was reluctant to go in without permission. He would never have given it a second thought before that afternoon, but she had told him to leave her then, and now he wouldn't force himself on her.

"Livia," he called softly. "May I come in?"

There was still no response, and sighing, he turned away from the door, entering his own chamber. He knocked again on the adjoining door to her chamber but with little hope for a response. Either she was asleep or she still couldn't bear to lay eyes on him.

It was only just after midnight. He went to the window that looked down on the deserted street, drumming his fingers on the pane. He'd spent a wretched evening, trying to close his mind to the letters with drink and cards, but he couldn't find oblivion. Why had his father never mentioned their child in all those pages of passion? If Sophia had asked after her child, surely her lover would have answered her? To refuse to do so would be somehow punitive and there was nothing in those letters that indicated anything except the deepest, most enduring love.

He'd hoped that this house would give him some insight into the woman who had given birth to him. Instead he now had more questions than answers. Morecombe had so far resisted all attempts at friendly confidences and he could hardly go around questioning all and sundry about the character of the late Sophia Lacey without arousing general curiosity, and Livia's in particular.

He turned away from the window, looking at the door to Livia's chamber. He could probably make peace with those puzzles; he had lived with them all his life, he could continue to do so. But much more significant damage had been done to a completely innocent, uninvolved woman, and he was at a loss to know how to put it right.

He thought now that if he lost Livia he would have no difficulty finding within himself the fluent passion that had informed his father's letters to Sophia. But eventually such a loss, such a fruitless expending of love, would break him as he now suspected it had broken his father, finally changing him from a warm, passionate man into an unbending, withdrawn, emotionless man who couldn't love his own child.

He couldn't allow that to happen.

He crossed the room to the adjoining door and gently turned the knob, half afraid it would be locked against him, but it swung open onto Livia's darkened chamber. The fire was almost out, the candles guttered, the curtains at bed and windows open. It seemed as if she had gone to bed refusing any attentions from her maid.

He tiptoed to the bed and looked down at her. With a shock he realized that she was wide awake, her eyes open, gazing up at him.

"I thought you were asleep," he said softly. "I didn't mean to intrude."

"A little late, don't you think, for such delicacy?" Her voice was hoarse, little more than a rasp, and he could see in the dim gray light from the window how her eyes were red and swollen, her countenance blotched.

"Ah, Livia . . . please don't," he begged, reaching for

her hand where it lay on the covers. "Please, my love, let us try to put this right."

She drew a deep, shuddering breath and closed her sore eyes. "I'm so tired, Alex, I can't do this tonight."

He still held her hand as he looked at her in something akin to despair. Every instinct told him that to leave it there, to let her fall asleep filled with this wrenching anger, would be the worst thing he could do.

"Sleep, then, while I rekindle the fire and do something to make this room more comfortable," he said. "You've had no dinner?"

She shook her head on the pillow, a grimace of distaste crossing her face, her eyes still resolutely shut. "I'm not hungry. I just want to sleep. Leave me."

"I've done that once today," he said with decision, "and I don't think I'm going to do it again." He laid her hand back on the coverlet and moved away from the bed. He drew the curtains at the window, shutting out the dark. There was kindling and a scuttle of coals in the hearth and he set about getting a blaze going.

He fetched fresh candles from his own chamber and set the sticks on the mantel, leaving the bed in shadow. It soothed him to be doing something practical with visibly satisfactory results and he could tell from her breathing that Livia had not gone to sleep.

He went back into his own chamber for the cognac decanter that Boris always left out for him and poured two glasses.

He carried one over to the bed. "Sweeting, drink a little of this."

Livia opened her eyes. "You're not going to go away, are you?"

"Not yet," he agreed, holding out the goblet. "You look as if you need this."

Livia had never believed in pointless combat. She couldn't force him to leave her alone, and while she was tired unto death she knew she couldn't sleep. Cognac might help. She pulled herself up against the pillows and took the goblet, inhaling the fumes that were powerful enough to clear the stuffiness from her nose.

"Let me fetch you something to eat," he suggested. "Or hot milk?"

"No, thank you." She sipped the cognac. "So, how do you suggest putting this right, Alex? You've deceived me, betrayed me, pretended to love me—"

"*No*," he interrupted. "I will not allow you to say such a thing. I have never pretended to any of my feelings for you, Livia. I will grant you the moral high ground at present, but I tell you straight you will lose that advantage if you accuse me of things that are absolutely *not* true. Is that clear?"

His vehemence startled her out of the slough of misery, and in part of her mind Livia recognized that it was a timely jolt. Self-pity was a loathsome vice and she'd been in danger of sliding into its viscous depths.

"But you *have* deceived me," she said more moderately. "You *have* lied to me."

"Yes, I have." He sipped his cognac. "And for that I am sorry. But in truth, Livia, I don't see how I could have taken you into my confidence. I am spying on your government, when all's said and done."

"Oddly enough I had realized that for myself," she said with a welcome return to cynicism. "And how do you think that makes me feel?"

"Rotten, I would imagine."

"Nicely put. A cat's paw is the answer I would have chosen." She held out her empty goblet. "More, please."

He fetched the decanter. "Go easy . . . it's powerful stuff on an empty stomach."

"It can't make me feel worse than I already do," she said, then pulled herself up. More self-pity. It was a debilitating emotion; anger was much better.

"This house was the symbol of my independence," she stated. "I loved . . . no, love it. In my heart it's mine, and to be told on top of everything else that I have no claim to it is the worst kind of practical joke. Do you understand that? Are you even capable of understanding that?"

"Yes," he said baldly.

"And what does it mean to you? You have other houses, don't you?"

"Yes."

"So, why do you want mine? Oh, no need to answer that. I know, it's not mine and a man always has to claim his own property, otherwise he's less of a man. I understand that." Her tone dripped sarcasm.

"I didn't take it away from you," he pointed out. "If

you hadn't found those letters you would never have known the truth. I saw no need to tell you . . . to hurt you unnecessarily."

And Livia was obliged to admit the truth of that. Without the letters she would have continued in happy ignorance, married to her prince, unaware of his deception and therefore unhurt by it.

She chose another tack. "As a matter of interest, once your work here is done, where were you intending that we should continue this life of married bliss? I assume your czar will have other missions for you? Was I to be a part of them?"

This was territory he couldn't go into. There was no knowing the outcome of this enterprise. "That's an insulting question," he stated. "You are my wife, and my life is not whole without you. For the duration of this war, we will remain in London. Afterwards . . . who knows? I will go where duty takes me, and you, my wife, will be at my side."

"A loyal and obedient wife," Livia murmured. "Just as a Russian husband expects."

"Now you are really beginning to annoy me."

She shrugged. "Deny it."

He looked at her in frustration. "Just how different is that expectation from one that an English husband would have? Wives are chattels in law in your country too, Livia."

"Checkmate." Livia finished her cognac. "You may lay down the law, husband, and I am legally bound to accept it. However, as you know perfectly well, legality is not always the final arbiter. I have a father, powerful friends . . . if I choose to leave you, then I will do so, and there will be nothing you can do to prevent me."

Alex took an involuntary step back from the bed. "How did we get onto this byway, Livia? I love you. And I believe you love me."

Livia closed her eyes for a second, then she said in a soft, defeated voice, "Yes, for pity's sake, I do."

Alex nodded. "Then let us have done with foolish talk about legality and possessions. A deep wound has been inflicted and we have to heal it . . . but we have to heal it together, sweeting. I am guilty, I accept my guilt, but I swear to you I will do everything in my power to make it up to you."

"You will tell me everything about your spying? About who you are, what you are, what you intend doing?" She watched him closely. "You will take me absolutely into your confidence, now and always?"

Oh, what a tangled web we weave. He couldn't possibly promise that, not yet. Not while so much remained to be done. "I cannot promise that," he said with deep regret. "And you must swear to me that you will not confide what you do know of my activities to anyone."

Livia closed her eyes again. "I swear it. And now we have nothing more to say to each other."

Alex stood helplessly by the bed for a moment, then he turned away, drawing the bed curtains around her. He picked up the candles, took them back to his own chamber, and closed the door softly behind him.

Livia slept eventually, but it was a restless sleep plagued with confused strands of dreams that left her filled with a vague sense of premonition and the absolute knowledge that something was very wrong, but in her dreams she couldn't identify it.

When she awoke memory was bitterly clear and she had no difficulty identifying the source of her unhappiness. Her eyes felt sore and dry and her head ached. She dragged herself out of bed and went to the dresser mirror. Even in the dim light in the bedroom she could see what a fright she looked, her hair standing out around her head in a tangle of curls like Medusa's snakes, her face pasty white, her eyes red. She couldn't ring for Ethel looking like this.

There was some cold water in the ewer and she poured a little in the basin and splashed her face, holding a washcloth over her eyes. It brought some relief. Then she tugged her brush through her hair, trying to restore some order to the tangle.

She paused, her hairbrush in midair, at the sound of voices from the adjoining room. Alex and Boris, of course. She wondered dully if Alex would come in to her this morning. And if he did, what she would do . . . say. She seemed to have cried away all coherent thought, all rationality. She was just a bundle of confused emotions.

She pulled the bell for Ethel and went to draw the window curtains back. The previous day's rain was gone and a watery sun shone from a washed-out blue sky. Soon it would be spring and the square garden would be a mass of yellow forsythia and daffodils.

"Good morning, m'lady." Ethel bustled in with a tray of morning chocolate. "Oh, you're up and about already." She set the tray on the dresser and gave her mistress a concerned look. "I waited for you to send for me last evening, ma'am. Are you quite well?"

"Yes, quite well," Livia said, hearing how listless she sounded. She tried to inject a little spirit into her voice as she said, "I fell asleep early last night and couldn't believe it when I only awoke a few minutes ago. I must have been really tired."

"Yes, m'lady." Ethel didn't sound too convinced. "You had no dinner, though."

"I wasn't hungry," Livia said in a tone that she hoped would close the discussion. "I believe I'll ride to Mount Street this morning, Ethel. Please put out my habit."

"Yes, ma'am. Will you take breakfast in the parlor, ma'am?"

Livia debated. There was no sound from next door now; presumably Alex had already gone downstairs. "No, bring a tray for me up here, Ethel, I'll breakfast by the fire when I'm dressed."

Cowardly, she knew, but she wasn't ready to bump into Alex accidentally and she was by no means prepared to face him for the next round of this miserable business. And there would be a second round. It was by no means over. She would have to make a decision, more than one, and she was far too muddled at this point even to frame the question, let alone the solution.

∽◦∾

Alex surveyed the breakfast table without enthusiasm. He had no idea what to do. And it was such an unusual situation for him to be in, it left him feeling oddly bereft. He couldn't take his wife into his confidence, at least not at this juncture, and if she insisted that reconciliation depended on his confidences, then it was an impasse.

He poured coffee and glanced at the post that Boris had left beside his plate. Invitation cards and bills. He had no interest in the former and the latter were merely a necessary nuisance.

He looked up sharply at an alerting cough from the door. "Excuse me, sir." Boris bowed. "There is a visitor . . . Monsieur Tatarinov." Boris managed to indicate what he thought of the gentleman in question simply by a downturn in his voice.

Alex frowned. It was far too early for social calls, not that Tatarinov was in the habit of making such calls. It had to be pressing business. "Show him in, Boris."

Tatarinov entered the breakfast parlor before Boris had the chance to summon him. "Prokov, good, you're at home."

"I usually am at this hour of the morning," Alex said amiably. "Please, sit down. Coffee?"

"No, vodka if you have it." The stocky Russian came up to the table.

"Of course . . . Boris?" Alex signaled to the major-domo, who instantly departed. "Won't you sit down, Tatarinov?" He gestured to a chair opposite.

"No . . . no, I have no wish to sit down . . ." The man was visibly agitated.

"You appear troubled, my friend," Alex observed, spooning sour cream onto his plate of smoked mackerel.

"With good reason," the other said. He sniffed. "That smells good."

"Sit down, man." Alex waved his fork at the chair and pushed the platter of smoked fish across the table. "Whatever it is will keep long enough for you to eat and drink."

Tatarinov sat down and piled a plate with smoked fish, spooning sour cream lavishly on top. He reached for a dish of chopped egg and took a liberal helping, then took a hunk of black bread from the basket.

Boris set the vodka bottle and a stubby glass at Tatarinov's elbow. "Will that be all, Prince Prokov?"

"For the moment, yes, thank you, Boris."

"So, what's amiss, Tatarinov?" Alex asked when they were alone once more.

"Sperskov's gone missing," Tatarinov said through a mouthful of mackerel. He poured vodka into the glass and tossed it down his throat, smacking his lips with satisfaction.

Alex frowned. "I don't understand. How could that be?" He took a sip of coffee.

"No idea." Tatarinov shrugged. "But he didn't sleep at home last night."

"He has a mistress," Alex reminded him, dabbing at his mouth with his napkin.

"Yes, but the woman's married. He never spends all night in her bed. I went to his house this morning and they said he hadn't come home last even." Tatarinov helped himself to more bread. "I went to that little love nest of his, in Half Moon Street. The servant there told me the duke left soon after midnight and his lady a little later." He stuffed a piece of fish-laden bread into his mouth, chewing stolidly as he regarded Alex across the table with the air of one who has just presented a fait accompli.

"He could have gone anywhere after he left the house," Alex said, shaking his head with a touch of impatience. "The man has friends in this city." He shrugged. "More than one lover, I shouldn't wonder. Sperskov's always had a taste for the softer side of life."

His visitor grimaced. "Aye, an aristocrat through and through, that one. I've always thought him too soft for this business. He's only half a mind on it, the other half's between a woman's thighs."

"You're harsh, my friend," Alex protested. "Sperskov is an idealist."

"We've no need of such in our ranks," Tatarinov declared. "We need warriors."

"We need both," Alex said firmly. "Nicolai is loyal to the cause, blindly so, and his contacts make him indispensable. Why did you go in search of him in the first place?"

"The man's in charge of communications. He should

have received something from Nystad by now. I went to discover if there was anything."

Alex nodded. They all had clearly defined roles in this business and Sperskov's network of friends and acquaintances across Europe made him the perfect conduit for communications. "Where else have you looked for him?"

"Nowhere as yet. I thought to find out if you knew anything first. You're the one who keeps tabs on them all." He poured more vodka and tossed it back with the same flick of his wrist as the first glass.

"Well, I know nothing. I suggest we cast our net wider. I'll visit the foreigners, the French and English he numbers amongst his acquaintances, you take the Russians. If we draw a blank then, then we'll start to worry."

"Very well." Tatarinov pushed back his chair. "And I thank you for breakfast, Prince. Makes a change from the slop they serve in this benighted city." He gave himself one last gulp of vodka.

"Just one more thing, Tatarinov . . ."

"Yes?" He paused, the glass halfway to his mouth.

"If he doesn't turn up, what exactly do you think happened to him?" Alex dropped his napkin to the table.

Tatarinov shook his head. "Only one thing as I can see . . . Arakcheyev's men."

"I thought you had them under watch," Alex said sharply.

"I do, but I can't watch them every minute. I don't know every communication they get. You can be sure Arakcheyev knows every member of this little cabal, except . . ." He paused, looking at Alex, his black eyes narrowed. "Except you, Prince. You are the czar's friend, his observer and reporter on the English scene."

"True enough," Alex agreed, aware of a strange prickle on his nape. "And your point, Tatarinov?"

"For the moment none, and God willing, there will be none," his visitor stated, heading for the door. "We'll talk again this afternoon?"

Alex nodded. "Five o'clock, at the Black Cock in Dean Street."

"I'll be there."

Alex stayed at the table for a while after his visitor's departure. There was no reason to suspect Arakcheyev's hand in Sperskov's mysterious disappearance, but it was an unnerving thought.

And it did nothing to help him deal with his other problem. Should he go to Livia? Try once more to thrash it out? Or would he be better served by leaving her for a while? Once the initial force of her anger and hurt had lessened, as it had to, then perhaps she would see things differently. He could not fulfill the terms of her ultimatum, therefore nothing would be gained by another confrontation. Time might soften her attitude, and maybe he could come up with some half-truth that would satisfy her. But the very idea left a sour taste in his mouth. There'd been enough half-truths and downright untruths in his marriage. There must be no more.

Chapter Twenty-two

Livia arrived at Mount Street soon after eleven o'clock without coming across her husband. Boris had informed her that the prince had called for his horse and left the house straight after breaking his fast. He had given no indication of when he would return. It was all to the good, Livia reflected. She needed time for reflection. When next she saw him, she would have to have come to some decisions.

"Is Lady Bonham in?" she asked Harry's butler.

"Yes, ma'am. The ladies are in her ladyship's parlor," Hector informed her.

"Good. I expect to be here for some time, so I've sent my groom with my horse to the mews."

"Very good, my lady." Hector bowed and showed her to the parlor door.

"Oh, Liv, there you are." Cornelia jumped up from her secretaire. "I was writing you a note. We've been debating whether to come to you this morning or wait for you to send for us."

"Yes, and since we couldn't decide, we thought we'd send you a note and see what you'd prefer," Aurelia said, laying aside her tambour frame as she too rose from her chair. "How are you?" She examined her friend carefully. "You don't look too robust, my love."

"I'm not feeling robust," Livia said with a wan smile, unpinning her plumed hat. "I'm only glad you're both in."

"We wouldn't have gone anywhere without contacting you first," Cornelia said. "We hoped you'd turn to us when you needed us." She too subjected Livia to a grave scrutiny. "Oh, you poor dear, you've had a bad time. Come and sit down."

Livia shook her head. "Not yet, I'm too restless to sit." She paced the elegant room and her friends watched her in silence, waiting for her to decide when to come to rest.

Livia was in a quandary. She needed these women's counsel more than she'd ever needed it, but she would keep her promise to Alex not to reveal anything of his real work. However much she believed she could trust her friends, she couldn't forget that Nell was married to a member of the English secret service and she would not under any circumstances put her in a position of divided loyalties. Somehow she must get their advice, elicit their opinions in an effort to make sense of the situation herself, without actually revealing the truth that lay beneath every one of Alex's otherwise seemingly despicable actions and deceptions. And however much she loathed the idea that he was working against her own country, rationally she could accept his desire to work for his own.

"Alexis Prokov was Alex's father, as I imagine you guessed," she said eventually. "And by the same token, Sophia Lacey was his mother."

"Why didn't he tell you that from the very beginning?" Cornelia asked, frowning. "Once he'd met you and he realized that you have the same surname as his mother, wouldn't it have been natural to have exclaimed at the coincidence?"

"Except that he knew it was not coincidence," Livia said. She gave a bleak sigh. "But he never knew his mother. Can you imagine how hard that must have been for a child? He knew she was alive and well, but he was not allowed to know her. He must have thought that she didn't want anything to do with him."

"It would explain why he didn't want to talk of her," Aurelia said cautiously.

"Yes," Livia agreed, "but there's something else that's not so easy to explain. The house in Cavendish Square didn't actually belong to Sophia Lacey. Either she didn't understand, or she simply forgot after so many years, but Alex's father gave her the unrestricted use of it throughout her lifetime. On her death it reverted to his estate. And you can guess who is the heir to that estate."

There was a stunned silence.

Eventually Aurelia said slowly, thinking her way through it, "He didn't need to marry you to get his hands on the house, he could simply have evicted you."

Livia shrugged. "He maintains he saw no need to do that, because he decided I would make him an ideal wife. He simply ensured that the house became part of the marriage settlements."

"It would have been honest of him to have explained all this to you when he proposed," Cornelia said, "but maybe he felt it would be indelicate, Liv."

"Yes," Aurelia put in quickly. "It would have been a mite awkward to propose to a woman in one breath and then tell her she's already living in his property in the next."

It was no good, Livia realized. Without telling her friends the whole truth, she could never get a view of the matter that would really be able to help her clarify her decisions.

"I suppose you're right," she conceded. "But I still feel betrayed. And I can't help wondering if getting his hands on the house didn't have something to do with that whirl-wind courtship."

She sat down finally, perching on the arm of the sofa. "You must admit it was somewhat overpowering . . . you had suspicions, Ellie, you know you did."

"Yes," Aurelia agreed. "But *you* didn't, Liv. And you said that if you burned your fingers at a fire that excited you so much, then it would be with full knowledge." She twisted her hands in distress. "Forgive me, love, I don't mean to speak hard truths, but the situation exists and you have to decide whether to live with it . . . or how to."

And there it was, Livia thought. A hard truth and a hard decision. They didn't need to know about the spying, it wasn't really the issue at all. "But should I not feel betrayed by his deception?" she asked.

"Do you believe he loves you?" Cornelia went to the decanters on the sideboard and poured three glasses of sherry.

Livia saw his face, his eyes as he'd made his declaration at her bedside. "Yes," she said. "He says so and I believe him." She took the glass Cornelia offered her with a nod of thanks.

"And you, Liv?" Aurelia took her own glass.

"Oh, yes," Livia said simply. "With all my heart . . ." She laughed a little sadly. "All my hurt heart."

"Then you have to decide whether his deception was somehow an error of omission, a mistaken attempt to save you some pain, or deliberate because the man's an unmitigated, lying scoundrel," Cornelia declared.

"So I do," Livia said, taking a sip from her glass. "So I do." And somehow she had made up her mind. As long as it wasn't the latter, and she knew in every ounce of her being that Alex was true in his feelings for her, then she would have to find a way to live with the man he was. And somehow, somewhere, she would find forgiveness for his deception.

"Let's take the children to Gunters for ices," she suggested suddenly. "It's a lovely sunny day, maybe a little chilly for ice cream but the children won't mind."

The other two women looked at her a little strangely.

"Is that the end of this, then, Liv?" Cornelia asked.

"The end of my going round and round in circles," Livia stated. "I've worried my head into a tangle of knots and I need to be distracted. So, let's go to Gunters. I've a fancy for that bergamot ice."

"The children will have had lunch in the nursery by now," Aurelia said, "but Linton will still complain that it'll spoil their dinner." She laughed. "Oh, why not, Nell? We haven't had a set-to with Linton in weeks."

Cornelia was already pulling the bell rope. "We'll take the barouche."

Stevie, Franny, and Susannah were a bubbling, excited distraction, thrilled at the prospect of an excursion with their mothers and without the watchful eye of their nurse. Ices at Gunters were always a treat, but one rarely indulged in February. They stopped the barouche outside the establishment in Berkeley Square and a waiter dodged through the traffic in the square to take their order.

The children shrieked their choices in a crescendo of excitement. Cornelia deftly extricated the essentials from the babble and gave the waiter a clear order. "Liv, you'd like the bergamot pear?" she added.

Livia was no longer sure that she fancied what had seemed appealing half an hour before, but she acceded.

"I want to try that parmesan ice," Aurelia said. "It sounds so interesting."

"And I'll have the coffee," Cornelia said.

The relieved waiter dodged his way back across the street into Gunters, returning in a few minutes with their order balanced on a tray. The children clamored to take their ices into the square garden under the now winter-bare maple trees and dispersed under supervision of the groom and Daisy while the women stayed in the carriage.

"You don't seem too enthusiastic about that berg-amot, Liv," Aurelia observed after a minute, watching Livia play with the ice in her glass, taking tiny tastes on the tip of her spoon.

"Perhaps it wasn't such a good idea," Livia said. "How does the parmesan taste?"

"Delicious," Aurelia said with a laugh. "But probably better at the dinner table. It's a combination of cheese and sweet."

"You should have stayed with the conventional," Cornelia declared, scraping the last morsels of coffee ice from her glass. "But it grows chilly, inside now as well as out. We should get the children home."

"Yes, and I need to go back to Cavendish Square," Livia said, leaning down from the barouche to put her empty glass and spoon on the tray the waiter held. She was ready now, her mind clear. Ready to make her de-mands, ready to look for the compromises that her father had told her she would have to find when inevitably they came to a crossroads. And Alex would be ready now.

"Would you like to take the barouche home?" Cor-nelia asked. "Your groom could bring Daphne back."

"No," Livia said. "I'll enjoy the ride . . . it's barely fif-teen minutes, after all."

"You're comfortable, Liv, with what you're going to

do?" Aurelia asked sotto voce as the children piled back into the barouche.

Livia gave her a quick smile. "With what *I'm* going to do, yes. How Alex will respond, I don't know."

"Don't forget that we're always here," Cornelia said, seizing Susannah's strawberry-sticky hands in her handkerchief before they smeared her pelisse. "Any time, Liv. Send for us."

"Yes, I know," Livia said. "And I thank you both."

❦

She arrived back at Cavendish Square just as the day was fading. The streetlamps were not yet lit but the house lights were on as she hurried up to the front door.

Surprisingly it was Morecombe who opened it. At this time of day he was usually ensconced in his own quarters and Boris ruled supreme.

"Good evening, Morecombe." She stepped through the door. "Where's Boris?"

"Off for the evenin'," Morecombe stated. "Someone needs to keep the door."

"Yes, of course," Livia said. "Is Prince Prokov in?"

Morecombe shook his head.

"Oh." Livia was at something of a loss. "Have you seen him this afternoon?"

"Oh, aye," Morecombe said, closing and bolting the front door.

"And he went out again?" she asked, patient, because impatience would slow the process even further.

"Men come for 'im," Morecombe said. "You want yer dinner in the parlor, m'lady. Our Ada's made your favorite roast lamb wi' that there red-currant jelly."

"Delicious," Livia said absently. Something wasn't quite right here. "Did the prince say he wouldn't be in for dinner when he left with his friends?"

"Summat on those lines, my lady," Morecombe stated. "Shall I set dinner in t' parlor, then?"

The one issue that concerned the single-minded retainer, Livia reflected, knowing that nothing would deflect him until he had his answer. "Uh . . . yes, thank you," she said, going to the stairs. "Are you sure my husband left no message?"

"No, no message," Morecombe said, turning back to the kitchen. "Dinner'll be ready in an hour."

"Thank you," Livia said. On impulse she turned from the stairs and went into the salon. The image of Sophia Lacey gazed out serenely from above the fireplace.

But how serene was she? Livia stepped closer, looking up into those astonishing blue eyes. She should have known, she thought. They were the twins of Alex's. And they were so unusual it was extraordinarily dimwitted of her not to have noticed.

But then, how could she have remarked on something that as far as she was concerned had absolutely no relevance to her life? Such connections only became obvious when one was in possession of certain facts.

She was aware of an overwhelming sense of anticlimax, of frustration. The knowledge of having reached a decision had buoyed her during the afternoon and she'd been going over in her head the words she would use when she saw Alex. To find that he'd gone out without a word, without making any effort to communicate with her, brought a resurgence of anger. Perhaps he really couldn't care less whether they were estranged or not. It certainly seemed as if it hadn't bothered him unduly. How else could he calmly go off with his friends without a word to her? But then, of course, he was probably out and about on his country's business, she thought in renewed frustration. It seemed it took precedence over his marriage.

Livia went upstairs to change out of her riding habit. She pulled the bell for Ethel and then wandered through into Alex's room. The empty space was filled with the sense of her husband, but it felt wrong somehow. She looked around, frowning slightly. A crumpled cravat lay on the dresser, a coat was thrown carelessly over a chair, a pair of boots seemed to have been flung into a corner, the armoire was open, and the coverlet on the bed was rumpled.

Had Alex gone out in such haste that he hadn't troubled to summon Boris's assistance? Why hadn't anyone come in to tidy up after him?

A feeling of unease crept over Livia as she looked around. It was a vague feeling but it lifted the fine hairs on the nape of her neck. She turned and went back to her own room, where Ethel was setting a ewer of hot water on the marble-topped washstand.

"Did you see Prince Prokov this afternoon, Ethel?" she asked as she unbuttoned her jacket.

"No, m'lady. Will you wear evening dress?"

"No, I'm dining alone tonight, just bring me the velvet robe, please." She shrugged out of the jacket and unhooked her skirt. "What time did Boris leave?"

"About three o'clock, m'lady."

"Was that before or after my husband left?" She stepped out of the skirt and went to wash her face and hands at the washstand.

"I don't rightly know, madam." Ethel handed her a towel. "I didn't know the prince had gone out."

"Oh, I'll ask Morecombe, then, when I go down." Livia dried her face and hands and then slipped her arms into the wide sleeves of the robe that Ethel held out for her. She fastened the buttons down the front, then sat at the dressing table while Ethel unpinned her hair and brushed it out.

"Will you leave it loose, m'lady?"

"No, pass me the netted snood." Livia caught her hair up at the back, twisted it into a loose knot, and slipped the snood over it, confining it tidily on her nape. "That's all, thank you, Ethel. But would you go and tidy up next door? I can't understand why no one's been in since my husband left."

"Perhaps no one knew his lordship had gone out, ma'am, what with Boris not being here. Mr. Morecombe probably didn't think to mention it."

"No, I'm sure not," Livia agreed. It was a more than

likely explanation, and it wasn't that important when all was said and done. "Does anyone in the servants' hall know where Boris went?" Boris's absence struck her as rather odd. In all the time they'd been in London she couldn't remember his leaving the house unless specifically on Alex's business.

"Not as far as I know, m'lady. Probably his afternoon off," Ethel suggested.

"Yes, I suppose so," Livia agreed. "I didn't realize he ever took one."

"He doesn't, usually," Ethel said. "But maybe he knew the prince was going out and he wouldn't be needed."

"Maybe so," Livia said with a shrug. "See to tidying Prince Prokov's chamber anyway, please, Ethel. He won't want to come back to it looking like that. I'm going downstairs." She went down to her parlor and rang for Morecombe.

He appeared after about five minutes. "You want summat, m'lady?"

"Yes. Did you see Prince Prokov leave this afternoon?"

"Aye. He an' two men. They come for him about fifteen minutes earlier. I let 'em in an' Jemmy showed 'em up."

"Showed them up? What do you mean? Into the library, surely."

"Well, as to that, I know what 'appened. They asked for the prince, I told 'em he was above stairs, an' they said they'd go on up. So I tells Jemmy to take 'em up." Morecombe's gaze was a trifle truculent.

"I didn't mean to contradict you, Morecombe," Livia said swiftly. "I was just a little surprised."

"Oh, aye," he said stolidly. "Well, about fifteen minutes later they all three come down an' go off. There was an 'ackney outside waitin' on them."

Alex went off in a hackney? Livia stared at Morecombe. "The prince didn't send to the mews for his curricle . . . or his horse?"

"No, as I says, there was an 'ackney waitin' on 'em."

"Thank you, Morecombe." Livia gave him a quick smile of dismissal and the old retainer shuffled off. She left the parlor and went into the library, uncertain what she was looking for. It all seemed tidy and in order, papers neatly arranged on the desk, quill pens sharpened, and the faintest hint of Alex in the air.

But her unease increased. She wandered aimlessly around the room, looking for something, but she had no idea what. It was ridiculous to feel this sense of foreboding. Alex had gone out for the evening, as simple as that. He often went out with his friends, or his compatriots . . .

She turned and went back into the hall, looking for Morecombe again. She found him in the parlor setting a place on the table in the window for her dinner. "Were they foreigners, these men who came for the prince?" she asked.

"Reckon so," he stated, polishing a wineglass on his sleeve. "Spoke funny . . . kind of thick like. Not the usual kind of friend," he added somewhat obliquely.

It was a long paragraph for Morecombe, Livia reflected. "How do you mean not the usual kind?"

"Rough customers, I reckon." He set the wineglass in its place and looked over his handiwork. "You want a bottle of the '92 burgundy with the lamb?"

"Oh, yes, lovely, thank you." Livia frowned into the fire. The only acquaintance of Alex's whom she would describe as a rough customer was Tatarinov. But her husband was a spy, up to every kind of devious scheme, how should she know who his friends and colleagues were? She hadn't even known the truth about the man himself, and he'd gone out of his way to keep her well clear of the men he worked with. A couple of rough customers more or less was probably all part of a spy's world.

She poured herself a glass of sherry and sat down by the fire to await her dinner. She was not going to worry over this another minute. Alex would reappear later . . . of course, if he'd gone out for the evening, and knew he was out for the evening, he would have changed into evening dress.

She set down her glass just as Morecombe came in staggering a little beneath the weight of a laden tray. "Was the prince in evening dress when he went out?" she asked casually.

"Not as I remember," Morecombe said, setting a roast saddle of lamb on the table. "There now, there's parsnips an' a dish o' them scalloped taties that you like. Peas with onions, an' red-currant jelly. Our Ada wants to know if you'd fancy a brook trout t'follow."

"Oh, no, this all looks wonderful," Livia said hastily. "Prince Prokov doesn't know what he's missing."

Morecombe greeted this observation with a sniff and pulled the cork on the bottle of burgundy. "Right y'are, then. That'll do you."

"It certainly will, thank you." Livia sat down at the table and gazed unseeing at the feast laid out before her. She seemed to have no appetite but she couldn't risk upsetting Morecombe and the twins. Resolutely she carved herself some lamb.

Chapter Twenty-three

BY CLOSE TO MIDNIGHT, LIVIA was beside herself. She knew that Alex would have sent her a message if he intended to be out this late. He would not deliberately cause her concern, however at odds they were. He hadn't changed into evening dress so he obviously hadn't had any formal plans to dine with friends, or go to his clubs, or attend the theatre or the opera. Anyway, he would never have done the latter without seeing if she wanted to join him, or at least before yesterday it would have been unthinkable.

She paced the parlor, too restless even to try to read or sew. Perhaps he'd gone to a card party, an informal gathering where they played high and drank deep. She knew that he sometimes did. Not that she'd ever seen him even slightly the worse for wear. Whom could he be with? She racked her brains trying to think of someone obvious to ask, but no name came to her.

And anyway, she told herself, if he was merely at a

pleasure party, he would have sent a message to say he'd be late home. She couldn't get away from that certainty.

Could he have had an accident? Knocked down by a carriage? Fallen foul of the gangs of footpads who roamed the alleys? Images of his bleeding body sprawled in some dark, deserted lane filled her mind. She shook her head as if it would dispel the pictures. That was a ridiculous fear; Alex was more than capable of taking care of himself.

Controlling her rising panic with difficulty, Livia went into the library again. The terriers scampered ahead of her into the lamplit room and thumped down in front of the fire, regarding her with their bright button eyes beneath thick fringes. The curtains were drawn, the fire burning brightly, all just waiting for its owner's return. She sat down at his desk and tried the drawers. They were all locked, except one at the bottom.

She pulled it open and looked in surprise at the ivory-handled pistol it contained. She'd never seen Alex with a pistol; as far as she knew he didn't even go to Manton's shooting gallery for sport. But then he wasn't in the habit of telling her everything, as she already knew.

Livia took out the weapon gingerly, turning it over in her hands. Was it loaded? She had no way of telling, but Morecombe would probably be able to tell her. He was something of an expert with the blunderbuss, after all. Not that it mattered. She was about to replace it in the drawer when the front door knocker sounded, loud and urgent. The dogs leaped to their feet, yapping frantically.

Alex. He was knocking with such vigor because he

knew Boris wasn't on duty. Why hadn't he come back by now? she wondered. It was nearly midnight, after all. But Alex must have given him the whole night off, she decided, and Morecombe wouldn't hear anything short of the last trump at this time of night. Still carrying the pistol, she hurried out to the hall, her heart leaping with relief.

"Just coming," she called, pulling back on the heavy bolts as the dogs pranced and barked and leaped at the door. She hauled it open and then stared in disbelief and disappointment. Monsieur Tatarinov stood on the doorstep.

"Good evening, Princess." He raised his voice over the noise of the dogs and stepped disdainfully over them into the hall without waiting for an invitation. "Where's your husband? I need to talk to him." Again without waiting for an invitation he strode across the hall to the library, the terriers gamboling at his heels.

"He's not here," Livia said, following him into the room, instinctively closing the door behind her. "He went out this afternoon, and he hasn't come back since." She could hear the tremor in her voice. "Don't you know where he is?"

Tatarinov's nostrils flared as he inhaled sharply. "Since this afternoon, you say?"

"Yes . . . please, is something wrong?"

He didn't immediately reply, merely stood staring at the carpet, slamming one closed fist into the palm of his other hand. "Madame, did he go out alone?"

"I wasn't here myself, but I understand some men came to call and he left with them some time later." Livia knew now that something was dreadfully wrong, but strangely her fear had receded under the determination to get out of this taciturn and unpleasant man every scrap of knowledge he had.

"Men? How many?"

"Two."

"Russian?"

"Foreign certainly. Tell me, monsieur, does this have anything to do with my husband's work on behalf of his country?"

That brought his eyes up from the carpet. "What do you know of that?"

"I know that my husband is a spy for the czar," she said. "He told me so himself, so you may be quite frank with me." She looked at him, suddenly puzzled by his expression. He looked both startled and relieved. "So answer me, please. Is my husband's disappearance something to do with that work?"

"You'd best ask him yourself," Tatarinov said. "I must go at once." He took a step to the door.

Livia acted instinctively. She was still frightened for Alex but she was more frightened of not knowing what was going on.

She spun around and locked the door, dropping the key into her pocket. Of course if Tatarinov tried to overpower her he'd probably succeed . . . slowly she raised the pistol. She still didn't know whether it was loaded but guessed that Alex would have seen little point in having a gun that was no good in an unexpected attack. And it seemed obvious now that he had been prepared for such an event. And now so was she.

Tristan and Isolde, hackles rising, began to growl as they sensed the menace in the room. Tatarinov looked murderously at them and raised a foot to kick Tristan aside as the animal approached with bared teeth.

"*Sit,*" Livia commanded, and miraculously they backed off. Her hand was perfectly steady as she trained the pistol on Tatarinov's shoulder. She had no desire to kill him, but thought she could probably put a bullet through his shoulder at this range.

"What are you doing?" he demanded, outrage and astonishment on his face.

"I want you to tell me exactly what's going on," she said evenly. "Is my husband's life in danger?"

Tatarinov rocked slightly on the balls of his feet, assessing her determination. "If you shoot me, Princess, your husband will have even less chance of escaping his abductors," he pointed out.

"Abductors?" Livia frowned, but the pistol didn't waver. "Who would abduct him?"

"Madame, we are wasting precious time—"

"Then answer my question," she snapped. "And be quick about it. My patience is wearing thin. Who has taken my husband? And where have they taken him?"

He took another step towards her but both dogs leaped at his ankles, barking and nipping. He kicked out at them but it only made them more frantic.

"Get them off me," he demanded, and in different circumstances Livia would have found it amusing that he should be more alarmed by a pair of silly pink dogs than by a pistol trained on him.

"Sit down and they will too," she said. "As long as they think you're threatening me, they'll go on doing what they're doing."

He cursed in a language she did not understand, but the gist of it was clear in any language, then sat down on a straight-backed chair. Immediately the dogs settled back on their haunches with an air of complacence at a job well done.

"All right, Monsieur Tatarinov, tell me what's going on, all of it, and quickly."

He sat still, frowning at her. Women in his experience didn't behave like this, waving pistols around and setting dogs on a man. They knew their place and kept to it. He had had his reservations about Prokov's wife, an overly bold woman, he'd decided on first meeting. This conduct, however, went beyond bold.

"I'm waiting, monsieur. Have the czar's enemies taken my husband?" She waved the pistol.

Very well, if you want the truth, Princess, then you shall have it. "If the czar's enemies had abducted your husband, Madame, we would have little to worry about," he stated. "Prince Prokov was working to remove the czar. I believe Arakcheyev's secret police have him."

He glanced around the room. "If I get up and give

myself vodka from that bottle over there, will these wretched creatures attack me again?"

Livia lowered the pistol against her skirt and went over to the sideboard. She brought the bottle over to him. "Who is this Arakcheyev?"

"The czar's head of the Ministry of War." He tipped the bottle to his lips and drank deeply. "He also controls the secret police."

Just the sound of the term sent a chill of horror down Livia's spine. The fact that Alex had misled her as to his true allegiance would have to wait. At present it mattered little who held him captive. "How do we get Alex out of their hands?"

"I'm fairly certain they will be taking him back to Russia," Tatarinov told her. "They'll not torture him here." He saw her blanch but she didn't waver, her eyes remained fixed upon him, the pistol still held quietly at her side.

"Sperskov is a different matter, he's not a close friend of the czar's, they did what they had to with him and presumably he gave them Prince Prokov." He drank again. "Can't blame him for that. He must have held out quite a long time if they didn't come for the prince until this afternoon."

"I understand very little of what you're saying," Livia said. "Who is this Sperskov?"

"A member of our little band of brothers," Tatarinov said shortly. "Loyal to our cause, and an essential conduit . . . he knows all the right people. But he's not battle-hardened. He disappeared last night. I feared the worst, particularly when I could find no news of him and your husband did not make our agreed rendezvous late this afternoon."

Focus on the most important matters, Livia told herself, trying to rein in her imagination. *Don't let the horrendous images get in the way of clear thinking.*

"How will they take him out of England?" *Focus on the practical.*

"By ship, of course." His voice rose with sudden impatience. "They'll be in a hurry to get away so they'll probably go from Greenwich, as it's the closest shipping dock. There are always ships willing to take on an unorthodox passenger or two for the right coin."

He stood up and the dogs growled. "I'm wasting time. Unlock that damned door and let me get about my business."

"I'm coming with you," Livia said, snapping her fingers at the terriers, who came reluctantly to her side.

"You can't possibly . . . that's ridiculous . . . never heard such a thing . . . you'll be in the way," Tatarinov blustered, trying to push past her to the door.

"There's nothing you can do about it," Livia said calmly. "I shall simply follow you to Greenwich if you don't want me to travel with you. I can assure you I will not hold you up in any way, and I most certainly will not be in your way, but you should understand once and for all that my place is with my husband and if he is in danger then I *will* be at his side."

She turned to open the door. "Will you wait for me while I change my clothes quickly? Or must I follow you?"

"Madame . . . Princess . . ." He saw her adamant countenance and thought it was probably better to keep her under his eye. He would put her somewhere safely out of the way when they reached Greenwich. "I'll wait."

"Good." She turned the key in the lock and opened the door. "Do you have a carriage here?"

"I'm riding."

"Good, then I'll change and fetch Daphne from the mews." The dogs were on her heels as she ran up the stairs, calling over her shoulder, "Ten minutes at most."

Tatarinov eyed the front door. He could be gone from the house and on his horse in two minutes, but he knew the wretched woman would follow him and the gods alone knew what she would do on her own. He needed to collect a couple of others on their way to Greenwich, and he could only pray that the prince and his abductors had missed the evening tide and were waiting for the morning.

And if they weren't at Greenwich . . . ?

∽∾

Livia threw off her robe and scrambled into her riding habit. She dropped the pistol into the deep pocket of her jacket and sat on the bed to pull on her boots. Her mind was closed to anything but the urgency of the moment. She would not think of the possibility that the ship had already sailed. She would not think of the possibility that they had gone to Dover or some other port. She would not think of the possibility that Alex might already be dead . . .

She left her bedroom, closing the door on the dogs, their pathetic whine following her as she ran back down the stairs. Tatarinov was pacing the hall, a short, stocky, bull-like figure who somehow inspired confidence. She disliked him certainly, but she had the conviction that if push came to shove he would be a very useful ally to have.

"I'm ready." She hurried to the front door and pulled it open. It would have to stay unlocked, but there was nothing to be done about that. Tatarinov's horse, a sturdy and unbeautiful raw-boned gelding, was tethered to the square railing.

"My horse is in the mews, just across the square," Livia said. She ran to the mews and was leading Daphne from her stall when a shout came from the room above the stable.

"Eh, who's there? What's goin' on down there?" A tousled head appeared in a window.

"It's me, Jemmy. I'm just taking Daphne for a ride," she called softly, unwilling to wake the entire mews.

"Eh, m'lady, at this time o' night?"

"Just a fancy I have," she said. "Go back to sleep."

But Jemmy appeared in the yard in less than a minute, sleepy-eyed and tousled, but determined to saddle the mare. "Should I be goin' with you, m'lady?" he asked doubtfully.

"No, I have an escort, thank you," she said, gesturing

to the entrance of the mews, where Tatarinov sat astride his gelding. Jemmy led Daphne to the mounting block and Livia mounted quickly. "Tell everyone at the house not to worry about anything," she said. "I'll be back in the morning." She had no idea whether she would or not, but something had to be said.

Tatarinov merely grunted when she rode up beside him. "Got to make some stops," he said. "Pick up some others. I can't take 'em on alone."

"*I'm* here, don't forget," she said.

"I'm hardly likely to," he stated, and from then on they rode in silence.

They rode over London Bridge and then followed the river south. Three times Tatarinov turned his horse into a narrow side street, telling Livia brusquely to stay where he could see her. He knocked out the same rhythm on three doors and a hasty conversation that Livia could not make out ensued, resulting on each occasion in a man joining them on a sturdy pony.

The three men stared at Livia but offered no greeting; instead the men talked amongst themselves in Russian, leaving their female companion to her own unquiet thoughts.

It was an hour's ride to Greenwich, the longest hour Livia thought she had ever spent. They rode into the village and took the Norman road down to the docks. They passed a watchman with his lantern on a tall pole, making his rounds, his voice a mournful chant: *Three o'clock and all's well.*

He looked suspiciously at the group of riders as they passed him, and Tatarinov leaned down from his horse and tossed him a coin. The watchman deftly caught the glint of silver and pocketed it, then continued on his way, still chanting. The night riders could be bringing rapine and mayhem to the village of Greenwich, but a silver coin bought a watchman's silence.

The handful of ships swinging at anchor along the quayside showed riding lights in the dark, and a handful of buildings along the wharf had lanterns hanging outside. Sounds of shouting and laughter came from within several of them, and a door opened at one. Two men, forcibly ejected from the taproom, rolled onto the mud-slick cobbles in a violent tangle of limbs.

Tatarinov conferred with his companions and then spoke finally to Livia. "There's a boat shed over yonder. You'll be safe enough there."

"Judging by the type of person frequenting this wharf, I somehow doubt that," Livia said acidly. "And if it were safe for me to hide in a boat shed, what are you going to be doing in the meantime?" Her fingers closed reflexively over her pistol.

"Reconnoiter," he said. "No point running into anything if we don't know what's out there. Maybe the prince isn't even here."

This made perfect sense, but Livia had no intention of allowing them to go off without her. "Don't mind me," she said firmly. "I won't interfere in the least. I'll stay in the background until I can see something useful to do."

Tatarinov glowered. For two pins he'd call his companions over and they'd physically restrain the woman, but he couldn't help the reflection that if he offered injury or insult to Prokov's wife, the prince, assuming he came out of this alive, would not be best pleased. "If I were your husband I'd be mighty glad to see the back of you, shouldn't wonder," Tatarinov muttered, turning his horse into the shelter of a dilapidated lean-to beside a boat shed on the quay.

Livia smiled for the first time since this nightmare had begun. "Oh, I don't think he will," she said. "I really don't think so at all." She followed his lead and dismounted, tethering Daphne to a post in the lean-to close to a water-filled horse trough.

Tatarinov's men dismounted and tethered their own horses, then after a whispered discussion the four men split up, two going into the village, Tatarinov and the other taking different directions along the quay. Livia, after a moment's reflection, headed after Tatarinov. She had an idea, just a niggle of an idea at present, but if they were in luck and found Alex somewhere in this line of ships, she thought she could see a role for herself in his rescue.

Alex in the aft cabin of the good ship *Caspar* was cursing his own stupidity, even as he tried to think of how and when he had made a mistake. How had these two ruffians known to come for him? They'd said nothing of any significance since they'd appeared in his bedchamber. Boris, of course, would never have let them upstairs, but Morecombe, as he'd made very clear, did not work for Prince Prokov. He'd open the door and let a visitor in, but it wouldn't occur to him to inquire of the prince if said visitor would be welcome.

But they would have taken him somehow, Alex knew. These were Arakcheyev's men and failure was not an option. But with a little warning he could have been more ready for them. Sperskov's disappearance was the key, he now realized. He should have armed himself against discovery the minute Tatarinov had told him the duke had vanished. But he had always believed in a cool head. Make sure of something before you act. In this particular instance, with hindsight, not the best operating procedure, he reflected with grim cynicism.

He could have resisted when they came for him, of course, but that would have endangered Livia. He had expected her home at any minute throughout the confrontation, his ears straining for a sound from the adjoining bedchamber. Arakcheyev's brutish henchmen would have had no scruples how they used her, and with only a handful of women, an old deaf man, and a youth in the house to summon for aid, he could see little help for it but to go with them without a fight.

And now he was bound and gagged, tied to a chair in a dismal cabin in a yawl heading on the morning's tide for Calais, and from there the hell of an overland journey to St. Petersburg and the tender hands of Arakcheyev.

The emperor wouldn't speak up for him, and with a wry twist of his mouth beneath the filthy strip of sacking that kept him silent, Alex thought that he could hardly blame the man when his so-called friend had been part of a conspiracy plotting his death. He knew he had the czar to thank for the fact that he was still alive. Dried blood crusted a gash over his left eye and his lip was split, a purple bruise swelling on his cheekbone, courtesy of his captors, who hadn't been able to resist the opportunity to exert a little power over the usually powerful. But apart from these really minor injuries he was in essence unhurt.

The czar would insist on absolute proof of Prince Prokov's involvement in the conspiracy before anything really unpleasant could happen to him. But that protection would last only as far as his final interview with the emperor.

Oh, he thought he could manage to face the inevitable with some degree of dignity, even the degradation of pain, although that would be harder. But he was tormented by the knowledge that he was parting from Livia without reconciliation. She still saw only his deception, a monumental deception, he would freely admit, but unless he could be sure she saw also, and believed in, his love, then he would die a wretched death. Just five minutes, that would be all he needed.

But Livia was tucked up, snug and resentful and

angry, in Cavendish Square, and here he was. As helpless as a trussed goose.

The sound of voices brought him out of his grim reverie. Familiar voices. The captain of this scruffy yawl, sounding as if he'd hit the rum bottle rather frequently during the evening, and another voice, one that made his heart jump and cleared his mind of anything but the need to concentrate and be ready for action.

Tatarinov.

No point wondering how the man had known what had happened, Alex told himself, just concentrate on how to tell him that he was there, just below him. Alex looked around the small, dim cabin. The chair he was tied to was bolted to the floor, as was every piece of furniture. There was a lamp burning low on the table. He could think of many uses for it in his present predicament, but they all depended on his being able to hold it, and he couldn't do that.

His arms were bound at his sides by the rope that tied him to the chair. And the knots were masterly sailor's knots. His legs were tied together at the ankles but he could still move them in unison. He swung his legs up from the knees, kicking the underside of the table. Although its base was securely bolted to the decking, the wooden top shook and the lamp with it. He kicked again, a little more carefully; he didn't want the lamp to roll over. It could set light to this tinderbox in the blink of an eye.

Trying to strike a happy medium between making sufficient noise to be heard and not upending the lantern, he set up a rhythm that Tatarinov would recognize if he could hear it.

❧

Livia stood on the quayside in the shadows, watching the group on the deck of the *Caspar*. Tatarinov was talking with two men, and they struck her as a formidable trio. The sailors, as she assumed they were, were powerful figures, broad-shouldered and barrel-chested. Tatarinov himself, as she'd already reflected, reminded her of a bull.

They were taking no notice of her and she edged closer to the side of the yawl, hearing the lapping of the dark water below. It was quite a wide gap between the side of the yawl and the quay, and she tried not to look down into that sinister blackness as she leaned forward, attempting to peer through a grimy porthole even as she strained her ears to hear what they were saying. At least they were speaking in English.

"We'll be away at dawn on the morning tide," one of the two men said to Tatarinov. "Be in Calais by sundown tomorrow."

"Can you take a passenger? I'll pay well for passage." Tatarinov rattled his pockets and the chink of coin rang in the still frosty air.

"Oh, aye? Well, as to that, we've already got passengers . . . don't know if we've room for another," the other man said.

"I'll pay well," Tatarinov repeated.

"Eh, there's room enough," his colleague stated. "Cabin's occupied, but you can stay on deck. It'll be a mite chilly, but with a good thick boat cloak you'll manage, I reckon. 'Tis a daylight crossing when all's said an' done."

"Just a minute," the other said, cocking his head towards the hatchway. He pointed down towards the hatch. "Best do summat about that."

"Aye," the other said, hitching up his britches, which were fastened with a piece of rope. "We'll be back in a minute, sir."

Tatarinov nodded as if he had no interest in their conversation, but Livia saw his stony expression as he turned away from the hatch, thrusting his hands into his britches' pockets and staring grimly out at the quay.

She leaned closer to the porthole and experimentally rubbed at it with her sleeve. The strangest feeling gripped her, an odd excitement. She spat on the grimy glass and rubbed again, managing to clear a small circle.

She stared into a dimly lit space, all in shadow. It was impossible to make anything out clearly, just dark shapes and the glow of a lantern somewhere. But she could hear something, a steady thumping, and there was a vaguely recognizable rhythm to it.

Again that strange feeling gripped her, more strongly this time. Impatiently she spat again on the glass and rubbed vigorously, widening the clear space. Her view opened out and she saw into more of the cabin now.

And she saw the bundled figure on the chair, close to the table. And she saw him raise both his feet at right angles to his body and kick the underside of the table. That was the noise she had heard, and the rhythm was the one Tatarinov had used to summon his cohorts on the journey. It had to be Alex.

She raised a hand to tap on the glass and then reared back, almost losing her footing on the slippery quay. She felt sick. The two men had entered the cabin. She could hear the sounds of their fists but she couldn't bear to look. Alex's kicking had attracted more than just Tatarinov's attention. He would have known it would, of course. He would be prepared for what they were doing to him now, but such a realization did nothing to help Livia.

She moved away from the side, not knowing what she should do, her eyes searching for Tatarinov. Then she saw him turn towards the hatchway as the two sailors came back out, one of them rubbing his knuckles. Tatarinov glanced to the quay, saw Livia approaching, and with an infinitesimal movement of his hand told her to back away.

She had no choice but to let him conclude his business with the sailors, and then she would tell him what she intended to do. Anger had replaced her sick horror. She melted back into the shadows to wait.

Chapter Twenty-four

LIVIA, HUGGING THE SHADOWS OF a boat shed, heard the sounds of booted feet from somewhere behind her, and voices, slightly slurred and speaking in what she now recognized as Russian. Alex's captors . . . the secret police. That would put four men on the *Caspar* against Tatarinov and his three cohorts. Four against four. Good enough odds, particularly if she could give them the advantage of surprise.

Her heart was banging against her ribs so hard she thought it must sound like a drumbeat, but despite that her mind was cool and clear, her resolution hard and diamond bright. She watched the two men approach the yawl but before they could reach it, Tatarinov had jumped down to the quay and was hurrying in the opposite direction, head huddled into the turned-up hood of his cloak.

The men glanced at him briefly, then climbed up on deck. Livia thought their step was a trifle unsteady. If they were drunk, so much the better.

"Get back in here." Tatarinov's rough voice coming from behind her in a fierce whisper made her jump. She'd seen him go off in the opposite direction but now he was in the boathouse behind her. She didn't trouble to ask how he'd managed it.

"Was that the secret police?" she whispered, stepping back through the door into the dark space that smelled of wet canvas and tarred rope.

"Aye," he said shortly. "You're to get in here and stay here while we go about our business."

"No," Livia said with quiet determination. "I know Alex is on that ship, I heard him knocking, and I can guess what they did to him. I'm going to help you get him out . . . no, listen to me." She held up a hand imperiously as he began to interrupt. "You're four against four. If I distract them for you, you should be able to creep up on them."

"Distract them?" He looked at her in mingled disdain and astonishment. "Don't be stupid, woman. What can you do?"

Livia controlled her temper. She began to unbutton her jacket. "I need a bottle of liquor . . . rum . . . whisky . . . brandy, anything." She shrugged the jacket off and began to fumble with the buttons of her shirt. "They have whores on quays, don't they?" she demanded impatiently.

Tatarinov stared at her now with just the beginnings of interest. "Like as not," he said. "What d'you intend?"

"I intend to stagger on board as a half-drunken whore

offering my body and a bottle," she told him succinctly. "I'm certain I can attract their attention long enough for you and your men to get in position."

And now there was something akin to respect in his eyes as he watched her pull her hair loose of its snood and run her fingers through the curls until they stood out around her face in an unruly tangle.

"Fetch me drink, Tatarinov," she demanded with the same impatience. "There's taverns aplenty around here . . . a bottle of anything will do. I need to smell of drink myself." She looked around, still fluffing out her hair. "I need some dirt, something to grub me up a little."

"You swear you won't move until I get back?" he asked somewhat uncertainly. There was no knowing what this manifestation of Princess Prokov would do next.

"I need that bottle," she pointed out, rolling up her shirtsleeves. "I can't do anything until you're back with it. And there's no point in my going on that ship without you and your men being in place, now is there?"

"I reckon not." He nodded and disappeared behind her, presumably through a back door to the shed.

Livia rubbed some tar on her fingers and then smeared a thumb down her cheek. It would be the devil's own job to wash off, but needs must. She ripped the bodice of her shirt artistically, showing more than a hint of cleavage, and added a smear of tar between her breasts for good measure. There was dust aplenty in the cobwebby reaches of the boat shed and she rubbed and smeared with as much art as she could in the circumstances. A mirror would have been a help.

Tatarinov came back with his three companions. Silently he handed her an open stone jar. Livia sniffed and her stomach roiled at the raw fumes. "What is it?"

"Rough stuff," he told her, "but they'll drink it. You'd best take a swig."

Livia tried and choked as it burned down her gullet. She shook her head, for the moment speechless, and poured a little into the palm of her hand, dabbing it onto her pulse points at her throat and behind her ears, an eccentric perfume that in other circumstances might have amused her.

"All right, I'm ready," she said when the burning in her throat had died down and her eyes had stopped watering. "Tatarinov, they're expecting you to return to take passage with them, aren't they?"

He nodded, watching her in the dim illumination from the lamps outside that filtered through the ill-fitting slats of the boat shed. "What d'you have in mind?"

"Well, if we both go on board together . . . arm in arm . . . I could be a whore you picked up in one of those taverns. We're both drunk, I'm willing to spread my favors around . . . and we play it from there. Your . . . uh . . . your colleagues will watch and wait for their opportunity to join the fun."

"A good plan, except that I am known to Arakcheyev's men," he informed her.

"Then I go alone," Livia said, even though fear gripped her belly. It was a very different prospect to go into that lion's den without Tatarinov's supporting presence.

Tatarinov spoke quickly in Russian to the three men who had been staring in blank incomprehension at Livia since they'd entered the boat shed. There was a short burst of conversation among them, then Tatarinov nodded and turned back to Livia. "All right, let's do it."

He accompanied her to the back door of the boat shed. "Try to get them to the aft rail," he said. "If you can get them with their backs to the docks even for just a moment, it will give us a big advantage."

Livia nodded her understanding. "I think I can do that."

"Princess . . ." He started to say something and then stopped, but to her astonishment she saw something approaching a smile soften his hard mouth, and then it was gone.

"Monsieur Tatarinov," she responded, then went through the door onto the quay. She raised the stone jar and with a raucous, high-pitched, and distinctly vulgar laugh staggered towards the gangplank of the *Caspar.*

"Who goes there?" one of the sailors shouted down as he spied her swaying across the cobbles.

"Just a friend," she called back drunkenly, waving her stone jar. "Brought you some comfort if you've coin to give a girl."

Ribald laughter greeted this and the four men gathered at the head of the gangplank. "Come on up, girlie. We've an hour t'go before the tide and coin aplenty for the right service."

Livia waved her jar freely and giggled, tripping as she reached the top. Huge arms enveloped her and a mouth swamped hers in a beery kiss. She thought of Alex, helpless below, and she let herself fall into the part, flinging her arm around her embracer before reeling away from him to another one. They passed her from hand to hand, fumbling her breasts inside her shirt, pinching and pawing her backside, swigging from her stone jar.

She flung her arms wide and sang out with a drunken gurgle, "Come one, come all," and they surged on her as she fell back against the aft railing, laughing, dodging kisses.

And as they surrounded her, Tatarinov and his men came silently up the gangplank, knives in their hands. Then one of Livia's would-be clients heard or sensed something. He spun around with a shout of warning.

Livia rolled away from the rail. Tatarinov and his men had the advantage of surprise but the others were all armed, and drunk though they were, they all knew how to brawl. It was not going to be an easy victory for either side. Livia didn't hesitate. She ducked low along the railing, trying to keep out of the line of sight, praying they were all too occupied to notice or remember her. She crossed the short strip of unprotected deck at a crouch and dived into the darkness of the hatchway, her heart racing, the sour taste of raw spirit rising in her mouth.

She half fell in her haste down the gangway and into the dark cabin. Alex was slumped in the chair, his head on his chest, a trickle of blood running sluggishly from a gash on his temple. They had hit him hard, and it looked to Livia as if the wound had been caused by a ring or something like it.

She would not allow herself pity, or horror, only action. She ran to him. He was unconscious, unmoving in his bonds. Desperately she looked around for water. There was none. But she still held the jar and what was left of its vile contents. She grabbed Alex's head and pulled it back, pressing the jar to his lips, forcing some of the spirit into his mouth. His eyes shot open and stared at her for a moment without comprehension, then he shook his head, wincing with the pain.

"What in the name of all the gods are *you* doing here?" He sounded blurred and as disoriented as he felt.

"I'm at your side," Livia said, fighting back tears of relief. "Where else would you expect me to be?"

A tiny spark of light showed behind his dazed blue gaze. "Nowhere else," he said, and then choked as she forced more of the spirit between his lips.

"Good God, woman, what are you doing to me? I'm half dead already, do you want to finish the job?"

"Oh, Alex." She kissed him on his bleeding mouth. "Are you all right?"

"At the moment, yes, but we won't be for much longer. There's a gutting knife on that locker in the bulkhead. I've been eyeing it for hours."

Livia couldn't believe how strong he sounded, but common sense also told her that such a surge of energy could not last long when a man had been so ill-treated.

She fetched the gutting knife and sawed at the ropes at his wrists, then dropped to her knees to cut the bindings at his ankles. "Tatarinov—"

"On deck, I know. How many?"

"Four to four."

"If they weren't dealing with Arakcheyev's puppies, I'd say Tatarinov and friends needed no help from me," he said. "But . . . give me the knife, sweeting."

Oh, how she had longed to hear that endearment again. "I have your pistol," she said prosaically.

"You are a miraculous woman." Alex took the pistol from her. His eyes held hers. "I love you, Livia. I have been so desperate to tell you that. So afraid you didn't really believe me and I wouldn't get the chance to convince you."

"I am convinced," she said. "You don't need to tell me, my love."

His broken lips moved in a painful smile, then it was all business again. His voice was clipped. "Follow me up, and keep out of the way. I mean it, Livia. You must make certain they can't get hold of you. They will use you if they can and we will all be lost. The minute we get on deck you get down to the quay. Understand?"

"Certainly," she said without expression.

"Stay right behind me." He headed for the gangway and Livia followed him up on deck. Blood ran along the decking. Tatarinov and one of Arakcheyev's men were engaged in a knife fight, both men bleeding, both as fierce as Cossacks fighting to the death on the steppes. One of the sailors was an inert heap on a pile of rope, the other was struggling with one of the men who had accompanied Tatarinov. Arakcheyev's second man was in another death struggle with two of Tatarinov's colleagues.

"Let's bring this to an end," Alex said under his breath. He raised his pistol and waited for a second until the man fighting with Tatarinov had his back to him for a moment. Then he shot him. Only Livia heard him say, "I owed you that, my friend."

The sound of the gunshot brought everything to a sudden, almost surreal halt. The shot man crumpled slowly to the deck, and the second member of the secret police was taken off guard for only an instant, but enough for a man fighting two against one. He was quickly disarmed.

The sailor who remained on his feet dropped his cutlass as Tatarinov's man slipped beneath his guard and drove his knife under his arm. And a strange silence fell. Even the sounds from the taverns had ceased. Only the sky remained as starlit and cheerful as before, shining brightly down upon the blood-slick deck and the twisted, crumpled forms.

Alex turned and saw Livia standing at the head of the gangplank. She had not been able to tear herself away from the scene and get down to the quay as he'd instructed. He came over to her and spoke softly but with vehemence. "You are a wonderful, amazing woman, you achieve miracles, and I adore you, but just this once you are going to do exactly what I tell you. Is that understood, Livia?"

She nodded, numbed by the speed and wholesale destruction of the last minutes.

"I mean it, Livia." He took her shoulders, forcing her to look at him instead of the scene behind him. "Do you know where the horses are?"

"Yes, of course."

"Then you are to go down to the quay now and wait with the horses."

"What will you be doing?" But she knew the answer and she knew she didn't want to hear it spoken.

"Take this and go." He gave her the pistol; the barrel was still warm.

"Is it loaded?" she asked, puzzled.

"No, but only you will know that if anyone accosts you. Now go." He turned her to the gangplank with a little shove between her shoulders. "We will make this right, sweeting. But you must go now."

Livia went. There was an eerie quiet along the quay now, all the hubbub of the taverns faded as even the drunken revelers sought sleep in the few short hours before dawn. There had been no one to hear the pistol shot from the *Caspar,* but Livia thought that even if there had been, the sound would have gone unremarked in the general riotous chaos. She kept the pistol hidden in the folds of her skirt, finding it comforting even though it would do little good if she were threatened. But she was not really afraid. Now that Alex was safe, there was nothing really to fear.

She picked up her discarded jacket from the boat

shed and hurried along the quay to the lean-to where the horses were tethered. They whickered softly when she came up to them, and Daphne threw up her beautiful silver head and nuzzled Livia's shoulder.

"Not long now," she whispered, burying her nose in the mare's neck, inhaling the rich scent of horseflesh. She stroked down her flank and tried not to think of what was happening on the deck of the *Caspar*.

It was clear enough to her that Arakcheyev's men could not be left alive to take the tale back to the secret police. And she had to assume that the men of the *Caspar* had to suffer the same fate. There would always be the danger that the Russian secret police would trace their colleagues' disappearance to the *Caspar*, and from what she'd gathered about the fate of the unknown Sperskov, they would soon reveal all there was to know about Alex.

Spying was a dirty business, assassination even more so, but Livia was no innocent ingénue. She could understand the hold that patriotism had on some men. She could look at the hard facts even if she didn't like them, and Alex's safety was all that mattered.

She heard footsteps beyond the lean-to and moved away from Daphne to the front of the ramshackle shelter. Alex was alone, limping, wincing with every step, his cut and bruised face looking even worse as the first streaks of light appeared in the east.

She ran forward as he stumbled slightly. "Put your hand on my shoulder, love. Daphne will carry both of us back to London."

"We'll not ride all the way to London immediately," he stated, resting his hand on her shoulder for a moment. "We'll get away from here and find an inn on the road. I'm done in and you've done enough for one night. You need to rest."

"*Stuff and nonsense,*" she declared. "I'm the only one among you all who is whole. I've done almost nothing."

He looked at her then and raised an eyebrow. "Somehow, my love, judging by your appearance, I rather doubt that."

"I was playing the whore," she said, hastily rebuttoning her shirt. She thrust her arms into the sleeves of her jacket. It would do something to hide the strategically placed rip. "I had to look the part."

"Yes, of course," he agreed with mock solemnity. "But was it really necessary to smother yourself in tar to achieve the desired effect?"

"If you weren't already hurt, Alexander Prokov, I'd be very tempted to kick you," she said with feeling. "That's all the gratitude I get." But her heart sang. Despite it all, he was himself.

"Where are the others?" she asked, looking back along the quay. "Are we waiting for them?"

"No," he said shortly. "They have something to do when the tide comes in."

"What?" she asked. "I need to know, Alex."

He looked at her with a frown. "They will take the *Caspar* out into the North Sea and scuttle her," he stated, taking his hand from her shoulder.

"How will they get back?"

"She carries a sailing dinghy. Tatarinov is a good sailor." He moved past her into the lean-to. "We'll take their horses. They won't return here; there are plenty of small coves and villages along the North Sea coast where they can make landfall safely."

"And all knowledge of the events of tonight, of Alexander Prokov and his plans, will go down with the *Caspar*," she said, stating the grim truth.

"Yes," he agreed. "And that's enough of this for now. Mount up. You'll need to lead one of them; I'll manage the other two."

Livia led Daphne out and scrambled inelegantly but without assistance onto her back, sitting astride, taking the reins of one of the ponies. "Can you ride, Alex?" she asked with concern as he mounted Tatarinov's rawboned gelding. "If you fall . . ."

"I won't fall," he said. "But we won't ride far. We'll go away from the river and find an inn."

"But Alex, how will we explain the state you're in, not to mention me." She gestured to her torn and disordered garments. "And why do we have three extra horses?"

"Just follow my lead," he said. "In fact it would be better if you say not a word. Shock has deprived you of speech. Just do as I tell you."

"You're very dictatorial for a man whose wife has just rescued him from certain death," Livia declared. "I would have thought some of that Russian authoritarianism would be blunted by now."

He laughed, although it was clearly painful for him to do so. "I'm still the same man you married, sweeting. But that's something we should perhaps talk about later, when we've had time to collect ourselves and you've had time to reflect on a great many things." His voice was serious, the laughter gone, and she knew what he meant.

And it was true. She did need to reflect on a great many things. And that most important question of all: *Was love enough to get them and their marriage through this and out the other side?*

They rode out of Greenwich village and headed further inland, while keeping parallel to the river. Alex clearly needed all his remaining strength to stay mounted and Livia didn't speak, just watched him with growing concern. As the sun rose they began to have company on the road. A farmer with a wagonload of cabbages passed them on his way to Covent Garden market, and a young girl herding a gaggle of geese stared at them from the hedge as they rode by.

"There's an inn up there," Livia said, seeing a sign outside a thatched-roof building ahead of them. "I think we'd better stop now, Alex."

He gave no sign of having heard her—his face was a mask of pain—but he directed the horses around the back of the building to a rough-and-ready stable yard. An ostler was currycombing a shire horse as they rode in. He looked at the two disheveled riders, and his eyes widened as he took in Alex's battered countenance.

"Eh, what 'appened to you then, sir?"

"Footpads," Alex said curtly, dismounting. He staggered as he reached the ground and grabbed the gelding's stirrup to steady himself. "See to the horses. They need watering and a bran mash. You'll be paid well."

The ostler looked rather doubtful about that, but even weak, injured, and disreputable in appearance as he was, Alex conveyed an absolute authority. The man put down his currycomb and went to take the gelding's reins.

Livia swung off the mare and went to Alex, offering her arm. He shook his head carefully and murmured, "You're in shock. Just lean against me as if you're about to collapse and keep quiet. This will be over in a very short time."

She closed her lips firmly but refused to add her weight to his burdens, walking upright beside him as he made his way to the back door of the inn.

The landlord emerged from the taproom as they entered a narrow, dark hallway. "What can I do for ye?" he asked, peering suspiciously at them in the gloom of the passage.

"A bedchamber and hot water," Alex said. "We were set upon by footpads a while back. They killed my groom and took four of our horses. I managed to beat them off in the end, but my wife is hurt and in shock."

The man examined them closely. "Eh, right bad you look," he observed. "Shall I send for the sawbones?"

"No . . . no." Alex waved aside the suggestion. "My wife will tend to me. She's suffered nothing worse than a fall from her horse and a bad fright."

The landlord was still looking suspicious. "I'll fetch

the wife," he said, and disappeared through a door behind him. Several minutes later he returned with an angular woman whose iron-gray hair was severely pinned back. Her eyes were hard and sharp and every bit as suspicious as her mate's.

"What's all this, then?" she demanded. "Footpads hereabouts? Never 'ad any trouble afore."

"Be that as it may," Alex said, "my wife and I were set upon. We were taking a train of horses to a horse coper in Southwark. We left our stables outside Greenwich at dawn and they were lying in wait for us." His voice hardened. "If you can't be of service just say so and we'll be on our way."

"That's all well and good," the woman declared. "But how'll we be paid? That's what I'd like to know."

"In coin," Alex said shortly.

"I thought you said you was robbed?" she demanded.

"Of my horses," Alex said. "Not of my purse." He put a hand on Livia's shoulder.

She could feel what little strength he had ebbing from him as his weight bore down upon her but she kept her silence, her gaze firmly fixed upon the floor.

"Eh, woman, you can see they're done in," the innkeeper said. "If they can pay, what's the 'arm in givin' 'em a room?"

"None, I suppose," she said. "Come along a' me, then." She turned to the foot of the stairs and they followed her up to a small, ill-furnished chamber under the eaves. "This'll 'ave to do," she stated.

Alex had eyes only for the bed. He staggered forward and dropped onto the straw mattress.

Livia decided it was time she took the initiative. She spoke in a very soft, subdued voice. "Please, mistress, could you supply us with water? I need to wash his wounds."

"Oh, aye," she said. "Thought the cat 'ad got yer tongue."

"And witch hazel if you please," Livia pleaded in the same subdued tone.

"Aye" was the only response and the landlady went off, leaving them alone.

"Do we have money?" Livia asked.

"Take my boots off," Alex replied.

Livia decided he wasn't capable of being questioned about anything. She hurried over to the bed and bent to pull off his top boots.

"Inside the left one," he muttered, his eyes closing against the pounding in his head. "Under the inner sole."

She reached inside and felt over the inner sole. It felt normal enough, but the leather lifted easily at the side and to her astonishment she felt a small depression in the heel of the boot. Her fingers encountered a chamois pouch nestling snugly into the depression.

"Another trick of the spy's trade," she murmured, lifting out the pouch, opening the drawstring to peer inside at the glitter of gold. "Do you always carry an emergency fund in your boot?"

"It has its uses," he said. "For the love of God, Livia, don't talk to me anymore. I have to sleep."

She looked helplessly at him. He was the color of dead ashes, the bruises livid against his normally taut skin, which now seemed to sag off the bones of his face. His brow was furrowed in pain and his eyes when they flickered open for a minute were bloodshot.

She paced the small chamber, waiting impatiently for the landlady to return with water. It wasn't the landlady, however, but a young scullery maid carrying a ewer of tepid water, a jar of witch hazel, and a skimpy towel. She set them on a rickety washstand. "Mistress says d'you want to break your fast, ma'am?"

Livia glanced at Alex. There was no possibility of his eating anything at this point and she didn't feel hungry herself, merely desperately weary. "No, but please thank your mistress. Maybe later when we've slept a little."

The girl curtsied and disappeared, leaving them at last in blessed isolation.

Livia swiftly went to work. She washed Alex's cuts gently with a corner of the towel and dabbed witch hazel on the bruises. When she opened his shirt she gasped a little at the mass of purple bruising on his ribs. "*Bastards*," she muttered under her breath, smoothing the witch hazel over the discoloration.

Alex's eyelids flickered, but he barely moved as she went about her work. She took off his stockings and loosened his britches, then eased the coverlet from beneath him. She put it over him and he gave a little sigh of relaxation as his body sank into the crackling straw.

Livia did what she could to clean herself up of the

worst of the carefully applied grime; the tar, as she'd expected, was utterly resistant to tepid water without the aid of soap, and she needed needle and thread to sew the tear in her shirt, but her jacket was still intact and would cover the worst of it.

Satisfied that she'd done all she could, she slipped beneath the coverlet beside Alex, snuggling close to his warmth as her own fatigue and the aftermath of the long night took its toll and she began to shiver. At last her body warmed and she fell into a dreamless sleep, curled up against his side.

Chapter Twenty-five

THE SUN WAS HIGH WHEN Livia awoke. At first she had no idea where she was and lay bemused for a minute, wondering why she appeared to be fully dressed. Then she became aware of Alex beside her and everything made sense once again.

Carefully she sat up and looked down at him. He was still asleep but she was relieved to see that the ashen pallor had gone. The cuts and bruises were still very much in evidence but his skin had a healthier tinge to it. She leaned down and kissed his brow.

"Is there an angel in my bed or am I dreaming?" Alex murmured dopily, his eyes still closed, but a tiny smile on his swollen lips.

"This is certainly not an angel's bed," Livia said. "I'm sure this straw is full of livestock. I'm beginning to itch." She slid off the mattress and shook out her skirts, glad that she hadn't taken anything off before climbing into bed. "How do you feel?"

"As if I've been run over by the entire field at Newmarket races," he said with a groan, at last opening his eyes. "What's the time?"

"Late morning I would guess," she said. "But there's no clock in here and I don't have a timepiece. What happened to yours?"

"One of Arakcheyev's henchmen took a fancy to it," he said, sitting up gingerly. His head swam and he closed his eyes again until the spinning stopped.

"What is it?" Livia asked, unable to conceal her anxiety. "Is it your head? Do you have a headache?"

"Yes to both," he said, opening his eyes again. "That bastard Igor concussed me when he knocked me out."

"Lie down again," she said urgently. "We'll stay here until it's better."

"No, thank you," he said, swinging his legs carefully off the mattress. "God knows what's living in this straw, but I can hear them moving." He stood up, resting a steadying hand on the bedpost. "Help me with my boots, sweeting. I don't think I can bend my head."

"No, no, you mustn't," she said, fetching his boots. "Sit down." She gave him a little push in her anxiety. "I'm sure we shouldn't go anywhere until you feel a little better." She dropped to her knees by the bed.

"We're going home," he said grimly, lifting a foot for her.

Livia struggled with the tight-fitting boot. They had no shoe horn and the boots were made to fit like gloves. Alex reached down, trying to keep his head up, and pulled the leather top up his leg, while she fought with the second one.

"There." She sat back on her heels. "Should you eat something, or drink something, Alex?"

"No, I'll throw it up," he said firmly. "But you should get something. Go down to the kitchen and see what that poker-faced landlady can produce."

"No." She shook her head. "I'm as anxious to get out of here as you are. The sooner you're home and I can send for the physician the better I'll feel." She stood up and held his coat for him. "Stay here and I'll pay mine host and get the ostler to saddle the horses. We're still taking the others back?"

"Yes, I'll keep them safe in the mews until our men come for them." He followed her downstairs, ignoring her protestations that he should wait on the bed until they were ready to move.

The landlady, her husband on her heels, emerged rapidly from the taproom as they reached the bottom step, and Livia had the distinct impression they'd been lying in wait for them, presumably to make sure they didn't do a moonlight flit.

"How much do I owe you?" Alex asked, opening the chamois pouch.

The landlord's eyes widened at the sight of gold, but his wife, unimpressed, said curtly, "Half a sovereign. There's the care for the horses as well."

Alex gave her a sovereign and said, "Let me give you

this. I thank you for your courtesy and consideration, madam."

For the first time a look of uncertainty crossed her hard eyes as she took the sovereign. Then she sniffed and turned back to the taproom.

Livia gave a choke of laughter. "She didn't know what to make of that. But you shouldn't have been so generous, Alex."

"It was a gesture that gave me great pleasure," he declared. "Come on, let's get out of here."

They rode back to London much more slowly than Livia and Tatarinov on the way out, but Alex was still not strong enough to keep up a fast pace, particularly when he was controlling the two ponies he was leading. It was early afternoon before they crossed London Bridge and almost an hour later when they reached Cavendish Square.

"I'll take some of the horses to the mews, I can manage mine and two others," Livia said. "And Jemmy can come and fetch the others. You go on inside."

Alex didn't argue. He gave her the reins of Tatarinov's gelding, tethered the other two to the rails, and went up the stairs to the front door. Boris opened it before he reached it and exclaimed in horror. "What's happened, Prince . . . have you been in an accident? I've been in despair, no one knew where you were, and the princess just told young Jemmy that everything was fine and she'd be back in the morning, and—"

"Yes, I know, Boris," Alex said soothingly as he stepped into the welcome haven of his own hall. His head ached abominably but he couldn't rest yet. "But I'm home now. I need you to send messages to Count Constantine Fedorovsky and Leo Fedotov. Ask them to come immediately."

He didn't know whether Sperskov had been forced to give them up as well; it seemed unlikely since as far as he knew they hadn't been picked up, but they needed to be warned and the entire situation had to be reassessed. Sperskov, poor devil, was presumably floating somewhere in the river Thames.

"Bring a bath up to my bedchamber, Boris, and have Ethel do the same for the princess."

Boris bowed. "I'll attend you, Prince. Should I send for the physician?"

"No, I don't need a sawbones." Alex set foot on the stairs, grasping the banister rail firmly.

Morecombe was manning the front door when Livia entered the house twenty minutes later. "Eh, my lady, what've you been an' gone an' done?" he demanded, staring at her. "Runnin' off in the middle o' the night like that . . . an' just look at you."

Livia gave him a weary smile. "It was an emergency, Morecombe. I'm sorry if I alarmed you."

"Right worried we were," he declared. "Our Mavis was beside 'erself when we found you gone this morning. Couldn't think what 'ad 'appened to you."

"Oh, dear," Livia said, wishing she could have slipped

in undetected. "I had to leave in a hurry, Morecombe. The prince sent for me," she improvised. "I couldn't wake you, it was the middle of the night."

"Strange goings-on in a gentleman's 'ouse, I must say," Morecombe muttered. "An' you look as if you've been dragged through a hedge backwards. Ethel's taken a bath up for you."

"Oh, thank you, Morecombe." She managed a warm smile and then asked, "Is Boris back yet?"

"Aye, come back this mornin', ready to see to 'is master's foreign breakfast," Morecombe declared, every muscle expressing disapproval. "In a right state he's been when 'e found the master not 'ere."

Livia nodded. Silly to have had doubts about Boris's loyalty. "Could you please ask Mavis if she could make me one of her possets? I can't think of anything I'd like better . . . oh, and one for the prince too, if she wouldn't mind." Alex might not acknowledge it, but he needed the soothing mixture of hot milk and wine flavored with cinnamon, cloves, and honey as much as she did.

"Aye" was the only response, and Livia dragged herself upstairs, conscious now of an overpowering weariness in no way relieved by the absolute conviction that nothing would ever be the same again. Her marriage, her husband, this life that they had led . . . wasn't real in the way that she'd believed it to be.

Now that the excitement of the chase and the sweet relief of having Alex safe was over, cold reality was a bitter pill to swallow. She loved Alex and he loved her, but that hadn't prevented him from doing what he'd come to London to do, even though it had nearly taken him away from her. Had he given her a moment's thought? Had he tried to imagine how she would have felt with his abrupt and final disappearance? And even if he had, it didn't make any difference to him. He'd still gone ahead with his plans. If Tatarinov had not come to find him, he would be on his way to his death in Russia now, and she would never know anything about it . . . about who he really was.

And somehow that felt like the ultimate betrayal. They had shared the most intimate secrets of their bodies, but his spirit, his very self, had been kept hidden from her. She loved him, but could she go on living with him when he withheld so much of himself from her?

Ethel greeted her with a torrent of questions and exclamations that Livia allowed to wash over her as the maid helped her out of her stained and torn garments. "Eh, m'lady, that's tar, that is?" Ethel observed in astonishment as she took Livia's chemise and saw the black smudges between her breasts. "Where on earth did that come from?"

"It's a long story, Ethel," Livia said, sliding into the hot bath. "Pass me the soap and I'll scrub it off while you wash my hair."

She could hear only a subdued murmur from Alex's room and after a moment, soothed by Ethel's hands in her hair, kneading her scalp, she closed her eyes and drifted into a trance . . . a trance that grew deeper as she sipped the posset Mavis sent up, and the warm wine and honeyed milk drugged her senses.

She wasn't aware of the adjoining door opening until Ethel said, "Good afternoon, sir. Should I leave the princess now?"

"Just for a few minutes, Ethel," Alex said as he came over to the bath.

Livia opened her eyes, looking up at him. He was once again immaculately groomed, clean-shaven, his wheat-colored hair well coiffed and glossy. The cuts and bruises were still there, of course, but they seemed less noticeable. His blue eyes drifted down her body and he smiled, a smile that she remembered so well from their lovemaking. It started in his eyes, a deeply sensual glow of appreciation, and then his mouth curved in a perfect bow. And despite her unhappiness, her nipples hardened beneath the water.

"How are you feeling?" she asked, trying to ignore her arousal, which in the circumstances was just plain perverse.

"Much better," he responded. "That drink one of the twins made was a remarkable pick-me-up."

"I thought it might do you good."

He continued to look down at her and his expression was now grave. "I have to see some people, sweeting," he said. "But when that's done, we must talk."

"What people?" she asked. "Fellow assassins?" She bit her lip, hearing the acid in her voice.

"You could say that," he responded dryly, the sensual

glow banished from his eyes. "I suppose Tatarinov told you everything."

. "Only under duress," she said. "I threatened him with your pistol, and the dogs chewed his ankles."

For a moment his expression brightened with amusement, then became grave again. "My meeting won't take long. Will you be up here or in your parlor?"

"In the parlor," she said. Somehow the bedroom didn't seem the right place for such a conversation, and she certainly didn't want to be naked.

"Very well, I'll come to you there." He turned to the door. "Shall I send Ethel back?"

"Yes, please."

He left her chamber and went downstairs to the library, where his fellow conspirators were already gathered, the vodka bottle passing freely between them.

"Good God, Prokov, what happened to you?" Constantine asked in horror.

Alex told them, sparing no details.

"Sperskov is gone?" Fedotov said in disbelief. "Arakcheyev's men?"

"Sperskov is probably at the bottom of the river now, poor devil, and Arakcheyev's henchmen at the bottom of the North Sea, or they soon will be. The question, my friends, is how do we proceed from here?"

"Cautiously," Constantine said grimly. "Someone put them onto Sperskov."

"I think we can assume that our man in the army in Finland has been picked up," Alex said calmly. "They'll get what they can out of him, but fortunately he knows no names. Only that someone paid him well to abduct the czar."

"He was paid in English gold," Fedotov pointed out. "That'll pinpoint us."

"Yes, but they won't move without more information," Alex said, pouring himself a glass of cognac, hoping it would do his head some good. "It's to be assumed Sperskov only gave them me, since no one came knocking on your door. And since Sperskov is gone and Arakcheyev's henchmen also, we're safe enough for the present."

He took a cautious sip and then put the glass down. It did nothing at all for his headache and he couldn't afford to be fuddled when he talked with Livia; there was far too much at stake.

"So what now?" Fedotov asked.

"We lie low," Alex said decisively. "Let the talk die down around the czar and then we see."

"And in the meantime, Mother Russia allows herself to be governed by Napoleon Bonaparte like some province of France," Constantine muttered dourly. He drained his glass. "Very well. We can't do anything until Tatarinov turns up again anyway."

Alex saw his visitors out and then went to Livia's parlor. He gave a perfunctory knock on the door and went in. The terriers rushed at him in ecstatic greeting and on this occasion he neither put them out of the room nor subdued them.

Livia was sitting on the window seat, a book open in

her lap, but it was clear she had not been reading. She was very pale, her pallor accentuated by her afternoon gown of pale yellow muslin. Ordinarily the color suited her, but this afternoon it made her look sallow.

She was aware of this but had decided once the gown was fastened that as she had no interest in enchanting her husband at this time, it mattered little if she didn't look her best.

"Have they gone?"

"Yes." He leaned against the door at his back and regarded her closely. "You know I love you."

"Yes." She clasped her hands loosely in her lap and the book fell to the floor, but she made no attempt to retrieve it.

"And you love me."

"Yes."

He steepled his hands against his mouth in a gesture so familiar to Livia that she could feel tears welling behind her eyes. "And you know now who I am, what brought me to London, and what I intend to do."

"Yes." She began to wonder if this litany of the obvious would ever end. "Are you still intending to do this thing?"

"I don't know," he said. "That will depend on many factors. But you need to know that I have not given up, and that I will work for my country in whatever capacity strikes me as opportune at any time."

"I see. And if I asked you to give that up, for my sake, for the sake of our marriage . . . our love . . ."

"I could not agree."

"Well, at least you told me the truth for once," Livia said, not caring that she sounded bitter. "I'm grateful for that. At least I know how I stand, and where I come in your priorities."

"If you wish it . . . if you decide that that's what you want . . ." he began, painfully feeling for the right words, "then I will leave you and return to Russia. There need be no scandal. You will remain my wife, Princess Prokov, with this house and a very generous income. It will be said that I was summoned by the emperor and had no choice but to go. We decided you should stay here rather than risk the rigors of a journey across war-torn Europe. My continued absence can be explained in many ways, and if you decide you would like to remarry, then I will arrange for a divorce in Russia and you will be free."

Livia said nothing. She gazed at the bleak prospect of such a future and knew that she would never want to remarry. She would remain in a separated limbo for the rest of her life.

"Is that what you would wish, Livia?" he asked quietly.

"I don't know," she said. "Probably, but I need time to think."

"Of course." He bowed with a little click of his heels and left her.

Livia sat on the window seat for a long time, as the shadows lengthened and the winter dark set in. Ordinarily her instinct at such a time would be to go to

Mount Street and seek comfort and counsel there. But she couldn't face her friends with this. This was something she had to wrestle with alone.

❧

Alex went downstairs, filled with a bleak despair. This journey had been so long in the planning, so complex in the execution, and it had taken so many twists and turns for which he had been utterly unprepared. He had not expected to find this love . . . this absolute need to nurture and protect. And he had never expected to find himself the recipient of such a need. He didn't even know *how* to both give and receive it. He had never been taught how to open himself to such emotions.

He walked into the salon, where the lamps had just been lit and a soft glow suffused the room. His mother looked down at him from above the fireplace. Her eyes . . . his eyes . . . clear and steady. *Were they saying anything to him? What would she say to him . . . to her son?*

"What was she to you, then?"

Alex turned, startled at the soft Yorkshire burr behind him. Morecombe, soft-slippered as usual, stood looking up at the portrait.

"My mother," Alex said simply.

Morecombe nodded. "Aye, the lassies an' me thought 'twas summat o' the kind," he said. "Ye've 'er look about you . . . O' course it was afore our time, but we knew there was summat not right. Our lady 'ad a sadness to her . . . broke our hearts it did, when it came on her bad."

"My father had it too," Alex said quietly.

"Best not let 'istory repeat itself, then," Morecombe declared laconically.

Alex shook his head. "I had come to that conclusion myself."

"Good, then ye'd best be about it." The old man turned and left the salon.

Alex stood in front of the portrait for a moment, then he nodded and went upstairs.

⚬✦⚬

Livia was still exhausted; the few hours sleep she'd snatched in the inn that morning seemed to have happened in another lifetime. Every bone and muscle in her body ached and her eyes were tight and sore, as if she'd been weeping for hours. As soon as Alex left her, she went into her bedchamber, locking the door behind her. She could face no solicitous servants at the moment. She threw off her clothes, letting them lie where they fell, and dropped her nightgown over her head, turning wearily to the bed.

She had one upraised knee on the mattress when the adjoining door from Alex's chamber opened. She looked over her shoulder to where her husband stood, his face white, his blue eyes filled with fire.

His voice, however, was quiet, although the determination, the fixed purpose behind his words was as clear as a thunderclap. "My father sacrificed his love for his country, there can be no other explanation for those letters, for his empty wasteland of a life," he said. "But *I* will not. Livia, you are mine, and you are not leaving me and I am not leaving you. I can't imagine why I even had such a ridiculous, asinine idea."

He crossed to the bed in three strides and lifted her off, setting her on her feet in front of him, his hands gripping her shoulders.

"Look at me, Livia, and tell me you don't belong to me. Tell me that I do not belong to you." He shook her a little in emphasis. "Come on, Livia. Tell me."

She looked up at him. "You know I can't."

"Yes, I do know it." He pushed up her chin and kissed her so hard she was sure it must have hurt his battered mouth, but he held her thus for a long time, his mouth against hers, his breath rustling across her cheeks, his free hand tracing the line of her body from her breast to her hips.

He held her until the blood began to move warmly through her veins again, until the rigid sinews of resistance melted and she leaned into him. Then he lifted her against him and lay down on the bed with her, cradling her head in the hollow of his shoulder, trailing his fingers through the tumbled cascade of dusky curls.

"I am defeated, sweeting, unmanned," he said softly. "I will give up my country if I must, and settle down and become an English gentleman with nothing on my mind but sports, and hunting, and cards."

Livia smiled into his shoulder as a curious peace filled her. He meant it, but he didn't know what such a sacrifice would mean for him. "What nonsense," she said. "You can't do that, you wouldn't be you. Harry Bonham manages to serve his country and his wife perfectly satisfactorily, why shouldn't you be able to?"

Alex smiled ruefully. "I wondered when you'd take me into your confidence about Bonham."

"It wasn't my confidence to break," she said. "Did you know all along?"

"For quite a while," he admitted. "But the situation is a little different, my love. Bonham serves the country he lives in and his loyalties are very clear-cut. It is rather different for a Russian and always has been. Loyalty to king and country makes sense for an Englishman, but not always for a Russian. The emperor is not good for his country."

"Then you must work to remove him," Livia said simply, remembering again her father's advice on the issue of compromise at a crossroads. "I understand *that*, what I don't understand is why things must be kept from me. Particularly things that make you the man you are, the man I love. I don't like secrets and I loathe deception."

"And I am guilty of both," he agreed, bending an arm behind his head to pillow it. "I am by nature secretive, my love. It was the way I was brought up. My father kept everything about himself from me, everything about my mother. Until I saw those letters I never dreamed he was capable of any real emotion other than devotion to country and duty."

"How lonely you must have been," Livia said, hitching herself onto an elbow and stroking his cheek.

"I was," he agreed, "but no lonelier than most children in my country. Russian parents tend to be distant at best." He sighed a little and attempted a rueful laugh that failed miserably. "But I do wonder why my mother never asked about me in those letters. If she had, my father would surely have answered her in one letter at least."

"No, I think it's quite the opposite," Livia said. "I think it was too painful for Sophia to think of you at all, let alone to ask about you. She had to go on living; surely it was easier for her to pretend that you did not exist for her. She must have been so young when she lost you and the love of her life. She had an entire life to live without what made it whole for her." She shuddered a little, thinking how close she and Alex had come to just such a destiny.

"What a wise woman you are," he said, bringing his arm down to stroke along her back. "I've married beauty, wisdom, and amazing courage and fortitude. I don't quite know why I deserve such good fortune, but if you promise to be gentle and not squeeze me too tightly, I will endeavor now to show you how utterly and totally I love you, wife of mine . . . how I complete you, and you complete me."

"Then show me, my prince," she murmured, moving herself over him, her fingers deftly unfastening his britches. "But in deference to your bruises, I shall do all the work in this demonstration."